Highland Princess

AMANDA SCOTT

Highland Princess

NEW YORK   BOSTON

Warner Forever is a registered trademark of Warner Books, Inc.

Cover design by Diane Luger
Cover art illustration by Franco Accornero
Typography by David Gatti
Book design by Giorgetta Bell McRee

Warner Books

Time Warner Book Group
1271 Avenue of the Americas
New York, NY 10020
Visit our Web site at www.twbookmark.com

Printed in the United States of America

ISBN: 0-7394-4636-3

The Curtain rises on Act III with the entrance of Lady Peel:

Sue Bengston Steele
12 December 2003
Requiescat in pace

Author's Note

In the fourteenth century, the surname Stewart was in transition from an occupational term to a surname. Robert the Steward, having descended from Robert the Bruce's sister, Marjory, assumed the throne in 1371 (five years after this story takes place) as Robert II, the progenitor of the Stewart dynasty of Scotland and, later, England. Robert's daughter, the princess Margaret, was known as Margaret Stewart.

For readers who enjoy knowing the correct pronunciation of names and places mentioned, please note the following:

Ardtornish = Ard-TOR-nish
Clan Chattan = Clan HAT-tan
Duart = DOO-ert
Eilean Mòr = EE-lee-an MORE
Gillean = Jill-ANE
Hebrides = HEH-bri-deez
Isla (or its present-day spelling, Islay) = EE-lah
Lubanach = LOO-ban-ock
Maclean = Mac LANE
Macleod = Mac LOUD
Reaganach = RAY-gan-ock
Tioram = CHEER-em

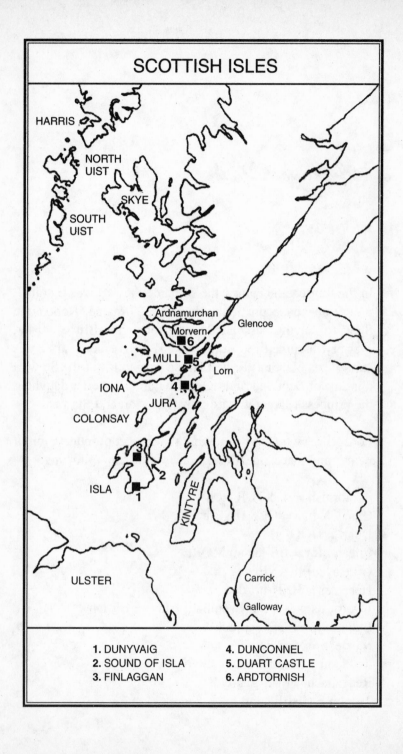

SCOTTISH ISLES

HARRIS

NORTH
UIST

SKYE

SOUTH
UIST

Ardnamurchan

Glencoe

Morvern
■6

MULL ■5

Lorn

IONA

■4

JURA

COLONSAY

■3

2

ISLA ■1

KINTYRE

ULSTER

Carrick

Galloway

1. DUNYVAIG   **4.** DUNCONNEL

2. SOUND OF ISLA   **5.** DUART CASTLE

3. FINLAGGAN   **6.** ARDTORNISH

Prologue

*Loch Gruinart, the Isle of Isla,
Scotland, March 1366*

The tide was going out, and still he had not come to her, despite his promise to arrive at the loch early so that she could get home before dark. Already she was late starting, and it would be as much as her life was worth if she failed again to have supper ready on time.

She walked along the sand toward the cliffs on the north shore, determined not to look as if she were impatient for him. As always, a thrill rippled through her at the thought of the danger in what she did. She liked a bit of risk, though. It added interest to her otherwise humdrum existence.

He had said he had to go to Kilchoman and would meet her on his way back, so he would come soon. He had to come. He had to take care of her, too, and the bairn, because he had promised he would. He was not always able to keep his promises, but he had to keep this one. He had to make her feel safe again.

As the sun sank nearer the horizon, she stood staring at the sea, forcing herself to relax, to enjoy the changing patterns of light. The dull gray clouds drifting overhead would turn to brilliant, rosy colors as the sun set, although she dared not linger long enough to see it, and the sight would not be as splendid from home.

A twig snapped, and she whirled with a smile of welcome that vanished when the man she saw was not the one she expected.

"You!"

"Aye, 'tis me, right enough," he snarled, striding up to her and putting both hands on her shoulders, gripping so tightly that she cried out.

"Don't! Let me go!"

"Nay, then, ye were warned no t' play off more o' your tricks, lass. Ye've done it now for the last time, I'm thinking, if ye ken what's good for ye. But afore I teach ye t' mind your betters, ye'll be paying a wee tribute, as his grace might say."

She screamed, but no one heard her except the one collecting his tribute, and her screaming was no more to him than the gulls' shrieks overhead. Indeed, it added spice for him to know she was paying dearly now for the wrongs she had done him in the past.

Although she did not know it then, she had already seen her last sunset.

Before long, her screams faded to silence.

# Chapter 1 ————————————

Near the eastern coast of Isla, a fortnight later

Dense fog blanketed the sea, flattening the waves and creating a world of eerie silence where water, land, and sky merged into impenetrable grayness. That fog was stealing the last hours of Ian Burk's life.

Each passing minute drew the hangman's noose nearer, but without wind, the slender royal galley bearing his hopeful rescuer could only drift with the tide. Its great square sail was useless and its eighteen oarsmen, unable to judge their exact location or course, had long since stopped rowing. They and their three passengers sat in silence as thick and heavy as the fog-muffled surroundings, listening intently.

Seventeen-year-old Lady Mairi of Isla pulled her hooded, fur-lined crimson cloak more snugly around her, stifling impatience. Even her father, the most powerful man in the Isles if not in all Scotland, could not successfully order fog to dissipate.

Beside her, her woman Meg Raith muttered, "'Tis cruel o' the fog t' blind us after the stars and wind we had when we left Dunyvaig. In troth, one canna help but wonder now what lies beneath us." Her voice shook on the words.

"No sea monster stalks these waters," Mairi said firmly.

"None would dare," Meg agreed as if no thought of monsters gliding through the dark depths below had ever entered her head. Less resolutely, she added, "Be ye certain, mistress?"

"Aye, and in any event, the sun is up or soon will be, because everything around us was black a short while ago," Mairi said, pushing a damp, dark curl back under the shelter of her hood. "Moreover, Meg, it is the very nature of fog to creep up on unsuspecting travelers. This one would not seem nearly so eerie had it not swallowed us in the darkness before we realized it was so near."

"Mayhap ye be right, mistress, but 'tis unsettling all the same."

Mairi agreed. Highland galleys usually moved swiftly, especially when wind and tide were favorable, and she loved the sea. The journey from her father's castle Dunyvaig, on the southeastern coast of Isla, to his administrative center on Loch Finlaggan in the north was nearly always a safe one and—at just over twenty miles—relatively short. But even the longest journeys on the water were seldom boring, because the scenery changed constantly and playful otters or seals often accompanied the galleys, amusing passengers with their antics.

She had rarely made any journey on a moonless night, however, with only stars to guide her helmsman, and now, thanks to the fog, the trip had taken hours longer than usual. And hours, for Ian, were precious.

Just then, the helmsman blew two notes on his ram's horn, as he did at ten-minute intervals, both to give warning of their presence to anyone else daft enough to be on the water in such murk and to demand a response from the lookout at Claig Castle when they drifted near enough. The massive fort on the Heather Isle guarded the south entrance to the Sound of Isla, a waterway of great strategic value to Mairi's father, MacDonald, Lord of the Isles and King of the Hebrides.

She turned her attention to the galley's stern, where her fair-bearded half brother lounged on a pile of leather skins beside the helmsman, looking grimly annoyed through the thick mist that billowed about him.

Knowing her voice would carry easily in the silence, she said quietly, "How much farther do you reckon it is, Ranald?"

His expression softened as he shifted his gaze to her. Like all three of her elder half brothers, twenty-one-year-old Ranald was a large, broad-shouldered, handsome man who bore the natural air of authority that sat easily on each of them. A little smile touched his lips as he said, "Near, lass, but not so near that I can promise ye'll be warming your toes by a fire in less than an hour or two."

"The water seems so still," she said. "I can scarcely tell if it is the fog or the boat that moves. Has the tide begun its turn?"

"Nay," he said. "It still carries us northward, and I warrant we'll reach the Sound's entrance soon. Doubtless the men at Claig hear our horn already, but fog distorts noises on the water, and they'll want to be certain of us afore they answer."

She nodded. Like anyone who had grown up with the sea as a constant companion, she understood its moods and movements well enough to know she would feel a distinct difference when they met the swifter flow of the tide through the narrow Sound. As for the helmsman's horn, not only was it the duty of the men at Claig Castle to respond to it but also to collect tribute from those permitted by the Lord of the Isles, rather than by birthright, to take the shorter passage through the Sound. The Claig watchmen would therefore be paying close heed.

But time passed so quickly that minutes now seemed like heartbeats.

Her thoughts returned thus abruptly to the subject that had occupied them since the previous night, when she had learned of Ian Burk's peril upon Ranald's return to Dunyvaig from Knapdale. He had been away two days, leaving her in charge of the castle, although her responsibility was light, since the castle's captain was one of MacDonald's most capable men.

The Lord of the Isles believed, however, that his offspring should know as much about what kept his castles and Lordship running smoothly as the people who did the work, and Dunyvaig was one of his most important holdings. It served both as guardian of the sea-lanes to the south and as safe harbor for his galleys, birlinns, and larger ships of war. From the castle's high, cliff-top site, its view encompassed much of the Kintyre coast and a vast panorama of the sea to the south. The harbor below, in Lagavulin Bay, was hidden from passersby and well fortified.

Ranald's present duty at Dunyvaig was to oversee the careening of MacDonald's ships, a chore done twice a year when scores of men rolled each ship ashore over logs so that they could scrape its bottom clean of barnacles.

This was the second year Mairi had accompanied him to Dunyvaig, entrusted with seeing to its household, to make sure the larders were full and that all was in good repair. For, as competent as the castle's captain was, he was yet unmarried, and therefore her mother, the lady Margaret, had formed the habit of looking in on Dunyvaig at least once a year to see that all was in order. That duty having devolved upon Mairi, she had acquitted herself well the previous year and had returned confidently a month before to do so again.

Thus, when Ranald had said MacDonald desired him to invite a new Knapdale chief to attend the annual Council of the Isles that week at Finlaggan, she had not turned a hair at learning she would be alone overnight among a household of men-at-arms with only her maidservant for protection. No man loyal to her father would harm her or Meg, and few men were more loyal than those at Dunyvaig.

The family would remain at Finlaggan for only a fortnight after the Council adjourned, because they would spend Easter as usual at Ardtornish, MacDonald's favorite seat, fifty miles to the north on the Morvern coast of the Sound of Mull. In midsummer, they would return to Isla so Lady Margaret could take the children to Kilchoman, their summer residence. It was a splendid palace, built only two years before on the west coast of Isla, but it was no place to be in a howling spring storm. Ardtornish, better protected against the winds, was infinitely preferable.

In any event, no household as large as theirs could occupy any residence for long. The demands made on the garderobes, not to mention stores and cellars, made it essential to move about frequently if only to let the servants attend to the cleaning in peace without having to deal with constant demands of family members.

Lady Margaret had sent word to Dunyvaig with Ian Burk a fortnight before, reminding Mairi and Ranald that his grace expected them to have completed their duties there by the time his Council adjourned, because they would both need time to prepare for departure to the north.

That her duties at Dunyvaig would mean missing the Council of the Isles had not distressed her, for although a few men sometimes brought family members, most waited until his grace moved north before bringing wives and marriageable sons and daughters to attend his court. Not only was Ardtornish more centrally located, but everyone was eager to take part in his Easter tinchal, the grand deer hunt that had begun to provide fresh venison for the Easter feast at Ardtornish and had soon grown into an annual social event.

No sooner did she greet Ranald's return to Dunyvaig, however, than she saw from his expression that something was wrong and demanded to know what it was.

"We met one of his grace's birlinns on its way to Loch Tarbert," he said. "They said that most of the councilors have arrived at Finlaggan, and he means to begin the court of grievances tomorrow, and . . . well . . ."

"And what?" she asked bluntly when he avoided her gaze.

"You won't want to hear it, lass," he warned her, adding reluctantly, " 'Tis gey possible that his grace will hang Ian Burk."

"Ian?" Her senses tilted, and a sickening chill swept over her. "But how can he?" she demanded. "Ian is infinitely trustworthy, Ranald. Why, he has looked after my ponies from my childhood—aye, and me, too! What can he possibly have done to warrant hanging?"

"The charge is murder, Mairi, and though I ken fine that you'll be wanting to return to Finlaggan straightaway, we can do naught to prevent his hanging if his accusers prove their charge. Under our Brehon laws—"

"I know our laws, Ranald, but his accusers must be daft. Who was killed?"

"Elma MacCoun," he said. "They say Ian pushed her off a cliff."

"That cannot be so! I tell you, Ranald, Ian has no violence in him."

He did not argue but neither could he placate her. She dismissed his attempts, saying flatly, "We have no time to lose."

He said calmly, "We can scarcely go this minute, lass."

"Mayhap we cannot, but we must go as soon as you can order a galley prepared and we pack our things."

"Tomorrow at dawn will be soon enough," he said. "There will be a host of grievances to hear, because there always are. Moreover, the men I met said only that most of the councilors had arrived, not all."

"But that was yesterday, was it not?" When he nodded, she said, "And his grace does not need any of them to hold his trial, sir, as well you know. Moreover, we cannot turn back the hours, and if we spend too many, Ian will suffer their waste through eternity. I mean to prevent that, Ranald, so do make haste!"

He rolled his eyes at what he clearly believed was a futile promise but made no other effort to dissuade her. Easily the most compliant of her six brothers and half brothers, he rarely proved awkward. But she would have expected assent from the others, too, because as stubborn as some could be, she could be more so.

Having agreed to do as she asked, he lost little time, and now here they were with the fog growing thicker, colder, and eerier until even her own practical mind began conjuring monsters.

At last, however, the tenor call of the horn they had been waiting to hear sounded through the fog from the fortress ramparts of Claig Castle.

The oarsmen's hands tightened on their sweeps.

"Hold water," Ranald warned. "Sound our signal again, and listen well."

The helmsman obeyed, blowing his two-note call.

As the sound faded eerily, Mairi heard the rhythmic splashing of oars that Ranald's quicker ears had already discerned.

Through the fog a deep voice boomed, "Who would pass here?"

"Ranald of Isla, you villain," Ranald bellowed back.

"Guard your steerboard oars, my lord," the deep voice replied with an appreciative chuckle. "We'll be upon ye straightaway."

The dark shape of another galley's prow loomed alongside them on the same side as the helmsman's rudder, and as Ranald's oarsmen on that side raised their sweeps high, she heard the other man order his to hold water. Their oars dug in instantly, bringing the approaching galley to a stop with commendable quickness.

"Welcome, my lord," the deep voice boomed, and Mairi recognized Murdo of Knapdale, captain of Claig. "Be ye returning t' Finlaggan, sir?"

"Aye," Ranald said. "You did well to find us so quickly, Murdo. Would you have done so had we not sounded our horn?"

"We would," Murdo said confidently. "I can hear fish swimming through my waters, sir. Moreover, in the unlikely event that my ears should fail, I've six more boats along the Sound, alert for any fool who might try t' slip past us in this devilish fog without paying his rightful tribute."

"Faith, sir, will each of those six stop us and demand to know our business?" Mairi demanded, fearing further delays.

"Nay, my lady," Murdo said. "I'll signal our code for safe passage t' keep them at bay. Each will pass it on t' the next, and we change our codes each night at uncertain times t' prevent any enemy from using them to our peril. Hark now."

He made a gesture and his helmsman sounded a series of notes from a horn pitched higher than theirs or Claig Castle's.

A moment later, the single long note from Claig sounded again, followed almost immediately by a higher single note in the distance.

"An ye keep the high notes t' larboard and the low ones t' steerboard, ye'll ha' deep water under ye all the way, my lord," Murdo said.

"Aye," Ranald said, nodding to his helmsman.

Taking their beat from the helmsman, the oarsmen rowed smoothly, trusting him to steer a safe course through the Sound.

Meg peered fearfully ahead, but as near as they were now to Port Askaig, the harbor closest to Finlaggan, Mairi felt only relief. Listening as intently for the horns as they all were, no one talked, leaving her again at the mercy of her thoughts. However, now she felt more confident reaching Finlaggan in time to speak for Ian, it occurred to her that the present fog bore a similarity to the mists beclouding her future. Certainly, her progress toward it had been becalmed for some time.

Many times had her father described what that future would be and how someday, in what seemed most unlikely circumstances, she might even become Queen of Scots. But meantime she drifted with the political tide, waiting for political winds to rise and blow her in the direction his grace desired her to go. And a political tide, like any other, could turn without warning.

She had no more power to control her drifting life than to control natural or man-made tides, and in truth, she had not sought to do so. Surrounded by a loving family and esteemed for her capabilities, at times even for her opinions, she was happy enough. Unlike her younger sister Elizabeth, who flirted with every man she met, Mairi had no great longing to marry. Nor did Alasdair Stewart, the man her father had selected to be her husband, show any interest in her or in their future together. But Mairi cared even less for Alasdair, her least favorite of her royal grandfather's multitude of sons by two wives and a long string of mistresses.

For one thing, her relationship with Alasdair lay within the second degree of consanguinity, and the Holy Kirk forbade marriage between such close kinsmen. He was four years her senior and handsome enough, she supposed, but although her father and grandfather believed the Pope would grant the necessary dispensation when the time was exactly right for requesting it, she did not want to marry her uncle.

Her half sister Marjory, on the other hand, had hardly been able to wait to marry Roderic Macleod of Lewis and Glenelg. Mairi did not envy her, though, because she now lived on the Isle of Lewis, far from Isla and Ardtornish, off the northernmost reaches of Scotland. The proud mother of three small children with a fourth on the way, Marjory would not even join them for Easter at Ardtornish.

Land loomed darkly now on both sides of the galley, and it was not long before a high-pitched horn blew the four notes that she recognized as Port Askaig's call. Soon afterward, she heard voices and discerned the shape of her father's wharf ahead. Men bustled about in the mist, and their helmsman shouted to make ready.

Containing her impatience only until the galley bumped against the landing and was made fast, she stood, gathering her skirts in one hand as she stepped onto a rowing bench and extended the other hand to a lad on the dock. The instant he grasped it, she stepped nimbly out onto the timber planks.

"Hold up, lass," Ranald commanded sternly behind her.

"I've told Ned here to run and saddle our horses, but we must wait until our baggage—"

"You may wait if it pleases you, sir," Mairi interjected. "I've no time to deal with baggage if I'm to save Ian. Just saddle my horse and one for Meg as quickly as you can," she told Ned, "for we must make haste." Glaring at Ranald, she dared him to countermand the order.

Instead, he sighed, saying, "Saddle mine, too, Ned." Then with a straight look at Mairi, he added, "Doubtless your lady mother is impatient to see you."

"Aye, sir," Mairi said. "But do send another man to help Ned, for we must not tarry. Your need for haste is not as strong as mine, so you may certainly stay to supervise the unloading if you believe it necessary. It would be good to know when his grace means to begin Ian Burk's trial, however," she added with a quizzical look at the lad who had helped her step onto the dock.

Frowning, he replied, "I dinna ken, my lady, though men ha' talked o' nowt else these past days. They did say his grace would begin when the chapel bell rings Terce, but I warrant he'll wait till this fog lifts, or he—aye, and everyone else, too—will be gey wet afore yon trials be over."

"But I've no notion what the hour is now," Mairi said.

"You've time enough yet," Ranald said.

"Unless," the lad said, "his grace ha' decided t' try Ian Burk first, and indoors. If he does that, I'm thinking he'll begin when he likes."

"We must lose no more time then," Mairi said with a surging horror that Ian's fate might already be decided. "Do you come with me, Ranald, or not?"

"He'll hold no trial within doors, Mairi. The law requires that all such gatherings be open to all. He'll hold this trial on Council Isle as he always does."

"He would not be so cruel as to make Ian wait," she said fiercely. "Only look about you, Ranald. So dense a fog could last for days."

Sighing, he told the helmsman to oversee the unloading of their baggage, holding on to Mairi's arm as he did, as if he feared she would go without him.

"His grace should have taught you obedience," he muttered a moment later as he hurried her along the jetty toward the steps leading up to the village. "I'm thinking he did you no service by encouraging you to speak your mind to men, but I warrant your royal husband will deal firmly with you after you are safely married."

Grinning impudently, she said, "I am not married yet, sir, or even betrothed. Nor do I think any perhaps-someday-king Alasdair will prove a trial to me."

Ranald chuckled. "Every one of the Steward's sons has the Bruce's blood in his veins, Mairi, and such men know their worth. Moreover, Alasdair is older than you, as large and strong as his father, and as likely as anyone to join his grace's court here or at Ardtornish. We'll see then how tolerant he is of female backchat."

Mairi lifted her chin, determined to show no concern about Alasdair Stewart. She would deal with him later. Right now, she had a hanging to prevent.

Their horses were quickly saddled and the three miles from Askaig to Loch Finlaggan were soon behind them.

Finlaggan served as the administrative hub for the Lordship of the Isles. From the top of the rise overlooking the loch, through the still-heavy curtain of fog, the riders could barely discern the tiny village of cottages on its western shore or the sprawling, low-walled palace complex on Eilean Mòr, the larger of two islets just offshore. A stone causeway connected the islet to the village.

Council Isle, the much smaller of the two, still lay hidden in mist. Connected by a second stone causeway to Eilean Mòr at the latter's southeastern tip, it served as a meeting place for the annual Council of the Isles, the gathering of chiefs, chieftains, lairds, and other councilors loyal to the Lord of the Isles. Only fourteen to sixteen of them served as official councilors at any time, but deliberations were open to all. No business of the Lord of the Isles was conducted in secret.

Isla's trials, as well as appeals of decisions made elsewhere by Brehons, the hereditary judges who served throughout the Lordship, also took place on Council Isle or at Judgment Knoll, a hillside overlooking Loch Indaal on the southern end of Isla. Generally, men condemned to death in either place were hanged on the Knoll.

At the annual gathering, the councilors and his grace customarily sat around a great stone table so ancient that men said Somerled himself had held his councils there. The lad was right though, Mairi decided. If they sat around that table today, they'd be soaked through in minutes. Indeed, in so thick a fog, someone might even tumble off the causeway or stumble into the water along the shore.

From her position on the rise, she heard a rat-tat-tat of hammers that told her men had already begun their day's work on the chapel's new slate roof, but she could discern no activity within the complex, let alone see any on the tiny, fog-shrouded islet. Nevertheless, the sense of urgency that had driven her since learning of Ian's trial continued to plague her. She spurred her pony forward.

No sooner had she and her companions crossed the causeway from the village to Eilean Mòr and dismounted in the grassy enclosure there than a lad of ten or eleven summers came running to help Ned with the horses.

"Has his grace already gone to Council Isle?" Mairi asked him.

"Nay, my lady, for wi' this fog, he ha' decided t' hold council in the hall."

"But can that be legal, Ranald?" she asked as Ned led the ponies away and the younger lad fell into step beside them.

"Legal enough, I warrant," Ranald said as they passed from the grassy stable enclosure to the next one, which housed the chapel, guardhouses, and cottages. "'Tis his grace who interprets the laws, after all, and he is ever a fair man."

"Aye, that he be," their informer said earnestly, trotting beside Meg to keep up with them. "The laird did say the great hall will hold all who come, my lady, and he did set men like me t' direct them there. I'm thinking his grace will begin Ian Burk's trial first, since it be the local one, and new. That'd be within the hour."

"I'll just have time to change my dress then," Mairi said, relieved that she would not have to appear before the company in her present soggy attire.

Commanding Ranald to make her excuses to her mother, and taking care to avoid anyone else who might try to delay her, she and Meg hastened across the roofed and stone-paved forecourt and up the steep stairway within the ten-foot-thick wall of the family's private quarters, to the bedchamber she shared with her younger sister Elizabeth. There, with Meg's help, she quickly donned an ermine-trimmed tunic and kirtle of the rich scarlet wool known as tiretain, because it had come all the way from Tyre.

Meg plaited Mairi's glossy black hair into twin coils, pinning one over each ear, and concealed the whole beneath a delicately embroidered gold-mesh caul. Atop the caul, she set a narrow gold circlet to denote Mairi's rank.

"Your gloves, mistress," she said sharply when Mairi stood and turned toward the door. "And, too, you should carry a lace handkerchief."

"Don't be daft, Meg, I've tarried long enough." But she took the gloves, knowing her mother would scold if she appeared barehanded before such a company. Then, without further comment, she hurried out and down the steep stairway, holding her long skirts away from her feet with her left hand. Her right hovered near the stone wall, but so great was her hurry that she barely touched it.

From the top of the stairs, she heard male voices below in the forecourt, but by the time she reached the doorway, silence reigned outside. Even the hammering on the chapel roof had stopped, doubtless so the workers could attend Ian's trial.

Emerging into the empty forecourt, she bundled her skirts awkwardly over her left arm to keep them out of her way and pulled on her gloves as she hurried across the pavement and through the arched gateway into the courtyard of the vast rectangular great hall. Hurrying up the wooden steps at the hall's southeast corner, she entered the antechamber to hear male voices again from the great hall beyond.

The door into the hall stood open to allow two tall men to pass through, one behind the other and gentlemen both if their short, brightly colored velvet cloaks and tight-fitting silk hose were any indication. As she crossed the chamber, the second man, a bit shorter and slighter than the first, reached to pull the heavy door closed behind him. The voices inside the hall were fading, telling her that her father had already mounted the dais to begin the proceedings.

"Hold there," she commanded in a low but urgent tone as she held her skirts higher and increased her pace, fearing the man might attempt to bar the door.

It continued to close, but she caught its edge before it did.

"Wait," she said more loudly, struggling against the strong grip that threatened to pull the door from her grasp. "I want to come in."

The door stopped, but as she sighed her relief and moved to pass through the narrow opening, she found herself facing a broad, immobile male chest clad in sky-blue velvet, and instantly realized that she had misjudged the size of the gentleman she had thought was the smaller. The top of her head barely reached his shoulder.

At Finlaggan and elsewhere in the Isles, most men wore the skins, saffron-colored shirts, and blanketlike garments that barelegged Highlanders belted around themselves, but many of the galley-owning Islesmen, who treated the seas as their highroads, wore richer, more courtly garments that they had seen and purchased in their travels.

Thanks to her older brothers' interest in similar garments, she recognized his short tunic as being of French design, and recalled her mother's oft-expressed dislike of the blatant display of male backsides and sexual organs encased in thin hosiery that the fashion for such short tunics so often provided. Resisting temptation to let her gaze drift downward, she said, "Pray, sir, stand aside. Surely you know that you must leave this door open."

"His grace, the Lord of the Isles, is about to try a man for his life, lass. Open or not, this hall is no place for a maiden today, however beautiful she may be."

His voice was low-pitched but touched with humor.

Fighting to control her irritation, she looked up to tell the impertinent, self-appointed doorkeeper how irrelevant his opinion was to her, but she swallowed the words when her indignant gaze met his twinkling blue eyes.

The sensations that held her in thrall then she would later find difficult to recall clearly, let alone to describe. Warmth swept through her, doubtless stirred by that impudent twinkle, but the warmth included a sense of surprise. She would try to persuade herself that the latter was due only to having never before seen eyes of so clear and pure a blue, like calm water in the Firth of Lorn when the tide was on the turn and the sun high and shining from a clear sky. She felt a strange tingling, too, in places where she had never felt anything similar before.

"Let me pass," she said, but her mouth was suddenly dry and the words emerged in a harsh whisper.

He shook his head.

Dampening her dry lips, she tried to swallow, to look away from that spellbinding gaze, but she seemed to have lost control over such actions.

"What the devil's amiss here?"

The obstacle in front of her turned, shifting aside slightly as he did, but before Mairi could sufficiently gather her senses to take advantage of the opening and slip past him into the hall, the second, even larger man blocked the gap and stared at her in astonishment.

"By heaven," he said impatiently to the first, "I'll remember this when you next take me to task for lingering over a pair of bonnie eyes. Send her away, Lachlan, and close this door. His grace is glowering at us, and I warrant he'll not begin until it is shut."

Irritation returned. Mairi stiffened and squared her shoulders, saying sharply, "This door must remain open. Our law requires it."

"What do girls know about our laws?" the second man demanded.

"Perhaps nothing," the first said equably, adding before Mairi could contradict him, "Nonetheless, I believe she is right. This being the first time we've attended such a proceeding indoors, I'd forgotten that the usual openness is due to law and not merely to circumstance. Thank you, mistress, for the reminder. We would not want to displease his grace."

"If you think my father is displeased now, sir," she said, "just wait until he hears that the pair of you tried to keep me from entering. It is as much my right to do so as it is yours."

Both men's eyes widened in astonishment, revealing those of the second to be nearly as pure a blue as those of the first.

In unison, they exclaimed, "Your father!"

"Aye, for I am Mairi of Isla. Now, stand aside and let me pass."

Instead of being properly abashed, the one called Lachlan caught her gaze again and held it, the twinkle in his eyes deepening as he continued to block her way. This time, however, the only emotion the twinkle inspired was fury.

Her hand shot up, but even as it did, his flashed up quicker and caught it.

His eyes still twinkled, and his leather-gloved grip was light, but she could not pull away.

Chapter 2

Lachlan Lubanach Maclean of Bellachuan on Seil, and Knapdale, fought to keep from grinning at the lass's dismay. He should, he knew, have guessed who she was at once, because not only was she richly dressed but she also lived up to her legendary reputation for being the most beautiful woman in the Isles. Doubtless, that incredible beauty had bewitched him and caused his wits to desert him.

Looking at her, he felt something stir within that he had not felt for a long time. Her eyes had a bewitching, message-sending clarity, her voice a rich musical resonance that was deeply sensual. Her temper was legendary too, however, and by the way her ivory cheeks reddened and her dark blue eyes flashed, he was certain that had she wielded her father's power of the pit and gallows, he would soon be hanging from a good strong rope. Nonetheless, he felt drawn to her.

Beside him, his brother Hector made a warning sound in his throat, but Lachlan ignored him. Hector cared more for the ancient Clan Gillean battle-axe he wielded so dexterously than he did for anything else, but he also had a finely honed eye for the fair sex. Lachlan's skills extended to many things other than battle, too, and he welcomed any challenge or puzzle. The comely lass offered both.

"What goes on here?" a gravelly voice growled behind them as a strong hand grabbed Lachlan's shoulder, startling him. He still held the lass's wrist, but in that instant he realized that whoever had grabbed him had also put a hand on Hector's shoulder, doubtless meaning to pry them apart to see what was going on.

Quicker than thought, he released the lass and caught Hector's other shoulder as he wheeled to deal with the intrusion. By the look in his eyes, Lachlan was barely in time, undoubtedly saving the intruder from a stunning blow if not instant death.

"Steady," he muttered, but Hector had already recalled their surroundings, and the light of battle quickly faded from his eyes.

The two turned as one to face the interloper, and Lachlan stifled a sigh when he recognized Niall MacGillebride Mackinnon, Chief of the Mackinnons and High Steward of the Household to the Lord of the Isles.

Behind Lachlan, the lass pressed both small hands against his left side, trying to shift him out of her way. Hoping to protect her from Niall's displeasure, he stood his ground until she said, "Niall, make them move. I want to come in."

When Mackinnon glared at him, Lachlan obligingly stepped aside.

"This be no time or place to stand chatting," Mackinnon said curtly. Then, softening his tone, he smiled at the lass and added, "Welcome home, Lady Mairi. 'Tis relieved we are that you've enjoyed a safe journey despite this wretched fog."

"Thank you," she said. "But pray, sir, will you show me

where I should sit? I want to speak for Ian Burk, you see, but the hall is exceptionally crowded."

Mackinnon frowned and glanced over his shoulder.

The thirty-by-sixty-foot-long hall teemed with men. Not only did they occupy every bench, they also crowded each long side aisle from its line of pillars to its outer wall, leaving a walkway only from the door where Lachlan and the other two stood with Mairi, up that short side aisle and around to the dais.

Beyond Mackinnon, between two of the nearest line of pillars supporting the barrel-vaulted ceiling, Lachlan could see MacDonald of the Isles seated behind the table on the dais in a full-length black robe edged with gold braid. He was flanked by two golden banners bearing the Nyvaig, the "little black ship," that was both his device and the Great Seal of the Isles. Nearby stood his ever-present body servant.

As Mackinnon tried to espy a suitable seat for her ladyship, MacDonald gestured to him.

"Forgive me, my lady," Mackinnon said with a bow before turning to obey.

"Look after the door, Hector," Lachlan said. "I'll look after her ladyship."

As the lass stepped aside to permit Hector to obey, she snapped, "What if I do not want you to look after me?"

He grinned as he raised his forearm, inviting her to place her hand upon it. "Faith, lass, but I have always wanted to witness an avenging goddess in action," he said. "Would you deny me that pleasure?"

Becoming color flooded her cheeks. "Don't be absurd," she said. "And you should more properly address me as 'Lady Mairi.'"

"Should I?" He chuckled, waiting pointedly, his arm still extended.

The chuckle had come from low in his throat, and the sound reached right inside her to inflame the very blood in her veins. She knew her cheeks were red, because she could feel their heat, but her anger had not fazed him. Indeed, she seemed only to amuse the wretched man, yet something about him fascinated her.

It certainly was not his appearance, for although he dressed with an extreme air of fashion and possessed undeniably intriguing eyes, she did not think he was especially handsome. Other women might disagree, she knew, but his hair was too ordinary a brown for her taste—like the dusky brown of a hawk's wing—and his features too sharply chiseled for beauty. Moreover, he was too tall.

She was not accustomed to craning her neck to meet any man's gaze. To be sure, her father and brothers were tall, thanks to Viking raiders who had mixed with their Celtic forebears, and yet the man facing her was taller even than Godfrey, the second eldest of her brothers, and so far the tallest. And the man's brother—for brothers they must be, so much alike were they—was taller yet, a veritable giant. They made a formidable pair.

"Come, lass. They're all staring at you, so we must find seats or risk drawing his grace's ire." He waited, arm out, clearly expecting her to accept his escort.

Knowing she could do her cause no good by creating a scene, and certain he would not simply stand aside, Mairi set her hand lightly on his forearm.

No sooner had she done so, however, than he put his free

hand over hers, gave it a decidedly familiar squeeze, and murmured, "Alas, my lady, but I see no room left on any bench unless you would have me order some man from his place, and that, I believe, would cause more of a stir than you'd like."

Deciding he was determined to stir her temper again, she tried to ignore the large hand entrapping hers as she peered around the hall, only to see instead, to her chagrin, that he was right.

Niall Mackinnon had already reached the far end of the dais, where he stood ready to begin, and although he glanced toward her, he did not meet her gaze. Nor, she knew, would he delay the proceedings to accommodate her.

With a little tug, she pulled her hand from its captor's grasp and stepped back against the wall, realizing only then that unless she had been so fortunate as to find a place in the front row, she enjoyed a clearer view now than she would have had from anywhere else.

The first hour passed slowly, for despite her young informant's prediction, MacDonald dealt first with a stream of petty grievances, albeit settling each one with dispatch. The appeal of a decision by a Brehon on the Isle of Lewis likewise went quickly, and at last, Niall called the case against Ian Burk of Isla, for murder.

"Is the accuser in the hall?" Niall demanded in stentorian tones.

"Aye, I'm here, right enough," declared a barelegged man in a short, shaggy black cloak, a long saffron-colored shirt, and leather shoes with the hair still on them, who stood by a front pillar not far from Mairi. His dark, shoulder-length hair hung in ragged tangles beneath his flat black cap, and he looked grim as he made his way along the crowded front bench and onto the dais.

"Hail forth the prisoner," Mackinnon commanded.

Two stout men-at-arms escorted poor, well-shackled Ian Burk into the hall through the very door near which Mairi and her two self-appointed guardians stood.

Between his escorts, Ian's lesser height and wiry build made him look thin and vulnerable. His tawny hair was tousled, and he looked frightened—as well he might, Mairi thought—but he stood straight between his two guards and faced his liege lord bravely as the three passed within arm's length of her.

Although Ian had not glanced at her, she had no doubt that he had seen her. Even had she been across the room, she knew she must stand out in that assembly of men and would have done so even without her scarlet dress. She likewise had no doubt that Ian would take comfort, however small, from her presence.

That knowledge gave her pause, for the first time since she had learned of his trial, to consider the wisdom of her actions.

She had never spoken up at such a proceeding before, and although she did not doubt that her father would allow her to speak, she could not be certain that any words of hers would sway him if he believed Ian had committed a crime for which he should hang. That her presence might give Ian false hope seemed cruel.

However, that thought lingered only long enough to be dismissed. Ian had been loyal to her from her childhood. He was a staunch friend who had served her well and deserved her loyalty in return. To abandon him to his fate without doing everything she could to protect him would be a much crueler act.

MacDonald let the silence lengthen until Mairi felt her nerves straining and her fears returning in double measure. He was generally a mild man, more diplomat than warrior, known for looking first to his own advantage and that of Clan Donald. To the best of her knowledge, he had never taken part in a battle, but he defended his clansmen and supported other leaders, such as the Pope, the High King of Scots, or the King of England, when he agreed with their acts or intentions.

However, above all, he was a practical man, and thus unlikely to release any prisoner just because his daughter asked him to. MacDonald believed in the rule of law, and as Lord of the Isles and King of the Hebrides, he *was* the law of the Isles.

"State your name," Niall Mackinnon directed the accuser.

"As God and all here ken fine, I be Mellis MacCoun," the man snapped.

"With what crime do you charge Ian Burk?"

Red-faced and narrow-eyed, Mellis MacCoun put his hands on his hips and glowered at poor Ian. "I charge him wi' murder, that's what, for causing me poor wife Elma's death, and I'll have justice, I will. The villain should hang!"

"Before God and this company, Ian Burk, how do you plead to the charge?" the Lord of the Isles inquired in his quiet but clearly audible voice.

The hall was so silent that Mairi could hear herself breathing and could nearly hear her heart pounding in her chest.

"'Twas not me who caused Elma MacCoun's death," Ian said. "By my troth, your grace, and before all here, I dinna think I even clapped eyes on the woman the day she went missing, though I dinna ken for a fact what day that were."

"The accused swears that he is free of guilt," MacDonald said. "Mellis MacCoun, what manner of proof do you offer us that Ian Burk swears falsely?"

"He were with her," MacCoun declared angrily. "Others saw them together."

"Call forth your witnesses then," MacDonald ordered. "But first, to make the matter plain for us all, on exactly what day did this meeting between them occur?"

"Why, the day she disappeared, o' course."

The words stirred a ripple of laughter through the hall, but it broke off when his grace's gimlet gaze snapped from accuser to audience.

Again, he let the silence stretch tautly before he looked back at Mellis MacCoun and said, "You must forgive me, for even if I could say what day your wife disappeared, the accused declares his belief that he was not with her and says he does not know the day. Therefore I must ask you to supply us with the exact date of her disappearance so we may know that we all refer to the same day."

"But all here ken the day, your grace."

Mairi frowned. She did not know. Indeed, she knew little about the murder. She had known Elma MacCoun, because she knew everyone on Isla, but she had not known her well. She recalled that Elma had been Mellis MacCoun's second wife, rather pretty, and sadly childless.

"He must know that everyone here is not of Isla," a low voice murmured near her ear. His breath caressed the side of her neck like a warm breeze but was scarcely as soothing, agitating her nerves instead.

She had been trying to ignore his presence, to concentrate on her father's questions and the answers to them, but her awareness of him had not diminished one whit. Nonetheless, his voice startled her, and his comment stirred her to look around the hall again.

Isla was a well-populated island, and the Finlaggan complex alone employed and housed numerous servants and guardsmen, but Mellis MacCoun should certainly have realized that at least half of those present in the hall were off-islanders, present only for the Council of the Isles. She decided that he simply thought everyone in attendance would somehow already know the details of the crime without his having to relate them.

To be fair, such news would normally travel quickly, carried by seanachies to the remotest areas of the Lordship. Murder was not a common event in the Isles—not without a blood feud between clans or a war in progress, at all events, and her father's rule of the Isles had been generally peaceful despite his being now, as so often before, at odds with David Bruce, the High King of Scots.

Murmuring had begun again in response to Mellis Mac-Coun's insistence that everyone knew the details, but this time it took only a glance from the Lord of the Isles to restore silence.

"What day was it that your wife disappeared?" MacDonald asked. "Come now, man, think. Was it a year ago, a month, a sennight?"

Mellis looked at the vaulted ceiling and sighed. When his frustration was met with more silence, he said abruptly, "No more than a bit past a fortnight, I warrant, but I'm no a priest, am I, counting each day o' the sennight? Nor each hour, neither, from Prime t' Sext t' Prime again. I dinna ken nowt o' time without yon chapel bell telling me when t' work or sleep!"

"Then what more can you tell us about that day?" MacDonald asked, his patience apparently undiminished.

Mellis shrugged. "I'm recalling Elma were no there t' get me supper when I come in late from the stable. 'Twas no till Ewan Beton found her days later that I saw her again. Saw her dead body, that is t' say," he added with a bitter look at Ian.

"Have you duties on a Sunday?" MacDonald asked.

"Nay, and I'm thinking ye ken fine I do not. Sunday be a day o' rest."

Several grunts indicated that it was no day of rest for some among the company, men that Mairi knew were likely guards or household servants.

"I'd have you think now with your day of rest in mind," MacDonald urged. "Might Elma have disappeared the day after a Sunday or the day before one? Did anything else unusual happen on that day or near it?"

Frowning, Mellis shook his head. "I dinna ken . . . hark, though! I do, by me troth. I were late in from the stables because I'd ridden wi' me lord Godfrey t' Kilchoman and back that day. I should ha' recalled straightaway, but we've been again since, and what wi' everything . . ." He shrugged.

A near memory twitched in the back of Mairi's mind as her father said, "Did anyone else accompany you and Lord Godfrey to Kilchoman?"

"Aye, for did we no take three lads t' begin cleaning yon great house for when Lady Margaret takes the bairns there? And we took two men t' repair a wall."

"Very well," MacDonald said. "Name your witnesses against Ian Burk."

"Gil Dowell, Fin MacHugh, and Shim MacVey," Mellis said tersely.

"Which of them saw Ian Burk with your wife?"

"Shim did, for one."

"Then 'tis Shim MacVey we'll be hearing from next," MacDonald decreed.

Niall Mackinnon snapped the order, and a lanky man with fiery red hair made his way forward, climbing over benches, between men until he stood on the edge of the dais. He gaped from Niall Mackinnon to MacDonald to Mac-Coun, fixing his gaze at last upon Ian Burk.

"Tell us what you saw, Shim MacVey," MacDonald said.

"I did see him—Ian Burk—walking wi' Mellis Mac-Coun's Elma across the causeway from Eilean Mòr t' the mainland o' Isla. Gil were wi' me. Fin, too."

"Are Gil Dowell and Fin MacHugh here, as well?"

"Aye," Shim said, gesturing toward the company.

"Stand up then, the two of you." When two dark-haired men of the same age and general build as MacVey got reluctantly to their feet, MacDonald added, "Do you both swear that you saw Ian Burk with Elma MacCoun?"

"Aye, laird, I did," the first growled, echoed by the second.

"What day was that, Shim MacVey?"

Looking as bewildered as Mellis had, Shim said, "I dinna ken the day, your grace, but 'twas the day Mellis said, the last day ever we saw Elma, and she were looking grim, too."

"Grim?"

"Aye, sure. I'm thinking 'tis likely she were that scared o' being murdered!"

"Did you see Ian Burk kill her?"

"I did not! But then, I never clapped me eyes on the woman after."

"Are you sure it was the same day described by Mellis MacCoun?"

"Stands t' reason, I'm thinking, 'cause we never did see Elma again."

"Do you agree with that, Gil Dowell?"

"Aye, I do. Like Shim and Gil, I ha' never seen the lass since."

"Fin MacHugh?"

"Aye."

MacDonald gazed thoughtfully back at Shim, then at Mellis, and then at Ian.

But Mairi had heard enough. She took two steps forward, ignored the large hand that clamped hard onto her left arm, and said clearly above the hush, "If it please your grace, I would like to ask a question of Mellis MacCoun."

MacDonald nodded.

Looking sternly at Mellis, she said, "Did you see Elma for yourself the morning of the day she disappeared, before you and the others rode to Kilchoman?"

"Aye, me lady, o' course I did. She fixed me breakfast like always, or I'd ha' sought her out t' see that she did and given her a clout besides."

"And that was here on Eilean Mòr?"

"Aye, sure, it was. We've our wee cot in the stable enclosure, as ye ken, and I'm thinking now 'twere Elma what brought out me bundle, too, wi' a bit o' meat and bread for me dinner, and me dirk t' cut it with."

Mairi nodded, turning to face her father. "I beg your indulgence, your grace, to ask one or two questions now of Ian Burk?"

MacDonald glanced around the hall as if he expected to hear an objection, but the hall remained silent.

"You may," he said.

"Thank you, sir," Mairi said. Turning to look as directly at Ian as she had at Mellis MacCoun, but speaking in a gentler tone, she said, "Ian, do you remember crossing the main causeway with Elma MacCoun?"

Even with the distance between them, she could see the lad swallow hard and hoped he retained sufficient courage to speak the truth. Everyone there would detect a lie, and if he lied, his fate would be set and sealed.

He looked frightened out of his wits, but he locked his gaze with hers and answered, "Aye, m' lady, I do recall the walking, and I recall too that she spoke sharp t' me, because she thought it were time and more I be thinking o' marriage. But although I didna want t' marry her sister, Jane, which Elma thought I should, I did the woman no harm then or ever. That I swear t' ye by God Hisself!"

Ignoring snorts of laughter that rippled through the audience, Mairi said, "What day did you walk with her, Ian? Do you recall that, as well?"

"I do," he admitted, his words barely audible. Apparently realizing as much, he straightened and said more clearly, albeit as reluctantly, "It were the day afore I left for Dunyvaig wi' your lady mother's messages for ye and for Lord Ranald. I remember, 'cause Elma were a great one for talking about Dunyvaig, having lived there as a child, ye ken, and I'd never gone there, so afore she mentioned marriage, she were telling me what I must look at and all."

With a sigh of relief, although she had already deduced much of what he would say, Mairi said to her father, "Ian Burk cannot have killed Elma MacCoun, your grace. Mellis proved as much just now when he told us that he and the others saw her on Eilean Mòr shortly before they departed from Finlaggan. The galley that carried Ian to Dunyvaig departed at dawn from Askaig on that same day, and my lord Godfrey's party would not have left for Kilchoman before dawn. Indeed, if I know Godfrey, they departed hours later."

A few knowing chuckles greeted these words, but Mairi barely waited for them to fade before she added, "Elma was still alive then, sir, and Ian was miles away. He did not return until three days later, well after she had disappeared."

Exclamations burst from the assembly until Niall roared for silence.

As the last few voices died away, Ian said as if he were speaking to himself, "Aye, that be true about me leaving the same day. I rode to Askaig gey early, too—afore dawn—'cause the captain said he'd leave me behind were I no there when he were ready t' go. Lord Godfrey were shouting at men in the forecourt when I left, but I'm thinking he hadna yet broken his fast."

"Why did you not tell us all this earlier?" MacDonald asked.

Ian spread his hands and said regretfully, "I didna ken that were the day. I did stay at Dunyvaig that night and the next and part o' the day after that. We reached Askaig well after dark, too, so I stayed wi' me cousin there. The first I did hear about Elma going missing were a day or two after when someone said he thought she'd run off. It were days more afore they found her body on the sand, and no till three days ago that anyone said I'd been the last one wi' her and so I must ha' done it. I knew I'd walked wi' her, and I thought it must ha' been the day she went missing. No one said otherwise, so I didna ken I'd been away when she vanished."

MacDonald nodded, then said in his placid way, "Does any man here have evidence he can produce to disprove the lady Mairi's interpretation of this case?"

No one spoke.

"Very well. I therefore declare Ian Burk innocent of the charge of murder. You are free to go, lad."

Swiftly, Ian knelt and said with deep sincerity, "Thank you, your grace. I am your loyal servant, as ever I was."

Mellis MacCoun snapped, "But what about me wife? Who killed Elma if the lad did not?"

"That is not for this court to determine," MacDonald told him. "It is clear that Ian Burk did not kill her, and so that concludes the morning's business."

"All rise and depart now right hastily, so that this hall may be prepared for the midday meal," Mackinnon commanded.

As the men on the benches rose noisily to their feet, Mairi realized that although her self-appointed escort had released her arm, the moment her father granted her permission to speak, he still stood beside her—much too closely beside her.

MacDonald left the dais, and the company surged toward the door. There was but the one suitable exit, because the only other lay beyond the screens at the rear of the hall, through the pantry, buttery, and kitchen. As the crush of men swarmed around her, a hand cupped her elbow firmly, urging her toward the door at a more rapid pace than she might have set for herself.

"I'll escort you to the laird's hall, lass," the now-familiar deep voice said.

She needed no escort at Finlaggan, but the men surging around them were all talking now, and she did not want to raise her voice above theirs to be heard, so she allowed him to guide her out of the hall. On the steps outside, however, she turned to him and said firmly, "I thank you, sir, but I require no escort here."

His huge brother stood behind them, and others crowded behind him.

"We cannot stand here," Lachlan said as he urged her down the stairs to the courtyard. "How could you be so certain that the lad did not do it?"

Seeing nothing to gain by arguing or refusing to explain, she said, "I have been at Dunyvaig for a month with my brother Ranald, attending to the household there whilst he supervised the careening of his grace's ships that harbor there. A fortnight ago, Ian brought messages from Finlaggan and happened to mention that Godfrey had left that morning for Kilchoman to begin preparations for my mother and the children to spend their usual time there this summer. So when Mellis described the day he last saw Elma and said Ian had been seen walking with her on the causeway before she disappeared, I knew that it could not be so."

"Then 'tis odd that the others did not note as much long before now."

"Mellis and his witnesses seemed certain of their facts," Mairi pointed out, "and the events they described clearly took place over a sennight or more. Elma and Mellis often bickered, and when they did, Elma would go off alone to pout. I suspect that no one thought of murder until they found her body, and doubtless by then all the days had run together in their minds."

"Not in yours, however."

"No, but I had the benefit of distance and my own certainty that Ian could not have committed such a foul crime. Moreover, I had spent the hours since learning of his trial trying to think how to save him. I meant to speak for him in any event, but when I saw that the truth would speak for itself, I own I was much relieved."

"My lady," Niall Mackinnon said, interrupting from behind, "you should not be out here like this without your woman. I will escort you to the laird's residence."

Feeling guilty, albeit uncertain why she should, Mairi hesitated.

"I have already said that I will escort her ladyship," Lachlan said.

Mackinnon looked down his long nose at the younger man. "Unless I am mistaken, sir," he said coldly, "you have not been properly presented."

"That is true," Lachlan admitted with an easy smile.

"Perhaps you would present me now, and my brother as well."

"I do not present upstarts to ladies of the blood royal," Mackinnon snapped. "Come along, lassie," he added, taking Mairi's elbow with the familiarity of one who had known her all her life. "I warrant your lady mother has learned of your return by now and must be wondering where you are."

"You know, Hector," she heard Lachlan say as Niall hurried her across the yard toward the laird's hall, "that slanderous scoundrel is beginning to irk me."

Mairi hid a smile. Mackinnon frequently irked her, too.

—————————————————————

Chapter 3

"Niall, I beg you, slow down," Mairi said midway between laughter and annoyance. "It is not necessary to propel me across the yard. Consider my dignity, if you please!"

"You should consider your own dignity," he retorted. "To be seen in such company as that does you no honor."

"Who is he? I know only that his brother called him Lachlan—if, indeed, the huge one is his brother."

"Aye, they be brothers—twins if you can believe it—and devil's spawn, the pair o' them. The bonnie one is Lachlan of Bellachuan on Seil. His father, Ian Dubh, is chief of Clan Gillean and one of his grace's official councilors. Nonetheless, the sons of Gillean are upstarts, for all that they claim cousinship with your family."

"Surely you must know if they are cousins," Mairi said, frowning.

"Ian Dubh did marry a descendant of your great-grandfather's younger brother," Niall said. "I do not question her ancestry, certainly, but Clan Gillean knows little about its own. You should have naught to do with any of its sons."

"But if their father is a chief who sits on the Council of the Isles—"

"Och, aye, he is that, and yon Lachlan, in his puffed up arrogance, expects to follow after him in both positions, although I believe he is the younger twin."

Mairi stiffened but said evenly, "But did his grace not decide that when he dies my wee brother Donald will inherit the Lordship instead of John or Ranald or Godfrey or, indeed, some other, older kinsman of ours? Does the law of tanistry not allow the chief to suggest his successor to the clan?"

Niall did not answer at once, which did not surprise her, for although the law did allow suggestions, the clan usually made the final decision, and the successor could be any member of the chief's family. That meant it could as easily be his brother or nephew, or even a female, as any of his sons. Indeed, the chief's brother, being closer to the clan's progenitor than anyone in a subsequent generation, was often selected. But MacDonald had flatly decreed that the first son of his second marriage would succeed him, rather than any of his older sons, and that declaration was a sore point for many, not least because Donald was still a very young child.

However, Amy Macruari, MacDonald's first wife—and mother of John Og, Ranald, and Godfrey—although a great heiress, was not of royal blood. Mairi's mother, Margaret, on the other hand, not only was the granddaughter of Marjory, sister to Robert the Bruce, the great king who had united and freed Scotland, but also the daughter of Robert the Steward, present heir to the Scottish throne.

Thus, MacDonald had named wee Donald because of his royal connections. And that was not the only area in which he had gone against the law of tanistry, for it also required equal division of a man's wealth among his heirs. Believing dynasties were more apt to retain control of what they held,

MacDonald had declared that all his Clan Donald holdings would go to Donald. However, he had generously decided to divide the vast Macruari lands he had inherited through Amy among her sons.

As for his remaining unmarried daughters, MacDonald expected to dower them all handsomely and marry them into powerful families whose connections would further extend the increasingly vast power of Clan Donald.

Realizing that Niall still had not answered her question, she said, "Well, sir? Do you disapprove of his grace's naming Donald to be second Lord of the Isles?"

"It is not my place to approve or disapprove of his grace's decisions."

His calm austerity made her wonder if she had imagined emotion earlier when he had spoken of the brothers Maclean. Now he seemed intent only upon crossing the yard to the laird's hall gateway without allowing interruption from any member of the palace staff bold enough to speak to them.

Still curious about the two men and determined to probe further into Niall's reaction to them, she said, "Pray, tell me more about those brothers, sir? You say their acquaintance can do me no honor, yet surely if their father is one of his grace's chiefs, they are honorable men."

"If you want to know more, my lady," he said stiffly, "I shall ask his grace to explain the matter to you."

Mairi grinned. "I suppose you expect me to drop the subject rather than risk my father's wrath, sir, but experience should tell you that such a ploy will only fire my curiosity. Are they truly so dreadful?" When he grimaced, she added provocatively, "I thought them both rather handsome and charming."

"You should not even be having this conversation with

me," he said sternly, "but if you must know what I think, they are not suited to tread the same ground you do. The one they call Lachlan Lubanach, or 'Lachlan the Wily,' has set himself to become the most knowledgeable man in the west of Scotland, and pursues aspirations that far exceed his appropriate station in life."

"How so?"

"Many do say, and I believe that he has created a vast network of spies to bring him news of happenings throughout the Lordship and beyond."

"Spies!"

"Aye, and 'tis a most unsavory business that. Surely, you must agree."

Knowing he would not appreciate it if she admitted that the only emotion his words stirred was envy of a man who could gather so much information, she said, "Is his giant brother the same sort of person?"

His response resembled something between a grunt and a sigh.

"Come, Niall," she said as they neared the gateway to the laird's hall forecourt. "They are guests at Finlaggan, so I shall see them again, perhaps frequently. The more I know, the better I can protect myself."

The look he cast her told her as clearly as words that he recognized her curiosity for exactly what it was, but he said, "The brother is worse, if anything."

"What do men call him?"

"Hector the Ferocious."

"Mercy! Why?"

"Because he is a fierce man who carries a battle-axe everywhere save openly at his grace's court. That fearsome weapon is said to descend from their progenitor, Gillean of the Battle-axe, and they say Hector the Ferocious wields it as if it were part of him. 'Tis Lachlan has the brains, Hector the brawn, but both are dangerous, lass. Promise me that you will keep your distance from them."

To avoid a promise she knew she would break, she said, "I will take care, sir, but a murderer is far more dangerous. Who do you think killed Elma MacCoun?"

"Faith, lass, I don't know. It was only Mellis and his witnesses being so certain that persuaded anyone the woman had been murdered. I'll wager 'tis as likely she fell off a cliff and was swept ashore at Loch Gruinart with the tide."

"I heard only that they'd thought Ian pushed her and that Ewan Beton found her. Did he find her at Loch Gruinart?"

"Aye, on the sand there, washed up by the sea. 'Tis a pity, too. She was a better wife than MacCoun deserved. But you do not fool me, lass. I know you too well, and I want your word that you'll heed my warning about the sons of Gillean."

Solemnly, Mairi said, "I do understand, sir, thank you. I will take care."

He glanced at her again, but this time she met his skeptical look directly, easily maintaining her somber expression.

After a long moment, he nodded and said in the annoying paternal tone he often took with her, "Good lass. Let us go now and visit your lady mother."

Stifling a sigh, Mairi allowed him to escort her up to her mother's solar.

The Maclean brothers watched the pair from the great hall porch until they disappeared through the gate into the roofed forecourt of the laird's hall, when Hector said gruffly,

"I'm thinking that man's not singing your praises t' the lass."

"Nor yours," Lachlan said, revealing his amusement at last with a wry smile. "Niall MacGillebride Mackinnon does not like us or our ilk, but although he may worry about how much I know of him, I warrant he'll not trouble us much."

"He might if you continue to cast hungry glances in her ladyship's direction," Hector warned. "Aye, sure, but she's a fine-looking wench."

"She is," Lachlan agreed, thinking he had never seen one finer. Her skin looked like ivory, making him yearn to touch her, to see if it was as smooth.

"Who would have thought she'd be MacDonald's daughter, though?"

"Both of us should have known the moment we clapped eyes on her, had we thought at all," Lachlan said, still enjoying the bubble of laughter that had filled him from the moment he had first engaged her in conversation.

"Indeed, I was fair spellbound by her beauty and failed to consider who she might be," Hector agreed.

"I, too, but who else would wear ermine and red tiretain at his grace's court, and a gold circlet atop her caul? That should have told us if naught else did."

"Her lady mother, mayhap, would wear all that, or mayhap her sister."

"But 'twould be the same then, as to identity and rank. Moreover, we know Lady Margaret and Elizabeth. The others are all bairns yet or married and gone."

"She might have been a chief's daughter," Hector suggested, clearly unwilling to agree that they both should have guessed her identity.

"Few men have brought their wives, and none has brought a daughter."

Hector nodded. He might question Lachlan's judgment but rarely for long.

"She's a brave lass," Lachlan added, idly fingering the gold ring on his right little finger, "or she's a foolhardy one."

"Aye, a woman should not speak up as boldly as she did," Hector said, "but by my troth, she seems canny enough. I'm thinking someone should have seen afore she did that the lad, Ian Burk, could not have committed that murder."

Lachlan shrugged. "Men do not always see what is beneath their noses. As she said, by the time anyone realized the woman had been murdered, enough time had passed that few folks knew exactly where they were when she disappeared. I'd wager the first time anyone even considered the possibility that the lad might have been elsewhere was when her ladyship did. I own, though, I'm curious."

"About what?"

"I'd like to know who did kill that woman, and why. 'Tis a puzzle, that is."

"Aye, and you were ever the one for puzzles."

Lachlan nodded, then frowned and said, "Have you heard anyone say just how they know she was murdered?"

"Nay, then, only that she died. Do you want me to look into it?"

He nodded. "See if you cannot glean at least such facts as are known beyond what we heard at that trial, but take care. Many will talk about it, so opportunities to learn more should present themselves, but we'll be here just a few more days, and no one will thank us for putting our noses into Isla business." He paused, smiling reminiscently, and added, "I agree with you, though. She's a clever lass."

"Still, she should have told someone else, and quietly," Hector said. "I'm thinking no woman should speak up so boldly in a court of law."

"Perhaps," Lachlan agreed, "but I like a bold lass better than a dull one."

"You like any lass, as long as she's pretty," Hector said, grinning.

"I learned that from you."

Still grinning, Hector said, "Aye, that's true." After a moment's thought, he added more seriously, "I like bold lasses, too, my lad, but I'm thinking that one treads perilously near becoming insolent."

"She does," Lachlan agreed. But her insolence was not what kept his thoughts fixed on the lovely Mairi of Isla for the rest of that day.

Lady Margaret greeted her daughter's arrival with visible pleasure, as did Mairi's sister Elizabeth and the two waiting women who bore them company. The latter two had served her ladyship since her marriage, and Mairi generally thought of them as the Rose and the Weed because of tall Adela's predilection for bright colors and shorter, plumper Clara's habit of dressing in russet and brown. All four women set aside their embroidery, the better to express their delight, and the Rose and the Weed stood politely to make their curtsies to her.

As Mairi made hers to her mother, Lady Margaret said with a smile, "I did not anticipate your return for yet another sennight, dearling."

"No, madam, but we had completed our duties at Dunyvaig, and so Ranald and I were able to return sooner."

Lady Margaret raised one thin, delicately arched eyebrow, but Elizabeth laughed. "Indeed," she said as she tucked a stray nut-brown curl back under her caul, "and here were we, suspecting that 'twas the shocking news of Ian Burk's trial that drew you home—and that so swiftly as to risk your life in a dangerous fog."

Suppressing irritation with her sister in order to meet her mother's quizzical gaze, Mairi felt guilty heat surge to her cheeks. She was searching her thoughts for a persuasive way to explain her concern for Ian and her determination to prevent his hanging when Niall Mackinnon, still beside her, interrupted her thoughts.

"Her ladyship's recklessness must concern us all, madam," he said to Margaret. "Doubtless his grace will have much to say to Lord Ranald for allowing it, but that she cared so much about a mere servant's fate does bear testimony to her kind heart. Moreover, you will be pleased to know that Ian Burk managed to prove himself innocent of the charge."

"Praise be to God for that," Lady Margaret said, adding gently, "You may leave us now, sir. I would be privy with my daughters."

Recognizing a touch of her own annoyance with Mackinnon in her mother's tone, Mairi nonetheless braced herself as he bowed and took his leave.

Lady Margaret Stewart rarely lost her temper or displayed strong emotion. A handsome woman handsomely garbed in gold-embroidered, sable-trimmed ivory silk, she displayed a regal manner reflective of her heritage. Her father was hereditary High Steward of Scotland as his father and ancestors for over two hundred years had been before him. He was also heir apparent to the Scottish throne, because David Bruce, despite being in his forty-third year and on his second wife, had no offspring.

When the door had shut behind Mackinnon, and the Rose and the Weed had discreetly returned their attention to their embroidery, Mairi met her mother's gaze and said, "I hope you are not angry with me, madam."

"No, dearling, although I confess I am glad we did not know your intent and thus endured our brief reaction to your recklessness only after your safe arrival."

Elizabeth said, "You should have been more thoughtful, Mairi."

"We did not know the fog would come," Mairi pointed out.

"Neither did you have to depart in the dead of night, as you must have done to arrive so early this morning," Lady Margaret said.

Knowing better than to insist that Ian's peril had put the necessity for speed ahead of that for caution, Mairi held her tongue, albeit with difficulty.

That her mother understood that difficulty was evident in the half smile that touched her lips, and more so when she said, "Am I correct in believing that young Ian did not prove his innocence alone, as Niall's words might lead one to assume?"

Mairi returned the smile. "I was able to show that he could not have killed Elma," she said. "I do beg pardon if my actions distressed you even briefly, madam, but having known him most of my life, I was certain he could not have done it."

"If anyone did murder her, I'd guess it was Mellis Mac-Coun," Lady Margaret said with more tartness than she was accustomed to display.

"I own, I should like to know how she died," Mairi said.

"Do you think Mellis did it, madam?" Elizabeth asked, her blue eyes wide.

"I do not encourage anyone to gossip, as you know, but I have heard him described as a hard man, and she was much younger than he, and beautiful," Lady Margaret said. "I know the difficulties that can arise when a woman marries a man twenty years her senior, and few men are as fair-minded as your father."

"Mellis MacCoun is not," Mairi said.

"Aye, but even so, I should think it more likely that Elma had some sort of accident, for as you doubtless know your-self, she liked to wander along the shore when she was dis-tressed or angry with Mellis. There are places along the Sound, certainly, where one might slip and fall into the sea."

"Niall thinks she fell, too, but at Loch Gruinart, not along the Sound."

"Is that where Ewan Beton found her?" Elizabeth asked.

"Aye, for so Niall told me."

Lady Margaret said, "Gruinart is five miles from here, but a woman in a temper can cover a good distance, walk-ing or riding, and I'd warrant Elma could reach the sea cliffs north of here even more easily and be swept west on the tide."

That was true, and few women on Isla could swim. With the long skirts and underskirts most wore, even fewer would survive falling fully clothed into any but shallow, calm water, and none would survive falling off a cliff into surf crashing against the rocks below. At least they had found Elma. Often, inexplicably, victims simply sank in the cold seawater, never to be seen again. Just imagining such a fate sent a shiver up Mairi's spine as a new thought stirred.

"Does anyone even know when Elma left Finlaggan?"

"Aye," Elizabeth said. "Someone asked the guardsmen at the causeway, and they agreed that she left sometime that af-ternoon, well before suppertime."

"Then Mellis cannot have killed her," Mairi said, "unless

he somehow met her at Loch Gruinart before Godfrey and his party returned to Finlaggan."

"Enough of this sordid talk," Lady Margaret said. "Tell us the news of Dunyvaig; and then, whilst I change my attire to dine with our guests, you can visit the children and amuse them until it is time for us to walk to the great hall to dine."

"They will be glad to see you," Elizabeth said. "They have been plaguing us for days to know when you would return. But first, do tell us all about Dunyvaig."

As they discussed the cleaning and new stores at Dunyvaig, and such news as Ranald had gleaned in his travels to Annandale and Loch Tarbert, temptation stirred more than once to ask if either Margaret or Elizabeth had taken notice of the sons of Gillean, but Mairi stifled each impulse. Knowing that her mother strongly approved of MacDonald's plan to marry her into the royal family, she decided she would be wiser to satisfy her curiosity on her own. Niall had said the two men were popular, which assured her that they had drawn Elizabeth's attention, but she thought it unlikely that her well-guarded younger sister would know much about them.

The chapel bells rang the midday hour of Sext a short time later, and less than a quarter hour after that, Mairi entered the great hall again with Lady Margaret, Elizabeth, and the two ladies in waiting.

A transformation had taken place in the meantime. Rows of white-draped trestle tables stood where crowded benches had been before, and the high table on the dais at which her father had presided over his grievance court had been extended to accommodate his noble guests. It was likewise draped in elegant white linen, but embroidered round the hem with his ubiquitous little black ships.

Frequently, the Lord of the Isles, like other wealthy, powerful men, dined separately in the laird's hall with his family, but MacDonald made it a habit to dine in the great hall regularly, wanting to maintain a close connection to his dependents. He had not come in yet, but Ranald and Godfrey stood on the dais and Mairi joined them with her mother and Elizabeth. Her eldest brother, John Og, had not come to Finlaggan because his wife, Freya, expected to deliver their second child soon, and John Og hoped his presence at home would produce the son he so fervently desired.

As Mairi greeted Ranald and Godfrey, Ranald clapped her on the shoulder and said, "You slipped out too quickly, lass. Ian Burk was looking to thank you."

"I only did what was right," she said as one of Godfrey's big hands wrapped around hers. Turning to receive his welcoming kiss, she saw her father emerge from the chamber behind the dais, flanked by the two sons of Gillean.

"Close your mouth, lass," Godfrey murmured. "Ye're gaping like a trout."

"Welcome home, daughter," MacDonald said as she hurriedly curtsied to him. "We've missed you. But before I forget my duty, it has come to my attention that no one has yet presented the sons of Ian Dubh, Chief of Clan Gillean, to you."

He extended a hand to her, and she gave it a loving squeeze as she rose from her curtsy and said, "I am glad to be home again, your grace." Meeting his gaze, she relaxed. She had been confident he would not deny her the right to speak or scold her for it afterward, but the warmth in his expression was nonetheless reassuring.

MacDonald continued to hold her hand as he said, "It is a pleasure for me to present two new ambassadors to my court to you, daughter. This gentleman is Lachlan, son of Ian Dubh, son of Gille Coluim, son of . . ."

He continued the formal introduction through six or seven more generations, but she had already shifted her gaze to Lachlan Lubanach. Her intent had been to display an air of condescending formality, even hauteur, but the wretched man caught her gaze and held it, his eyes alight with that wicked twinkle.

She nearly interrupted her father to demand of his guest if he dared to laugh at her, but well aware of what her brothers' reaction would be to such a demand, not to mention her father's to such an interruption, she held her tongue.

". . . and this is his brother Hector," MacDonald added at last. "The two of them serve as Ian Dubh's ambassadors from Clan Gillean."

"Welcome to Finlaggan," Mairi said, striving for grace but too aware of that lingering twinkle to believe she sounded anything but dazed. Gratefully aware that Lady Margaret had led her two faithful attendants and Elizabeth away, and knowing that if she wanted to deal satisfactorily with the impudent man she first had to gain the upper hand, she said innocently, "Do men really call you Lachlan the Wily?"

His quick smile caught her by surprise, because she had been certain her comment would annoy him. His teeth flashed white, strong, and even as he said, "Aye, your ladyship, they do, especially those who envy my wiles, wishing they were as agile of mind. But one need not wonder long about who whispered such information into your beautiful ears."

Feeling heat in her cheeks and struggling to ignore a temptation to cover ears that her headdress already covered, Mairi realized that her father had spoken.

"I beg your pardon, your grace," she said. "I was not attending."

"I asked who was so impertinent as to repeat such a thing to you," MacDonald said, looking stern.

Although Niall had annoyed her, she knew he had warned her out of concern for her safety, and she did not want to betray him.

The awkward moment became more so when Hector said bluntly, "'Tis no great leap of thought, your grace, to guess that it was your Master of Household."

The stern gaze snapped toward him, but he met it with easy calm.

Lachlan said with similar ease of manner, "I fear that Niall Mackinnon does not love us, your grace, or any man of Clan Gillean. As you know, my father holds property on the Isle of Mull, where Mackinnon aspires to control all."

"Not all, I think," MacDonald said dryly. "I control the Isle of Mull, so both Niall Mackinnon and Ian Dubh hold their properties only at my pleasure."

"Aye, your grace," Lachlan said. "But doubtless Lady Mairi grows bored with talk of property and hungry for her dinner." Glancing at the high table, he added, "I warrant you would have Hector and me take our places below the dais today."

"Nay, I would not," MacDonald said with a relaxed smile. "Not only do you stand in your father's place at my council, but I invited you to dine with me, and do not rescind my invitations so easily. Indeed, I enjoy your company and would that Mairi and her lady mother may enjoy it, too. Take your place between them if you like, for I mean to keep your brother by me to tell another of his amusing tales."

Thus did Mairi find herself seated beside the man who

rapidly was becoming something between an enigma and a nemesis to her.

A glance at the end of the table to her right revealed Elizabeth shooting dagger looks at her, but it was Mairi's privilege as the elder to sit at her mother's left, and with so many men at the high table, she was certain Lady Margaret had commanded Elizabeth to sit, well guarded, between the Rose and the Weed.

No sooner had the chaplain spoken the grace before meat than Lachlan Lubanach said ruefully, "I hope you are not too vexed with me, lass. I could see that my mentioning Niall Mackinnon displeased you."

Turning her head with the firm intent of reminding him that he should address her properly, she encountered a boyishly rueful look that instantly caused her to reassess her first appraisal of the man.

The day outside still being decidedly gray, the iron candelabra in the hall had been lighted, including the pair hanging over the high table, and his eyes reflected the warmth of candle glow. She felt as if she were being drawn right into them.

"In this candlelight your eyes look like dark, bottomless pools," he said.

"Don't be silly," she retorted, as if she had not been staring into his and thinking similar thoughts. Wrenching her gaze away and striving to sound only casually interested, she said, "Why should you think I was vexed with you?"

"Do you deny it?"

"Nay, I do not, but you are an impudent man, Lachlan Lubanach."

He grinned, and again she noted how his quick smile altered his features, warming and softening them. "Surely," he said, "I have given you greater cause than that to think me impudent, lass."

She surprised herself with a gurgle of laughter. "I warrant, sir, that if I should be so foolish as to deny that, you would soon *give* me greater cause."

"Aye, I would," he murmured, his smile growing more tantalizing.

"Mairi, lass, out of pity, unless you mean to starve the rest of us, let that gillie serve you your fish," Godfrey commanded from her left, startling her.

Godfrey and Ranald both burst into laughter, but she caught a look from Lady Margaret that warned her to remember her manners, and a more speculative one from her father that caused her to turn quickly to the patient gillie behind her and ask for a small slice of salmon from the wooden tray he held.

Relieved when her father turned back to Hector, she allowed Lachlan to serve her an onion pasty from the platter before him on the table.

"Would you like claret, lass?" he asked as he held a saucepot for her with one hand and signed with the other to a second gillie to fill his wine goblet.

"No, thank you," she said, spooning a small amount of mustard sauce onto her pasty. Then, drawing breath to steady her suddenly uncertain nerves as she returned the spoon to its pot, she said, "I should not have said that about giving me more cause to think you impudent."

"Nor should you have flung that insolent name men call me in my teeth."

"I wanted to annoy you," she admitted. "I will apologize for that, too, however, because you are my father's guest, and it was discourteous of me."

"Nay, lass, don't apologize. Your boldness gives me hope."

"Hope?"

"Aye. I'm thinking the time has come to take a wife, you see."

Swiftly she raised her eyes to look beyond him at her mother and father, but both appeared to be listening to Hector Reaganach.

Diverted, she said, "Does your brother truly tell such entertaining stories?"

"Aye, he does," Lachlan said. "And 'tis a good one he's telling now, and appropriate, too, about a contrary wife."

"How can you know that?" she demanded. "You cannot possibly hear him."

"I asked him to tell it," he said. "I knew it would amuse your parents and keep them occupied so that I could talk to you."

"You should not talk to me of wives though, sir, unless you only meant that you intend to tell me that tale yourself."

"I'll gladly tell it to you sometime, but not just now," he said, smiling again.

"Then why did you tell me you are thinking of taking a wife?"

"Because I believe I may have found the one I want," he said, still smiling.

"Pray, do not be nonsensical," she said, guessing what he meant. Then, realizing that he might not be thinking what she assumed he was, she said quickly, "I am no one to advise you on such an important matter, sir."

"Faith, I don't want your advice," he said, chuckling.

Knowing then that he had meant exactly what she had thought, she exclaimed, "But we've only just met. You do not even know me!"

"I know you live up to your legend," he said. "You are every bit as beautiful as men say you are."

"Pray, sir, cease prating absurdities to me. Legend, indeed! Surely, you want more in a wife than mere beauty."

"There is nothing mere about your beauty, lass. Not only have you a lovely face and unmatched grace but I have never seen skin so unflawed or eyes so dark and mysterious. I thought at first they were black, but they are not."

"No, merely blue," she said. "Like your own."

He shook his head, still smiling, and she realized that she was flirting with him. Oddly, the notion did not shock her, and that realization convinced her at last that Niall had been right. Lachlan Lubanach was a very dangerous man.

$\mathcal{C}hapter\ 4$ ————————————

Lachlan enjoyed that meal more than any other he could recall. He had long admired MacDonald of the Isles for his acumen and ability, but found that he liked him more than he had expected to like any man wielding such power. And he admired Lady Margaret for her gentle grace and unfailing courtesy.

But Lady Mairi stirred more than admiration.

Although her demeanor was cool, calm, even aloof, that little gurgle of laughter that had escaped her stirred a strong desire in him to hear her laugh again and with abandon. He sensed suppressed passion in every move she made, and a strong sensibility, which led him to wonder what delights she held in store for a man who could release those passions.

She was regarding him curiously, clearly wondering what outrageous thing he would say next, so he said, "I warrant Hector must have finished his tale by now, so if you will excuse me, I should converse with your lady mother, lest she believe me discourteous."

Mairi nodded regally, instantly refilling the bubble of delight he had felt since their first meeting. Even so, as he turned to engage Lady Margaret in dutiful conversation, he wondered how the lass would display the temper that others had warned him about. If she threw things at him, such passion might amuse him until his own unpredictable temper took fire. Then only God knew what would happen unless he quickly broke her of the habit.

Mairi was annoyed. She would have liked to grab Lachlan Lubanach by the ears and force him to explain exactly what he had meant when he had so glibly spoken of taking a wife. To be even slightly concerned about such a thing in a man she barely knew seemed ridiculous, but even so, she could not stop wondering.

Godfrey engaged her in conversation as soon as she returned her attention to her trencher, and she discussed family matters with him, laughing when he said that their eldest brother, John Og, truly believed he could affect the gender of his child by hovering over his unfortunate wife until the babe arrived. But as they chatted, half of her attention remained fixed on the murmured conversation to her right. She heard little of what they said, but when Margaret laughed, she wondered what he had said to amuse her, and twice she lost the thread of what Godfrey was saying.

"You like him."

Her breath caught, and her jaw dropped. "What?"

"You like him," Godfrey repeated, his voice low. "I can see it in your eyes and feel your awareness of him even as you converse with me. It won't do, lass."

Grimacing, Mairi said, "I wish you would not tease me, Godfrey. I do not know what you are talking about."

"I do not tease," he said seriously. "He's a charming fellow. Everyone says so. Even his grace likes him. Faith, he likes them both, for all that Hector the Ferocious has more the reputation of a predatory warrior than a courtier. I warrant that when his grace's court gathers at Ardtornish, the ladies will like them both even better than their men do now. Only heed how hungrily Elizabeth eyes them."

"Will those two be at Ardtornish, then?" Mairi asked, careful to include Hector, although she did not much care if he joined them at Ardtornish or not.

"Aye, they'll be there, for I'm told that their father, Ian Dubh, has grown less interested in politics and is passing his candle to Lachlan. And Bellachuan being close to Ardtornish, they have both accepted his grace's invitation to join us for his annual Easter hunt on the Isle of Mull."

"There is at least one person who does not like him . . . them," Mairi amended quickly.

Godfrey nodded. "I have noted for myself that Niall Mackinnon expresses no compliment for any son of Gillean. But Mackinnon is an excellent high steward, lass. He thinks only of our welfare and that of his grace."

Knowing that in his own gentle way Godfrey was warning her, she changed the subject to Dunyvaig, because the mention of passing candles had reminded her that one of the men had accidentally started a fire in the garderobe tower there.

"I can guess how," Godfrey said, laughing. "He took a candle in with him and it fell off the ledge into the pile of fresh hay they keep there for wiping."

Mairi nodded, enjoying his merriment, although similar accidents happened frequently, sometimes with astonishing, even terrifying results.

A lock of the tawny hair that Godfrey had inherited from his mother Amy had fallen over one eye, and he brushed it aside, still grinning at Mairi. He was the largest of her half brothers, with the biggest hands and feet, but also the kindest.

Sobering, he said, "That was a brave thing you did, lass, standing up for Ian."

"I knew he did not do it," she said, "but I wonder now who did."

He shrugged. "Not Mellis MacCoun, if that is what you're thinking, because he was at Kilchoman with me. We did not return until that evening, after she'd disappeared. But stop changing the subject," he added sternly. "If you've taken a liking to Lachlan the Wily, you're wading into dangerous water."

She was tempted to tell him Lachlan had said he was thinking of marrying, to ask what he thought about that, but she knew what Godfrey would think of any man discussing that subject with her rather than with their father. She knew, too, that everyone expected her to marry Alasdair Stewart if only because—presuming that a cumbersome number of persons obliged him first by dying, and the fractious Scottish Parliament agreed—he might one day become King of Scots.

Even if he did not, her grandfather Robert would be king unless, through some miracle of God, David finally managed to produce a son or daughter. And since her father's primary reason for marrying her to Alasdair was to help fulfill his goal of forming as many royal connections as possible, the better to protect every member of Clan Donald, she doubted that he would change his mind.

Fingers touched her right knee, nearly startling her out of her skin.

"What is it, lass?" Godfrey asked. "Art cold?"

Managing a rueful smile, she said, "I think I nearly fell

asleep as I sit here, sir. Much as it pains me to admit weakness, I'm dead tired."

"And no wonder, since Ranald tells me you insisted on starting for Finlaggan nearer midnight than dawn and then were becalmed for hours. Did you sleep at all?"

"I wasn't tired then," she said. "Even becalmed and unable to see my hand before my eyes, the current carried us safely enough, albeit slowly, and it was exciting to be on the water in such darkness. Although," she added, remembering, "Meg Raith kept imagining sea monsters."

Godfrey chuckled again, but then said gently, "You neglect our guest."

She had known from the moment Lachlan Lubanach's fingers touched her knee that Lady Margaret must have returned her attention to his grace, but she had thought it would do him good to study patience.

Turning to him now, she said with polite dignity, "I trust you find our meals to your liking, sir."

"They are excellent, my lady, as are his grace's minstrels."

She had not heeded the minstrels, because they played wherever her father dined, but she glanced obediently at the little gallery halfway up the east wall. A narrow stairway in the wall led up to it, she knew, for as a child she had often sneaked up there to listen while her father and other men discussed kings and princes in faraway lands and wars that one or another wanted the Lord of the Isles to help him win. She did not approve of war, for although her father was not combatant, the politics of war often took him from home for long stretches of time.

Niall Mackinnon had caught her eavesdropping once when she was eight or nine, and had spanked her soundly before bearing her to MacDonald and telling him what she had done. But although he had scolded her for slipping away from the women without permission and thus worrying a number of people, and had *not* scolded his high steward for her humiliating and painful punishment, MacDonald had always, patiently, answered her questions. He had also, in time, taught her to play chess, explaining that much of the game's strategy imitated war.

Realizing that Lachlan was sitting quietly now, watching her, she said, "Will you tell me the story now that your brother related to my parents?"

"Another time, perhaps," he said. "Your lady mother is nearly ready to depart, and I warrant you and the lady Elizabeth will go with her."

"Aye, but there is time enough for you to explain what you meant," she said, mildly annoyed because a true gentleman would have complied with her request.

He looked puzzled. "What I meant by what?"

"Good sir, you know perfectly well. You said you are interested in marrying, and you said it in such a way that I'd have to be a noddy not to take your meaning. But surely you know that my father would never permit such a connection even were I to consent to it."

"Would you consent?"

His gaze had intensified, and every fiber of her body threatened to betray her as she gazed back. It took enormous strength of mind to say calmly, "You must not ask me such a thing. 'Twould be most improper under any circumstance, but to ask when we know so little of each other . . . Faith, to ask me at all when neither you nor your father has approached mine. You step beyond all the bounds, sir."

"Aye, I do that, and often," he said. "I have found it is the best way."

"The best way for what?"

"To get what I want, of course. Necessity acknowledges no bounds."

Lady Margaret chose that moment to stand up, and Mairi, stunned by his casual attitude toward such an important topic, felt only gratitude that she need not continue the outrageous conversation. That she would have liked to continue it confused her, for she had never had such an experience before and knew not how to cope with it. Indeed, she had never known a man like Lachlan Lubanach and had no idea how to cope with him.

He fascinated her at the same time that his behavior outraged and appalled her. Often had she heard troubadours sing of men who fell hopelessly in love in the face of all opposition, and rode off in triumph, the ladies of their desire riding pillion behind them. Mairi had long believed those tales to be apocryphal, for what possible end could such defiant couples meet but disaster.

Obediently she returned with her mother and Elizabeth to the laird's hall, knowing that MacDonald and his councilors, including the sons of Gillean, would be busy all afternoon with the business of the Council of the Isles. If her thoughts frequently slid away from her duties, she nonetheless performed them and did not protest when she learned that the family would take supper privately, for by then she was exhausted. Moreover, she wanted to think about Lachlan Lubanach and devise a way, somehow, to keep him safely at arm's length. He offered excellent opportunities to practice the art of flirting, but that was all she wanted of him.

She was certain of that and told herself so several times before she climbed into bed beside Elizabeth. She was still telling herself so when she fell asleep.

The next morning Mairi woke with the dawn, and when her waking thought was for a pair of teasing blue eyes, she mentally scolded herself and resolved that flirtation would not be the order of the day. After Lady Margaret arose, the entire household would assemble for morning prayers, but that would not happen for another hour, and by then Mairi intended to be a good distance from Finlaggan.

At Dunyvaig, every waking hour had been duty-bound. Determined to show her father and mother that she was perfectly able to handle such responsibility, and having no social obligations of note, she had devoted as much energy to her tasks as Ranald had to his. Since Ranald was likely to knock heads if work on the boats or fortifications progressed too slowly to suit him, Mairi's diplomatic skills had been required occasionally as well, after such incidents.

Plainly, she now deserved a holiday.

Dressing quickly, without assistance and without waking Elizabeth, she brushed snarls from her long hair and carelessly replaited it, deciding to leave it uncovered until her return, when Meg Raith could arrange it properly and encase it in its usual, formal caul. Finding gloves and donning the hooded crimson cloak she had worn in the boat the morning before, she hurried downstairs and across the open, south-facing forecourt without encountering another soul.

Loch Finlaggan stretched southward, gray, calm, and peaceful. The previous day's fog had lifted, but the sky remained overcast, the air still. As she crossed the great hall courtyard, a pair of gulls soared silently overhead. Beyond the hall, she hurried along the narrow road linking servants' cottages and chapel, then continuing through the enclosure to the stone causeway and the main island of Isla.

Her skin prickled as she strode past the chapel, for although workers had not begun work for the day on the roof, it was always possible that her father's chaplain or one of the monks who served him might step out and call to her. He might want only to bid her good morrow or welcome her return, but could as easily demand to know where she was going and wonder aloud if she would return in time for prayers. Answering either yea or nay to him could well land her in the suds later.

No one called to her, and as she passed through the gateway to the stable enclosure, she released the breath she had been holding.

"Ian, are you here?" she called as she entered the barn.

"Down here, mistress, wi' the lad."

Smiling, she turned toward his voice and found him in the end stall brushing her favorite mount, a sleek, long-tailed, light gray gelding she called Hobyn.

Patting the horse's flank, she eased past it to its head, murmuring endearments and reaching to stroke the blaze on its face. Instead, Hobyn pushed his soft nose into her palm.

"He missed me," she said.

"Aye, he always does," Ian agreed, still brushing. When she said nothing more, he glanced shyly at her and said, "'Tis that grateful I am t' ye, my lady. Nae one else would believe I didna kill Elma."

"I know, Ian. It is plain now to everyone that you did not, however."

"Still, I'm glad ye came home when ye did and that ye spoke up so strong at his grace's court. Had ye no done that, Mellis MacCoun would ha' demanded me hanging straightaway."

"The charge against you was weak, Ian. I've yet to hear anything to prove Elma's death was not an accident. In any event, I mean to ride this morning."

"Aye, sure, mistress, I'll just saddle Hobyn and get me own pony."

"I want no saddle today, nor do I need you with me," she said. "I mean only to ride to Loch Gruinart and back before I break my fast."

"Sakes, mistress, 'tis safe enough for ye anywhere on Isla, I ken well, but if ye should suffer a mishap—"

"I won't," she said, laughing at his concern. "Nor will anyone scold you. It is not as if I have not done the same thing many and many a time before."

"Aye, 'tis true, that," Ian said. "I'll just put the lad's bridle on then and give ye a leg up."

Minutes later, free of care and comfortably astride as she had ridden since childhood, she rode out of the enclosure and across the causeway, keeping an eye on the cottages along the shore on the slight chance that one of her brothers had come out early to speak to a guardsman or someone else who lived there.

Ancient woodland lay before her split by a narrow track that ran alongside one of the many burns feeding into Finlaggan. She followed it to the top of the low ridge, and as she rode north along the ridgeline, the eastern sky beyond the pointed twin Paps of Jura grew pink and then orange, spreading color into and under the thin cloud layer above.

Riding downhill to Loch Car Nan Gall, she paused to watch the sun peep over the horizon, splashing golden rays through the narrow space below the cloud layer. The wooded dale was narrow, and she crossed a second ridge a short time later. From the top, she enjoyed her first view of the sea at the north end of the island. Following a tumbling river through more patches of woodland, she soon came to the craggy point where Loch Gruinart met the sea.

To her right lay the cliffs from which Elma might have

fallen. Others loomed above the seashore on the other side of the loch mouth, for she had often seen them from boats on the water. But she thought it unlikely that Elma would have walked so far, and unlikely, too, that she had taken a boat, since someone surely would have known of it and spoken up before now.

It occurred to her then that Elma might have followed Godfrey's party to Kilchoman, perhaps to take Mellis something he had forgotten. But even if Godfrey had not followed his usual route south to Loch Indaal and across its head, his party would have ridden closer to the head of Loch Gruinart. From where she was to the loch head was at least five miles from the sea, too far from any cliff off which Elma might have fallen.

One of Mairi's favorite pastimes was to ride along Loch Gruinart's shore and back to Finlaggan by way of jewellike Loch Cam, and the temptation was strong to do so today if only because she might find some indication as to exactly where Ewan Beton had found Elma's body. But that likelihood was remote, and the journey would take too long. As it was, she risked missing breakfast and would likely have to endure her mother's displeasure.

Nevertheless, she could not return without first galloping on the sand. Loch Gruinart was blessed with wide, rolling sand dunes along its shore, and she could ride full out on them. Indeed, one of her greatest pleasures in summertime was to run barefoot through the warm sand. Just thinking about that now made her smile.

From the ridge above, Lachlan watched the lass ride down to the shore. She was a pleasure to watch, no matter what she did, but on horseback, she was breathtaking. He had never known an Isleswoman who rode so easily and so well, as if she were an extension of her horse. The silvery gray was splendid, too.

He had spent an hour after supper the previous evening building an acquaintance with young Ian Burk. Easily deducing that Lady Mairi cared about the lad, and that Ian might thus prove a font of valuable information if handled deftly, Lachlan had employed his considerable skills of interrogation to excellent result. Although Ian was plainly devoted to his mistress, the task had not been difficult after Lachlan expressed his satisfaction that Ian had proven his innocence, and his certainty that Lady Mairi's relief must have been profound.

The result had been as if a dam had broken, releasing a torrent of praise for her ladyship. Directing the conversation after that had been child's play, and he had soon learned that her ladyship delighted in early-morning rides, that she had been unable to indulge that pleasure at Dunyvaig, from whence she had just returned, and that she would almost certainly want to ride first thing in the morning.

Thus, Lachlan had set himself to wake before dawn, had ordered his horse saddled, and had ridden across the causeway into the woodland before her, soon finding a concealed vantage point from which he could watch for her to follow.

Keeping her in sight had been easy, although for a time he'd had to be careful not to let her see him. But the only time she had nearly done so was when she had paused to watch the sunrise, and after that she had seemed to care only about her destination, because she had ridden without once looking back.

She lingered on the headland only a moment or two, gazing northward at a calm sea. Then, abruptly, she wheeled the gray, leaned over its withers, and urged it forward. Responding at once, it galloped across the strip of sand, its long tail banner high. The lass's glorious ebony hair, loosed from its plaits, streamed like a second banner behind her. Despite the distance between them, he could see her wide smile, and found himself grinning in response.

Without further thought, he spurred the powerful bay he rode, and it too leaped forward, as eager for the run as he was.

Mairi breathed in the tangy salt air, wanting to shriek her delight as Hobyn pounded along the sandy shore toward a line of boulders that formed an uneven barrier from the waterline into the thick growth of shrubbery at the high-water mark. As she drew near, she reined to a slower pace, then to a halt.

The day was fine despite the overcast. The sea was calm, the shallow loch even more so, and the sand looked warm and inviting. Impulsively, she slid to the ground, retaining her hold on the reins as she did. Then, taking off her cloak, she heaped it on one boulder as she sat on another to pull off her soft leather boots.

Barefoot, she stood and wriggled her toes in the sand. Then, chuckling to herself like a merry child, she pulled the gray higher onto the shore and looped the reins over a branch of scrub. Then, hoisting her skirts above her knees, she ran between two of the boulders to the flat, clear stretch of sand beyond. Water lapped at the shore, rhythmic and gentle with airy foam in place of the surf that often thundered in from the north, so the tide was clearly on the turn. Although thoughts of surf and tide distracted her briefly, the temptation to test the water soon proved too much, and she ran onto the wet sand, finding it cool to her bare feet but not cold enough to discourage her from testing the water.

As the next wave spilled onto the beach, she splashed through it, squealing as the chilly water kissed her ankles. Then, laughing, she ran on, skipping and kicking the water with a child's delight until she stopped to watch two brown and white redshanks fighting over flotsam they had found on the beach, their long red legs making them easy to identify. The victor took wing with its snatched prize, and the other followed with angry, excited babble. The flight of both—fast, erratic, with jerky wing beats—held her fascination briefly until she heard hoofbeats thudding toward her across the sand.

Whirling, she saw the horseman bearing down on her, having barely slowed to negotiate the line of boulders. She knew instantly who it was, and her heart, although still pounding hard from her run, quickened its beat.

He slowed his mount, reining it to a halt while still some distance away, as if he were afraid he might frighten her if he rode too close.

Moments passed. At last, moving cautiously, still watching her, he eased a leg over the horse's withers and slid to the ground.

The moment his feet touched sand, Mairi turned, snatched up her skirts, and ran, keeping to the hard, damp sand at the water's edge. She did not glance back, certain that he would remount and follow, not daring to lose time by looking.

Exhilarated, she quickened her pace, listening hard for more hoofbeats on the hard-packed sand. After several moments of hard running without hearing them, she glanced back.

What she saw startled her nearly out of her wits, because without a sound to warn her, he was right behind her. Shock stirred new speed, but it was useless.

He caught her by her right shoulder, swinging her off balance and making her stumble, but she did not fall because without missing a step, he scooped her into his arms, kept running for a few steps, and then slowed to a stop.

He did not set her down, nor would the words come to demand that he do so.

Her gaze locked with his. Her heart pounded harder and faster than ever.

Chapter 5

Lachlan was of two minds. Common sense said he should set her down at once and apologize for frightening her. But her body was warm and soft in his arms, and with roses coloring her lips and cheeks, her dark eyes sparkling, and her breasts heaving in that tantalizing way, he knew it would take a man of stronger character than his to do anything so daft when he wanted only to kiss her.

Gently, he said, "You've caused me to ruin an excellent pair of boots, my lass, so if that horse of mine decides to return to his stable without me, I'm going to be sorely vexed with you."

"I am not your lass." Her voice was as rich, resonant, and musical as he remembered, and the sound of it struck respondent chords throughout his body, making him want even more to kiss her.

When she licked her lips, he nearly gave in to the temptation and briefly wondered if he was crazy to ignore the opportunity.

Forcing himself to speak calmly, he said, "Why did you run from me?"

She did not answer at once, but a twitch of eyebrow and

a tightening of lips told him she was weighing her answer, perhaps even deciding between possibilities.

"Before you reply, I would ask a boon," he said in much the same tone that he might have used to calm a nervous mare.

She cocked her head, but he did not accept the clear invitation to ask what he liked, waiting instead until she said, "You deserve no boon."

"I know that," he said, "but still I do ask one."

"A gentleman would set me on my feet first."

He waited, inwardly smiling at what was apparently a natural inclination on her part to negotiate with him.

After a longer silence than he had expected, she sighed and said, "What boon would you ask then?"

"Only that you be truthful rather than kind or clever in answering my question. What was the first thought that crossed your mind when I asked it?"

"That I did not know why I ran," she replied readily. "I just did, but that seemed a stupid thing to say to you."

Her dark eyes were wide open, and when her rosy lips twitched in a small grimace, he knew she spoke the truth. Her breasts no longer heaved with such fervor, but the color in her cheeks had not faded, nor had his intense desire to kiss her. And, oddly, she had not repeated her earlier suggestion that he set her down.

He did so now but put both hands on her shoulders so that she had to face him as he said, "You may always speak your mind to me, lass. I may disagree with you or point out errors if I detect them in your feminine logic, but I will not laugh at your opinions or call them stupid."

"I have six brothers, sir. I know what men think of women's opinions."

"Faith, do you dare to equate me with ordinary men?"

"Are you so extraordinary then?"

He smiled, searching her eyes for any indication that she was frightened of him. Seeing none, he moved a hand to cup her chin, holding it gently as he bent to taste her lips at last.

His mouth was soft at first, so soft she could barely feel it with hers. She stood perfectly still, fighting a longing to press her lips hard against his. And despite his gentleness, or perhaps because of it, the sensations that swept through her made her feel as breathless as she had felt while running away from him.

Her breasts swelled, pressing against her bodice as if they tried to escape its confines, and then, when he moved his hand from her chin back to her shoulder and pulled her against him, she felt her nipples harden, as new, wondrously stimulating sensations flooded her body.

His lips, demanding now, began to explore hers, to taste and savor them, and Mairi wondered how she had ever, for a moment, thought he was not a handsome man. His kisses grew harder, hungrier, and his arms slipped around her, hugging her closer until it felt as if the entire length of her body pressed against him. Indeed, she could feel his body moving against her in at least one place that she had not known a man's body could move—not unaided, at least.

Somehow, her hands found their way to his waist beneath his short cloak. His velvet doublet felt soft to her exploring fingers. As if it were perfectly natural to do such a thing, she eased her hands around him until she was hugging him back.

He pulled away abruptly and, shifting his hands to her shoulders again, set her firmly back on her heels.

She looked up in confusion. "Did I do something wrong?"

"Nay," he replied with a rueful smile. "I did."

"But why did you stop?"

"Because I have no wish to make an enemy of the Lord of the Isles or of his beautiful daughter," he said dryly.

"Oh," she said, trying to decide if the surge of disappointment she felt was because he feared her father's wrath or because he had stopped kissing her. She looked down, as if enlightenment might come from the sand beneath her bare feet.

His fingertips found her chin and tilted it up again. His eyes danced. "I enjoyed it, lassie," he said. "Don't think I did not."

"Well, you should not have done it," she said tartly.

"Faith, I ken that well enough."

"My father intends me to marry my cousin Alasdair."

"Aye, so you said, and I warrant 'tis wise for him to forge as many royal ties as he can, particularly with our Davy vexed with him again, as so often he is."

"He certainly is now," she agreed. "But I cannot think why the King should expect every lord of high estate to contribute to a ransom that most had small if any part in negotiating. The taxes he demands are absurdly high and will go to the English king, who is no friend to us. 'Tis no wonder so many refuse to pay."

"Most of our Davy's nobles have not refused. Only your father."

"That is not so, sir. Many chiefs and chieftains in the Isles have refused. Has your father paid what David demanded of him?"

"Faith, lass, even a king's demand cannot create money

where there is none. We of Clan Gillean have naught to offer him save our swords and loyal support."

"But your loyalty should be to the Lord of the Isles," she protested.

"Aye, sure, and so it is, and the Lord of the Isles commands our boats as well. If he should order us to support the King of Scots, we will as we have before, and right loyally. However, in point of fact," he added gently, "his grace refused payment of those ruinous taxes on behalf of all his Islesmen. Davy's anger arises from the fact that others, not just Islesmen, have followed MacDonald's lead."

She knew he was right. Somehow, she had lost sight of that point in her determination to prove him wrong. But in fairness to him, he had not said she was stupid to have done so, as John Og or Ranald might have done, or dismissed her opinion out of hand, as Niall Mackinnon so often did. She remembered something the latter had said to MacDonald while discussing the king's ransom.

Lifting her chin, she said, "Mayhap my father believes that having served as a hostage in England for nearly a year to guarantee David's promise to negotiate a ten-year truce with his nobles, and that infamous ransom, he had done all that was required of him. He holds small respect for our cousin, the King, doubtless because David is weak, unprincipled, and unworthy to call himself the Bruce's grandson."

"Faith," he exclaimed, "your father may think such things, but I hope that in general you have the good sense and discretion to keep such opinions to yourself."

She nibbled her lower lip. "I do, of course. Indeed, sir, I cannot think how I came to blurt that out to you, as I did."

His smile then warmed her to her toes, and the hand that gently squeezed her shoulder felt unnaturally warm, too.

"I meant it when I said you may say anything you like to

me," he said. "I do insist, though, that you exercise particular caution when expressing your opinion of the King to others or, indeed, your opinion of any other powerful man."

Mairi stiffened. "How dare you issue such a command to me?"

"'Tis merely wiser, I'm thinking, to trust few others with any confidence."

"Nonetheless, sir, you have no right to give me orders."

"I become ever more certain, however, that I want to have that right."

She could not mistake his meaning now, not when he loomed over her as he did, his hands still firm upon her shoulders, and gazed so intently into her eyes. Nor could she deny that her body responded instantly and with unfamiliar excitement to the thought of marrying him and letting him forever have his way with her.

Nevertheless, she said with a calmness that surprised her, "Since you raised the point of wisdom, sir, I take liberty to suggest that you would be wiser to accept what is real. You will never have the right to command me."

"We'll see," he said.

She stepped back, suppressing a sigh of relief when he made no move to stop her. "We should collect our horses."

"Aye," he agreed, "and your boots."

Disappointment stirred at the readiness with which he turned back, but she was glad to see that his horse still waited patiently where he had left it.

She knew he would not take hers if his had bolted, but she knew too that she did not want to ride pillion with him, and was certain that he would neither let her ride home alone and leave him to walk nor agree to walk beside her while she rode.

He did not mount the bay straightaway when they

reached it, gathering its reins instead and leading it as they returned to the line of boulders and Hobyn.

She did not speak; nor did he. The birds' whistles and shrieks overhead, even the rhythmic whispers and gurgles of water lapping at the shore, grew unnaturally loud to her ears. The aromas of the sea wafted stronger than usual, too. She could think of nothing to say, it being clearly ineligible to demand to know if he had sensibly given up the hopeless notion of marrying her.

"Sit on that rock yonder," he said.

"Why?"

"I'll help you put on your boots."

Ignoring an urge to tell him that she could perfectly well put them on by herself, she did as he told her and then nearly smiled in response to the sudden twinkle she detected in his eyes.

As he gently rubbed sand from her feet, warming them between his big hands, he said, "Why did you come here this morning?"

She hesitated but could think of no reason to distrust him. "I came to see where Elma MacCoun died."

He frowned. "Do you know then exactly where that is?"

"No, but they say she may not have been murdered at all, but instead may have fallen off a cliff and been washed ashore."

Thoughtfully, he said, "I wondered what made them so sure, but one would think that if they weren't, they would have hesitated to charge Ian Burk."

"I thought of that, but I thought of something else, too," she said, adding as he picked up one of her soft leather boots and slipped it onto her foot, "The cliffs are in the wrong place."

His eyes danced again, but he said only, "How can that be?"

She knew she had phrased her thought badly but went on without hesitation. "The only cliffs easily accessible to Elma, if she walked as they say she did, are just north of us here. The tide comes in from the west, so had she fallen hereabouts, it would have carried her eastward toward the Sound of Isla."

"And the ebbing tide would have swept her out to sea, where she'd have sunk to the bottom, her fate forever unknown."

Mairi nodded, grimacing at the image his words produced.

"So knowing the exact place they found her matters only if such knowledge will lead us to her killer, but we do know now that the killer must exist."

"Aye." Hearing the statement spoken aloud made her shiver, but a moment later, both boots back on her feet and securely tied, she stood, shook her skirts into place, and went to the gray, stroking its muzzle as she untied its reins from the shrub. She turned then to lead it toward a rock onto which she could climb to mount, but two strong hands caught her at the waist and lifted her onto her horse.

Settling herself, she let him straighten her reins, thanking him politely when he handed them back to her.

"Do you dislike saddles, lass?"

She shrugged. "Ladies' saddles are cumbersome things, good only for a palfrey's ambling gait. I prefer to ride astride so I can more easily sense my horse's movements. I have ridden so since I was a child. My brothers taught me."

He chuckled. "Do you hunt, sail boats, and swim, too?"

"Aye, of course, but 'tis no odd thing, sir. Many

Isleswomen swim and sail, and noblewomen everywhere hunt, I believe."

"Perhaps, but I'll wager that you do all those things better than most."

Modesty forbade agreement, so she kept silent, but the compliment shot a surge of satisfaction through her. Watching with approval as he swung himself onto the bay, she decided that he, too, probably swam and sailed as well as he rode. Indeed, Lachlan Lubanach struck her as a man who would make a point of doing well anything that he did at all, but she would certainly not tell him so. He was far too sure of himself already.

They rode in silence along the beach until they reached the track leading up the heather-clad hill, when he said, "I should apologize for startling you when I rode up behind you earlier. I thought you had seen me."

"Why would you think that?"

His lips twitched. "I could imagine no reason other than a strong desire to avoid me that would send you darting off along the sand like a frightened deer."

Refusing to take umbrage at that unfair image, or to reveal how much she enjoyed the unladylike pastime of running barefoot on the sand, she said only, "Had I wanted to flee, sir, I would not have dismounted first."

"I thought you were afraid to ride your horse through that wee hindrance of boulders," he murmured provocatively.

"Did you?"

"Whatever your reason, you did try to run from me."

She nibbled her lip at the reminder, having no wish to admit that darting away as she had, had most likely been an act of unwise, instinctive flirtation and nothing more. She would not give him the satisfaction of hearing that, however, nor would she repeat such foolishness in future. If she had learned anything about the man in the past twenty-four hours, she had learned that if it served him, he would take advantage of any weakness.

He did not pursue the topic, for which she was grateful. Instead, some minutes later, he said, "Were you living here at Finlaggan while your father was in Flanders earlier this year?"

"Nay, my mother prefers Ardtornish from November to mid-January. The walls are thicker there, the hall fires warmer, and the outside air is colder."

"Aye, privies don't stink so much in an icy winter, 'tis true."

She chuckled. "Do you always say exactly what comes into your head?"

"Don't be daft. Of course I don't, and I hope you don't either."

"I don't suppose I do. Why did you ask that, about where we lived?"

"I like to know things, and I knew that your father had served as Royal Envoy to Flanders. In fairness to our Davy," he added, "he has made numerous, albeit unsuccessful, efforts to please his grace, such as naming him his Envoy."

"Oh, aye," Mairi said. "Years after my father persuaded the English to release him after he stupidly invaded England, he expressed his gratitude by naming him Constable of Edinburgh Castle. Last year it was Envoy. But titles won't please him, because David is stupid. Three years ago, he decided that an English prince would make a better successor to the Scottish throne than a Scot who bears his own blood and that of the Bruce. Do you want the English to rule Scotland, sir?"

"Nay, lass, I do not. Clan Gillean supports your grandfather to succeed Davy, as do most Scots. Little likelihood exists that we'll ever bow to an English king."

"Aye, but only because Parliament honored the Bruce's will over David's objections by naming my grandfather his successor."

"Aye," he agreed, "and one can only imagine what a defeat it was for Davy, but even so, he sensibly named Mac-Donald to assume your grandfather's position as High Steward of the Royal Household."

She shrugged. "I don't know how sensible it was. More likely, he was being practical because he dislikes change, and whilst my father holds the title, my grandfather still tends to the duties. Had David appointed anyone else, that man would doubtless have insisted on taking control."

"I still think Davy has made more attempts to please his Lord of the Isles than MacDonald has made to please his king."

"My father does not recognize David as his sovereign, sir, as you must know. He is King of the Hebrides as well as Lord of the Isles, but when he refused to make or allow such exorbitant 'contributions' as David demanded to pay the ransom he had refused for eight years to pay, Parliament declared against my father and accused him of fomenting rebellion. And they did that at the King's instigation."

"The English have been pressing hard to get their ransom," he pointed out.

She shot him a challenging look. "That has naught to do with the Isles. We have ever supported the position in which we most strongly believe."

"Or the position his grace most strongly believes will benefit us," he said.

"By heaven, sir, do you dare—"

"Peace, lassie," he said, grinning at her. "I've no wish to fratch with you."

"I'm not fratching!"

"If those daggers in your eyes were real weapons, I'd be a blood-covered mess by now," he insisted. "I meant that last bit as a compliment to your father."

"It did not sound like a compliment."

"In troth, lass, and despite anything I may have said during this interesting discussion, I believe your father to be the greatest politician and diplomat in all Scotland, if not in all Britain, and I mean to learn as much as I can from him."

"Truly?"

"Aye, because he united the Isles as no one had since the days of the great Somerled, and has ruled them peacefully for forty years through often difficult and turbulent times."

"A magnificent accomplishment, indeed."

"Aye, sure, and he succeeds because he never commits himself too far to one side or the other. He plays a clever game instead, increasing or consolidating his power with every move he makes. His legal institutions alone should sustain the Lordship of the Isles for centuries to come."

"You *do* admire him," Mairi said, pleased.

He nodded. "Your father is blessed with an acute political sense, lass. He always knows which way to jump, and like a cat, he always lands on his feet. A wise man can learn much from him."

They continued conversing in this vein until they topped the last rise and saw Finlaggan below. Only then did Mairi realize how swiftly the time had passed. Although her father nearly always answered her questions and had provided her with an education nearly equal to that of her older brothers and such nobles' sons as fostered at Finlaggan, she could not recall ever before having enjoyed so easy a discussion of such subjects.

She had long been fascinated by history and politics, because she adored her father and had always longed to know what he did and where his travels took him. From the time she had learned to talk, perhaps even before, MacDonald had spent time with her on his return from any venture, relating exciting tales of what he had seen and done. Her interest in his stories had soon stirred a passionate curiosity to learn more about the world beyond Finlaggan and the Isles.

Her brothers teased her when she tried to question them about royal politics or take part in their discussions of history. Their tutors, although patient with her questions, tended to dismiss her ideas and opinions. Niall Mackinnon had punished her the one time he had caught her eavesdropping. And her mother, although well versed in her own role as a pawn on the political game board, did not talk about politics or history, believing such topics were solely for men to discuss and decide.

Thus had Mairi learned long before Lachlan Lubanach had ordered her to keep her opinions to herself that if she wanted men to let her listen to their discussions, as much as it frustrated her, it behooved her to stay silent. She longed to tell him so now, but she believed that after she had so easily betrayed her opinions to him, he would not believe her. She longed to talk more about Elma's murder, too, but since he knew little of Isla and less about its inhabitants, such discussion would avail her nothing but the pleasure of conversation, and she feared he would think it odd of her to ask him what he thought about it.

The clouds had broken, and from the top of the rise, they saw splashes of sunlight beaming down on landscape and loch, and paused to enjoy the view.

After a long moment's silence, he said quietly, "Do you have any notion who Elma MacCoun's killer might be, lass?"

Startled by the abruptness of the question after her own shift of thoughts to the murder, she said, "What made you ask me that?"

He shrugged. "I told you, I like to know things. Curiosity is my besetting sin. So, who do you think did it?"

"I don't know," she admitted. "I've been away for a month, but Mellis MacCoun is a quarrelsome man. You heard him yourself when he said he'd have clouted Elma on the head if she had not fixed his breakfast that day."

"What do you know of Ian Burk's accusers, or the man who found Elma?"

"Ewan Beton found her. He is the son of Agnes Beton, our herb woman, and he is very kind. As for Gil Dowell, Shim MacVey, and Fin MacHugh, they are loyal men, I believe. Shim is Niall Mackinnon's man, and Gil and Fin were born on Isla. I don't know them as well as I know Ian or Ewan, but I know nothing to suggest that they might be dishonest. Doubtless, they were just mistaken about when they saw Ian and Elma," she said, adding, "We should go, sir. I am very late."

He nodded and lifted his reins to ride on toward the palace complex.

"I wish we could linger," she said, "I have enjoyed our conversation."

"I, too," he said, meeting her gaze. "I know of no other woman who possesses such a diverse knowledge of the world beyond her own walls, lass. Moreover, I believe you have inherited much of your father's astuteness."

Mairi's voice seemed suddenly to have deserted her, because no one had ever said such a thing to her before, and she had no idea how to reply. Merely to say thank you would not express a thimbleful of what she felt. She looked at him searchingly, wondering if he had meant it or had said it only to flatter her.

When he met the look easily, she said, "You are kind in your compliments, sir. I shall never develop a particle of his grace's skill, but it is good to know that I have not made a fool of myself, conversing on such topics with you."

"You'll rarely make a fool of yourself in any conversation, lass, but you do seem bent on condemning yourself to a tedious future."

"Indeed?"

"Aye, because Alasdair Stewart is a man of little brain or knowledge of the world. His interests lie solely in adventuring, and nearly always concern conquests of the fair sex rather than political intrigue or understanding."

"You should not speak so to me," she said, sounding so unduly prim to herself that she surprised herself by adding curtly, "Does he have so many women?"

His grin flashed wide. "You make my point for me," he said.

"Then I have missed your point, sir."

"'Tis plain enough. Would you have dared ask anyone else that question?"

Aware that she was blushing warmly, she found it nonetheless easy to answer him. "By my troth, sir, I ask you because I do not know anyone else impertinent enough to give me a plain answer. Does he?"

"He does, and is faithful to none of them. You would be wiser to marry me."

She swallowed hard, wishing she could think. "Even if I wanted to marry you, sir, I could not."

"Ah, but we make progress now, I'm thinking," he said with satisfaction.

"You continue to prate absurdities! How can that be progress?"

"Because 'tis plain now that you are no longer strongly opposed to the notion. I call that excellent progress."

She stared at him. "You are daft. I have just said, *again*, that I cannot marry you, that my father will never allow it."

"Nay, lassie, you said that even if you wanted to you could not. Were you so strongly opposed to the notion, you'd have told me to go and boil my head, and you'd not be so plainly enjoying our conversation."

She pressed her lips together, knowing that if she said more, she would just reinforce his opinion because, whether she liked it or not, what he said was true.

Chapter 6 ————————

Although Lachlan was certain that Mairi wanted to say much more to him, she remained silent, staring straight ahead as they approached the causeway.

Deciding to see how long she could keep quiet, he tried to emulate her by looking straight ahead, but it was not long before he gave in to the urge to look at her again, and then again moments later.

By heaven, he thought as he glanced at her for the third time, fascinated by the rosy smoothness of her left cheek and the fullness of her soft lips, she is not only the most beautiful woman in the Isles but also the most alluring.

Abruptly he said, "Could you not persuade him?"

She looked at him, nibbled her lower lip in the way he had decided meant only that she gave thought to her answer, then said, "I have little say in it, sir."

He wanted to nibble that lip for her, to lick it, to savor its taste, to—

"I don't know why you look at me like that, for surely you must know my father won't change his mind simply because I ask him to," she added.

Quickly regaining focus, he said evenly, "I believe that you wield more influence than you know."

"His grace will not alter his plan for me any more than your father would if your sister tried to persuade him to let her choose her own husband."

"I have no unmarried sisters."

"If you had one," she said, audibly gritting her teeth, "or if one of them had tried to persuade him to— Mercy, sir, you know perfectly well what I mean!"

Ignoring her irritation as well as the subject of sisters, he said, "I'm thinking 'twould be more useful to know why your father did not formally betroth you to yon fool Alasdair Stewart long ago. He might easily have done so as soon as you achieved your seventh birthday. Faith, by law, he could even have arranged for the marriage to take place on the day you turned thirteen."

The very thought that she might already have been married to Alasdair Stewart annoyed him enough that he drew a deep, steadying breath as she said, "But I know why he did neither of those things."

"Why, then?"

"'Tis plain enough," she said. "My grandfather may stand next in line to the throne, but the King and his present wife have been married only two years and may yet surprise everyone by producing any number of children."

"Davy was married to Joanna for thirty-four years before she died, and they produced no offspring," he reminded her.

"Be reasonable, sir. They were both children of four when they married, and Joanna spent the last five years of her life in England."

"That may account for half of their years together, but they still had plenty of time to produce offspring," he insisted. "Moreover, he visited her often in England."

"Aye, well, perhaps she was at fault. Margaret is much more . . . That is to say, I'm told that she . . ."

When she stopped without finishing for the second time, he said helpfully, "Margaret is indeed a lustier wench. She certainly would have produced a child by now, could she have done so, because she is just that sort of troublemaker."

"Perhaps," she said, "but then perhaps my father was not so eager to see me married and living elsewhere that he pressed for an early marriage."

"Or perhaps your grandfather is not sure he wants you to marry Alasdair, or Alasdair is such a profligate fool that he does not want you," he added gently.

Mairi opened her mouth to deny that last suggestion indignantly but shut it again when she realized she did not know what Alasdair thought. Although she had met him several times, he did not interest her, even though her father meant her to marry him. She trusted MacDonald, dutifully believing that he must know what would suit her as well as he knew what would suit his kingdom and Clan Donald.

Her awareness of how late she was increased as she and Lachlan crossed the causeway. Although Lady Margaret was generally mild of temperament and slow to anger, Mairi knew that if MacDonald had looked for her or if someone had seen her with Lachlan and suggested that she had behaved foolishly or dangerously, her mother would be displeased. And she found Margaret's mildest displeasure more discomfiting than outright anger from nearly anyone else.

Lachlan had not spoken since suggesting that Alasdair might not be delighted to marry her, and she missed their easy discourse. She had not known any man before who seemed so interested in what she had to say.

Ranald and Godfrey were easy enough to talk to, although the former was as likely to laugh at her as to take anything she said seriously. Godfrey was the easiest one to discuss family issues with, but she frequently suspected that he was just kind, that he often humored her without really agreeing with what she said.

John Og was no confidant at all, being married and living in Kintyre. He and Freya were presently interested only in the arrival of their second child, hopefully the son he so desperately wanted that he had even asked Niall Mackinnon's brother, Fingon, the Green Abbot of Iona, to bless one of that Holy Isle's green stones for Freya to wear on a chain around her neck to bring them luck.

Mairi's half sisters were all married and living elsewhere. Her younger sister Elizabeth was too much of a chatterbox to make a good confidante, and the other children were simply too young to fill that role.

She and Lachlan were nearing the entrance to the stable enclosure when he broke his silence at last to say, "Will you ask him?"

Mairi rolled her eyes. "You must be daft."

"Nay, lass, just purposeful, and to learn the answer to any question, it is first necessary to ask it."

"Then you ask it," she said. "'Tis your place to do so, not mine."

"Not after I've been told you are spoken for," he pointed out. "Moreover, I'll warrant your father will more likely think before he replies if you ask him."

"I'd still be wasting my breath."

"You will not know that until you speak to him."

"I know it now," she insisted.

His gaze intensified as it caught and held hers. "Will you ask him anyway?"

His voice was low-pitched, sensually so, and her nerve

endings tingled in response. She told herself she could look away if she wanted to, and then wondered how it was that he made it so hard for her to do so.

At last, with a sigh, she said, "I will consider it, but it seems senseless to ask him a question to which I already know his answer."

"But you will think about it?"

"I have said that I will."

"Good enough, then."

They had reached the barn, and Ian Burk and a second gillie came running to hold their horses. Mairi greeted Ian with a smile, and swung her leg over to slip off Hobyn as usual, but Lachlan had already jumped to the ground, and he grasped her firmly around the waist. Lifting her off the gelding without further ado, he set her on her feet and offered an arm to escort her back to the laird's hall.

His attitude was nearly avuncular, so much so that she said provocatively, "Thank you, sir, for lending me your escort. I felt quite safe, I promise you."

Without a blink, he said, "'Twas my pleasure, lassie, I promise *you*."

"You sounded a hundred years old," she muttered the moment they were beyond earshot of the gillies.

"Sometimes, you make me *feel* a hundred years old."

She chuckled. "At least no one will be telling my father that we arranged some sort of clandestine meeting."

"Not yet, at all events," he said, smiling.

The smile shot new sensations along her sorely tried nerves, but she managed to walk beside him with her head high, knowing better than to engage him in a battle of wits in full view of anyone who chose to glance their way.

As they crossed the great hall yard, the chapel bell rang

the midday hour, and she realized the men had already come down off the roof.

"Mercy," she exclaimed, "I paid no heed to how high the sun had risen. I knew 'twas late but not *so* late! 'Tis nearly time to dine."

"Have you so many duties to attend before we do?"

"Nay, not today, but my mother will be vexed by so long an absence, and when she is vexed, my father's temper can likewise be uncertain."

"I have no doubt you will know how to manage them," he said. "You will certainly have better sense than to annoy your father whilst you are pondering the best time to ask him so important a question."

She made a face at him but did not deign to reply.

They had reached the forecourt, and when he showed no inclination to leave her, she stopped and turned to face him.

"Do you intend to escort me all the way up to my mother's solar, sir?"

"If you invite me, I shall accompany you gladly, but if you've no further need of me, I'd like to find my brother and be sure he has not created any mischief in my absence. Shall I see you in the hall?"

"Of course. I doubt anyone will forbid me to dine."

"This evening, too? Will you sup with the rest of us tonight?"

"I believe so. His grace rarely sups privately when he has guests at Finlaggan."

"Until then," he said, "I depend on you to think hard, lass."

Knowing of nothing she could say to that, Mairi bobbed a curtsy and fled upstairs to her mother's solar.

Learning that his brother had left Finlaggan with Lord Ranald, bent on some mysterious mission, Lachlan hurriedly made himself presentable for the midday meal. But he decided he might have spared himself the effort when he learned that the meddlesome high steward had moved him to the left end of the high table and put MacDuffie of Colonsay, hereditary keeper of the records, at Lady Mairi's side.

Heretofore he had spared little thought for Niall Mackinnon despite the man's obvious distaste for Clan Gillean. Having been sure it stemmed from land issues on the Isle of Mull, he wondered now if it might signify something other than simple lust for larger estates. The man certainly seemed protective of Lady Mairi.

Although Lachlan could see her occasionally from where he sat, he could not converse with her, and he had better sense than to keep looking toward her like a lovelorn lute player. Thus, he focused his attention on those nearer him at the table, and soon initiated a lively conversation rife with political opinion, in the course of which he learned a few interesting things that he had not known before about goings-on at King David's court.

He knew that many Islesmen believed he had more knowledge than anyone else of what went on in the western Highlands and Isles, even at the Scottish royal court. He both treasured and encouraged that reputation, cultivating contacts with many strategically placed gentlemen, and even the occasional rattle-tongued lady. And he maintained a vast correspondence with the former if not with the latter. Gifted with the ability to make friends easily, he rarely made enemies. Thus, the attitude of Niall Mackinnon was an aberration and one he would investigate.

Having already heard rumors that Mackinnon thought himself indispensable to MacDonald, and knowing that since his wife's death three years before he had remained unmarried, Lachlan wondered if it could be possible that Mackinnon's attitude toward the lass was more possessive than protective.

He would look into that, but for the moment, he contented himself with making one or two casual, complimentary remarks about Mackinnon, knowing that they would be repeated in the right quarter. If the tactic accomplished nothing else, it might at least lead Mackinnon to decide that Lachlan the Wily was a fool, and if it did that, the "fool" might well gain the upper hand.

Even with so many to serve, the meal was a speedy one, as midday meals were in most households, and only those who were not councilors or interested spectators lingered afterward to talk. Most followed MacDonald to Council Isle, where the Council of the Isles would continue its official duties.

Noting that Lady Margaret had already left the chamber and had taken her daughter with her, Lachlan knew he had no choice but to attend to his duties with MacDonald and the other councilors at least for the afternoon, and postpone further dalliance until evening. And if the family failed to join their guests and retainers for supper, or to linger afterward for conversation and amusements, he would simply continue to enjoy the companionship of his new friends.

As experienced as he was in the art of negotiation, he knew well that an apparent lack of interest in any outcome could prove helpful, whereas too much interest could spoil the brew. Although maintaining a disinterested air for any length of time was always difficult, the prize this time was worth the effort.

That Lachlan Lubanach had not been seated near her again at the high table did not surprise Mairi, because that honor was rarely accorded to the same person at every meal. However, the wave of disappointment she felt surprised her, especially since she had been dreading the question he was sure to ask.

Although Lady Margaret had not scolded her or even asked where she had been, she did give her a look that led Mairi, in her guilt, almost to wish that her mother had reprimanded her. Instead, Margaret had asked her to walk to one of the cottages near the stable enclosure after they dined to look in on Agnes Beton, who was ill. Since Agnes was Ewan Beton's mother and a cousin of Elma MacCoun's, she looked forward to the visit, if only to learn more about Elma's last days.

She had not seen MacDonald, for he had ordered food served to him in the sole building on Council Isle, where he kept a table and chair, and where much of the paraphernalia for the council meetings was stored. And although she was glad to have missed any opportunity to ask him how firmly he was set on her betrothal to Alasdair, she knew that merely telling Lachlan that she had not seen him would not satisfy him. He did not care about Alasdair. He clearly wanted her for himself, but she did not know how she could propose that to MacDonald. Young women simply did not tell their fathers whom they wanted to marry.

The thought startled her, and she mentally amended it. It was not that she wanted to marry him. If any young man wanted to marry her, he should present himself to her father as a suitor and ask the question himself. Moreover, Lachlan Lubanach, with his reputation for skilled negotiating, would doubtless have a more facile way with words than she ever would on such a topic.

She had thus decided to put the matter to him in just that way, and that, she told herself, explained her disappointment at his absence.

As her mother hustled her out of the great hall afterward,

Mairi resigned herself to a dutiful afternoon. Lachlan had not spared her even a passing glance, so doubtless he was playing a game of sorts, or did not care about the outcome.

Determined to fix her mind wholly on her duties, she returned to the kitchen to fetch a basket with two small manchet loaves and a pot of soup, and then walked straight to Agnes Beton's whitewashed cottage. Men were back at work on the chapel roof, and the musical rat-tat of their hammers accompanied her.

"Bless all in this house," she called as she opened the door. "Agnes, I've brought you hot soup and rolls. I hope you feel well enough to eat them."

"Bless ye, my lady, and a good morrow to ye," Agnes wheezed from her pallet as Mairi entered. A fit of coughing overcame her, but when she could speak again, she said, "I'm better today, for I've distilled one o' me own potions, but that soup smells tasty. If ye'll set it on the hob, my Bessie will help me with it anon."

Since the fire in the tiny fireplace had gone out, Mairi could not see that putting the pot on the hob would accomplish anything, so she said, "It's still hot, so if you'll tell me where I can find a spoon, I'll help you with it myself."

"'Tis an angel ye are, lass. Ye'll find a mug on the table yonder and a wee spoon in the basket, and I'm thanking ye straightaway lest I die afore I drink it."

Mairi grinned. "You'll not die for years yet, Agnes. You're as tough as whitleather. My father tells me so frequently. Moreover, he needs you, for no one else kens the herbs or the healing skills as well as you do."

"Aye, but there be many hereabouts as think I should never get sick," Agnes said with a weak smile that revealed a mouthful of crooked or missing teeth. "Are those wee loaves from the high table?"

"They are. I stole them from the kitchen myself just for you," Mairi said as she drew a joint stool near the old woman's pallet. "Here now, just taste this."

"Wi' permission, mistress, I'm thinking I'll drink the broth first."

Mairi helped her until the soup was gone, then handed her a roll, which the old woman carefully broke into pieces to eat.

"Such a fine meal," she said. "I vow, my lady, I feel nearly well again."

"Have you been sick long?"

"Nobbut a few days," Agnes said. "In troth, my lady, it come upon me after our Ewan found Cousin Elma's body on the shore. Such a shock as that was!"

"Do you know what happened to her?"

Agnes's watery eyes narrowed as she shook her head. "Nay, my lady, I dinna ken. Some say 'twas that feckless brute Mellis; but some still say 'twas Ian Burk."

"Ian could not have done it," Mairi said firmly. "He was not here."

"Och, I ken that fine now, but wi' some, once an idea enters their heads, it'd take a lightning bolt t' strike it out. 'Tis a pity our Elma were so bonnie a lass."

"She was," Mairi agreed, remembering, "but why should that be a pity?"

Agnes gave her a long look but made no reply.

"Come, Agnes, if there is aught you know of this, you must tell me."

"Nae good comes o' loose tongues, my lady, but I will say that Elma didna get on well wi' Mellis, and she did seek her comforting elsewhere."

"With Ewan?"

"Och, nay then! Me Ewan be a good lad, and finding our

Elma like he did near did him in as well, I tell ye. Fishing, he were, and expecting t' find Gruinart fair leaping wi' salmon, but he found Elma afore he caught even one!"

Having known Ewan almost as long and as well as she knew Ian Burk, Mairi could easily believe that he had simply gone hunting for big fish, and she could see that Agnes was weary, so she did not press her further. Setting the empty mug and spoon on the table for Agnes's daughter to wash later, Mairi took her leave.

The rest of the afternoon passed slowly until she retired to the bedchamber she shared with Elizabeth to change for supper, but the time then passed too swiftly, for she could not decide what to wear. She tried on first one dress and then another until Meg Raith threw up her hands in frustration.

"Faith, mistress, if ye dinna decide soon, your lady mother will be upon us."

"I'll wear this one," Mairi said, indicating the sky-blue silk gown she was wearing. "Arrange my caul please, Meg, whilst I slip on my shoes."

Meg obeyed, grumbling that Lady Margaret would be sending one of her ladies to hurry them before they were done. No such dire thing occurred however, and Mairi soon descended to her mother's solar, where she found Lady Margaret, her women, and Elizabeth on the point of departing.

"Good, you will not delay us," her mother said with a smile. "The bell rang several minutes ago, however, so if we do not want to be caught up in the bustle, we had better make haste."

In the hall, the bustle had already begun, with people finding their places at the trestles. Once again, Mairi saw, Niall had seated the sons of Gillean at the far end of the high table. Hector Reaganach was looking pleased with himself, though, and she remembered that she had not seen him or

Ranald at the midday meal. Lachlan sat beside Hector but did not glance her way.

Noting that Ranald stood near his own place, his expression exactly like Hector's, Mairi said, "Do you know where Ranald was all afternoon, madam?"

"He does not confide such things to me," Lady Margaret said.

Their secret was soon told, however, for Godfrey said to Mairi as they ate, "Ranald has a surprise, lass, and 'tis one I'm thinking you'll enjoy."

"Do you mean to tell me what it is, sir, or must I guess?"

"I can tell you only what I know, that he heard about a troupe of strolling players at Tarbert Castle—splendid guisers," Godfrey said with a grin. "He went there and abducted them for our entertainment tonight, or so Ranald says."

She chuckled. "I warrant he will not describe it so to his grace, however. I doubt he would look kindly upon the abduction of any Islesmen or their guests." Nevertheless, she thought it a delightful treat. Their own minstrels were skilled, but their tunes had grown familiar to all, and new entertainment was always welcome.

She sensed that the others in the hall were as excited as she and knew that the news had spread.

Gillies quickly cleared away the trestles after the meal, opening a space in the center of the hall for the guisers, who wore masks and colorful costumes. All of them were men, but some were dressed as women, drawing hoots of laughter from the audience. Their play was simple, a familiar Isles tale about the great Somerled's victory over the Viking raiders. Every member of the audience knew the story, but the guisers were new to them and skilled at stirring both laughter and cheers.

They had clearly conferred with MacDonald's minstrels,

because the musicians accompanied them with ease. When everyone had taken bows, the minstrels began to play for a sword dance and several gentlemen arose to take part, including Lachlan Lubanach and his brother.

Laying three pairs of crossed swords down the center of the hall, the men took turns showing off their skill at the ancient *Gille Callum* that had begun as a weapons dance in the days of the Roman Empire to develop military skills.

Despite Hector's reputation for ferocious fighting, the audience soon saw that Lachlan was the more skilled dancer of the two. His steps were nimble, his grin infectious, and soon the audience was clapping in time to the music and steps. The two brothers danced side by side in their group of three, and Mairi noted that Hector kept glancing at Lachlan as if he were taking his cues from him.

He managed to accomplish all his steps, kicking a sword but once, and then lightly. However, when the three dancers bent to pick up their swords, he tried to do so without missing his steps, and tripped over his own two feet. As he tried to catch himself, both swords flashed up dangerously. Had Lachlan not swiftly intervened, the third man in their group might have found himself abruptly headless.

The audience roared with laughter, as if the entire business had been planned and rehearsed for their delight, but Mairi had been watching the brothers closely, and the darting looks that passed from one to the other told her plainly that such had not been the case. A glance at her father's frowning face told her just as plainly that MacDonald had interpreted the incident as she had, but when the dancers finished their round, and all three clapped each other heartily on the back, evidently having enjoyed themselves hugely, the Lord of the Isles nodded approval.

When the gentlemen had had their fill of sword dancing,

the players formed a line and invited the audience to join them in a ring dance. Merriment ensued, with MacDonald, his lady, and their offspring taking places in the line, mingling with councilors, guests, and retainers. There being far more men than women and children, everyone joined as he or she chose.

One masked guiser left the line to bow low before Mairi, laughing beneath his mask as he took her hand and pulled her to the head of the line, flinging a necklace of tinkling bells around her neck as a sign that she should lead the dance. Then, inserting himself between her and the next man in line, he took her hand and urged her to lead the way.

Laughing, she obeyed, and the line of dancers grew merrier. The music of the minstrels' lutes and pipes skirled faster and faster as the line wended its way, gathering dancers as it went, until nearly everyone was dancing. Her merry captor left the line, having first placed Mairi's hand in that of the gentleman behind him, and he soon returned with a grinning Lachlan Lubanach.

Believing that the guiser meant to replace her as leader, Mairi raised a hand to her necklace of bells, but he shook his head, inserted his new captive between Mairi and the man behind her, and the dance went on until the music stopped and she came to a breathless stop in front of Niall Mackinnon.

"You should be dancing with us, Niall," she said merrily.

"You forget, my lady, that my brother, Fingon, is the Abbot of Iona," Mackinnon said austerely. "The Roman Kirk does not approve of such wild dancing, and particularly dislikes ladies who lead, or wear the bells to do so."

"Faith, sir, if my father sees naught amiss with it, I certainly do not."

Beside her, Lachlan said, "What's wrong with the bells?"

With a look of dislike, Mackinnon said, "The Kirk deems

such bells to be the devil's instruments. A cardinal o' the Kirk likened such dancing to a man who binds a bell to his cow's neck that he may hear the sound and be sure she is still there."

"By heaven," Lachlan snapped, "would you liken her ladyship to a cow?"

"I but quote Cardinal de Vitry," Niall said austerely.

"I have read much," Lachlan said, "but I do not know de Vitry."

" 'Even as the cow that leadeth the rest hath a bell to her neck, so the woman who leadeth the dance may be said to have the devil's bell on hers. For the devil, hearing it, is easy in mind and sayeth, "I have not lost my cow, she is safely mine.' "

Mairi heard Lachlan's sharply indrawn breath and felt him stiffen beside her.

Chapter 7 ——————————

"Calm yourself, lad," the Lord of the Isles said, appearing apparently out of nowhere to rest a hand on Lachlan's shoulder. "Niall's but having a game with you."

Noting that Hector had put an even larger hand on his other shoulder, Mairi said to Mackinnon, "I know you did not mean to offend me, sir, but I think it would serve you well if my father ordered you to lead the next ring dance, bells and all."

Niall shot her a look of annoyance, but before he could speak, Hector said, "Beg pardon, my lady, but I've promised Rory Macleod that I'll serve a penance now for near lopping off his head during our sword dance." With a droll grin, he added, "Although it might have improved his looks."

"Take care wi' our Rory," another wag said loudly. "He's seeking favor wi' the Lady Elizabeth, and may soon become another son t' his grace."

Someone else demanded to know what Hector's penance was to be.

"I'm to sing a song or two," he said. "But if we're to dance another—"

Cheers broke out, giving Mairi to realize that despite his ferocious reputation, he was popular and had apparently, in his short time at Finlaggan, already established himself as an entertainer. Her teasing suggestion that Niall lead the next dance was forgotten when Hector took a lute from one of the minstrels, sat on a nearby bench, and plucked the strings in turn, testing each note. The instrument looked tiny in his hands, but his touch was sure when he began to play.

Mairi knew the diversion was intentional and was grateful for it, because she realized that her tactless comment might have set more tempers than Niall's alight.

A hand touched her arm, and she looked up to find Lachlan still at her side. "Will you walk with me whilst he sings?" he asked, his carefully calm tone making her wonder if he was still angry with Niall, or maybe even with her.

She glanced at her father, but MacDonald's head was bent toward Lady Margaret, who was nodding and smiling. "I should not, sir," she said, "and well do you know it. I fear you mean only to plague me with questions I cannot answer."

"Then you have not yet spoken to his grace."

"No, for I have scarcely seen him. 'Tis Council time, I'd remind you. He spends most of his hours with his nobles and other men, not with his womenfolk."

"Then ask him to walk with you," he suggested. "He appears to be in an excellent humor now."

Glancing at MacDonald again, she saw that he was laughing at something her mother had said. It seemed a pity to disturb them, but Hector had begun singing a humorous ballad that she knew had numerous verses, and she realized that it might well be the best chance, perhaps the only one, that she would have. The Council of the Isles would continue to devour his time for three more days, and afterward everyone would leave, including the sons of Gillean.

When Lachlan nodded encouragingly, she drew a steadying breath and moved to her father's side.

"Forgive me, sir," she said in an undertone, "but if you can afford me a few minutes, I would speak privately with you."

"Of course," he said at once. "Shall we step outside?"

She waited until they reached the porch, but then, knowing it would avail her nothing to couch her words tactfully, she came straight to the point. "I wondered, sir, how firmly you are set on my marrying Alasdair Stewart."

His surprise visible in the light of the torches flanking the porch and lighting much of the courtyard, he said, "Why do you ask, child?"

When Lachlan had said she must do it, it had sounded easy, but now it seemed absurd. She scarcely knew him and should not have to do the asking. She remembered that she had been going to remind him of that, but it was too late now.

Drawing a deep breath, she said, "Lachlan Lubanach . . . that is, I should like to know, sir . . . that is, he would like to know if you might possibly consider—"

"Faith, does the man want to marry you, daughter?"

"Aye, sir, he says he does. 'Tis true that I scarcely know him, or he me, but he is most amusingly attentive in his conversation, sir, and he seems kind." She did not think Mac-Donald would be swayed by the argument that Lachlan's voice stirred emotions she had not known herself to possess or that his slightest touch heated her blood so that it felt as if fire flowed through her veins.

He said, "The sons of Gillean are popular with everyone here, daughter, so it does not astonish me that you like him. Nor does it surprise me that he has fixed his interest with you. But desire, popularity, and kindness are hardly the most important attributes in my daughter's husband. Moreover, your kinship falls within the forbidden degrees, so such a marriage would require papal dispensation."

"Faith, sir," she said. "You've told me yourself that if one follows the rules of the Kirk, nigh well every man and woman in Scotland lies within them, and Alasdair Stewart is my uncle!"

"Alasdair Stewart could one day be King of Scots, however."

"With respect, your grace, that is unlikely."

"Nevertheless, the Pope is much more likely to heed a request for a marriage between a daughter of the Lord of the Isles and a son of the future King of Scots than he is of that same daughter to a son of a little known Islesman."

"But—"

"Faith, lass, what could a member of Clan Gillean—"

"His father is chief of that clan, a position to which Lachlan will succeed!"

"Even so, what can he offer to MacDonald's daughter, or to MacDonald?"

"I would not have to leave the Isles, sir."

"A woman belongs with her husband, Mairi. I cannot deny that your mother and I will miss you, but you will see more of your grandfather and will certainly enjoy life at the royal court. You won't care then about leaving the Isles."

Her throat tightened, and she felt a sudden desire to cry. That she would not have to leave had just popped into her head, but she knew that she cared very much.

MacDonald gave her an impatient look. "Doubtless Alasdair will allow you to visit us from his castle at Lochindorb as often as you like. Do not speak of this again, daughter, nor complain of it elsewhere. I will not have scandal."

"No, sir." Shivering a little, as much from the knowledge

that she had displeased him as from the chilly air, she returned quietly with him to the hall.

Gillies were brewing punch by the fire. A piper accompanied Hector's lute, and Hector was singing another ballad, this one less ribald, more haunting. Folks had drawn benches up and were nodding and tapping toes in time to the music.

Mairi moved closer. It was hard to imagine Hector being ferocious, and she decided that someone must have named him so in childhood as a jest. When the song was finished and he began to sing another bawdy one, she noted that his eyes twinkled exactly the same way that his brother's did.

As the thought crossed her mind, Lachlan touched her arm, startling her because she had not sensed him near before that moment.

He smiled, but when she did not respond, he said, "I'm guessing your mission proved unsuccessful."

"You must have known it would," she said, glad he did not seem vexed.

"Nay, lass," he said. "One never knows, so it is necessary to do the asking."

"But 'tis the man's duty, not mine."

"I explained that. He would simply have told me that you are as good as spoken for. I'd hoped your words would have more effect."

"Well, they didn't."

"Then there is but one thing remaining for us to do."

"Aye," she said with a sigh.

His smile widened to a grin. "I believe you're sorry he said no."

Resisting an impulse to smile back, she said wistfully, "If I am, it is because I would like to know you better, sir. I did much enjoy our conversation."

"Aye, well, I've more to me than conversation, lass, as you'll discover if you'll but follow my lead."

"I must obey my father."

"Aye, you must, so we'll give him no cause to issue orders we do not like."

She frowned. "I do not like such talk. You said there is only one thing to do."

"Aye." He raised his eyebrows. "But mayhap you lack the steel I believed you had in you. If that is so, 'tis as well I've found out before it is too late."

Bewildered, and realizing they had been assuming different things, that he did not intend to submit to her father's decision, she said, "Too late for what?"

"I told you," he said. "I have decided that I must marry, and I believe you are the perfect choice for my wife. However, grand goals necessitate bold steps. Thus, I require a wife whose courage matches that of the powerful Islesman she marries."

Suppressing indignation at the suggestion that she lacked courage to match his, she said, "But you are not so powerful a man."

"I shall be one day though, and soon."

She believed him. His air of confidence and the near smile tugging at the corners of his lips made it impossible to doubt him. Tempted almost beyond endurance to insist that she was courageous enough for any man, but certain that was what he expected her to say, she resisted, lifting her chin and glaring at him.

He chuckled, saying blandly, "Art afraid to walk with me?"

"I wish you would not be so absurd."

He offered his arm, and she let him escort her to the side aisle, where they could stroll and still hear the music. How-

ever, instead of turning at the end and strolling back, he continued toward the anteroom door.

"Where are you taking me?" Mairi demanded.

"Outside where we can talk undisturbed. No one is paying us heed."

She doubted that that was true. Folks might not be staring at them, but she could not believe that no one would note
their departure.

At first, the air felt chillier than when she had gone outside with her father, but when Lachlan put an arm around
her shoulders, she suddenly felt too hot. She would have
liked to lean into that arm and feel it tighten around her, but
she said firmly, "Please, sir, you must not."

He took his arm away, and the chill settled over her
again.

In the light of the torches flanking the hall entrance,
Lachlan could easily read her expression, and he knew she
was wary. He would have to tread carefully if his plan was
to have any chance of success.

He walked silently toward the grassy terrace leading to
the chapel and was relieved when she walked beside him
and made no objection, less pleased that she did not speak at
all. Still, he was a patient man, and he needed to think.

They had left the torchlight behind, and the darkness was
peaceful. The moon was up, no more than a white, crescent-
shaped sliver amidst a blanket of stars. A slender, translucent
cloud drifted across it, glimmering dimly in its light.

As they approached the grass, he remembered that her
slippers were thin and realized the grass would be damp.
Moreover, if anyone came in search of them, there would be

less to condemn in a quiet stroll at this end of the paved courtyard than one that led them into darker reaches of the complex.

She fascinated him. Not only was she the most beautiful woman he knew, but delightfully unpredictable. The flash of anger in her eyes had told him the wee dart he'd thrown, questioning her courage, had hit its mark, but she had barely flinched. Instead, she had looked him in the eye, daring him to call her a coward.

He did not think any such thing, because she had more nerve than most men he knew. He had learned that the first time he'd seen her, when she had stood before MacDonald in his own court and demanded to be heard. And he had watched her make her case and save the lad, Ian Burk, from certain hanging.

Nevertheless, the very traits that drew him to her likewise provided obstacles to his plan. She would not be easily swayed by dulcet words or enchanted by his wit or charm. That she reacted with anger was a good sign that he could touch her emotions and stir her passions. That he felt a strong connection to her, almost as if he could step into her mind and listen to her thoughts, was encouraging too.

It had been years since he had known a woman with whom he felt such a connection and had never expected to feel it again. Still, it was not a constant factor in their relationship, which puzzled him. Such a connection, if it existed, should be more reliable. In a perfect world, one of his creation, it certainly would be.

Smiling at the sacrilege, he tried to focus on finding a solution to the puzzle at hand, but her very presence distracted him, and that, too, was unusual. He could think on his feet in nearly any circumstance, a trait that had saved him more than once from death or disaster. Now, instead, he was overly aware of the whisper of her skirts, of the wafting floral scent of her perfume, of the way she moved silently yet ever so gracefully beside him.

Mayhap she thought he was angry with her for saying he should not put his arm around her. He was not, for he had done it just to see how she would react. He believed in subtlety, particularly when he was negotiating for something, and even more so when it was something he particularly wanted, but sometimes directness served his purpose better.

"Art vexed with me, lass?"

Her answer came instantly and calmly. "Should I be, sir?"

"Nay, but I did wonder. You have grown so quiet."

"I'm thinking that I should feel guilty, wandering about out here with you, especially since my father has forbidden us even to think of marriage."

"Did he truly say we must not even think of it?"

She thought, her brow delightfully furrowed. "No, not in those words," she said at last, "but he did say I must marry Alasdair, and 'tis the same thing, is it not?"

"Not if he did not say it," he replied firmly.

"He said I must not talk of it or complain. He does not want a scandal."

"Then we must speak of it only between ourselves. Will you ride out again tomorrow? I mean to do so, and we can ride together if you like."

She shook her head. "Although I may choose to ride, sir, we must not ride together. My father has not forbidden that either, but he would not like it."

"Very well then," he said with a sigh. "I did expect as much."

"Because you think me a coward?"

"Nay, lass, only an obedient daughter, and I find naught amiss in that."

Nevertheless, he was content to let the notion that he might somehow think her a coward play in her head for a time. He would disabuse her of it soon enough.

"Have you truly read so much?" she asked abruptly.

"Aye," he said. "Clan Gillean is one of the hereditary learned clans. For centuries, men of each generation have devoted much of their lives to study. My father is one of those. He taught both Hector and me, and then sent us to France to learn more. I showed more aptitude for study than Hector did, and he showed more aptitude for weaponry. Do you want to learn to read, lass?"

"I can read," she said. "My father, too, believes in educating his children, sir, even his daughters, but I wish I knew more."

"One can spend too much time in study," he said, thinking of his father, and his mother's complaints before her death that because Ian Dubh saw study as a solemn duty, he neglected matters that were, in her eyes, much more important.

"I suppose one can spend too much time at anything," Mairi said. "Niall told me that you and Hector are twins. You must be the elder."

"Nay, Hector is, by nearly an hour."

"But you will be chief."

"My father said he thought 'twas time for brains rather than brawn to lead Clan Gillean, and Hector agrees."

"I see," she said, adding with a sigh, "We should go back to the hall."

"In a moment," he said, putting a hand on her shoulder and turning her to face him. The top of her head barely reached his chin. With a single finger, he tilted her face up. Her eyes reflected distant torchlight, making them sparkle despite her solemn expression. She did not blink or try to pull away. No one else was in sight.

Gently he bent toward her, touching his lips to hers. With delight, he felt her sharply indrawn breath. She did not draw back.

Slipping his free hand behind her head, cradling it gently, wishing he could feel her hair instead of the rough netting of her caul, he kissed her firmly, savoring the taste of her lips.

Pausing, he murmured, "I want you for my own, Mairi of the Isles."

"I know," she murmured back. "Will you kiss me again?"

"Aye, I will, but let us first move into the shadows nearer this building, where we shall not draw unwarranted attention."

"This is where our house servants sleep," she said, but she made no objection when he drew her into the shadows.

Pulling her against him, he kissed her more thoroughly and fervently than before. When she responded with equal fervor, it was all he could do not to sweep her into his arms and carry her to an even more private place where they could learn as much about each other as they liked.

Deciding to see how much she would allow, he touched her lower lip with his tongue, pressing gently to see if she would let him explore within.

The answer was a low moan from her throat, and hearing it, he pressed harder until his tongue filled the warm interior of her mouth. His body stirred, aching for her as his hands moved over her slender curves. One hand paused to cup a soft breast. Her only reaction was to press harder against him.

Her hands rested lightly at his waist now. Her tongue

began to dance with his, and he knew her attention was engaged. He began searching for her laces.

Hearing a sound from the direction of the hall, and aware that guardsmen were about, although none stood in plain sight, he broke away, inwardly cursing the complexities of female dress as much as the interruption.

"Someone has come out," she said quietly. "I think it is Niall."

"Fiend seize that man!"

She chuckled but said, "We must go back in. It would never do for him to find us like this. Come this way, through this passage to the terrace. Then it will appear as though we merely strolled to the chapel and back."

"You seem mighty experienced in the ways of deception, my lass," he said as he followed her. "Have you slipped away to kiss many men like this?"

With laughter in her voice, she said, "I shall keep my own counsel on that."

Quickening his step, he caught her arm and pulled her to face him.

"Will you indeed?"

It was too dark in the passageway to read her expression, but she said calmly, "Art angry, sir? You have no right to question me so."

"Not yet," he said, "but Alasdair Stewart does not deserve you, lass, and I swear to you by all I keep holy that he shall not have you."

The fierce words sent a thrill through Mairi's body, but she said, "We must go now, sir, and quickly. Those voices are nearer."

"Very well," Lachlan replied, "but I shall not change my mind."

She was glad she had not admitted that except for relatives and friends, in greeting or farewell, he was the only man she had kissed. She hoped he would kiss her again, but he did not, and they hurried through the passage to the terrace.

His words had been wonderful to hear, and his purposeful tone delightful, but she set no store by any of it. However wily he might be, he was no match for the Lord of the Isles, who was far too powerful and utterly set on marrying her to Alasdair. Even if by some miracle of God, the Fates, or the wee folk, MacDonald should change his mind, her grandfather Robert the Steward would not.

He and her father had frequently discussed the need to unify and centralize power in Scotland, and to do that Robert needed support from the Isles. Her marriage to Alasdair would do much to solidify that support. Her marriage to a member of Clan Gillean, learned or not, would accomplish nothing useful.

As they emerged onto the green, two figures approached them.

"Who goes there?" a voice called.

Recognizing it, Mairi said clearly, "'Tis I, Niall. Did you fear an enemy had somehow managed to invade Finlaggan?"

"You should not be out here alone," Niall Mackinnon said sternly.

"I'm not alone," she said, stifling a jolt of the guilty, childish fear he could so easily rouse in her. "The hall grew too warm and smoky, and I craved fresh air."

"His grace will not be pleased when I tell him that you came out here with only that fellow as escort," Niall said.

"You need not tell him, for I mean to do so myself," Mairi said, "and he will not thank you, sir, for interfering in what can be only our concern."

To his credit, Niall did not debate the point, and she was glad, because he retained a strong tendency to treat her as if she were still a child and he a second father or favored uncle. He had often said that he cared as much for her as for any of his own family, and had been part of her life for as long as she could remember. Nonetheless, she resented his habit of telling her what to do and how to behave. The fact was that he was not a family member, and he had become a distinct annoyance.

"You may leave us now, lad," he said tersely to Lachlan. "I will escort her ladyship back to the great hall."

"Don't be a fool, Mackinnon," Lachlan said lazily. "If your purpose is to protect her ladyship's reputation, you will hardly do so by making such a point of rescuing her from my clutches. That will serve only to suggest that she is not to be trusted in any man's company, including your own."

"How dare you!" Niall snapped.

"Peace, Niall," Mairi said, managing a light laugh despite the fact that her heart had leaped into her mouth at the sudden tension between the two men. "You know he is right, sir. If you interfere every time I stop to speak to a man, what will people think, if not exactly what he says? I am perfectly capable of looking after myself, I promise you. Or do you honestly believe Lachlan Lubanach is such a villain that he would try to abduct me from Finlaggan, or worse?"

"Nay, lass, and I beg pardon if I have offended you. But in truth, I do believe that you should not trust this man. He has come here only to wheedle his way into your father's good opinion and benefit from his generous nature."

"So you think my father is a fool, too, do you?" Mairi inquired gently but with a distinct edge to her voice.

"Never!"

"Then take care what you say, Niall. Lachlan Lubanach and his brother are here as official councilors and ambassadors from the chief of Clan Gillean. See that you treat them with the same respect that we accord to all of his grace's guests."

Niall's lips tightened, but he said only, "Yes, my lady. Good night, my lady."

He and his slim, dark-haired companion, whom Mairi had barely noted but saw now was Gil Dowell, turned back toward the hall, and strode briskly away.

She and Lachlan strolled after them in silence for a time before she said ruefully, "I should not have spoken so sharply to him."

"No," he said. "It was unwise."

A sudden ache in her throat stunned her with the realization that she had wanted to impress him.

"I'll admit," he went on easily, "that it delighted me to hear you take the wind out of that puffed-up rooster, but I should advise you in future to issue your rebukes in a more private manner."

"He made me angry."

"Aye, and that was another mistake."

She managed a smile as she said, "Aye, it was, for I've a fearsome temper when it's roused."

"Thank you for warning me of it, but that is not what I meant."

"No?"

"Nay, lass. The mistake was not his but yours, in allowing your temper to govern your actions. One rarely gains ground by letting emotions point the way."

"Do you never give way to yours?"

"Never," he said firmly. "At least, never since I grew old enough to understand the consequences, which are rarely what one hopes they will be."

"Oh."

"If you'll agree not to snap my head off, I'll offer another bit of advice."

"What?"

"You should apologize to him."

"I don't want to, but I suppose you are right," she agreed with a sigh. "It was unkind of me to take him to task in front of Gil Dowell—or you—particularly when he was only trying to protect me."

"Nonsense, that man is an interfering nuisance who cares about nothing that does not increase his own power or position. You should apologize to him only because it will disarm him and give you the advantage of having behaved well."

"He did not behave well, did he?"

"No, for he can scarcely fear that you are at any risk here amidst your own people and your father's guardsmen. He meant only to insult me, which he has attempted to do at every turn since my brother and I arrived."

"But why?"

"I am not entirely sure. He and my father clash some, because both want to control more land on the Isle of Mull, but Mackinnon has taken it to extremes here."

"He told me that you have a reputation for knowing everything that goes on in Scotland," Mairi said thoughtfully. "Mayhap he fears you are here to spy on us."

"Then he is twice the fool I've thought him. If I acquire information easily, it is because, over the years, my father has fostered many sons of noble families at Seil and I maintain contact with them all. But his grace is welcome to share in any knowledge that I possess. We of Clan Gillean are loyal to our liege lord."

"But surely Niall does not dislike you for no reason at all."

"Hector believes he is jealous because the other men here for the Council of the Isles have taken kindly to us. Our popularity makes him envious, Hector says. 'Tis true that Mackinnon seemed to take us in dislike from the first, but you may have hit upon the reason for that," he added thoughtfully. "Although he'd be wrong to think we'd do aught to harm his grace or the Lordship, he may still suspect such things. 'Twould be unwise of me, at least, to discount that possibility."

That he had heeded and accepted her comments gave her a warm feeling, and she would have liked to pursue the conversation, but as they approached the steps to the hall, MacDonald and Lady Margaret appeared in the doorway.

"There you are, daughter," MacDonald said cheerfully. "We wondered where you had gone. 'Twas kind of you, lad, to look after her."

"It was my pleasure, your grace," Lachlan said lightly. "I trust that my brother has ceased sullying everyone's ears with his bawdy songs by now."

"Hector Reaganach is a most entertaining minstrel," Lady Margaret said, smiling. "His music gives us all great pleasure."

"I shall relay your compliments to him, my lady," Lachlan said with a graceful bow. "They will gratify him immensely."

"Good night, sir," Mairi said.

"Sleep well, my lady," he said with a look that warmed her to her toes.

"Well, lass, did you tell that young man what I said?" MacDonald demanded as they walked back to the laird's tower.

"Yes, sir."

"Good. He seems to have taken it well enough, which is just as I'd expected, since he seems both sensible and loyal."

"He is certainly loyal to you, sir," Mairi agreed. She was not certain that she could say as much for Lachlan's being sensible. In fact, she decided, her lips still burning from his kisses, she rather hoped he would not be.

Chapter 8

Lachlan entered the great hall to find most folks departing and Hector flirting with a maidservant. The lass was attempting to gather up dirty mugs and goblets but seemed entirely willing to endure his blandishments.

Suppressing a smile at the familiar sight, Lachlan gestured to him to join him near the fire. It had grown chilly outside, but he had not realized he was cold until he had come in. He hoped that the lass had been warm enough, although he doubted that she would complain of the cold. She did not seem to be one to coddle herself.

"You found your way back," Hector said, clapping him on the back hard enough to make him brace himself, then adding in an undertone, "I've been seeking information, but most folk claim cloudy memories with regard to the dead lass. One of the few things they agree on is that she left after Godfrey's party did and wasn't seen again until Ewan Beton came upon her body at Loch Gruinart whilst fishing."

"Lady Mairi is certain someone killed her, and I agree," Lachlan said, explaining what she had said at Loch Gruinart about the cliffs.

"But Elma's husband was with Godfrey both going and coming," Hector said. "That much is also agreed to by all, so I don't see what opportunity he had to kill her, unless he persuaded someone to do it for him."

"Unlikely that he'd trust anyone else with such a plan," Lachlan said.

"I agree. I do have some other notions I want to discuss, but I'd given up looking for you. Thought you'd got lost."

"You thought nothing of the sort," Lachlan retorted. "I was but taking a stroll in the moonlight, a perfectly harmless thing to do."

"Aye, because with your great wits, you'd do nowt to make it otherwise, such as seducing the beauty or abducting her."

"I am not in the habit of abducting innocent wenches," Lachlan said.

Sobering, Hector gave him a direct look. "You were away long enough."

"We had things to discuss. Lady Mairi asked her father if he might consider favoring a marriage between us."

"Nay then, she did no such thing."

"She did."

Hector gave a low whistle. "That'd be a stroke of luck for us, right enough."

"It would," Lachlan agreed.

"But stay, is the lass not promised to Alasdair Stewart?"

"His grace and Alasdair's esteemed, almost royal father have discussed such a connection, but they have not yet signed any papers."

"Sakes, do you expect to change their minds? What did MacDonald say?"

"That he expects her to marry Alasdair and not to cause any scandal."

Hector grinned. "He did not say no, then."

"You are learning the ways of our political world. Blessed be the intelligent mind," Lachlan said with a smile.

"Do you think you can bring the thing off?"

"I know I mean to try. I've made progress, but the next step is the riskiest."

"What do you mean to do?"

Hesitating, knowing that Hector was unlikely to approve, he said at last, casually, "I'm thinking I'll give her father good reason to approve our marriage."

"Marriage to a son of Gillean instead of marrying her into the royal family? What could possibly induce the man to want that?"

When Lachlan rubbed the gold ring on his little finger and did not respond immediately, Hector frowned. Then, quietly, he said, "I noted before that although you denied a habit of abduction, you did not address the possibility of seduction."

"She likes me well enough, and if I can get her with child—"

"You are daft. If you get her with child . . . Faith, if you even succeed in seducing her, you'll more likely end on MacDonald's gallows than as her husband."

"Nothing worthwhile comes without risk," Lachlan said, as he had many times over the years. "Thus one must take bold steps to achieve any worthy goal."

"She's beautiful, I'll grant you, but I'm thinking that no marriage, however beneficial to Clan Gillean, is worth risking your life."

"Mayhap because you have not yet found the right woman."

"Mayhap because I look for more in a wife," Hector snapped. "You may have wits, my lad, but you are six times a fool to see wealth and political power as necessities of life and marrying that lass as your way to acquire them."

Lachlan did not answer, for once giving his brother the last word.

The following morning Mairi awoke before dawn and knew she would not go back to sleep. Getting up quietly so she would not wake Elizabeth, and tiptoeing about in the dark, she found a kirtle she could put on without help. After tugging her boots on and throwing her crimson cloak over her shoulders for warmth, and to conceal the loose lacing up the back of her kirtle, she plaited her hair into two long, thick braids and went down to the forecourt.

Standing in the darkness, she savored the silence, for only servants in the kitchen, bakehouse, and stables were up so early. The chaplain and his minions would be at prayers and guardsmen at their posts, but from the roofed courtyard she saw no other human and heard only the soughing of a breeze through the shrubbery.

Even the loch was silent. Night birds had ceased their murmuring, and those of daylight still slept.

She walked over to the low wall separating forecourt and residence from the rest of the complex. Above her, the dark sky blazed with millions of stars, for the moon had set, and beyond the wall, at the bottom of the slope, the water of the loch lay mirror calm, reflecting each twinkling point of starlight.

Although she had come outside to think, she found it difficult to focus her thoughts even in such solitude.

When it came to Lachlan the Wily, feelings and emotions seemed to bar all rational thought. She had only to hear someone speak his name, or to think of him, and it was as if he touched her, because a sense of warmth spread through her body in much the same way as it did when he stood beside her.

So foolish, she thought, to conjure a man's image and produce only feelings, the strongest of which, if she but dared to admit it, was desire.

Her fingers itched to stroke his soft tunic again, to smooth the errant lock of hair that persistently fell over his brow. She remembered how he had held her and touched her the night before, and her breasts tingled at the memory. For all Alasdair Stewart's supposed success with women, he had never stirred such feelings in her.

She sighed. Surely, knowing she had to marry Alasdair, she ought to feel some irritation at his excesses with other women, but she felt none. Doubtless that would change after they married, but even that thought brought only another sigh.

Grayness nudged the dark away at last, and then, slowly, golden fingers of sunlight stretched from the east to touch land and water. Deciding that the morning bade fair to be a fine one, she hurried upstairs to find Meg Raith, who slept in the tiny wardrobe room adjoining the bedchamber she shared with Elizabeth.

As Meg was lacing the kirtle properly, Mairi said, "I don't want to wear a caul this morning, Meg. Just tidy it and put it in a net. I am going to ride."

"Surely ye'll break your fast first, mistress, and learn what duties your lady mother desires ye to attend."

"She won't mind," Mairi said, knowing that if she encountered her mother, there would be tasks to perform or children to amuse. She meant to have her ride first. "I have promised to help this afternoon, so I'll return before Sext, but if I am a trifle later, pray don't send a search party after me."

Meg frowned but did not attempt to dissuade her.

Hurrying to the stable enclosure, Mairi found that Ian had Hobyn waiting. The gray gelding nosed her affectionately.

"Thank you," she said to Ian, "but how did you know I would want him?"

He shrugged. "The morn be gey fine, mistress. Ye nearly always do ride on such a one. Will ye be wanting yon saddle on the lad, or me t' ride wi' ye today?"

"No need," she said. "I mean to ride only toward Loch Indaal and back."

"Ye'll no be going the whole way!"

"Faith, and why not?" she said. "'Tis no farther than I rode yesterday to Loch Gruinart. Indeed, I shall make better time, because the track goes alongside the hills instead of over them as the Gruinart track does, and is smoother."

"Aye, sure, but 'tis more heavily traveled, too, so I'm guessing that his grace or her ladyship would prefer ye take me wi' ye, is all."

Mairi eyed him narrowly. "I know you desire to please them, Ian, but if you would please me, do not question my decisions. If anyone disapproves of my riding, let that person speak to me."

"Aye, mistress," the lad said hastily. "I didna mean t' vex ye."

"I know," she said quietly. "Give me a leg up, will you?"

She was halfway across the stone causeway before she remembered that she had meant to ask him if anyone else had ridden out. Telling herself that it did not matter one way or the other, she urged the gelding to a trot and decided to enjoy the fine, brilliant morning and to think of nothing and no one else.

From the shelter of the woodland track she had followed the day before, Lachlan smiled as he watched her, deciding when she grimaced and glanced back at the stable enclosure that Ian Burk had successfully evaded any questions she had asked, or had simply denied serving anyone else that morning. Lachlan had done no more than give the lad a coin and ask politely that he not make news of his departure, adding that he had an important matter to attend to.

He knew it was possible, even likely, that Ian believed he attended to business for the Lord of the Isles, but Lachlan had not said so. If his conscience pricked him, the prick was small, for he held by certain maxims he had encountered in his study of Roman philosophy, not least among which was that if one's cause was good a small wrongdoing could become a virtue.

Since the first duty of any son of Gillean, like any of Clan Donald, was to increase the power and substance of the clan, his cause was certainly good.

He had relayed no information to anyone about his direction or plan, so if Ian did betray him, the lad could say only that he had left Eilean Mòr. But he believed Ian would earn his coin by denying knowledge of him unless MacDonald himself inquired. Then, of course, he would have to answer honestly, because MacDonald was his liege lord and a man had to serve his liege without question or hindrance. But if MacDonald even asked such a question, the fat would already be in the fire.

Her crimson cloak framed and set off her astonishing beauty. She had not bothered to tie its strings at the neck, leaving it open down the front, and as she rode across the

causeway toward him, he saw that the sky-blue kirtle beneath it fit like a second skin. More enticingly, its low-cut
bodice revealed a more-than-generous portion of her plump
breasts.

After they were married, he would strictly forbid her to
ride out looking like a prime invitation to seduction, but for
the present, he would account it his duty to see that no other
rascal dared try to accept that invitation.

Keeping her in sight without being seen proved easy, because the crimson cloak was visible for miles. Moreover, the
hillside where he rode was thick with trees and shrubbery,
giving him cover despite branches yet thin of leaves, because evergreens grew among the deciduous beeches, elms,
and black poplars. He let his pony pick its own way through
the woodland, keeping his eye on the lass.

She glanced over her shoulder occasionally, but his gray-
green doublet and hat, and tan leather breeches, blended
with the hillside colors. His horse was more visible, but its
bay coat merged into the shadows well, and so far she had
not seen it.

They followed the River Sorn, and after less than a mile,
the landscape opened into flat meadowland with downy
birch groves, willows, and aspens replacing the beeches,
pines, and poplars of the hills. Although willow and alder
thickets sprouted along the river and the burns and rivulets
emptying into it, he knew he could not conceal himself
much longer and spurred the bay to a faster pace.

Despite Ian's warning, Mairi had seen no other riders.
The only sounds were the gurgle and rush of the fast-flowing
river, the thuds of her pony's hooves on the dirt track, the

whoops of curlews overhead, and the chirps of woodland and river birds.

The morning fulfilled its promise, and although the breeze gathered strength as she entered the meadow, sunlight splashed on spring meadow grass and the myriad white daisies and yellow dandelions that cut wide, undulating swaths through it. As the dirt track dipped near the water, three coots swam rapidly away, warning others with their echoing hoots.

A kingfisher on a nearby alder branch, having taken no notice of her or of the coots, lifted its head and looked toward the woods behind her. As it did, she heard solid, thudding hoofbeats and turned sharply to see who came.

When she saw him, her breath caught in her throat. She had suspected he would come, but now that he had, she did not know if she was glad or sorry. If her heart's pounding was any indication, she was glad, but her head was not so sure. She waited for him, striving to look unconcerned, even cool and self-possessed.

He slowed and drew to a halt, facing her as he said evenly, "You should not ride alone, lass."

"And you should not follow me, sir," she said, raising her chin.

"Should I not?" His eyes danced.

"You know better." But she was having difficulty. Her lips wanted to smile.

"Had you any particular destination in mind?" he asked.

She shook her head. "Just to ride in the sunshine toward Loch Indaal until it seems time to turn back."

"I thought perhaps you might be seeking more answers to your mystery."

"No, just to think," she said. "I did learn more yesterday,

that I did not tell you, though." She told him what Agnes Beton had said about Elma.

"So Elma took comfort from men other than her husband," Lachlan said thoughtfully. "A dangerous course, especially if Mellis is a brute. What of the witnesses? Could any of them have been her lover?"

"I doubt that Ewan was. I don't know about Gil or Shim, or Fin MacHugh."

"Then we should find out more about them, but it can prove dangerous to track a killer, lass, and it is no task for a woman. Have you no duties at home?"

"I do, of course, because the council meetings continue through tomorrow, as you know, sir, since you serve as a councilor. But Niall is one, too, because as chief of the Mackinnons he serves as master of weights and measures for the Hebrides."

"So he will be out of your hair for a time."

"I should not put it so," she said with a smile. " 'Tis more that in his absence I must see to some things that he would generally attend to."

"Are his duties not taxing, added to your own?"

Her smile widened. " My duties are generally light, and presently involve only supervising our people as they see to the councilors' needs. My sister Elizabeth can see to it if I'm late. Indeed, sir, should you not be at this morning's meeting?"

"I attended the one yesterday afternoon, so Hector is there today," he said. "Apparently, the King has renewed his demand that his grace pay his share of the royal ransom to Edward of England, so they'll be arguing over their reply. I warrant I shan't miss anything that won't be discussed at length this afternoon, so like you, I decided to ride. Do you, perchance, know a place called Loch Cam?"

"Of course."

"I have been told it is most beautiful."

"Cam is much like any other loch on Isla," she said, "albeit higher than many and closely guarded by steep-sided bens."

"I thought I would ride along that ridge we crossed yesterday," he said.

"'Tis easier to follow the burn yonder and approach from the south."

"Will you show me?"

She hesitated. Here on the main track she was safe, but the way to Cam lay through thick woodland, with no track except deer trails by the burn that would not take them all the way. The ride would be too private, and she ought not to go.

"Art scared, lassie?" he said, his voice low, caressing. Again, the sound of it struck chords that vibrated through her, touching nerves and tensing muscles in her midsection and below, some that she could not remember ever feeling before.

She swallowed hard.

"Well?" he said, arching an eyebrow. "'Twas only yestereve, after all, that you were alone with me and came off safely, but if I frighten you . . ."

"You don't," she said, hoping she spoke the truth. "What could you do, for mercy's sake? If you molest me, I need only tell my father to see you hanged."

"I thought he threw offenders off a cliff," he said.

"Not here on Isla," she said. "Here, he hangs them on Judgment Knoll. You are thinking of the cliff at Ardtornish called *Creag na Corp*, the Cliff of the Corpses, from which condemned criminals are hurled to the rocks below."

"You would not let that happen to me," he said, gazing

steadily into her eyes. "So, tell me, dare you show me this beautiful loch of yours, or not?"

She knew the correct answer to that question was no, if only because such a trip would mean once again staying away from Finlaggan longer than she had planned, but instead and without hesitation she said, "Aye, if you like."

He smiled warmly. "Lead the way then."

They rode side by side to the burn she had indicated, then up the sloping meadow until thickening woodland threatened to engulf them again. Finding a deer track, Mairi moved into the lead.

A few moments later, spying a bright carpet of pink ground ivy and yellow primroses ahead, she said quietly, "There, sir, look. Spring is truly upon us."

"Aye," he murmured, "and you'll see more proof of it if you look into the shadows to your right beyond those white anemones."

She saw the doe and her fawn at once, as still as statues in the dense shadow of a tall poplar, but she knew she would not have seen them if he had not pointed them out. Looking back at him, she smiled.

The way steepened, but before long they crested a hill and looked down the glen where Loch Cam, a third the size of Finlaggan, lay dark blue and peaceful, an elongated cup between steep parallel ridges. To their right lay a formidable spill of boulders, interspersed with clumps of heather and bracken. To the left, sheltered from the harsh sea winds that could roar through from the glen's open northwest end, the hillside was tree-dotted and splashed with yellow and white daisies.

Picking their way amidst rocks and shrubbery, they rode down to the water.

"Let's tie the horses and walk from here," he said.

She hesitated. "I should not stay away too long."

"'Tis but a short walk," he said easily. "I'd like to see the view from the end of the loch, and it will do us good to walk for a time."

She doubted that he needed exercise, for surely he had ridden longer distances without respite, but when he dismounted, tied both horses to a shrub, and slipped his hands beneath her cloak to lift her down, she did not object.

His hands were warm and firm, and he lowered her slowly, gazing into her eyes as he did, his expression unreadable. Setting her down, he released her, his fingers brushing lightly against her breasts as he did, sending tingling heat waves through her body. Apparently unaware of the sensations he had stirred, he turned away and gazed out over the loch.

"This is a lovely, peaceful place," he said.

"It must look much like a hundred other lochs you have seen," she said.

"Seil has no lochs."

"Mayhap it does not, but you have traveled, sir, even to France. Moreover, your father holds land on Mull, which boasts many lochs."

"Aye, but the scents and sounds are different here, don't you think? Mull is more heavily laden with trees."

"I love the Isle of Mull," she said. "Duart Castle is my favorite amongst my father's many fortresses, because it boasts the most spectacular views."

As they talked, he set a light hand against the small of her back and guided her toward the left shore of the loch, choosing a route above the rocky shoreline across the grassy, tree-dotted slope. As they neared the opposite end, they had a clear view of the sea miles to the north and of the twin Paps of Jura, jutting into the sky to the east. No one else was any-where in sight.

Reminded of their isolation, Mairi pulled her cloak more closely about her.

"Art cold, lassie?" he said, putting an arm around her and drawing her near.

Telling herself that to pull away from him might stir him to take even greater liberties, she stood still, saying nothing.

"What is it, Mairi?" His voice was gentle and kind, with the softly beguiling undertones that she had begun to recognize.

"It feels lonely here," she said.

"How can it be lonely when we are together?"

"But for me to be alone with you like this is unseemly, sir."

"Would you prefer to have others about?" he asked, turn-ing her to face him.

"You know that is not what I mean," she said, looking up and then wishing she had not. But when she would have turned her head, he caught her chin and held it. He was too close, too warm, too . . . too everything!

"I may know what you mean," he said in that same gen-tle tone, "but I prefer to be alone with you, without a host of prattling tongues to watch over us."

Stifling a bubble of laughter, she said, "Tongues cannot watch people."

"You know what I mean," he said as he bent to kiss her.

Her body leaped in response, and although a stern voice in the back of her mind shouted at her to stop him, she did not try. She could not be sure he would stop if she asked him to, but her body was singing in response to his touch, and she knew she did not want to find out, either way. She also knew, although she would tell no one else, that she had been waiting, hoping, for just such a kiss.

His arms slipped around her, his hands caressing her shoulders and back, and hers sliding beneath his cloak to his waist. The cloth of his jerkin felt rougher to the touch than the velvet doublet he had worn before, but its roughness suited her mood, and she clutched the material tightly, holding him close.

The kiss began softly, as the one at Loch Gruinart had, but his lips hardened quickly against hers, and she could tell that his passions were stronger than before, his yearning more dangerous to her. Still, she could not find it in her to protest. She had never known caresses like his, never known a man like him, and had never known that her body could take fire as it did when he touched her.

She kissed him back, teasing his tongue with hers as if the two were soft-edged swords, and when he moaned, the sound sent a thrill through her stronger than any she had felt before.

How they came to be sitting atop his cloak on the ground with hers in a bundled heap beside them she would never recall, for her senses were filled by the sensations his hands stirred as they caressed her breasts and belly. When he hugged her tight, she gloried in the warmth of his body pressed so closely to hers, little realizing that his fingers were busy with her laces until her bodice relaxed its tight hold on her body and chilly spring air touched bare skin.

Holding her gently away from him by her shoulders where the material had slipped down, he said, "I want to touch you, lass, to stroke you all over, to see if what I cannot yet see is even softer to the touch than what I have already felt. I want to kiss your breasts, to suckle them like a bairn."

Fighting the astonishing sensations sweeping through her in response to his words, she said in little more than a whisper, "You mustn't."

"You don't want me to?"

She bit her lip, unwilling to lie, but unwilling to admit the truth.

"If you do not tell me to stop, I will assume that you want me to continue."

Mairi said nothing. She could scarcely breathe, let alone talk.

His movements as gentle and as mesmerizing as his tone had been, he pulled her closer, loosening her laces more until he could slide her kirtle all the way off her shoulders. She wore only her thin shift beneath it, and that too was easily untied and lowered, baring her breasts first to the sun's kiss and shortly thereafter to his.

"You are so beautiful," he murmured as his lips skimmed over her right breast, pausing near its nipple, his breath as soft and warm as a summer breeze. Then his lips closed around the nipple and his tongue teased it, creating wondrous ripples of pleasure that spread through her body.

Raising his head only to claim her lips, he kissed her thoroughly while his hands roamed at will, making her squirm and moan with pleasure. Pausing, he smiled down at her and said, "I want to make you my own—now, this moment."

"We mustn't," she said, feeling a sense of urgency as she said the words but feeling so much at one with him that she was unable to put any of that urgency into her tone. As a second thought, she added, "I am as good as promised to Alasdair."

" 'As good as' is neither a promise nor a betrothal, sweetheart. As to your father's saying we should not marry, leave that to me to mend afterward. Do you believe I cannot do it?"

"I don't know," she said, "but I have never before known anyone able to persuade him to change his mind after he's made a decision. In any event, I do think we would be wiser to stop before truly coupling."

"And I believe we'd be wiser to couple at once and often," he said gently. "I want you for my wife, Mairi of the Isles, and I believe the only way to achieve that now is to present your father with the accomplished fact of our union."

She was silent, trying to imagine what would happen if she let him seduce her. She knew only what she had gleaned from the few women who spoke freely of men and marriages in her presence, despite her maidenhood.

He said, "I'm thinking you want me as much as I want you, and boldness is necessary if we are to persuade your father. Do you want me for your husband?"

She nodded, feeling uncharacteristically shy. "Aye," she murmured. "I do, for I have never known a man like you."

"There are no others like me," he said with a sudden grin as he reached for her and pulled her close, capturing her lips and kissing her hard.

Forcing herself to ignore her body's instant response, she put both hands against his chest and pushed hard.

He raised his eyebrows. "No?"

"No," she said, sighing with both relief and disappointment at her success. "I want to. I would not lie about that even if I thought you'd believe me. But not here, like this, and not until I can think more sensibly about what I'd be doing."

"Then we should return at once," he said, getting to his feet and moving to pick up her cloak and shake it out.

"Are you angry?"

He shook his head. "Nay, sweetheart. Disappointed, yes—more even than I thought I'd be—but if we must stop, 'tis best we stop at once. I have a strong will, but strong passions as well, and I'd not trust myself to stop later, or you. And, too, I've heard tales about that temper of yours. The last thing I'd want is to stir it."

"I imagine that's why they call you Lachlan the Wily."

"I should perhaps tell you," he said, "that I prefer 'Lachlan the Astute.'"

She cocked her head thoughtfully. "And what would you name your brother, if not Hector the Ferocious?"

He chuckled. "Hector the Stubborn, I think, and doubtless you will find as many to agree with me as with those who dub him ferocious."

As they talked, she slipped her shift and kirtle back into place. Standing now, she turned so he could tie her laces, and thought as he did that he was the first man ever to do so. When he smoothed the material over her shoulders and turned her toward him again, she had all she could do not to fling herself back into his arms.

He held her away, inspecting her from top to toe.

"You look just as you should," he said, kissing her lightly on the lips and then cupping her elbow as he added, "See if you can keep up with me."

The pace he set as they returned was faster than before, but she held up her skirts and trusted his firm hand to keep her from stumbling on the uneven terrain.

When they reached the horses, he lifted her onto Hobyn and mounted the bay. She led until they reached the sloping meadow with the burn tumbling down through it to the River Sorn. Then he rode up beside her, saying, "You'd best ride to back to Finlaggan alone, sweetheart. And mind you be wary of strangers."

"There are no strangers on Isla," she said, savoring the endearment but raising her chin. "I'll talk to anyone I please."

He shook his head. "I'd as lief you don't stop to talk to any men, that's all."

Cocking her head again, but with a teasing smile, she said, "Why not?"

"Because most of us cannot be trusted," he said more sternly. "You should consider that when you think about me."

"How arrogant you are," she said, "to imagine that I should waste my time thinking about you at all."

With a grin, he wheeled the bay and rode off toward Loch Indaal.

Chapter 9

Mairi's return to Finlaggan was barely noticed at first. Council members and onlookers were still meeting on Council Isle. Lady Margaret was with the children in the nursery, and when Mairi found her, said only that she hoped she had enjoyed her morning ride and suggested that she change quickly for the midday meal.

However, Elizabeth met her as she was returning to their bedchamber to change, and said with a relieved sigh, "I'm so glad you're back. I've been looking for you everywhere."

"What's amiss?"

"One of the lads dropped a tray of manchet loaves in the bakehouse, and Niall says they cannot serve them for dinner. We shan't have enough without them, Mairi, but I dare not tell Niall to go and wash his head."

"I'll see what I can do," Mairi said. "Just let me tidy my hair first."

Elizabeth hurried away, and after a cursory attempt to smooth her hair and tidy herself, Mairi went to the bakehouse to find the plump little baker near tears.

"Any other day, mistress, we'd brush off them loaves and set them out," he said. "'Tis no as if they fell in the dirt, or worse. Well scrubbed my floor be, I swear t' ye, but Niall

Mackinnon were a-standing right in yon doorway when
Sym tripped over his own feet and pitched every one o' them
off his tray."

"I thought Niall was at the council meeting."

"Aye, sure, and as one o' his grace's chief councilors, he
should ha' been there," the baker said indignantly, "but that
man pops up like one o' the wee folk, making mischief just
when he's least wanted."

"What did you do with the loaves?"

"Faith, what d'ye think? They be in yonder basket, ready
t' go out t' the lower tables. Them folk will be thinking
they've moved above the salt, having such fine bread for
their dinner. But I've no time t' let new loaves rise afore
they'll be wanted, so what I'm t' do about his grace's noble
guests I dinna ken."

"You'll simply give them the new loaves you've baked."

"What new loaves?"

"Why, the ones in yonder basket, of course," she said,
grinning.

He stared at her for a long moment and then smiled.
"Aye, then, I'll do that, my lady. But willna Niall Mackinnon—"

"Never mind that," Mairi said. "Bread is more to be desired now than perfection. Slip them into the oven to warm,
and then serve them as usual. I'll tell his grace that your
great talents allayed disaster, and that will be that."

Cutting short his thanks, she left the bakehouse, looked
in on the laundry- and dairymaids, and the cooks in the
kitchen, and then went into the great hall, where she found
the trestles up, cloths spread, and all in readiness for their
guests. The servants had departed, all except one young
gillie who had lingered to encourage the fire in the great
fireplace.

More than an hour remained before her father and his councilors would return to Eilean Mòr for the midday meal, but she would require much of that time to make herself presentable. Deciding she should go at once, she hurried off the dais into the side aisle toward the door, but as she passed the archway to the minstrel gallery stairs, a hand shot out, caught her arm, and pulled her through the opening.

Recognizing Lachlan before the shriek at her lips could explode into sound, and noting with a hasty glance over her shoulder that the gillie by the fireplace was too engaged in his task to have paid any heed, she let her captor pull her farther into the dusky stairway.

"What are you doing?" Fearful of being overheard, she barely whispered the words, but her indignation was clear.

Grinning, he put a finger to his lips and drew her up the first few steps until they were out of sight from the hall. Then he pulled her close and kissed her hard.

With a sigh of pleasure, she melted against him.

"I've missed you," he murmured against her curls, free yet of any headdress.

"I thought you were riding to Loch Indaal," she said, keeping her own voice low. "You must have returned not long after I did."

"A nice ride, I'm sure, but I grew bored after you left. 'Twas a rare penance."

"You sent me away," she reminded him.

"Aye, for I did not trust myself. Now hush, sweetheart, or that gillie may hear us," he said, kissing her again. "Come up here with me for a time. Or will his grace be wanting his minstrels to play," he added as a clear afterthought.

"He always wants them," she said. Then, against her better judgment, she added, "But they will not begin until the food is served. Still, someone might hear us if we go up there, and how would we get down again unseen?"

"You worry too much," he said, pulling her into a tight embrace, his hands roaming over her body at will, sending delightful sensations through it. "Ah, lassie, my arms have ached to hold you again."

A vision of Lady Margaret arose in her mind's eye, but she pushed it away. Somehow, when she was with him, thoughts of propriety were merely intrusions.

Lachlan breathed in the herbal scent of her hair and skin. Having ridden only a half mile before realizing he was going the opposite way to the one he wanted, he had waited for her in the minstrel's gallery, certain she would come.

His disappointment at her refusal to couple with him had been strong, although he had already experienced second thoughts about the necessity of his plan, because Hector's words haunted him. Once he realized that he had become more concerned about hurting her or losing her good opinion than about winning points in their discussion, the decision had been easy. He had returned to Finlaggan only minutes after she had left the stables.

Except for servants, the place had seemed deserted, but knowing that she would likely look in on the preparations for the noonday meal in the great hall, he had gone there. Servants were scurrying to and fro when he entered, but aside from one or two who glanced his way to see if he wanted assistance, no one paid him heed as he slipped through the archway to the stairs and up to the gallery.

He watched with pleasure as she walked onto the dais and looked over the high-table arrangements. She walked the way a princess should, with her head high and her movements regal. He enjoyed the way her hips swayed, and the way she smoothed a wispy dark curl off her cheek. He had come to think that every move she made sent an enticing message to him. He had obeyed his instincts earlier, as always, in giving way so easily to her wishes, but he wanted her as badly as ever.

She still wore the temptingly low-cut blue kirtle, so sleekly formed to her seductive body that it stirred his to life and would likely stir the blood of any man worthy to call himself one. He shot a swift glance at the gillie by the fire to see if he dared cast his eyes her way, but the lad was safely intent on his task.

When Lachlan saw her step from the dais, he slipped back down the stairs to wait for her, and the moment he touched her, his body began to hum. He could barely wait to get her out of sight of the lad before kissing her, and as he urged her up the narrow steps ahead of him, he wished only that they had more time.

The gallery with its waist-high parapet was only large enough to contain three or four minstrels. The stone floor was bare, and without showing himself, he dropped his cloak, spreading it hastily and drawing her down on it beside him. Sitting against the wall, he pulled her gently into his arms and kissed her again.

She moaned low in her throat, making him ache to take her right there on the floor, but as the thought entered his mind, he heard voices below in the hall.

She stiffened.

His sharp ears caught a casual exchange of pleasantries, and he murmured reassuringly, "Just another gillie, come to fetch the one tending the fire."

Both left the hall, but her amorous mood had vanished.

"We cannot stay here," she said, her tone urgent. "It is too dangerous."

"Perhaps," he agreed, smiling at her and watching for the return smile he knew would come. In the shadows, as they were, her eyes looked black and huge. He kissed her eyelids, one after the other. "Sometimes danger improves an experience in much the same way that spices improve meat," he said.

"Aye, perhaps, but too much spice spoils the meat."

Chuckling, he said. "We'll go, lass, for we don't want to spoil what we have. You can just slip outside tonight instead, and we'll seek a trysting place together."

"I could never do that!"

"But I think you will," he murmured. "I want to marry you, and you want me, too. We're both agreed to that."

"Aye, but agreement counts for naught when our union is forbidden."

"As I said before, we must give his grace reason to change his mind unless the Steward's son's remote chance to sit on the Scottish throne sways you more than I've had cause to believe."

"You know it does not."

"Then go, and I'll see you tonight. Wait until the Compline bell rings. Nearly everyone should be inside by then, and I'll wait for you in the laird's hall forecourt."

"I can't."

"You can."

She was still shaking her head as she moved to stand, but he caught her and kissed her again, hard, deep, and thoroughly. Then he stood, glanced down at the hall to be sure it was empty, and pulled her to her feet.

"I'll watch from here whilst you go," he said. "Just remember to behave as calmly as ever, for you have every good reason to be leaving the hall and walking back to the residence." As he spoke, he smoothed the errant curl from her cheek, delighting in its soft, springy touch. "And, lass, when you change for the meal, leave your hair unbound. I prefer it so."

Without another word, Mairi snatched up her skirts and hurried down the stairs and along the aisle to the anteroom and outer door. There, remembering his advice, she paused to draw a deep breath and release it before she opened the door wide and stepped onto the porch.

No breeze stirred now, and the sun's warmth enfolded her in strong contrast to the chill of the empty hall, despite its now roaring fire.

The warmth calmed her and ordered her senses again. She strode across the yard and through the forecourt, forcing herself to think about what she could wear that would take little time to put on without undermining her reputation for elegance.

He had told her to leave her hair unconfined. Dared she obey him? It was one thing to defy convention when she rode early in the morning or tended her chores, quite another to do so at a meal in the company of noblemen, tenants, and servants—not to mention her parents.

"Good day to you, my lady."

With a start, she realized that she had been so lost in her thoughts that she had failed to notice Niall's approach from the residence.

"'Tis a fine day, sir," she said, recovering swiftly.

She thought he looked narrowly at her, but he said only, "You will find his grace with your lady mother."

"Then the council meeting is over?"

"Aye, though many stayed to talk more." He frowned. "You must take more care, lass, with so many men about. I'm thinking you should keep your woman or one of our lads at your side. I'd not like anyone to trouble you."

"Then you will not hamper me with attendants, Niall," she said. "No one would dare molest me here."

"Doubtless, you are right, my lady," he said with a bow. "Pray forgive the undue concern of one who has cared deeply for you since your childhood."

She knew that was true, and likewise meant to rebuke her, but she had detected an increasingly annoying, increasingly possessive attitude in him over the past year. Although the change had developed slowly, he treated her with less of the tolerant respect he had shown her as a child and more of what she had come to consider a fatherly manner or, indeed, one more intimate than that.

The memory of the day he spanked her leaped startlingly to mind. Pushing it aside and forcing calm reason into her tone, she said, "Thank you for your concern, Niall. I know you mean well, but I must hurry if I am to be dressed in time. I doubt that my father will delay his midday meal to await my pleasure."

He chuckled. "Nay, lassie, that he will not, for I wager every man at the council meeting is as hungry as I am."

"Then I'll bid you adieu," Mairi said, stepping past him. The strait look he gave her seemed out of keeping with their conversation, but she paid it little heed, her thoughts returning at once to memory.

Although she had spared few thoughts for the humiliating incident in years, suddenly it had been as if she were transported back to it, as if she could feel his big hand again on her bare, childish bottom. She had never told anyone that he had raised her skirt, and when the day came that she realized he should not have done so, the distance of time, the humiliation of even thinking about it, and the near certainty that anyone she told would laugh, had kept her from telling.

That the incident had returned to her thoughts so abruptly was troublesome, but she fixed her mind firmly on what she would wear and hurried upstairs.

Meg Raith awaited her impatiently, and when Mairi said casually that she had decided to leave her hair unbound, flatly vetoed the plan. "Ye'll do no such thing unless ye want to endure the rough side o' your lady mother's tongue and a stern command t' tidy yourself at once," she said. "What her gracious ladyship would say about it, I dinna want t' think. Such a notion!"

In that instant, Mairi was reduced to childhood status again, and she knew that Meg's displeasure was nothing to Lady Margaret's. Silenced, she wondered what demon had possessed her to make the suggestion. That a mere comment from Lachlan the Wily had stirred her to do such a thing without so much as considering the consequences was irksome, but even more so was that she had actually considered obeying his far more scandalous suggestion. Indeed, telling her to meet him in the forecourt at Compline had sounded more like a command.

From that point, she paid scant heed to the pale green gown Meg helped her don, or to the arrangement of her hair under a proper caul and veil. She turned when Meg said to turn, sat when she said to sit, and chose between two pieces of jewelry that Meg held out to her without heeding what either one was.

What had the man done to her? He seemed to negotiate everything, and he seemed to win every negotiation. If she gave an inch, he pressed for an ell. Already he had pressed her to exploit the freedom of movement she enjoyed, dismissing her qualms as if they were of no concern. She seemed to have no defense against him. Indeed, even now, as she considered the likely consequences of meeting him later, she felt no trepidation. Instead, her traitorous body sang, apparently finding the secrecy of the tryst as delightful as the tryst itself promised to be.

She could not do it. That much was as plain as could be.

Assuring herself that she was a sensible, obedient daughter, and not a mouse to dance at every move of the lion's paw, she went to her mother's solar, where she found the rest of the family on the point of descending to dine.

At table, most of her father's councilors stood on the dais, ready to take their seats, and somehow Lachlan Lubanach, despite being absent from the council all morning, stood in the place next to hers. Tempted as she was to make Elizabeth switch places with her, to teach him he could not always win, she did not. The right to sit at Lady Margaret's left was hers. Elizabeth would take her usual place, flanked by the Rose and the Weed, at the end of the ladies' side.

At a truly formal meal, with other noblewomen present, the men would all sit on her father's right, strictly by rank, the women on his left in a similar manner. As a child, when the Council of the Isles met, Mairi had not dined with the councilors, nor had her mother. But as his grace's daughters reached marriageable age, Lady Margaret insisted that they dine at least once or twice with everyone during council days, if for no other reason than to draw the attention of powerful councilors to the fact that his grace had daughters available to marry their sons.

Keeping her gaze modestly fixed on her mother's back, Mairi followed her to the table and stood at her place while her father's chaplain spoke the grace before meat. She could not continue to ignore the gentleman on her left throughout the meal, however, because they shared saucepots and courtesy required him to serve her from various platters as the gillies presented them. Only her father had a body servant to attend to such tasks for him and his lady.

The minstrels in the gallery began to play as the company echoed the chaplain's "amen," but the sounds of lute and harp were nearly drowned out by the shuffle and bump of so many taking their places on the trestle-table benches.

At the high table, the taking of seats was quieter and more orderly. MacDonald's servant assisted both his grace and Lady Margaret, but when Lachlan signed to the gillie behind Mairi's chair that he would assist her, she did not object, telling herself that she could scarcely do so without drawing unwanted attention to them both. As it was, she saw Niall look their way with a thoughtful frown.

The procession of food began as soon as everyone was seated, and Mairi bit her lip as the pantler, under Niall's stern eye and followed by the butter lad, strode to the high table with his basket of manchet loaves and offered the first to her father and the next to her mother. When Mairi's turn came, she took one of the small loaves as casually as everyone else, certain that her parents would be no more distressed than she to know that the manchets had fallen for a few brief moments onto the baker's well-scrubbed floor.

In the lower hall, the pantler's minions were distributing bread trenchers to the company, and the butler and his many helpers were already bringing in that heady drink of the Isles called brogac, as well as claret for the high table and beer and ale for the lower hall.

"You seem unusually fascinated by the gillies today, my

lady," the gentleman to her left said, his tone touched with laughter, as it so often was.

Looking straight ahead, she said, "One of the men caught a huge salmon this morning, sir, and it is to take pride of place in the first course."

"That would explain your considerable interest, 'tis true." The laughing tone had altered slightly to mockery, but still she refused to look at him.

She wanted to think, but with him so near, it was impossible. His brother sat at his other side, but Hector might as well have been in France for all the good that did. Beyond him sat Sir Ian MacSporran, his grace's hereditary purse bearer, and Mairi wondered why MacSporran, a man of higher rank, sat farther from his liege than the sons of Gillean.

At least Lachlan Lubanach had not taken her to task for covering her hair.

The minstrels had changed their tune, and it occurred to her that normally she would not have noticed. Today, it reminded her of her few moments with Lachlan in the gallery. She knew that had the gillies not interrupted their mood, she might have let him have his way. And she knew, too, that if she were such a goose as to meet him at Compline, she would not return to her bed afterward as a maiden.

He said something, pulling her from her thoughts.

Fixing her gaze on her bread as she tore off a piece, she said airily, "Forgive me, sir. I was not attending to you."

"Nay, lass, you were not. Are you always so rude to your dinner companions? For if you are, you will have to mend your ways after we are wed."

He spoke in a tone that might easily have carried to Lady Margaret's ears, and nearly choking on the bit of bread she had just put in her mouth, Mairi looked at him at last to see him grinning with delight at having made her do so.

As soon as she could talk properly, she muttered severely, "You, sir, should be well smacked for such insolent behavior at this table."

"Should I? You may punish me later if you still wish to, sweetheart."

This time, to her relief, he lowered his voice, but she fixed her attention on her dinner from then on, determined to ignore him. Even so, her awareness of him was palpable. She did not have to look at him to know every move he made, and when his near hand brushed her thigh, she nearly jumped out of her chair.

The meal was over at last, however, and the men did not linger. To her further relief, Lachlan accompanied the others back to Council Isle.

Walking with Hector and the other men, Lachlan smiled as he recalled Mairi's reaction to his teasing during the meal. Hector gave him a quizzical look, but not wanting to stir his brother's displeasure again, he said nothing until they approached the causeway to Council Isle.

Then, under his breath, he said, "Hold here a moment. Fix your shoe or something." As the others moved onto the causeway, two abreast, he said, "Elma MacCoun apparently liked men other than Mellis."

"Who can blame her?" Hector said. "Although if Mellis was the tyrant everyone paints him, she took her life in her hands if she smiled at anyone else."

"Aye, sure, but see if you can discover who she favored."

"I'm a step ahead this time," Hector said, "but it avails us little. By what I'm hearing, the lass favored anyone who fancied her. A bit of a hizzie, that one was."

MacDonald had taken his place at the great stone table, leaving them no more time for discussion. "Keep listening," Lachlan said as they hurried to join the others.

Having noted that Agnes Beton had not been at dinner, Mairi's sense of duty sent her to the kitchen to collect manchet loaves and soup again, and she hurried to the Betons' cottage, determined to keep her mind on her duties. Finding Agnes much recovered, she asked her if Ewan had been looking after her.

"I did not see him at dinner either," she added with a smile as she put the bread and soup on the table.

"Nay, mistress, bless ye," Agnes said. "Ewan ha' gone back t' Kilchoman t' help wi' the work there. He'll no return until just afore we depart for the north."

Remembering that Lachlan had said they should find out more about Shim MacVey, Fin MacHugh, and Gil Dowell, she asked Agnes if she knew any of the men well. "Are they particular friends of Ewan's?"

"I wouldna think it, my lady, but in troth I dinna ken. I'm thinking ye should ask the high steward, since like our Ewan, they mostly work for him. They went wi' Ewan t' Kilchoman today," she added. "Mellis went again, too."

"Did they all go with Lord Godfrey that day, then?"

"I dinna ken that, but they do be always the ones the steward sends out and about. Likely, he'll do the same when we go north, too. Ewan ha' said there be work aplenty at Aros and Mingary and at Ardtornish, too."

But Mairi decided not to ask Niall, certain he would not

approve of her interest in so sordid a crime, and might not agree with her conclusion that it even was a crime. Nor could she tell him that Lachlan supported that conclusion.

The rest of the afternoon passed in a haze. She spent much of it in the solar with Lady Margaret, her waiting women, and Elizabeth, but if she took part in any sensible conversation, she retained no memory of it later. As Meg was helping her change for supper, Elizabeth entered, took one look at her, and said, "Mercy, but why are you putting on your best velvet tunic when we are all to sup *en famille*?

"Are we?" A surge of disappointment washed over her.

Elizabeth's fair eyebrows shot upward. "You know we are. Our lady mother told us not an hour ago that his grace had decided we should."

"Of course," Mairi said, adding for Meg's benefit, "I was woolgathering at the time, I expect. I am glad you reminded me, Elizabeth."

"His grace will join his guests in the great hall for amusement afterward, but I fear we're condemned to a peaceful evening. 'Tis a pity, too, because Hector Reaganach has promised to sing the Crusade song again, and he is most amusing."

"Aye, but I recall only the vulgar songs he sang," Mairi said, certain that she must have been outside with Lachlan when Hector sang that particular song.

Elizabeth chuckled. "You would remember the lewd ones. Sometimes I think you must be quite wanton, Mairi. What would our lady mother say?"

Mairi said lightly, "They make me laugh, that's all."

She did not suspect that Elizabeth meant anything more by her words than what she had said, or that she suspected the burgeoning relationship between Mairi and Lachlan Lubanach. Her sister was not guileful or capable of subtlety.

Had she suspected that Mairi hid a growing interest in any man, she would have said so.

Nor did Mairi worry that Elizabeth might be forming an affection for Hector Reaganach. Her sister's destiny was as set as their half sister Marjory's or her own, because eventually Elizabeth would marry Black Angus Mackay of Strathnaver, destined like Marjory's Macleod to be chief of his clan. His support was of great importance, because the huge district of Strathnaver comprised the northwestern corner of mainland Scotland from Loch Naver and the Naver Forest all the way to Cape Wrath. Elizabeth was MacDonald's means of solidifying that support, just as Mairi was his means of reinforcing his connection to the Scottish Crown.

That evening, the sisters enjoyed an even quieter meal with their mother and her women than they had anticipated.

When Mairi inquired about MacDonald's absence, Margaret said, "His grace decided to sup with his councilors. They mean to continue their discussion of how he should most properly reply to the King of Scots' demand for payment of that dreadful ransom, as well as his complete submission to David as his liege lord."

"But how can David ask such a thing?" Elizabeth asked shyly.

"He should not," Mairi said flatly. "The King is not his grace's liege, and that stupid ransom is naught to do with us. Cousin David should be glad his grace helped to negotiate it, when he might as easily have left him in England."

Elizabeth sighed. "It is all very complicated, is it not, madam?"

Margaret smiled. "For us, perhaps, but a woman learns to

have faith in her husband, my dear. Men understand these things better than we ever could."

Mairi's hands clenched, but she dared say nothing. Although she was willing to believe that many men, especially powerful ones directly involved in great events such as the French war with England, were better positioned than most women to know and to understand political strategy, she would never agree that any man knew more about anything, simply by virtue of his gender, than a woman did.

Recalling the easy way that Lachlan the Wily had commanded her to wear her hair unconfined and to meet him at Compline, she hoped he did not expect to call every tune for her dancing if he should manage to persuade her father to let them marry. He'd get a big surprise if that *was* his expectation.

Chapter 10

Mairi felt edgy and unsettled after their meal, and had no desire to engage in polite conversation. As servants cleared away the table, Elizabeth took up her embroidery and asked Mairi if she wanted hers as well, but she shook her head. She desperately needed to think, but her thoughts refused to order themselves.

It was not long before her fidgeting attracted Lady Margaret's attention.

"My dear one," she said, "have you no task with which to occupy yourself?"

Before Mairi could reply, Elizabeth said, "I warrant she would prefer to be in the great hall instead of sitting quietly here, madam. I certainly would."

"Take care lest others think you frivolous," Margaret said sternly. "With Lent still upon us, you should be reflecting on piety, not on worldly pleasures."

"Yes, madam." But Elizabeth's tone was doubtful.

"Be patient," Mairi said. "Lent will soon be over, the men will bring their ladies to Ardtornish, and—" Catching her mother's stern eye, she broke off, adding hastily, "—and John Og will have his son at last, and we can celebrate his birth."

"When you say your prayers tonight," Lady Margaret

said dryly, "you might both take a moment to pray that John Og's child is born healthy and that our guests do not descend upon Ardtornish all at once or linger too long. We shall all have a more pleasant spring if the garderobe towers do not fill as fast as they did two years ago and force us to leave before your father has enjoyed his customary stay there."

"He won't let that happen again," Mairi said confidently.

The conversation meandered desultorily then until Mairi decided she could excuse herself without rebuke. As she hurried to her bedchamber, however, she knew Elizabeth would not be far behind.

Wondering at herself for being concerned about her sister, she wondered too how Lachlan had imagined for a moment that she could easily slip away to meet him. "Why am I even thinking such thoughts?" she muttered to the ambient air. "I am *not* going to meet him. 'Twould be utter madness."

She half expected to find Meg awaiting her, but it was early and she was not there. Without pausing to think about what she was doing, or why, she stepped into the adjoining wardrobe chamber where Meg slept and tended their clothing. Finding an old black cloak she wore as an extra garment when the weather was particularly cold, she hurried back into the bedchamber, and then stood holding it as she glanced around, her ears fairly twitching as she listened for Elizabeth's or Meg's approach.

Aside from a stool and washstand, the curtained bed built against the wall facing the wardrobe chamber and the candlestand beside it were the only furniture.

The blue velvet bed curtains fell short of the floor, revealing the stout legs of the bed's frame. Bending to see if she could push the cloak underneath without its being seen by anyone else in the room, she realized that as her mind was insisting she could not slip out later, her hands and body were preparing to do just that.

"But how?" she asked as her traitorous hands bundled the cloak under the bed. "What if Meg chooses tonight to see if the floor underneath has been swept?"

But by the time Meg and Elizabeth arrived, she had lighted candles and knew she would submit to her impulses. It was all she could do to avoid glancing toward the bed every minute to see if she had pushed the cloak far enough underneath.

Meg helped her out of her tunic and kirtle and, giving her a bed robe to wear, turned to assist Elizabeth.

Mairi cleaned her teeth at the washstand and washed her face, but her attention was on Meg. She could scarcely believe the woman did not suspect what she was about to do. Her tension seemed as if it should be noticeable to anyone.

Since everyone slept nude and she dared not enter the wardrobe after Meg had retired there, she could only hope she would hang the clothes they had removed on pegs outside the wardrobe door to air overnight, as usual, before stowing them in their chests the next day. Sometimes Meg did not go to bed when they did but stayed up to mend a tear or dab away a stain by the kitchen fire while she chatted with a friend, but only when she believed it was necessary to attend to such things at once, since she could see better by daylight.

The Rose and the Weed slept on pallets in the great chamber, outside the adjoining inner chamber where Lady Margaret slept with her lord. To get to the forecourt, Mairi would have to pass the great chamber, but since she knew from experience that both women slept like the dead, there remained only the small detail of her father and her brothers, all of whom would still be up.

Any one of them might decide at any time to return to the residence. However, none would seek her in her bedchamber, so she need only take care that she did not meet one on the stairs or outside in the forecourt.

Surely, she told herself as Meg brushed her hair, Lachlan would not want to linger in the forecourt. He had said danger lent spice to adventure, but foolhardiness would not, and he seemed sensible about most things, if a trifle overconfident.

She would just have to trust him to have a plan, but what it might be defied her imagination and made her body quiver with tremulous anticipation.

He would not take her to his room, because although Finlaggan boasted a number of guest chambers, there were not so many that the sons of Gillean would have rooms to themselves. The two would more likely share one, and might even share it with one or two other gentlemen.

She had had nothing to do with the accommodations for his grace's councilors, because that task fell within Niall Mackinnon's purview. And she knew that Niall would not have given special consideration to Lachlan or Hector.

"Mairi, where are your wits roaming?" Elizabeth demanded. "Meg has twice asked what you want to wear tomorrow."

Apologizing hastily, Mairi pushed all thought of trysting out of her head, told Meg what she would wear, and obediently shrugged off her robe and got into bed, giving thanks that her sister preferred the inner side near the wall. She would not have to creep over or around her to get out.

As Meg drew the bed curtains, Elizabeth murmured sleepily, "You seem distracted tonight, Mairi. You are not ailing, are you?"

"Nay, dearest, not in the least," Mairi said, hoping she spoke the truth but wondering all the same if madness counted as an ailment.

In the great hall, Lachlan toyed with the gold ring on his finger as he listened to apparently endless debate among the other councilors and cursed their verbosity. At least Mac-Donald had not insisted that they return to Council Isle to continue the day's discussions. He had feared throughout supper that he might, because it was plain to the meanest intelligence that the others had disliked leaving the islet to eat and had wanted to continue their talks there.

MacDonald had insisted that they eat, and that they adjourn to the great hall so the servants would not have to carry hot food to Council Isle. However, he had agreed that they could continue their discussion, since anyone who wanted to hear them could do so, just as they had at Ian Burk's trial. Lady Margaret clearly had not so chosen, and had kept her daughters with her, but that was just as well.

They had been over and over the same points since he had joined them after the midday meal, and according to Hector, those points were the same ones they had fought over all morning while Lachlan had enjoyed himself with Mairi. The most frustrating thing was that the answer to their dilemma was clear.

He would have liked simply to stand and explain it to them, but he had already suffered enough frustration to realize that they would reject any suggestion of his out of hand. Although their initial reception of him and Hector as their father's ambassadors had been kind, even jovial, they now clearly deemed him too young and inexperienced to understand the complex matters they discussed.

Hector had taken umbrage at this doubtless unintentional disrespect, more so on Lachlan's behalf than his own, as

Lachlan knew. Even now, Hector sat beside him, tense and twitching, like a hawk eager to hunt.

Lachlan's inner clock told him that the hour was fast approaching Compline. He did not care if the others wanted to sit up all night arguing, but he knew they would not look kindly on his departure before the matter before them was resolved or MacDonald sent them all to bed.

"They do not even ask us what we think," Hector muttered.

"They already ken fine what you think," Lachlan murmured back.

Hector shot him a look, but Lachlan met it with a half smile. "Don't look so fierce," he said. "You'll terrify someone, and then where shall we be?"

"Mayhap I'll terrify them into making a decision."

"More likely, your fierce looks will lend credence to certain rumors that you sleep with Gillean's infamous battle-axe instead of with any willing woman."

As he had hoped, that drew a reluctant grin as Hector said, "Lady Axe makes a fine bedmate." More soberly, he added, "I don't doubt you've already decided what they should do. Why not just tell them and be done with it?"

"Because they won't listen. Only recall how Mackinnon squashed everything I said yesterday, as if I were a brainless gowk. Now, hush; I want to hear this."

"Forgive me, your grace," brawny Murdoch Macleod of Glenelg said gruffly from the far end of the high table, around which they had gathered. "Although the hereditary keeper o' the records reminds us that the King ought t' be grateful t' ye for arranging his ransom from the English, I'm thinking the silly wee man allies himself more nearly wi' England than he does wi' us."

"Aye, that be fact," agreed Andrew MacSporran. "Were Scotland's Davy no married for a time to English Edward's sister, and did the wicked lad no suggest, nobbut three years since, that his successor on the Scottish throne should be Edward's eldest son, since Davy canna seem t' make any o' his own?"

As a number of the men muttered their disapproval, Macleod plowed back in, saying, "Another unfortunate fact, your grace, be that Davy kens fine that your marriage t' the lady Margaret—blessed be her name—allies ye wi' the Steward's faction, which he believes wants to unseat him and put the Steward on his throne."

"Aye," MacDonald agreed. "'Twould be in keeping wi' the King's character."

"If he had any," another voice muttered.

"With respect, your grace," Niall Mackinnon said, "the King has some reason for feeling so. He has made clear his disapproval of setting your first wife aside, without a proper annulment, to marry Lady Margaret. He has, in fact, at least twice suggested that you now stand possessed, illegally, of two wives."

Lachlan had little use for the King of Scots or his opinions, but gasps from several at the table warned him that with comments like Mackinnon's the debate would soon grow heated again if someone did not rein it in. He wondered if Mackinnon meant to stir trouble or had just grown bored. His reasons mattered little, however, since the primary difficulty lay in the fact that like most groups trying to make a decision, this one had raised many points, some of which pertained to the issue at hand but most of which were irrelevant, and to a man, they kept dancing around the main point without once touching upon it.

With a seemingly careless gesture, Lachlan knocked over his wine goblet, leaped to his feet as he did, and snatched a cloth from a passing gillie to stop the flow of wine before it spilled onto Mackintosh, chief of Clan Chattan, beside him.

"Forgive my clumsiness, sir," he said, smiling at the older man. "I swear to you that I am not ape drunk, although I must surely appear so. I fear I was paying more heed to the discussion than to my goblet."

"You are wise to attend to the debate, lad," Mackintosh said.

"Aye, sure, but I'm not certain I've grasped all the details," Lachlan said, shifting his gaze to MacDonald. "I wonder if I might ask a question, your grace."

"Certainly, lad," the Lord of the Isles said cordially. "Ask as many as you like. Sometimes our council discussions can confuse everyone present."

"Well, I'm certain everyone else here understands the situation, so pray correct me if I have taken aught amiss. 'Tis my understanding that the dilemma before us arises because the Scottish Parliament declared against you, your grace, for refusing to pay the so-called contribution to the Crown that the King of Scots demands to pay his English ransom, and also for supposedly fomenting rebellion because other Islesmen have followed your lead in not paying."

"Aye, ye've got that down, lad," Agnew, the hereditary Sheriff of Galloway, said approvingly. "That's it exactly!"

"Thank you, sir," Lachlan said. "Mayhap you will likewise agree with my understanding that the King also demands that his grace appear before him and give surety for his conduct."

"Aye, lad," Macleod of Glenelg said. "Ye've got that right, too."

"But surely I am also correct in believing that his grace is still King of the Hebrides and Lord of the Isles, am I not?"

"He is that!" many of them shouted as fists pounded the table.

Lachlan frowned, taking his time in order that they might

grow quiet again but also that they might think about the three points he had made.

"What's amiss, lad?" Agnew asked. "Be there summat else that puzzles ye?"

"I'm wondering when the King of Scots managed to assume sovereignty over the King of the Hebrides," Lachlan said, looking bewildered.

"He *never* did, and won't," Mackintosh declared. "A king be a king and equal to all other kings. Indeed, his grace's ancestor Somerled called himself King over the Isles *and* the Hebrides."

"I begin to understand," Lachlan said. "What you all managed to see before I did is that his grace is an independent prince and therefore free to make whatever decisions he chooses to make without help or hindrance from any other prince."

"Aye, that's it exactly!" Agnew and MacSporran announced together.

A silence fell as the others looked at each other.

Lachlan knew that he had made his point. Glancing at the Lord of the Isles, he met his quizzical look easily.

After a long moment, MacDonald's gaze drifted to the other end of the table.

Lachlan waited, saying nothing.

Feeling tense movement beside him, he briefly touched Hector's shoulder, felt him relax again, and knew he could trust him to stay silent, too.

Old Cameron of Lochaber, having remained silent throughout the evening's long discussion, stirred at last in his place of honor beside MacDonald. Holding the sole distinction in that company of having, forty-six years before, signed the Declaration of Arbroath, a vigorous letter written to Pope John XXII and signed by eight Scottish earls and thirty-one barons, declaring that Scotland would in no way, ever, yield to England, Lochaber held the deep respect of every man there.

The bell for Compline began to ring, and Lachlan stifled a groan.

When every eye had turned his way, Lochaber cleared his throat and said ponderously, "Every man o' ye kens that I be MacDonald's man and that I believe in freedom as ye do, and as all good Islesmen do—aye, and ordinary Scotsmen, too. So I'd remind ye that when we fight 'tis no for glory, riches, or honor, but always for freedom, which no man surrenders but wi' his life."

"Aye, that's so!" several shouted. Others nodded to show agreement.

"MacDonald, Lord of the Isles, be the prince o' our realm," Lochaber went on, "and like the King of Scots or England's Edward, he answers t' none save his own. That be the answer we send t' Davy. We'll tell him his grace willna contribute t' England's wealth by paying yon ransom and has nae need to offer or give surety for any o' his own royal decisions t' the King o' Scots."

Excited cheers broke out as MacDonald stood, and over them, he shouted, "Since you all agree, that is the reply I shall send!"

Turning to clasp Lochaber's hand, he waited for quiet again before saying, "I thank you all for your counsel and declare this meeting adjourned for the day. We'll meet again on Council Isle after we've broken our fast in the morning, to discuss all such matters of final business as may occur to you."

Leaning hastily to speak in his brother's ear, Lachlan said, "I need your aid."

"What would you have me do?"

"Sing to his grace and his sons or plague them, I care not

which, but keep everyone away from the laird's hall forecourt for as long as you reasonably can."

"Indeed, and dare I ask why?"

"You may ask, but I'll not answer. I must go at once!"

"Good luck to you, my lad. I'm thinking you'll need it."

As Lachlan hurried away, the echo of those words followed him.

Torches burning near the entrance to the laird's residence
showed Mairi the deserted forecourt. She had heard the
Compline bell only minutes after Elizabeth's deep breathing
had reassured her that her sister was asleep. Moving with
cautious haste, she had slipped out of bed and dragged her
cloak from underneath.

Meg had gone into the wardrobe and had not come out
again. Listening at the curtain, Mairi heard snuffling snores.

Slipping her kirtle over her head, she pulled the laces in
back as best she could alone and wrapped the cloak around her.
Then, picking up her boots from outside the bedchamber door
where she had left them earlier, knowing Meg would think she
expected to ride again in the morning, she tiptoed downstairs
past the great chamber before sitting on a step to pull them on.

Grateful that she had encountered no one else yet, and
having no wish to stand exposed in torchlight, she moved to
the side of the court overlooking the loch and stood in a deep
shadow there. Masses of stars filled the sky, and the golden
glow of a rising moon created a halo over the hills to the east.

Clutching her cloak about her and watching the open
gateway, she had just begun to wonder if she should go back
upstairs when she saw a tall figure striding confidently toward her. He was too far away for the torches near the front

of the forecourt to light his face, and the ones from the great hall porch cast a glow behind him, so she could not be sure it was Lachlan.

Aware that it might not be, she slipped behind a pillar, trusting her dark cloak to conceal her. To her shock, the figure turned and headed toward her.

"Don't hide; we've no time to dawdle," he said in a quiet but carrying voice.

"How did you know it was I?" she demanded quietly as he drew nearer.

"I saw you, of course."

"But I might have been anyone."

"Nay, sweetheart," he said, putting an arm around her, "you could never be just anyone. But come. The meeting has ended. Others may be on my heels."

"But where? Won't we walk right into them?"

His hand enfolded hers, warming it.

"You should have worn gloves," he said. "It's cold out here."

"By heaven, sir, I'm glad to have clothing on. My woman sleeps in the wardrobe. I had to get this cloak earlier and hide it under the bed. Had she not hung my kirtle to air on a peg in our chamber, I'd not have a stitch on under this cloak."

"I'd like that," he said in a teasing voice as he ushered her to the low parapet that faced the length of the loch. "But if it is the kirtle you wore this morning, I'll approve of that, too."

"'Twas not just my maid or my clothes," she said. "My sister sleeps with me. I don't know what demon persuaded you that I could slip out so easily."

"But you did, did you not? And you've left your hair unbound, too. We can, most of us, do what we set our minds to do."

"Perhaps sometimes, but not always."

"We can always do what is necessary. What's hard is recognizing necessity."

He swung a leg over the parapet and reached for her. As he clasped her waist, he said, "An unwelcome thought occurs to me. Will his grace lock that door for the night when he returns?"

"He never does," she said. "Guards stand at the causeway to the main island and patrol elsewhere, but none stands inside the residence enclosure or beyond. 'Tis Isla that protects us, not Finlaggan's guards."

"I expected them to be everywhere," he said. "One assumes that the Lord of the Isles will keep a great tail of men about him, as befits his princely rank."

"When he travels, he does take such an entourage. But the Isles are safe now, and few men lock doors. At Ardtornish, the main door boasts a key so large that I cannot lift it by myself to put it in the lock. My father let me try when I turned thirteen, but we never use it, because the whole of loyal Morvern protects us there."

"This way," he said, guiding her toward the southern tip of Eilean Mòr.

Dimly she could make out Council Isle at the end of its stone-and-timber causeway, surrounded by black, mirrorlike water that reflected the stars above.

"Where are you taking me?"

"Trust me. I know a place that will give us as much privacy as we like."

The words sent an anticipatory thrill through her until a dreadful thought stopped it cold. "You . . . you are not thinking that we should go into the building! My father's documents . . . 'Tis a sacred place, sir, as is the stone table!"

He chuckled. "Believe me, lass, I don't mean to desecrate any sacred place, even to be with you. Although if it should rain, I would not disdain shelter."

"The sky is clear."

"So it is," he agreed. "Now have a care as we cross the causeway. Some of the boards creak."

They did, but not so loudly that anyone would hear, and at least, she did not have to mind her footing as she had on the uneven ground. He had kept a hand under her elbow, and had seemed able to detect the slightest dip or hillock before it surprised her. She hoped his instinct for a safe trysting place proved as sound.

Her thoughts, no longer focused on footing or conversation, jumped to what lay ahead. With each step, her emotions teetered or entangled themselves. One moment she thought she must be mad, the next she offered thanks to God that her father was not a violent man. Other men had killed daughters who gave up their maidenheads to men not chosen for them. She did not think MacDonald would kill her, but she was not so sure about her brothers or her mother.

As she smiled at the thought of Lady Margaret wreaking physical violence, the stern image of her grandfather leaped to mind, followed a split second later by that of Alasdair Stewart.

"What is it, lass?"

"What?" They were approaching the building, some fifteen feet long and half as wide. The great stone table stood ahead to their left.

"Some notion struck you just then," he said. "I could feel it."

"I thought of Alasdair," she said, not even thinking about evading the question. "I could see him in my mind, tall and furious."

"Don't trouble your head about him," he said firmly, drawing her to the end of the building facing the south end of the loch.

"But what if I do have to marry him? He will find out, will he not, that—"

"You will not have to marry Alasdair Stewart, nor will we discuss him further. I find that I have taken a great dislike to the stupid man."

"Faith, sir, I thought you did not know him."

"I don't, but he must be stupid if he can claim you as his wife and has not done so. Here now, this way."

A moment later they reached the far end of Council Isle, where the building's mass concealed them from the palace complex.

He bent and began feeling around at the base of the wall.

"What are you doing?"

"I was here earlier," he said, "after the council adjourned for the midday meal. Someone might have found my bundle, but—"

"What bundle?"

"This one," he said, hefting it. "A jug of wine and two goblets, wrapped in two fine thick cloaks."

"You brought three cloaks with you? I thought you said you were poor!"

"One is Hector's," he said with the touch of laughter in his voice that she had come to love.

"And the other?"

"I don't know," he admitted, unwrapping goblets and jug, and spreading one cloak on the ground as he added, "Someone left it in our chamber, so I borrowed it for the occasion, knowing two cloaks would make a softer couch for us than one. May I pour you some wine, my lady?"

She surprised herself by giggling. She never giggled, but even as she did, she felt a sudden urge to turn and run away as fast as she could go. Instead, ruthlessly suppressing the urge, she said, "Yes, please."

Chapter 11

They sat for several moments with their backs against the stone wall of the building, sipping wine from silver goblets until Mairi felt warm all through.

She heard a horse's snuffling whinny from the stable enclosure. Otherwise, the night was so silent she felt as if her breathing might draw someone's attention, but both the wine and Lachlan's nearness reassured her. Had anyone told her she could feel comfortable sitting alone with a man she had met only three days before, she would have laughed, but she felt as if she had known him forever.

He put his arm around her, and she leaned her head against it, looking up as a star flashed across the sky, leaving a brilliant tail of sparks.

"Did you see that?" he asked.

"Aye, and made a wish, too. Did you?"

"Of course, and it is about to come true," he said, leaning closer and kissing her. A moment later he took the goblet from her hand, set it down somewhere, and pulled her closer while his free hand pushed her cloak away and touched the soft plumpness of her breast where the deep vee of the kirtle's neckline revealed it.

She gasped as his hand slid inside, moving the fabric off

her shoulders. She wore nothing underneath, because Meg had taken away her shift.

"This dress should be illegal," he murmured against her lips as his warm hand cupped her breast.

His hand was warm against her skin. Her blood flowed hotter still, like fiery rivers coursing through her veins to her core, making her body ache for him to touch it, to kiss her all over as he had once promised to do.

Stirring against him, she pulled him closer, holding him tight as he eased her down to lie on the cloaks he had spread. He kissed her again, thrusting his tongue deep into her mouth and exploring its interior as his hand eased over her body, sending new sensations through her everywhere he touched her.

He paused, leaning up on an elbow to look at her. The slim crescent moon peeped over the hill, casting its silvery light on them, revealing his tender smile.

"I want to make you mine, Mairi. I want us to have no doubt about that."

His words brought a quickening response from her body that she could not deny. "I don't know what you want me to say," she murmured.

"Don't say anything," he said, kissing her again.

His exploring hand moved lower on her body, skimming across her stomach to the juncture of her legs. As he eased her skirt up, she felt the chilly night air and wondered if she might grow too cold. But with his body atop hers and her blood racing, her legs felt the chill only for that instant. Then his fingers touched the bare skin high on one inner thigh, stroking her, and she could think of nothing else.

Her lips were soft and delightfully responsive, and her skin even softer than he had imagined it would be. Touching her encouraged him to play, to let his fingers stroke in reverence, and then, with his lips and tongue, to taste and savor. She showed no fear, only fascination, and briefly he wondered if she were more experienced in the art of lovemaking than he had thought.

But, no, she could not be, for not only were her reactions filled with virginal awe, but only the world's stupidest man, having experienced the delight of holding her so, touching her, and stirring her passions, could give her up. And a man that stupid would lose no time in crowing of his conquest to every other man he met.

He continued to kiss her, savoring the warm velvety interior of her mouth and anticipating a corresponding warmth elsewhere. As the image stirred his senses, he trailed fingers along her inner thighs until she gasped again. Flattening his hand, he moved it slowly, delighting in the silky softness of her skin against his palm.

She was moaning, and he feared she might be one to forget her surroundings and give voice to her passion, particularly at her climax. He wanted to taste more of her, to take his time, but even if she were quiet, they dared not linger long, for every moment increased the likelihood of someone catching them. Even as he savored the treats of her body, felt her squirm beneath him, and enjoyed her moans of pleasure, a part of him—the part that never slept—continued to evaluate the risk they faced.

He believed what she had said about the guards at Finlaggan, for he had already seen that they spent their days wrestling, practicing archery, hauling boats, or sailing on the loch or along the coast. He had seen only a few guarding anything.

Still, in his experience, a lord as skilled and successful as MacDonald would not suffer men about him who neglected their duties, and the safety of his family would be paramount. An army or navy might not be able to invade Isla without warning, let alone Finlaggan, but Lachlan believed that he and a few of his men in a boat could gain landfall at both places on any dark night, without being caught.

Whether they could as easily, with impunity, gain entrance to the apparently unlocked private quarters of the Lord of the Isles and his family was another matter, and one on which he would not bet heavily, especially with Finlaggan full of off-islanders. Were it as easy as it seemed if one accepted the lass's description, MacDonald would be dead by now and an invader ruling in his place.

While these thoughts tumbled through his subconscious, they stole nothing from his pleasure. His lips continued to savor hers, his tongue to dance with hers, and his fingers to explore. Wanting to examine her breasts more thoroughly, he moved lower, kissing her neck, the hollow under an ear, and her throat before he trailed a line of kisses over the right one and his lips captured its nipple.

Using his tongue, and feeling himself stir as he imagined the lass using her soft lips to such good purpose on him, he lingered over the right breast for a time before moving to the left one and then trailing more kisses down her belly.

She gasped again when his fingers invaded the moist area between her legs.

From their first meeting, Mairi had suspected that what she knew about couples and coupling was as nothing to the reality. When he touched her, she had been sure of it, but until that night, her knowledge of coupling had comprised only the curt answers received when she had boldly asked first her sister Marjory and later John Og's wife, Freya, to tell her what took place in the marital bed.

"Do people get children the same way that horses, dogs, and cattle do, or more like chickens and hawks?" she had naively asked the latter.

"Like horses, more's the pity," Freya retorted, adding with a blush, "Go tend your duties, Mairi. I do not want to talk of such things."

She had tried numerous times since, unsuccessfully, to imagine skinny Freya behaving like a mare in season, or John Og like a sexually aroused stallion.

"Art frightened, lass?" Lachlan asked quietly, raising his head.

His fingers stirred a new wave of aching heat between her legs, making her gasp as she said, "Nay!"

"I could tell that your thoughts were wandering and thought the only thing that could distract them right now must be fear."

"Not fear," she said. "Only curiosity about what you would do next."

"This," he said, moving so that she felt his warm breath stir the nest of curls near his tantalizing fingers.

"Oh! What are you doing?"

"Only kissing you everywhere, as I said I would."

"But surely not there!"

"Everywhere."

The warning voice in the back of his mind told him to get on with it, and complete the act that was his best hope for claiming her as his own.

As he kissed her nest, breathing in the womanly scent of her, he sent a prayer heavenward that his plan would succeed. Resisting the yearning to taste her and linger there, lest she protest more loudly, he moved gently up to kiss her lips instead, to still any protest before it flowered.

Freeing himself from his clothing was easy. The flat linked-metal belt he wore low on his hips clinked as he shifted it out of the way. His thigh-length tunic shifted easily, and his trunk hose opened just as easily. Reaching for her again, he gently used his fingers to be sure she was ready. Reassured by another gasping moan of pleasure, he fitted himself into her, careful to move with caution so he would not hurt her. The moment he touched her, however, his urge to take her increased so powerfully that it was as if he controlled a beast within.

His breathing quickened, and he could feel his heart pounding. His body throbbed, aching for release.

When Mairi realized that what touched her now was not his fingers she stopped breathing, wishing that part of her could perch on a tree branch and look down on them, to see exactly what he was doing. She could feel it—enormous in comparison to his fingers—and she remembered what Freya had said about horses.

But it did not hurt her. Instead, it seemed to toy with her, tease her, and the sensations it stirred were irresistible. She did not want them to stop.

She wondered what he was feeling.

His kisses were tender, light against her lips and cheeks, even her eyelids, and as she kissed his cheek and bristly chin, she felt herself surrendering, melting like warm butter beneath him.

Then he pressed harder, slid into her, and the ache of longing she had felt changed to a dull but sharpening pain. She squirmed and gasped, but he claimed her lips again, his tongue thrusting into her mouth. One hand moved to her right breast, stroking tenderly, teasing the nipple. Then with a moan, he shifted that hand to the ground beside her, balancing himself as he thrust into her, harder and harder, still holding her mouth captive so when the pain drew a cry to her lips, it went no farther.

Gasping now himself, he pounded against her, faster and faster, until at last he stopped, held himself above her for a moment, and then slumped atop her.

"Oh, sweetheart," he murmured.

"Did it hurt you, too?"

"Nay, it did not, and it will not hurt you either next time. 'Tis only when a woman has not done it before that it hurts her."

"How do you know so much about how a woman feels?"

He chuckled. "Hector told me."

Mairi's return to the residence was without incident, and lying in her own bed a short time later, with Elizabeth breathing softly beside her, she considered the events of the night and decided that lovemaking was neither as Freya had described it nor particularly amazing. Her body still ached, but she was no longer bleeding.

Lachlan had warned her afterward that she would bleed, and the pain she felt had made her sure he must be right, but she had nearly leaped out of her skin when he had said he would clean her himself. Once again he proved to be the most persuasive man she had ever met, and despite her initial resistance, she had let him, feeling no surprise whatsoever when he produced a large kerchief for the purpose.

Astonishingly, his touch had set fire again to her body, and remembering now, she readjusted her opinion. Some parts of lovemaking were pleasant, particularly so. She wondered if Freya could possibly have experienced those things and not mentioned them. Mayhap John Og was not as skilled as Lachlan.

She pondered the latter's skill for a moment, and the next thing she knew it was morning and Meg was drawing back the bed curtains to waken them, their bed robes in her hand. As Mairi slipped hers on and swung her feet out of the bed, she glanced at her kirtle on its peg to reassure herself that it had not become covered with grass or leaves on Council Isle. It was dusty around the hem, but although she did not recall its being so before her adventure, such a state was not unusual enough to stir her maid's curiosity.

She moved to the washstand as Elizabeth jumped out of bed and hurried to the garderobe, and was scrubbing her face when, behind her, she heard Meg say, "Why, what's this then? I didna see it last night or I'd ha' taken it down t' soak."

Lowering the wet cloth, she turned to see Meg examining the hem of the kirtle. "What is it?" Mairi asked, amazed that she sounded normal.

"A stain here at the hem." Meg shook her head. "I must be getting old, that's all. I'll see to it this afternoon, mistress. I ken well ye like t' wear this kirtle."

Mairi nodded, saying nothing, not trusting her voice, because Meg was examining the stain more closely.

"It looks like blood," she said, "but 'tis an odd place t' find blood."

Tempted to say she had somehow scratched herself, Mairi kept silent.

Meg shrugged, pulled the kirtle off the peg, and tucked it under her arm. "I'll just fetch Lady Elizabeth's tunic for her," she said. "I've put your things on the bed, mistress. If ye'll slip on your shift, I'll help ye wi' your lacing and all."

Exhaling with relief, Mairi obeyed and by the time Elizabeth returned, she was dressed and seated on the stool, letting Meg arrange her hair.

In the great chamber after prayers, they discovered that their father had broken his fast and had already gone to begin the final meeting of the council.

"Will everyone leave today, madam?" Mairi asked Lady Margaret when they had taken their places at the table.

"Many, I expect, but I shouldn't think that all of them will."

"Do we know yet who means to stay?"

Her mother's well-plucked eyebrows rose. "Whoever wishes to do so will stay, Mairi. Surely, you know that our laws of hospitality demand as much."

"Yes, madam, of course," she said hastily. "I was just curious."

The word slipped out without thought, and she winced when she heard it.

Lady Margaret's benevolent expression vanished and with ominous calm she said, "Curiosity is a poor excuse for incivility."

"Yes, madam. I beg your pardon."

"It displeases me when you speak so heedlessly."

"Yes, madam." She dared say no more, because Margaret

might forbid her to leave the residence if she believed such punishment would teach her a good lesson.

After a tense silence, her mother said, "Elizabeth, when you finish, fetch your embroidery, and I will show you that stitch you asked me about yestereve."

The moment of danger past, Mairi soon escaped, but she gained nothing by it. The only people she saw were servants, because everyone else was apparently attending the final council meeting. She considered joining them but feared she would find it impossible to keep her gaze from Lachlan and thus betray to others exactly what had happened. Therefore, she turned to her usual duties, although thoughts of him continued to hold her mind captive.

In daylight, especially after her mother's rebuke, the events of the previous night loomed unnaturally large and pricked her conscience sorely. Nevertheless, she had only to remember his touch on her hand, her shoulder, or her breast, to re-create echoes of the sensations he had stirred.

She wanted to see him, to reassure herself that he honestly cared for her, wanted to marry her, and believed he would win her. That she loved him would not weigh with her father, she knew, because noble marriages were too important to leave to any lady's predilections. An heiress, particularly one of so powerful a father, was but a pawn for him to play as he thought best.

She knew that her father loved her and that she was important to him, but her importance was the same as Lady Margaret's to Robert the Steward. The primary value of any powerful man's daughter was that he could use her to create or strengthen advantageous alliances.

Marjory's wedding to Roderic Macleod at Ardtornish had been so grand an event that everyone of note in the Isles and on the coastal mainland had come, their galleys festively decorated with banners, ribbons, and gilt. Even Robert the Steward had attended, and those unable to do so knew soon afterward that the ceremony had taken place, because beacon fires had burned from castle to castle to announce it. Folks had talked about that wedding for a full twelvemonth afterward.

Mairi expected signal fires and banners for her wedding, too, and if she married Lachlan instead of Alasdair, she would not have to leave the Isles. Also, she would enjoy many more nights like the previous one.

The more she thought about Lachlan, the more she feared he could not win her. By the time the Council of the Isles adjourned to the great hall for their final midday meal, her eagerness to see him had changed to anxiety for their future.

When she entered the great hall to find Sir Ian Mac-Sporran at the place beside hers, she searched for Lachlan, seeing him again at the far end of what would usually be the gentlemen's side, with Niall beside him. Neither looked her way, but as she gazed at Lachlan, Niall shifted his disapproving gaze to her.

Sighing, she looked away. Unless the Fates intervened, she would have no opportunity to exchange a word with Lachlan Lubanach until after they had dined.

The meal seemed endless. She liked Ian MacSporran, who was always patient with questions about fiscal matters, but had anyone asked later what they had discussed, she could not have recalled.

The company was boisterous, even celebratory, as if they had achieved great things, but she knew their joy was more likely due to the council meeting's having ended without major altercation. It occurred to her that she knew little of what they had done, which was unusual, since she took great interest in her father's affairs and generally wheedled as much information from him and from others as she could.

But since her return to Finlaggan, other than her efforts to identify Elma's killer, she had spared thought for little other than Lachlan the Wily. He had bewitched her, and she wondered uneasily if, having done so, he would vanish as mischievous fairies and other wee folk always did after wreaking their mischief. The thought depressed her, but she could not seem to banish it from her mind.

When the meal ended and Lady Margaret stood to leave, Mairi did as well, her depression deepening at the fear that she might not get to exchange another word with him. She certainly dared not turn and walk to the end of the table where he stood with Niall and other men, to demand speech with him. To do so would incite just the sort of scandal that MacDonald had warned her to avoid.

As she followed her mother in the opposite direction, she held her head high, determined that no one should guess her disappointment.

Elizabeth and Lady Margaret's women fell in behind her, and followed her ladyship outside. At the foot of the steps, Mairi paused to inhale the fresh air, willing herself to find a more appropriate subject to occupy her thoughts, when a familiar voice spoke from behind her.

"Your ladyship, pray forgive us for racing after you and accosting you so discourteously, but we would sadly disgrace ourselves did we fail to take leave of you after your many kindnesses to us, and I'm told that the horses his grace has provided to take us to Askaig await us even now in the stable enclosure."

Feeling instant heat in her cheeks at the sound of Lachlan's voice, she turned with a smile, only to realize that he had spoken to her mother.

Lady Margaret said, "'Tis no discourtesy, sir. We are pleased that you and Hector Reaganach would not leave without bidding us farewell."

"We thank you most sincerely for your gracious hospitality," Lachlan said, bowing deeply, as did Hector beside him. "We have much enjoyed our stay."

He was looking past Mairi at her mother as he spoke, and although she knew courtesy demanded that he keep his eyes on his hostess, she could not help feeling neglected. Catching Hector's gaze, and detecting a teasing twinkle in his eyes very like his brother's, she knew she was failing to hide her feelings. Accordingly, she smiled at him, only to catch a reproachful look from Lachlan when she did. That look, however, did much to warm her spirits again.

Her mother was assuring both brothers that they would always be welcome at Finlaggan, and their father as well.

When she finished speaking, before Lachlan could reply, Mairi said casually, "Do you mean to join his grace's court when he removes to Ardtornish, sir?"

"Aye, my lady, we do," Lachlan said with another bow. "Seil lies near there, as you know, and his grace has kindly invited us to take part in his great Easter tinchal. I neglected to ask him, however, if the ladies of his court customarily hunt the deer along with the gentlemen."

Lady Margaret said, "We do, sir, if the weather is fair."

"Which means only that the sky must not be weeping and grumbling," Mairi said. "Last year it dripped all day, but that did not stop us, and since the deer do not mind the wet, we managed to take two and enjoyed a fine, successful hunt."

They exchanged a few more platitudes before Lady Margaret bade the two gentlemen farewell and Mairi had, perforce, to walk away with her.

No further opportunity arose to speak to him, because the

brothers departed at once, and although Finlaggan did not see the last of its guests for three more days, the place seemed empty without the sons of Gillean.

Nevertheless, Mairi found much to keep her busy, because less than a fortnight remained before the household would remove to Ardtornish until midsummer. Ranald would return briefly to Dunyvaig, and Godfrey to Kilchoman, but they had servants aplenty to see to their packing.

With her own belongings to see to and her usual duties as well, the time passed more quickly than she had expected, until at last the evening before their departure arrived. After supper, she bade farewell to her particular friends among the household staff who would not go with them. A considerable number would remain, since administrative matters required constant attention, but Niall, Ian MacSporran, and many of their minions would go, as would Agnes Beton. As skilled as she was with herbs and potions, she always traveled with the family.

Thinking of the herb woman reminded Mairi that she had not looked in on her in nearly a sennight. Agnes had recovered from her illness by then, but recalling that she had said her son, Ewan, would be home from Kilchoman before they left for the north, Mairi decided to pay her a visit.

Dusk was already darkening to night when Ewan opened the cottage door and she entered with the customary blessing for everyone inside.

"God bless ye, too, m'lady," Agnes said, rising with much of her usual energy to greet her. 'Tis kind o' ye t' come."

"I wanted to assure myself that you are well enough to travel," Mairi said.

"Och, aye, I'm me old self again."

"Will you be going, too, Ewan?"

"Nay, mistress, there be plenty o' work needs doing here at Finlaggan, so I'll bide in the cottage and look after me mam's herb garden and all."

"Ha' ye learned aught more about our Elma, mistress?" Agnes asked.

"Nothing helpful, I'm afraid."

Ewan said quietly, "I'm thinking now that 'twere no accident, mistress. She were too high on the sand for the sea t' ha' put her there."

"I agree, Ewan. Can you tell me more about Gil Dowell, Shim MacVey, and Fin MacHugh? I don't know any of them well."

He frowned. "What manner o' thing d'ye want t' ken?"

"Whatever you can tell me. I'm particularly curious about how they came to mistake the day they saw Ian Burk talking with your cousin on the causeway."

"Sakes, mistress, none o' us recalls the order o' things that day. 'Tweren't till ye said Ian left afore dawn that I even recalled he'd gone t' Dunyvaig."

"Well, do either of you have any idea what Elma was doing that day?"

The two looked helplessly at each other.

Agnes said, "Days seem alike after a time, mistress. Like as not, she helped make beds, particularly them o' the high steward and purse keeper, and straightened their quarters, like every day, but some do say she left soon after the midday meal."

"What about the witnesses?" Mairi asked. "Do you know what any of them were doing that day?"

"Och, aye, I ken that fine," Ewan said. "There were wi' me at Kilchoman."

"But if that is true, they must know they saw Elma after

she spoke to Ian. They all said they had not seen her again after that, but she took Mellis's dinner out to him just before Lord Godfrey's party departed that day."

"Aye, well, they must ha' forgot about that," Ewan said.

Taking her leave soon afterward, Mairi mulled over what they had said. That the men had forgotten seeing Elma was possible, she decided, but that one or all of them had lied was just as likely, if not more so.

Returning, she detoured through the kitchen to bid farewell to members of the staff who were staying, and had stepped into the buttery when she heard MacDonald's voice from the great hall. He sounded weary and annoyed, so she paused, wondering if she should proceed or avoid possibly vexing him further by returning through the kitchen to the courtyard.

The next voice she heard was Niall's, saying, "I'd not have mentioned it to your grace, but I'm that concerned, and fear you must be as troubled as I am."

"I've noted that you have no great liking for those two lads, but I find them refreshingly candid, and the younger one astonishingly shrewd."

"'Tis the shrewdness that troubles me," Niall said. "Men call him Lachlan the Wily, after all, not Lachlan the Wise."

Mairi could not have walked away then if her salvation had depended on it.

"What is it you fear, exactly?" MacDonald asked with heavy patience.

"'Tis plain that our Lady Mairi is enamored with yon wily son of Gillean and he with her—though I suspect his true love is for her connections and inheritance."

"Neither his feelings nor hers can alter her future."

Mairi held her breath.

"And if they have acted on those feelings?" Niall said. "What then?"

MacDonald grunted. "Even so."

"Laird, only think what the Steward would say, or that devil's spawn of his that you have seen fit to seek as a husband to the poor lass! Think of—"

MacDonald interjected curtly, "Even if such a thing is true, Alasdair need only keep from her until he knows she cannot be carrying another man's child. With all his women, that should not inconvenience him, and he will still have a princess of the Isles as his wife, with all the power that the connection bestows upon him. He won't reject my daughter, Niall. That I promise you."

Mairi believed him if Niall did not, and learning that her father, much as she knew he loved her, agreed with Lachlan's and Niall's opinion of Alasdair's character made her feel sick. She knew he would insist that she marry Alasdair, and to do so when she was no longer a maiden was to face a horror beyond words.

No husband would forgive his wife for such a betrayal. Why, the law allowed any husband, noble or otherwise, to return such a wife to her family in disgrace and have the wedding annulled. Even if he did not send her back, all wives lived under their husband's rods. At Finlaggan, with MacDonald, that meant little, because he was not a man of violence, but everything she knew about Alasdair Stewart told her he was not anything like her father.

What would Lachlan think when she told him? He had promised she would not have to marry Alasdair, but he had also said they had only to tell MacDonald what they had done and he would agree to their marriage. Having been so wrong on the one point, how could he possibly be right on the other?

Chapter 12 ────────────

Soon after the five royal galleys passed below the formidable black mass of Duart Castle, Mairi's favorite among her father's many fortresses, she discerned his beloved Ardtornish ahead on the opposite shore. Both castles sat on high promontories and enjoyed wide views, but Duart, on the Isle of Mull's northeastern headland where the Sound of Mull met the Firth of Lorn, provided spectacular ones. The two formed part of a string of eight fortresses guarding the Sound and the Firth, two more of the inner sea-lanes strategically so important to the Lord of the Isles.

Sometime earlier, they had passed the tall, lonely-looking tower of the first of that string, Dunconnel, northernmost of the four tiny Isles of the Sea, on its craggy, nearly unapproachable rocky isle. Dunollie and Dunstaffnage, the next two, lay within sight behind them, and Castle Achaduin, seat of the Bishop of Argyle for over a hundred years, was barely visible on the Isle of Lismore to the north.

Aros and Mingary, the last of the string, lay west of Ardtornish, the former on the Isle of Mull's north coast, the latter at the west end of the peninsula called Ardnamurchan. The Lord of the Isles controlled all of them and a hundred more for Clan Donald and the people of the Isles.

As the royal galley and its four escorts sailed farther into the Sound, their little-black-ship banners waving gaily in the breeze, Mairi began to hear welcoming horns from the landing seventy feet below the castle, in Ardtornish Bay.

An impressive line of basalt cliffs towered above beech woods and a rocky shore to form the U-shaped bay. Thanks to recent rains, the numerous waterfalls called the Morvern Witches spilled more water than usual from the cliff tops. Most of the year, the Witches were so thin that on windy days a stiff southerly breeze could hurl their skirts upward instead of letting them fall in the usual way.

At the highest point of the cliff face squatted the large flat rock known as *Creag na Corp*, "the rock of the corpses," from which men that MacDonald or Morvern's Brehon court had condemned to death were flung to the rocks below.

Crossing the bay took only a short time, and soon the royal galley, with a splendid display of oarsmanship, slid into place alongside the stone-and-timber landing. Willing hands rushed to tie lines, others to help passengers disembark. His grace stepped onto the landing and turned to assist his lady.

Mairi and Elizabeth accepted lesser hands, as did her ladyship's two women. Meg Raith traveled in the second boat, which waited with the other three for the royal galley to row away from the pier. Then each in turn would land and unload.

After passengers and baggage had gone ashore, all five galleys would sail west around the point into Loch Aline, where his grace's ships harbored.

Mairi had no intention of waiting for her parents, let alone for Meg. Instead, eager to see what if anything had changed, she hurried up the steps carved into the stone cliff to the laird's tower. The entrance to its upper levels was on the east side and opened into a stairway ascending within the thickness of the wall. Hurrying up its yard-wide sandstone steps, Mairi passed the great chamber at the first landing and continued to the wall walk and parapets above. From the walk's south side, she enjoyed a panoramic view of the Sound and the Isle of Mull.

The day was so clear that she could see Aros Castle to the west and Duart to the east. On such days, and on clear nights, beacon signals could flash all the way from Mingary to Dunstaffnage and Dunconnel, or from Dunconnel to Mingary, to warn of danger or celebrate royal events such as Marjory's wedding. She wondered if Lachlan was on Mull now, visiting one of his father's holdings. If he were, and if they had devised a signal . . .

Reality struck before she completed the thought. She did not know what part of the large island contained Ian Dubh Maclean's holdings. They might lie far to the south or to the west, facing the Holy Isle of Iona near Niall Mackinnon's land. In any event, if Lachlan were at a window in Aros Castle this very moment, staring at Ardtornish and thinking about her, she would not know it.

Although she was aware that soon she would be missed below, she walked the rest of the way around the battlements surrounding the slate roof. The laird's tower, eighty feet from east to west and fifty north to south, was a solid fortress.

At an angle from the northwest corner, and sharing the garderobe tower, stood the new wing containing a kitchen and brewery on the lower level and guest chambers above. Ardtornish boasted outbuildings, too, including the great hall to the northeast, separated from the residence just as at

Finlaggan, and to the southeast, a barn with stabling for horses, a corn-drying kiln, and several boat shelters.

The promontory upon which Ardtornish stood provided its greatest protection. Its curtain wall was minimal, and so safe did his grace feel with all of loyal Morvern behind him, that no other defense existed north of the great hall.

As Mairi hurried down to the great chamber, she smiled, happy to be at Ardtornish but happier to know she would soon see Lachlan again, and could tell him of the conversation she had overheard between her father and Niall Mackinnon.

Thanks to Niall's skill, Ardtornish was ready to receive them and the many other guests who began to arrive the next day. Not until days later, however, on the Wednesday afternoon before Easter, did the sons of Gillean arrive.

Mairi's plan to confer with Lachlan suffered a setback soon afterward, when MacDonald, greeting the brothers, said he had arranged for them to stay at Duart.

"You will appreciate your accommodation even more Friday morning," he said with a laugh, "when being on Mull will allow you to sleep later than we can."

Friday was the day of his grace's grand tinchal.

Increasingly frustrated, and believing that Niall, not MacDonald, had arranged to house the brothers nearly five miles away, across the Sound, rather than more conveniently in the new wing, Mairi strove to contain her impatience. But Ardtornish suddenly seemed even smaller and more crowded than Finlaggan.

Opportunities arose that afternoon to speak to Lachlan, but none offered any promise of privacy, because guests wandered everywhere, even in the woods along the cliffs, and to the shore. Short of inviting him to accompany her to the garderobe, she could not think how they might conspire to be alone for even a minute or two. And if she were so desperate as to offer such an improper invitation, she could be certain they would find a line of people waiting to make use of the facility.

Three days remained of Lent, but the Lord of the Isles' court at Ardtornish had already become a lively social gathering. Meals were boisterous, the evening ones even more so than midday, for not only did they eat supper at five, as usual, but gillies served a late supper, as well, to those hardy enough to stay up until the small hours and still manage to rise in time for morning prayers.

Mairi had exchanged only a few polite words in company with Lachlan when he approached her just before suppertime, with Hector beside him, to say politely, "Do you still mean to join the hunt on Friday, my lady?"

"Aye, sir, I do."

"Will you and the other ladies carry bows, or do you go merely to observe?"

She raised her chin. "I will shoot, sir. I've had my own bow since I was ten."

"Then I'll wager you are a fine shot," he said, smiling.

"I strike where I aim, I believe."

He exchanged a look with Hector before saying, "I'd like to see you try your skill. Where hereabouts does one practice?"

"The archery field lies above the castle to the north," she said. "But I did not mean to imply that my skills match yours or Hector Reaganach's," she added. "My bow is shorter and less powerful than a man's."

"Then, for our contest, we'll shoot with your bow. How will that suit you?"

Several others, overhearing the exchange, immediately called for wagers and demanded that they arrange a party and a regular shooting contest. MacDonald, learning of the idea, agreed that it would be a fine way to prepare for his tinchal.

Mairi suppressed a sigh. For a few moments, she had believed Lachlan had found a way for them to be alone for a short time at least, but clearly he had not. She turned away, fearing she might reveal her disappointment to her father, and determined to think of a way to speak privately with Lachlan. But she had taken only a few steps before he caught her arm and said, "Don't run off, sweetheart."

She turned with a smile, noted that just then no one was within several feet of them, and said hastily in a low tone, "I must talk with you. Niall told my father that he suspects us of being enamored with each other."

"He is right, of course, but I wish a demon would fly away with him."

"But my father said—"

"Don't fret, lass. Your father already knew as much, did he not?"

"Aye, but—"

"Just leave everything to me."

"But—"

"We'll talk later," he murmured. "Now is not the time."

"Aye, I did hope we might be alone to shoot tomorrow," she said wistfully.

He smiled again. "We will be. It is going to rain."

"What difference can that make, and how do you know?"

"I know everything," he said, his smile widening to a grin as he added, "Remember that, and take heed what you do when I am not with you."

"I have heard that you are a knowing one," she retorted, not caring who heard her now, or who might accuse her of flirting. "Even if you do not set spies, sir, men do say that you have eyes and ears everywhere."

"And I encourage that reputation," he confided. "You'd be surprised at what I learn just because men fear I might have an eye on them. Often someone will decide it is better to tell me a tale himself than risk letting an enemy tell his version first and alter strategic details as he does."

"Do you gather information about my father?"

He leaned nearer, murmuring, "I gather information, sweetheart; I do not by custom share it, except with my liege. I will tell you this, however. I have learned from my most trusted man that Mellis MacCoun cannot have killed his wife."

Frowning, she said, "I own, I do not see how he could have, but can you be sure? Agnes Beton said Mellis is the most likely one, and she should know. Even my lady mother suspected that if it was not an accident, Mellis must have done it."

"He did not."

"Who is this henchman then, that you trust him so completely?"

"Ah, now, that would be telling."

"Did he find out more about the witnesses?" she asked. "I thought that Fin MacHugh, Gil Dowell, and Shim MacVey must have stayed at Finlaggan that day, but Ewan said they all went to Kilchoman. Surely at least one ought to have remembered seeing Elma when she took Mellis's things to him before they left."

"Aye," he said. "If they did not remember before they accused the lad, one or another should remember now why they did not. Of course, it may be too late to ask them unless they are here. We'll look into that."

"I think Gil and Fin may be here. Ewan and Shim are not."

"I'll look into it, but don't you trot about asking odd questions of people, lass. A man who would kill one woman may easily kill another."

She did not reply but glanced at Hector, chatting with Fiona MacDougall, the flirtatious daughter of Dunstaffnage's constable. Although she could easily believe he was Lachlan's most trusted man, she could not imagine how either one could know more about Mellis or the others than she did, or be so certain of themselves. But neither did she want to press him, lest he stop sharing what they learned.

She saw that he expected a reply to his command that she not ask questions, and realized that he had not yet answered the second one she had asked him.

"How can rain help us?" she asked again.

Confidently, but with a lurking gleam in his eyes that told her he knew she meant to divert him, he said, "You'll see."

She could not imagine how, but auburn-haired Fiona had abandoned Hector and descended on her now with friends, demanding that she go up to the wall walk with them to talk about men and other interesting things. Courtesy demanded that she agree, and in any event, Lachlan had slipped away as the girls approached.

No further opportunity arose the rest of the day to speak privately with him. Niall Mackinnon's notorious brother, Fingon, the Green Abbot of Iona, had arrived shortly after the Macleans, with his retinue, including the lady of his heart and two of his strapping sons, to take supper with MacDonald. In such elevated company—for it now included numerous clan chiefs and their families—the sons of Gillean figured as minor members of the court and thus, in Niall's all-important view, of insufficient stature to grace the high table.

Nevertheless, supper was excellent and the entertainment merry.

When the younger women moved to sit together and enjoy the antics of a troop of players after the meal, Fiona said in an undertone, "I warrant the Pope would heartily condemn this revelry should he chance to learn of it."

"Perhaps," Mairi said, "but although the Green Abbot has often condemned Lenten revelry, he is laughing as heartily as anyone else right now."

"Why do they call him the Green Abbot?" Ailsa Macleod, a young blond maiden from the Isle of Skye, asked her shyly.

"I'm not certain, but perhaps because the Pope still has reservations about him and refuses to recognize him as the Mitered Abbot of Iona," she replied.

"Fingon has many sons and daughters," Fiona said. "Most popes have an aversion to priests with children, do they not?"

Fiona had been a friend since childhood, and Mairi smiled as she said, "But Fingon follows ancient Celtic custom that allows all clergymen to marry."

"Aye, but the Roman Kirk is ever at odds with the old ways," Ailsa said. "I warrant they'll never see things as we Islesmen and the Highlanders do."

Another woman agreed but gave it as her opinion that it did not matter. "No one here pays heed to Rome," she pointed out. "Faith, we dinna heed the King o' Scots. Why should we heed someone from a much more distant place?"

Mairi enjoyed the evening. During a circle dance, she even held Lachlan's hand, but they exchanged no private words before he and Hector departed with a few others staying at Duart.

The next morning, she awoke to a heavy mist outside, but it burned off after the sun arose. High, scattered white clouds augured little chance of rain.

She performed her morning duties, keeping an eye out for the Duart boat, which arrived shortly before the midday meal. By then, the morning's fleecy white clouds had thickened, lowered, and increased in number.

The Green Abbot and his retinue had stayed, so the brothers again took places below the dais. But at a table where the ladies sat to Lady Margaret's left and the gentlemen to MacDonald's right, Mairi knew that short of wearing a skirt and veil, even Lachlan the Wily could not negotiate his way to a seat beside hers. Thus, her awareness that the clouds were darkening did much to sustain her through a tedious conversation with the lady on her left.

Several guests who had eagerly looked forward to the archery contest the previous evening had also noted the changing weather. One gentleman warned that the brewing storm might linger into the next day and spoil his grace's hunt. Others disagreed, insisting that what approached was no more than a squall that would hold off until evening and blow over before morning.

In the Isles, where survival depended on the sea, every man considered himself an expert on the weather. Mairi believed that Lachlan, though fascinating, was as undependable as any other when it came to weather prediction. She would welcome rain but only if it would gain them privacy without spoiling their hunt.

When Lady Margaret stood to signal the formal end to the meal, a number of other ladies elected to return with her to the great chamber. Only Ailsa Macleod and Fiona MacDougall continued to express interest in the archery contest, but both wanted to fetch cloaks and stouter footwear before leaving.

Mairi had dressed for the outing and had worn her cloak to the great hall, but she was content to wait for the others and said so.

"Where do you keep your bow, lass?"

Having been discussing cloaks and boots, she had not observed his approach, but turned with a smile, trying to ignore the way her body tensed and seemed to vibrate, even to hum, when he spoke to her.

She said, "I store my equipment in one of the outbuildings, sir. Ian Burk is fetching my bow, quiver, and shooting gloves now, as well as similar equipment for Ailsa and Fiona. I also told him to be prepared to accompany us."

"You should all carry your own equipment," he said with a smile. "Or do you hope, perchance, to tire the men out by forcing us to climb what is doubtless a very steep hill whilst bearing our weapons?"

Her lips twitched. "I thought you were going to shoot women's bows."

"We will for the contest," he said, "but Angus Macleod and Giles Duffy, the other two still courageous enough to go with us, want to practice with their own bows for tomorrow's hunt, so we're all taking longbows as well."

"Ian can carry your things, too, if the weapons are too heavy for you, and if you men have no servants of your own," she said mockingly.

"Faith, lass, my point is that we don't want any servants."

"Very well, then I'll tell Ian I don't need him, but it is a good thing that Fiona and Ailsa want to go with us. My parents would otherwise surely forbid me to go off with a pack of uncouth young gentlemen."

"Just what I feared myself, so Hector persuaded Fiona that she would enjoy the walk, and Fiona persuaded Ailsa," he said.

"But if you think Ian would be in the way . . ." She paused meaningfully.

He shook his head, and the girls returned then, so she said no more.

Despite Lachlan's professed concern, the climb to the archery field was easy, although the field, surrounded on three sides by beech forest, lay high enough above the castle to provide a wide view of landscape and Sound. The path they followed was well beaten, and the field, sheltered from wind by the beeches, was flat and grassy with swaths of colorful flowers. Although a few dark clouds spat rudely at them, the sun still peeked through occasionally, and no one suggested returning.

The four men selected several hay-filled butts and strode off the distance, marking a line in the dirt where they could stand to shoot.

When Lachlan reminded the other men that they could use only women's bows for the contest, Angus Macleod, a round-faced cousin of Ailsa's from the Isle of Lewis, replied with a challenging look, "Aye, sure, but I'm thinking the four o' us should hold a contest first amongst ourselves, t' see which man be the best shot."

Lachlan cast an eye skyward and looked at Hector. "What do you think? I own I'd like to rehearse with a proper bow before trying to shoot the shorter one."

The four debated the matter until Mairi said, "If you want your own contest, you should not waste any more time. It looks as if it may rain any moment now."

Lachlan nodded and deftly strung his bow. "Who will go first?"

Giles Duffy said he preferred a clean target and Hector said he wanted to see how the others did before he shot, whereupon Angus looked at Lachlan, who gestured for him to shoot after Giles.

The first two arrows struck within inches of the center mark.

Hector nodded at Lachlan, who said, "Nay then, you go

first. I won't have you splitting my arrow with yours as you did last time. I might need it tomorrow."

Chuckling, Hector put up his bow and let fly. As nearly as Mairi could tell, he did not pause to aim, but the arrow flew straight and true to the center mark. Clearly, she decided, he would win the contest.

Lachlan took his place at the line, squinting narrowly at the target as if it were hundreds of yards away. At last, he raised his bow with the arrow nocked.

With a thumping twang, the arrow struck shaft-against-shaft with Hector's.

"Faith, my lad, if you've broken my arrow off in that butt, I'll have something to say to you," Hector threatened as the four men strode forward.

Mairi followed to see if the two arrows were as close as they appeared, but she was not surprised when Lachlan dropped back to walk beside her.

"I don't know how well you shoot, lass, although I wager you'll hit your mark, but take your time. Don't be trying to shoot quickly to impress anyone. And see that you let the other lasses shoot first."

Annoyed as she was that he seemed to think she required lessons, she said only, "Aye, 'tis only polite, and I like the challenge of watching others do well."

He shot her a grin of approval, then said so quietly that she knew his voice would carry only to her, "I, too, love a challenge, sweetheart."

Heat flooded her cheeks, and she refused to look at him again.

They discovered that only a hair's width separated his arrow from Hector's, but as the men exclaimed their astonishment Mairi pointed out that if they wanted to keep their bowstrings dry for the next day's hunt, they had better get on with it, and everyone hurried back to the line.

Ailsa and Fiona agreed to shoot first when Mairi suggested it, but to her surprise, Lachlan said, "Those clouds are dripping already and will soon let loose a flood. I'm thinking, to speed things up, the women should shoot against each other as we did. Afterward, we'll have the women's winner shoot against the men's."

Laughing, Ailsa said, "You'll have to shoot again against Hector then to decide which of you competes against our winner."

"Aye," Mairi said, "and you should both shoot with smaller bows. Indeed, mayhap you ought to hold your men's contest again, using the short bows."

"Nay, for I've my reputation to consider," Hector said. "Bad enough to risk losing to a female. To try to outshoot one with a bairn's bow . . ." He shuddered.

"Coward," Lachlan muttered, but he smiled and Hector took no umbrage.

"No need for a second contest then," Angus said. "You equaled Hector's shot, and I've no more wish than he does to prove myself against a woman."

When Giles agreed, Lachlan said, "Then we are agreed that I'll shoot against the lass that wins the ladies' contest."

Mairi knew he expected her to win, but she also knew that Fiona was a fine archer. She did not know Ailsa well, because Skye was far away. But Dunstaffnage was not, and she saw Fiona whenever MacDonald was in residence at Ardtornish. They had often competed against each other.

The women each shot three arrows, and Ailsa proved at once that she was no match for Mairi or Fiona. Mairi's first two arrows hit the mark, but all three of Fiona's were near it, and Mairi's third was farther away. Not until everyone looked closely did they agree that since Mairi's two were right in the center and all three of Fiona's barely within the mark or just outside, Mairi had won.

Grinning his approval as he helped collect arrows, Lachlan said, "You shoot first, lass, and I'll use Fiona's bow. I'm thinking you'll make a fine adversary."

They took their places, and feeling suddenly nervous, Mairi drew a deep breath, took aim, and let fly. Her arrow had no sooner struck than Lachlan's first one followed it. Nocking a second arrow, she raised her bow.

So intent on the contest had they become that when the rain came—not with spatter but in a sudden, heavy shower—all three women shrieked. Mairi dropped her bow, and they grabbed for the cloaks they had taken off in preparation to shoot.

The men began to assist them, with Hector shouting at them to hurry, when Lachlan said in mild protest, "But we've not finished our contest."

Mairi looked at him in dismay, but his eyes were dancing.

"You'll be near drowned as it is, lass, running down the hill. What difference can a few minutes make but to decide a winner. Or are you afraid I'll win?"

Fiona, laughing again as she so often did, said, "We are not staying to watch, sir, beg how you will. But pray do keep my bow if you lack sense enough to run inside where it's warm and dry, with the rest of us."

Hector was shaking his head and frowning. "You cannot stay here alone, just the two of you," he said.

"True," Lachlan agreed. "So you will stay with us for propriety's sake. Unless you fear lightning," he added with a mocking grin.

Hector shot him a look but said nothing, continuing to shake his head.

Laughing at them, the others hurried off.

Another look passed between the brothers, and Hector turned away, moving to the edge of the field, where he could watch the others on their way.

"We are not really going to shoot, are we?" Mairi asked.

"Nay, we'll let the arrow closest to the center declare the winner. Come with me to the trees yonder though, and we can have our talk. Hector will watch to see that no one disturbs us."

The rain was pouring down, and she cast a sympathetic look at Hector. "Won't he mind getting so dreadfully wet?"

"Sakes, lass, he's been a sight wetter, I can tell you, anytime he's gone over in a boat or been caught in a storm on some journey or other."

"Well, we'll not stay long," she said as she let him pull her hand into the crook of his arm and urge her toward the trees.

"We'll see," he said, chuckling. "I own, I did not mean for our cloaks to be soaked before we'd taken shelter."

Laughing now too, she said, "Did you honestly think we'd have time to do more than talk?"

"A man seizes his opportunities," he said, pulling her under the spreading canopy of a beech tree and into his arms. "Kiss me first. We'll talk in a moment."

His lips claimed hers, and delighted, she kissed him hard and moaned when he thrust his tongue into her mouth. Briefly, she wondered if Hector could see them from where he was, but when Lachlan's hand moved inside her cloak to stroke her breast, she decided that she did not care. Even when he pushed her cloak off, letting it fall in a wet heap on the ground, she made no protest, and she knew that if he suggested they lay atop it, even if they got soaked, she would do as he asked. The thought sent tremors of hope through her body.

Lachlan's thoughts were following a similar track, but much as he would have liked to take her right there on the ground with the hushing of the rain in the trees to accompany her moans of pleasure, he knew Hector would strongly disapprove of any great delay, if only because they risked angering MacDonald.

He had explained that he wanted a chance to speak with Mairi in private, even to take a few moments' pleasure with her, but as much as he would have enjoyed lingering, he needed time to study MacDonald more before he decided his best course for winning his prize. To jeopardize that for a few kisses and cuddles, or even more, would be daft.

Recognizing that her fervent response boded well for any other liberty he might take, he nonetheless understood tactics as well as strategy, and knew he'd do better to bide his time. Therefore, with reluctance, he ended the kiss, held her close for a moment, and then loosened his embrace to look into her dark eyes as he said, "Tell me what you heard Niall and your father say."

She sighed and said, "I feared you'd not heeded me, because you only let me tell you what Niall said. His grace said our caring for each other changed nothing, so he said what if you took my maidenhood—might that not prove troublesome?"

"The man is a menace! What did his grace say to that?"

"That it would make no difference, that Alasdair need only lock me up until he was certain any babe I had was his.

He'd still enjoy all the benefits of having married a princess of the Isles. What are we going to do?"

"I must think, that's all," he said. "Just leave it to me."

"But it concerns me, too. I don't know why you always think—"

"It is a man's business to plan and make decisions about the important things in life, sweetheart. You must know you can safely trust me to do that."

"But I don't want to! I want to know what you are thinking and to tell you what I think. I have opinions, sir, and a brain that works perfectly well."

"And you are shivering," he said, kissing her again. "Let us see who won, and then we'll go down to the hall fire so we can get you warm again."

She glowered up at him from under her eyebrows, but he knew the ways of women and ignored the sour look, urging her to the target to collect their arrows and hoping she would not be too disappointed when she saw that he had beaten her.

She was not disappointed at all.

Her arrow sat dead center on the mark.

Chapter 13

Hector was waiting at the top of the track, and they hurried down the hill. The rain had eased before they reached the great hall, but they went no farther, opting instead to warm themselves at the great fireplace there.

The Green Abbot and his retinue had gone, but others remained, including their erstwhile companions, who demanded to know who had won the contest.

Mairi said nothing, waiting to see if Lachlan would tell them. He had not told Hector, nor had Hector asked, but to her surprise and delight, he said now with a rueful look, "Lady Mairi won."

Giles, laughing, said, "No one could expect a man to win with a short bow."

Angus agreed. "I warrant, even my cousin Ailsa would beat me did I try to win a contest by shooting her wee bow."

Ailsa and Fiona both cried out against such disrespect for their weapons, and Hector, who had turned from standing their bows against the wall near the fire and was straightening the bowstrings on a bench to dry, looked up and said to Lachlan, "Do you think 'twas merely the bow that cost you the contest?"

Mairi held her breath, but Lachlan shook his head.

"I wish I could say so," he said, "but I'd as lief not add thunder and lightning to that rain outside, and I've no doubt that if I told such a great lie, God would make His heavens ring." Smiling at Mairi, he added gently, 'Twas her ladyship's skill and mine own arrogance that beat me, not Lady Fiona's bow."

Returning his smile, Mairi moved near the fireplace and took off her cloak, spreading it over a second bench to dry while she warmed her hands. Her dress was still soaked, however, so when Ailsa looked outside moments later and said the rain had stopped, she left the hall with the others to go and change her clothes.

Although pleased that Lachlan had so easily admitted her victory, she was still annoyed with him for assuming she would be happy to put her future in his hands. Having never been one to sit by while others determined the course of her life, she wanted to have her say even if she could do nothing to change things. Her father understood that and encouraged her to form opinions and express them. Lady Margaret did not, however, and had often said that Mairi must learn to obey those in authority over her and submit gracefully to their commands.

Mairi knew she had too much of her father in her to do that. She could no more imagine MacDonald standing aside and letting others order his path than she could imagine him wearing a skirt and curtsying to the King of Scots.

Lachlan and Hector had brought clothing from Duart for supper and the evening's entertainment, and since the other men were housed in the guest wing, they easily arranged for a place to change. As they left the hall with the others,

Lachlan noticed Ian Burk near the kitchen wing, gesturing to him.

"I'll catch up with you," he told Hector, turning aside and waiting until everyone else had gone into the main tower before joining Ian. "What is it, lad?"

"Good sir," Ian said, "be it true that you and Lord Hector mean t' hunt wi' his grace's great tinchal tomorrow?"

"Aye," Lachlan said. "What of it?" When Ian hesitated, chewing his lip, he added tersely, "Do you disapprove of our doing so?"

"Nay, sir," Ian said hastily. "But a man has his loyalties, ye ken. I ken fine where me duty lies, and wi' respect, sir, it doesna lie wi' Clan Gillean."

Lachlan narrowed his eyes but held his tongue.

Grimacing, Ian looked straight at him as he said, "I'm thinking now that it doesna lie wi' the Mackinnons either, but solely wi' his grace."

"I begin to understand you, lad," Lachlan said. "His grace's high steward makes no secret of his disdain for the men of Gillean."

"He'd as lief see all o' ye laid underground, sir. 'Tis why I be thinking ye'd be wiser to occupy your time otherwise tomorrow."

"But surely, his grace's steward is not a man of violence," Lachlan said.

Ian barely managed to stifle a disrespectful snort. "Men do say he's a fine swordsman, sir," he said, "but he'll no be dirtying his hands an he can help it."

When Lachlan nodded without comment, he sighed and, measuring his words as if trying to explain the obvious to a dolt, added, "The steward has others who serve him, sir—at least two who be expert bowmen."

"Indeed," Lachlan said softly. "Do I understand then that you know these two marksmen and their purpose?"

Ian's expression froze.

"Come now, lad. Only a noddy could think that two such highly skilled bowmen acting on the steward's behalf might waste their arrows on deer."

"But I didna say that," Ian said, growing visibly more uncomfortable with each word. Finally, however, when Lachlan continued to eye him steadily, he nodded, his expression warier than ever, as if he feared the next question.

But Lachlan was not such a fool as to demand names from a valuable witness over whom he held no authority. Knowing he would gain more by letting Ian decide on his own to tell what he knew, he looked thoughtfully heavenward instead, as if he pondered an interesting puzzle. "I should think," he said, "that even a man with as much confidence in himself as the steward would hesitate to order the cold-blooded murder of two of his liege lord's honored guests."

"Aye, sure," Ian agreed. "But there be two fractious stags in Mull's herd that want culling, he says, and he'll be but setting a pair o' his best archers t' the task. Even the best man, he said, might miss his target and strike some poor innocent."

"I see."

"Aye, sir, so mayhap ye and Hector Reaganach should be elsewhere on the day. Me lady would be sore vexed, I'm thinking, should aught happen to either o' ye. She likes ye both gey fine, she does."

"I'll take care that no harm befalls us," Lachlan assured him. "You can do your part, however, by saying naught of this matter to anyone else, most especially not to her ladyship. Do you understand me?"

Ian swallowed and nodded. "Aye, sir, she'd worry, so I'll keep mum."

"See that you do," Lachlan said. Satisfied that Ian would obey him, he pressed two coins into his hand and went looking for Hector, finding that he had not changed but lingered yet in amiable flirtation with a curly-headed laundry maid.

"Leave that poor lass to her duties and take a turn on the ramparts with me."

Although Hector paused long enough to plant a kiss on the maid's rosy lips, he did not object or even mention the interruption until they reached the wall walk and could be sure no one would overhear. Then he cast Lachlan an inquiring look.

Lachlan said, "A problem has arisen that requires a solution."

"The lady Mairi proved uncooperative then? I had thought otherwise."

Shaking his head, Lachlan refused the bait. "'Tis not my lass who seeks our blood, nor would she."

"Our blood?"

"Oh, aye, for according to my earnest informant, we shall both shortly fall victim to a pair of badly aimed arrows."

"Ian Burk, of course. The deer hunt?"

"You are not always dimwitted. Almost do I see promise in you."

"I'll show you promise, my lad, if you serve me any more sauce," Hector said. "Does someone truly plot murder as a diversion for his grace's guests?"

"'Tis no anonymous someone. The villain, young Ian tells me, is none other than our good friend Niall MacGillebride Mackinnon."

"That man is stretching my patience," Hector said. "So now he prefers our deaths to our company?"

"Apparently," Lachlan said, and related what Ian had told him.

Hector's frown deepened as the tale progressed, and at its end, he said, "The plot is unworthy of the man. Does he not realize that one or both of his so-called experts might hit a true innocent rather than one of us?"

"I doubt he would consider anyone an innocent except another Mackinnon."

"You can't be including Lady Mairi," Hector said. "She means to hunt, for she said so, and you'll never suggest that he doesn't care what happens to her."

"Nay, I'll not say that," Lachlan said evenly.

Hector gave him a steady look, but he ignored it, forcing himself to think.

"I'd dislike missing that hunt," Hector said. "'Tis a great honor his grace bestows on us, and it pleases our father. 'Twould be churlish to disappoint them both. Still, we don't want to cause an innocent's death or injury. Mayhap we should create some excuse and forgo our pleasure in the greater cause."

"You would allow Niall Mackinnon to frighten us away?"

"I never said I was afraid," Hector snapped.

"Hold your temper, then, for I mean us both to hunt, and without risking death. No one will shoot a single arrow at us, I promise you."

"Aye, well, that's fine then," Hector said. "Does it occur to you that if the man is capable of such murder, he may already have committed others?"

"It does, indeed. Especially since the dead lass appears to have granted her favors to all and sundry. Mackinnon's wife died some three years ago."

"He's a bit of a stick, though," Hector said. "I don't see

him fornicating with a servant, although one of her duties was tidying his room. Ian MacSporran's, too."

Lachlan chuckled at the thought of the plump, self-important purse keeper seducing Elma, but Mackinnon was another matter. "Our Niall seems to care more about others' behavior than about his own. If Elma was handy . . ."

"'Tis certainly possible, but you may just be annoyed that Mackinnon looks at Lady Mairi the way he does, so your judgment may not be clear in his case—or it may, for that same reason, be clearer than mine," he added thoughtfully.

Lachlan thought his view of Mackinnon was perfectly clear, but he saw Hector's point and would not dismiss his subtle warning.

As they descended the stairs a few moments later, Hector said lightly, "I trust everything else is going well."

"Well enough, but we'll not discuss it here in the stairway, if you please."

"As you like. Tell me about tomorrow instead. I know we arranged for our own horses from Amalaig to be stabled at Duart, but I don't know more than that."

"Apparently, a swarm of gillies will cross the Sound to Craignure Bay tonight with supplies, and set up for breakfast before the hunt," Lachlan said. "In the morning, everyone else will pile into boats and go across, and MacDonald will provide mounts for the other hunters. I expect someone will explain it all at supper."

"No doubt, but I was sure you would know," Hector said. "Moreover, if we don't hurry and change, we'll miss supper altogether."

When Mairi entered her bedchamber to change her clothes, Meg exclaimed at her bedraggled appearance.

"Me mother would ha' said I'd less sense than a mouse did I get caught in the rain like ye've done, but we'll ha' ye out o' them wet things straightaway."

"We had a shooting contest, Meg. I told you."

"Well, thanks be ye didna wear anything nicer. Ye'd ha' it all over muck."

Resisting the temptation to point out that she had worn a plain skirt for that very reason, Mairi allowed Meg to divest her of her wet clothes and wrap her in a thick, warm robe. Then, sitting on a stool, she relaxed as the older woman began to brush her hair dry before the fire.

They were chatting quietly when Elizabeth entered, saying, "Oh, good, Meg, you are here. I want to change for supper, too, but I'll unbind my hair whilst you finish drying Mairi's. This caul has given me a dreadful headache."

"When you've taken it off, dampen a towel at the washbasin, mistress, and put it over your eyes. That will ease your pain some."

"I almost wish I'd gone shooting with you, Mairi," Elizabeth said, pulling off her caul and unpinning her hair. "Angus Macleod is a man I should like to know better, if only because he is kin to our Marjory's Roderic."

"He does seem kind," Mairi agreed. "But in truth, I think he has his eye on his cousin Ailsa. He is most protective of her, and teases her dreadfully."

"That sounds more like a brother," Elizabeth said. "Lovers do not tease, I hope. They should be more romantic."

"Fetch that wet cloth, Lady Elizabeth," Meg said sternly. "Ye can prattle all ye want when ye've settled yourself. Ye'll be unhappy an that headache lingers and ye ha' t' take one o' Agnes Beton's powders."

Elizabeth obeyed, lying on the bed with the damp cloth on her forehead and her eyes shut. She was dozing by the time Meg finished brushing Mairi's hair.

"She'll do better for a wee nap," Meg said. "I'll help ye into your dress."

Mairi was soon ready, and leaving Meg to tend Elizabeth, she draped her crimson cloak over her arm and went to the great chamber. Finding no one else there yet, she remembered she had not yet checked with Ian to be sure that all was in readiness for her to hunt in the morning.

He knew what she required, of course, but knowing she would not rest comfortably until she had seen for herself that he had remembered all her trappings and equipment, she threw on her cloak and hurried out to the barn. On the way, she watched for Lachlan but saw no sign of him.

In the barn, she found Ian brushing the beautiful gray mare that was her special mount at Ardtornish. She preferred grays and would hunt riding a silvery gelding from the same sire and dam, and kept at Duart for her use.

"Is everything ready for tomorrow?" she asked.

"Aye, mistress. Your scarlet trappings ha' been pressed out and polished and I've wound two fresh strings wi' your bow and added fresh arrows t' your quiver."

She asked more questions, which he answered with the respect he always showed her, but as they talked, she realized something was amiss.

"What's wrong?" she asked. "Is the mare off her feed?"

"Nay, mistress, nor her brother neither. I went across earlier t' look at him, and that lad seems as eager t' hunt as ye be."

"Good, for I mean to show certain people that a woman can shoot an arrow as well from horseback as she can standing still."

"Aye, sure, ye've a fine eye for a target, mistress," Ian said morosely.

"Ian, what is it? Tell me before I lose my patience!"

"'Tis only that I fear ye'll be disappointed in the company," the lad said reluctantly, looking wretched.

"Why should I be?" she demanded. "This court is as merry as any his grace has held. The hunt tomorrow should be wonderful."

"Some fear trouble may be brewing," Ian said lamely.

"Who would dare stir such a rumor?"

"I dinna ken who stirs them," he said hastily. "I just thought ye should ken that everyone may not hunt. I ken fine that ye've a strong liking for Lachlan Lubanach and Hector Reaganach."

"Surely you do not believe that he—that is, that *they* will stay away!"

"I did hear someone say that several people may, is all."

"Pooh," Mairi said. "They are neither of them such cowards. Furthermore, no one would disdain an invitation to his grace's tinchal, or dare to cause trouble on such a grand occasion."

"That be true, too, my lady," Ian agreed, looking miserable.

She wanted to shake him, believing he knew more than he was telling her, but his concern seemed absurd. Nonetheless, instead of returning to the laird's tower, she went directly to the great hall, where she found difficulty even pretending to be patient while she waited for Lachlan.

"You do both mean to hunt with us tomorrow, do you not?" she demanded without ceremony the moment he came in with his brother.

She discerned a flash of annoyance before he smiled in his usual warm way and said quietly, "You may be sure we will, sweetheart. We'd not miss such grand entertainment for anything. Why do you ask?"

"I just wanted to be sure," she said, relieved. "I don't want anything to spoil the day."

"Nay, we'll see to that," he said, adding lightly, "Should you be here alone before your parents arrive?"

"Do you think to issue commands to me, sir?"

He glanced at his brother, whose eyebrows soared upward, giving him a most comical appearance.

Lachlan said, "I've acknowledged that I have no right to command you, lass. I express concern only because I would counsel against angering his grace or your lady mother now—or ever, come to that."

"You need not fear they will be angry with me merely for coming to the great hall ahead of them, sir." She spoke calmly, but his tendency to issue orders to her recalled the day Ranald had said her husband would teach her obedience after she was wed. Ranald had been talking about Alasdair Stewart, of course, not Lachlan Lubanach. Nevertheless, the memory was discomfiting.

As if he were reading her mind, Lachlan said, "A gillie who waited on me said he had heard earlier that Alasdair Stewart might arrive in time for the hunt. Do you ken aught of his coming, lass?"

"Nay, I do not," she said. Her reply was curt, so she was not surprised when he frowned. Let him frown, she thought. He should know better than to irritate her. That was no way to woo a woman.

"Hector, I would discover more about Alasdair Stewart's plans," he said.

"I'll have a word with the lads." Hector bowed to Mairi as he took his leave.

"Is that how you do it?" she demanded. "You just tell him to find out what you want to know! It must be nice to play the lord over your elder brother."

"Will you take a turn about the room with me, sweet-heart? I warrant we should not stand here talking, lest we draw unwanted attention, but I'm sure no one will think ill of me for merely escorting you to the high table."

"We have already talked overlong, I think," she said coolly.

He held out his arm, his eyes dancing now in the way she found most difficult to resist. "I have vexed you," he said. "That much is plain, but I am not certain what I said or did that came amiss."

She raised her chin, but when he continued to twinkle at her, she finally put her hand on his arm. The great hall, like the one at Finlaggan, had a row of columns six feet from each long wall to support the roof and create a walkway. Lachlan escorted her up the near one to the dais, then bowed and walked away.

As she slipped off her cloak and draped it over her stool, she did not know whether she was angry or amused, but she did know better than to stare at his back. Therefore, she greeted Ranald's approach with so much enthusiasm that he gave her an odd look. Remembering what Lachlan had said, she asked Ranald if Alasdair intended to join them for the hunt.

"As he is not here now, lass, I doubt it," Ranald said. "His grace has not mentioned him, at all events. I think he is more interested in knowing if John Og's wee son has been born yet."

"I did expect to hear from them by now," Mairi admitted. "Do you think something may have gone amiss?"

"Only that John Og has long since received more advice than he wants," Ranald said, chuckling. "When our lady mother sent her last message to them, your Meg pressed her to tell him to put a spoonful of salt in the bairn's mouth as soon as it cries to safeguard him from the fairies. I told her I thought a spoonful of brogac would be more to the taste of any son born to John Og."

Mairi laughed, but as she did, she saw Lachlan and Hector talking to MacDougall of Dunstaffnage and Fiona. Her fingers curled, but she forced herself to relax. She would not behave like a child. Instead, when her mother and father stepped onto the dais, she asked Margaret if she might invite Fiona to sit beside her for the meal. Receiving permission, she stepped down to relay the invitation to Fiona, speaking warmly to MacDougall and Hector and politely to the others in their circle before returning to the dais with Fiona.

"Everyone is looking forward to the hunt tomorrow," Fiona said as she gazed out over the lower hall. "Will you think me childish if I own that I'm looking forward much more to the Easter feast on Sunday?"

Grinning, Mairi assured her that she, too, looked forward to the feast, but she knew that Fiona, denied meat throughout Lent, hungered for it more than she did. And in truth, she was wishing she could see what Lachlan was doing.

Guests lined both sides of the high table, but he sat at the men's end on the same side as she did, so she could not see him. She hoped they could exchange at least a few words afterward, but when the meal ended, Lady Margaret stood, saying matter-of-factly, "You and Elizabeth will need plenty of sleep tonight to last the day tomorrow, so you should return to your chamber now. Pray tell your sister, dearling."

Agreement being the only acceptable response, Mairi ignored a sympathetic look from Fiona as they exchanged good nights. Standing and concealing her movements as well as she could with her skirt, she slipped the cloak, on which she had been sitting, off the stool to the floor. Then, chatting politely with the woman who had sat to Fiona's left, she nudged it underneath the long linen tablecloth with one foot before going obediently to collect Elizabeth.

She hoped neither Fiona nor the woman beside her had

seen her drop it, and that neither would mention it if she had, but with so little time, she had known no other way to provide an excuse to return. The men would linger for hours, and she wanted to talk with Lachlan, because their earlier conversation and the stiff way in which they had parted had disturbed her. She did not want to be at outs with him.

As it was, she had to wait until Lady Margaret and her women had retired to the inner chamber, because Mairi knew her ladyship would just tell her to send a gillie to fetch the cloak.

At last, though, as Meg helped Elizabeth prepare for bed, Mairi exclaimed, "Faith, but I've left my red cloak in the hall and I'll want it in the morning. I'll just run and fetch it."

Meg shot her a quizzical look, but Mairi shot out the door before the woman could stop her. Hurrying downstairs, she saw as she crossed the courtyard that the great hall door stood open, the dark bulk of the building framing light from within.

A few torches lit the yard, two flanking the doorway, and she saw no one else as she approached. When she was a few feet away, she heard a voice from inside over the hum of general conversation. Recognizing it as Lachlan's but unable to catch his exact words, she increased her pace.

Then Hector spoke as a lull fell in the murmur behind them, and she heard him clearly: "So your plan marches smoothly withal, but do you still believe in the necessity of building Gillean wealth and power by any means you can?"

"Things march, certainly, but we'll not discuss that topic here, if you please."

Mairi held her breath, hoping Hector would ignore the request.

He did, saying sardonically, "I understand your desire for discretion, my lad, but that wily brain of yours has apparently neglected to consider one vital detail."

"And what detail is that?"

"That rather than give you his daughter, MacDonald might simply hang you or cast you off that rock they call *Creag na Corp*."

"Perhaps, but you'll concede that the prize is worth the risk."

Numb with shock, but terrified of discovery, Mairi whisked herself around the corner of the building.

Wealth and power? Could that be all she meant to him?

Until that moment, she had believed he loved her as she had come to love him, but Hector knew his feelings if anyone did, and despite Lachlan's comment about the prize being worth the risk, he had not denied Hector's words.

Chapter 14 —————————————

As soon as the yard was empty again, Mairi hurried back to the laird's tower, forgetting her cloak until she reached her bedchamber to find Meg awaiting her.

"Where's your cloak, then?"

"I . . . I didn't get it after all." Her throat ached, but when Meg looked skeptical, she added, "I'll send someone to fetch it in the morning."

"Where'd ye leave it, then?"

"I was sitting on it and . . ." She stopped, unable to think of anything to say that would not be an outright lie. "It . . . it might have slipped to the floor."

"I'll send a gillie t' fetch it straightaway," Meg said, eyeing her quizzically. "Ye should ha' asked me instead o' flying out in such a grand rush."

Unable to trust her roiling emotions any longer, Mairi simply nodded and let Meg prepare her for bed. When Elizabeth seemed disposed to chat after Meg left, Mairi said she wanted to sleep and turned her back.

She awoke to a rattle of bed curtains and candle glow, feeling as if someone had put sand in her eyes. She could scarcely remember sleeping, for she had spent much of the night trying to imagine anything the conversation between Lachlan and Hector might have meant other than the obvious.

Every effort met with failure. Tears had welled into her eyes from time to time, but she firmly suppressed them. She hated to cry, and if she could avoid it, was determined to let no man's behavior turn her into a watering pot.

Accepting his betrayal was impossible. Every fiber of her being resisted it, but parts of her flatly rejected it, responding instead to the plain fact that she was thinking of him. Disconcerting memories interjected themselves—memories of the way he had held her, the way he touched her and kissed her, of how easily he could make her body hum, and of the night he had made her his own. In the end, the result was emotional, but the chief emotion was anger.

"Hurry up, Mairi," Elizabeth exclaimed. "You know that our lady mother will not allow us to keep his grace waiting on this of all days."

"Ye look sick," Meg said bluntly. "Mayhap ye should stay abed. I can send for Agnes Beton t' give ye a potion that will put ye back t' sleep."

"I'm fine," Mairi said curtly. When the other two gaped at her, she added hastily, "I beg your pardon. I did not sleep well, that's all, but I'll hurry."

She dressed hurriedly, donned the crimson cloak that Meg held ready for her, and went downstairs with Elizabeth to find the others ready and waiting in the courtyard. Her ladyship's views on dallying were well known, and although MacDonald would willingly have arranged for any number of boats to transport stragglers across the Sound, no one wanted to disappoint him by tarrying.

As they made their way down the cliff stairs to boats waiting at the landing, the morning sky dawned leaden and low. Wispy curtains of mist clung like ragged cloaks to nearby hills and dipped into the Sound of Mull. No mist could dampen the hunters' high spirits, however, because they knew it covered scent and deadened sound, two attributes that would help in stalking their prey.

The procession of longboats was colorful despite the gloom. Black-ship banners waving, the royal galley led the way followed by Lady Margaret's boat with her ladyship, Mairi, and Elizabeth. Her ladyship's women and any guests who chose to bear her company on the hunt followed in the next boat, with a tail of other vessels behind it, large and small, all gaily decked with ribbons and banners.

Their destination, Craignure Bay, lay two miles west of Duart and four miles southeast of Ardtornish. With the boats heavily laden with passengers and high tide on the ebb, the journey took over an hour.

As they disembarked onto the long stone-and-timber jetty built against the steep cliff that plunged deep into the bay to form its eastern boundary, their helmsman said as he helped Lady Margaret out of the boat, "Take care here, my lady, and mind where ye step. This cliff plunges thirty or forty feet down, so the water here be gey deep. Ye others take heed, too," he added. "Folks ha' stepped off this wharf and sunk like stones, never t' be seen again."

They followed MacDonald and the others up the path, past an abandoned three-story stone watchtower, to their waiting horses, leaving the oarsmen to row on to Duart Bay, below the castle, where they would have their midday dinner and rest until time to collect their passengers and row home again.

The horses, supplied from MacDonald's holdings on Mull and stabled at Duart, had been delivered to Craignure earlier for the Ardtornish party and any guests who might choose to join them from nearby isles. Judging by the number waiting, Mairi deduced that several had already arrived.

The logistics for MacDonald's tinchal were complex, and more than one guest had asked why he did not simply hunt deer on the mainland of Morvern. His tactful answer was that he preferred hunting on the Isle of Mull, but Mairi knew the primary reason was that with a party comprised of nearly as many women as men, most of whom felt obliged to take part lest they offend their host, the quicker they could stalk their prey the better. Moreover, if not hunted regularly, the deer on Mull multiplied at a rate greater than the isle could easily sustain.

MacDonald had paused to talk with one of the gillies, and as he mounted, he said, "The lot from Duart should pass this way, but we'll not wait for them. They ken the route to the clearing where we'll break our fast, and should be along soon."

By the time everyone mounted, the boats had disappeared around the point, but the ride to the clearing was less than a mile, and they arrived soon afterward.

Mairi knew that Niall Mackinnon had crossed the Sound at least two hours before to oversee the preparations, and the result was nearly as splendid as if the meal were being served in the Ardtornish great hall. Three rows of linen-draped trestle tables stood in the grassy clearing, and the delicious aroma of roasting beef wafted to the riders as they forded the swiftly flowing burn nearby. The cooks at Duart had roasted the meat earlier, but Niall had ordered a spit set up over one fire to keep the meat warm while gillies broiled fresh salmon over another.

Some would doubtless complain that the Lenten fast still had two days to go before ending with the Paschal feast on Sunday, but since MacDonald liked meat, he provided it for those guests who, like himself and most other Islesmen, paid little heed to such intrusive edicts from faraway Rome.

"Where are the others?" Elizabeth demanded. "Being closer, the party from Duart should have arrived before we did."

As Mairi turned to say that it did not matter to her when they arrived, she encountered a speculative look from Mac-Donald, and since he was near enough to overhear, she decided she would be wiser to reveal nothing of what she felt.

With a slight shrug, she said, "I warrant they will come soon enough, Elizabeth. Are you pleased with the horse you are riding today?"

MacDonald turned to speak with Ranald as Elizabeth said in surprise, "Of course. Is he not from Duart, and have I not ridden him often these past two years?"

"I'd forgotten," Mairi admitted. "We should join our lady mother, should we not, before she sends for us?"

Casting a look toward the east, and Duart, she wondered what was keeping them. As Elizabeth had said, being only two miles away, they ought to have arrived by now, and when they did, she had a few things to say to Lachlan Lubanach.

Rarely noted as a man of exceptional patience, Lachlan was for once grateful to two of his fellow guests at Duart for their dilatory nature, because they had given him time to attend to some details of his own without drawing attention.

"You're gey quiet," Hector said a short time after their party set out at last. Like Lachlan, he wore his sword and had slung his famous battle-axe across his back as he usually did when he rode. Shifting its position slightly, he added, "I expected you'd be harrying that pair of sluggards like a shepherd with stray lambs."

"As so frequently happens, you misjudged me," Lachlan said. "I rarely advocate haste, but I do strive for efficiency."

Hector chuckled. "Aye, well, I don't doubt that you've been efficient, for I saw that you were up betimes and warrant I was snoring before you reached your bed last night."

"I set a few things in train after hearing what Ian had to say," Lachlan said, casting a wary glance at the four men and two women riding ahead of them.

"They are too far away to hear us," Hector said, clearly reading his thoughts. "Are we trailing behind because you have commands for me?"

"None but to keep your eyes open as you always do, and stay alert for anything that seems amiss," Lachlan said. "I've arranged a trap for our would-be assassins, but for it to succeed, we'll have to live long enough to spring it."

"Then we'll do that. Shall we catch up to the others now?"

"Not yet. I put no trust in that lad's assurance of our safety before the hunt begins, but a man would have to be a wretched archer indeed to hit one of those others if he were aiming at us."

"Do you mean to share the details of this wee trap you've laid?"

"Aye, but not until I know it is set. I'm glad you brought your axe, though, even if some folks might question its usefulness for hunting deer."

"No one who knows I always carry it will be so impertinent," Hector said. "Moreover, since half the men here are wearing swords and dirks, including us, I doubt that anyone will pay our weapons much heed."

"Niall Mackinnon is perfectly capable of suggesting that we leave all extra weapons at the gathering place."

Hector shrugged. "He can suggest what he likes." After a short silence, he added, "To my mind, the man suits the role as a villain well enough, but I know not why he would choose it. What can we have done to draw such ire from him?"

"We are sons of Gillean. Doubtless, that is enough, but if, as we suspect, he had a hand in Elma MacCoun's death, he may dislike the questions being asked. And apparently, I've given him another cause, as well."

"The lass?"

"Aye, the lass indeed."

"Do you believe that he would kill just to keep you from flirting with her, or does he suspect the truth?"

"He would kill because he wants her for himself. Even more, I think, does he want the wealth and power that accompanies her."

"And what of you? Is that not what you want?"

Lachlan hesitated.

"You did not answer that question last night," Hector said grimly, "but I think you must if you mean to condemn Mackinnon for wanting her inheritance."

Giving him a hard look, Lachlan said, "Do you believe that I would kill for the sake of winning her?"

"No, of course not, but surely Mackinnon cannot believe MacDonald would relinquish so important a piece on his board as the lass represents, to you or to him. After all, Alasdair Stewart is not the only eligible man with royal connections."

"You still doubt my capabilities, brother, but Niall Mackinnon does not. 'Tis precisely because he *does* believe MacDonald will give her to him if the betrothal to Alasdair fails that my appearance on the scene infuriates him. Before you and I arrived at Finlaggan, he believed he could bide his time, that the path to his victory was clear. But Lady Mairi makes no secret of her preference for me, and my age makes me a much more eligible husband. She looks on Niall much as she does her father, although she does not like or admire Niall as much."

"Mayhap you are merely blinded by your desire for her," Hector said bluntly. "You would not be the first man whose brain stopped working when lust for a beautiful wench struck—or lust for wealth and power, come to that."

Lachlan smiled. "I tell you, if Alasdair Stewart refuses to marry her and the Steward does not force him to do so, I stand in the best position to win her."

"Then, as usual, you know more than you have told me."

"Aye, but 'tis plain enough. Political winds shift, and my lads tell me Mackinnon persistently counsels MacDonald to wait until the omens for success are perfect, not to push the Steward or the Pope until the time is just right. Moreover, he exploits his kinship to the Green Abbot of Iona—a fiendish devil if ever I've met one—to warn his grace that the Pope may not be ready yet to approve the necessary dispensation for two such close kinsmen to wed."

"If the Pope were sensible, he'd reject Alasdair's application outright."

"I agree, but think you that a request from the future King of Scots and the present King of the Hebrides and Lord of the Isles would not sway his holiness?"

Hector sighed. "It would."

"Aye, so I'm thinking 'tis Alasdair himself who presents the obstacle. You will note that having made no appearance at Finlaggan, he likewise fails to make one here, although I did hear at least one rumor that he meant to join us today. It would not be strange if even that scoundrel balks at marrying his own niece."

"Still, Alasdair may not be the one who balks, especially since MacDonald is out of favor again with the King of Scots," Hector reminded him. "MacDonald and the Steward may be wary of approaching the Pope if David threatens to intervene."

"That, too, is possible."

"In any event, I'm thinking you'd be unwise to count Alasdair out when the rewards of marrying her ladyship are so great. Though young, he has revealed more than once that he has no scruples, and I don't believe that marrying his niece would trouble his conscience one whit."

"Perhaps not, but I'm counting him out because I have decided to marry her, so we need consider nothing else."

Hector nodded, and although the straight look he gave Lachlan made him wish it were easier for him to explain his emotions, or even to understand them himself, he knew that his twin would pursue the discussion no further.

They topped a rise, and the clearing they sought hove into view beyond a tumbling burn. Lachlan saw Mairi at once, and the fact that she was showing him her back as others turned to watch their approach made him smile. She was a puzzle, his Mairi, but he held the key, as she would soon learn.

With those in the clearing excitedly hailing their arrival, and their private conversation over, he and Hector spurred their horses to catch up with the others.

Mairi knew he was watching her. She felt his gaze boring into her back, but she kept her attention on Fiona, hopefully observing the breakfast preparations.

"That beef smells like something one might taste in heaven," Fiona said, "but my lord father would skelp me till I screeched if I tasted any. I tell you, the more the Green Abbot flaunts his leman and his many children the more closely my father insists that we keep to the rules of the Roman Kirk."

Mairi murmured sympathy, but her attention was more closely fixed on sounds of the arriving party. Despite her anger with Lachlan, something deep inside made her want to run and fling her arms around him, making her glad she dared not do so. Not only was Niall's stern eye upon her but MacDonald had glanced her way in that speculative manner more than once. And Lady Margaret would make her displeasure known at once if she caught either of her daughters engaged in more than light flirtation. Therefore, she hoped Lachlan had sense enough to ignore her but was disappointed when he did.

Everyone was soon at the tables, and for once, little ceremony reigned. After the grace before meat, MacDonald's body servant served his master's portion and Lady Margaret's, as the carver continued his swift slicing and gillies hurried to place heaping platters of beef and grilled salmon on the tables. Great rounds of bread sat ready to be torn apart at will, and wine and brogac flowed freely.

Mairi sat between Fiona and Elizabeth at a table of women, with Ailsa Macleod and her mother across from them. They had finished all but their wine when a cheer broke out and she turned to see his grace's huntsman running to kneel before him with his hunting horn held out.

"I've not hunted before," Ailsa said. "What is that man doing?"

"The huntsman and his men have found fresh spoor, which he is showing to his grace," Mairi explained. "They can estimate the size of the stag by measuring the distance between its tracks and the height of rubbed-off velvet on nearby trees."

"Velvet?"

"From the antlers," Fiona said. "Deer rub them against tree bark to shed the velvet as their antlers grow. The tracks must indicate a stag of good size," she added when Mac-Donald nodded his approval and the huntsman stood.

"What will they do next?" Ailsa asked.

Mairi said, "The huntsman's minions will stalk the deer whilst the dogs' handlers cut off its retreat and lads climb trees to watch which way it goes."

"You'd think so many would scare it away," Ailsa said.

"No, for they all know their business well. His grace pays his huntsman handsomely and gives him ten pence a day extra for each day he hunts."

She stood as a signal for the others to do likewise. "String your bows if you want to shoot," she told them. "I warrant we'll be mounting soon." To Ailsa, she added, "Wait for his grace to tell you to shoot before you do."

Ailsa smiled. "I've no wish to shoot in such company. As you saw yesterday, I am no archer, but I do like to try new things, so I'll ride with you."

Mairi had been keeping an eye on MacDonald, but her gaze shifted to Lachlan at the table beyond him, likewise preparing to depart. When the Lord of the Isles strode toward the horses, the other hunters fell in behind.

Keeping close to MacDonald and chatting with Fiona, Mairi realized that Lachlan was near only when his hands gripped her waist to lift her up just as she reached her gelding.

"Thank you," she said, surprised into smiling.

"'Tis an honor, your ladyship," he said with a polite nod.

Then, to her further surprise and profound annoyance, he turned away, mounted the black horse he was riding that day, and eased it to a position between her father and Niall. His brother rode at MacDonald's left, but after some moments, catching Mairi's eye, Hector dropped back to ride beside her.

"Good morrow to you, my lady," he said cheerfully. "Do you think we'll see any sunlight today?"

She responded politely. He was easy to chat with, and she was growing to like him very much, but she wished he would trade places with his irritating brother.

Taking care to stay close to MacDonald, Lachlan received the signal for which he had been waiting when one of the huntsman's minions came to inform his grace that the dogs and the stag were in good positions.

He had not known when his prearranged signal would come, or exactly how, but when it did, it was clear. The man looked at him and touched his forelock—an ordinary gesture of respect, but done this time with the three middle fingers straight, the thumb and little finger touching.

Lachlan gave no sign that he'd observed the signal.

MacDonald put his ivory oliphant to his lips and blew, signaling for the dogs to drive the stag toward them. With it caught between dogs and hunters, they soon brought it to bay, and to Lachlan's astonishment, his host nodded at him, giving him the honor of shooting the first deer of the day.

He loosed his shot swiftly and accurately, and the deer fell and was quickly still. The huntsman's men moved in to skin it and divide the meat. All but the dogs' small share of each kill would be carried back to the clearing to be guarded from predators, and taken later to Ardtornish to be roasted for the Easter feast. Since MacDonald had said they would take at least four bucks that day, there might even be enough meat for those who lived within a day's journey to share in the bounty.

"An excellent shot, lad," MacDonald said. "I'd been told you shoot well."

Lachlan smiled wryly. "If 'twas Lady Mairi who told you, your grace, I know she also said she beat me soundly yesterday in our contest."

"Aye, the saucy lass told me so before we broke our fast, but she said, too, that you shot with her bow to make the contest fair. I admire fairness in a man."

A dry note in his voice stirred Lachlan's instinct for trouble, but he said calmly, "I, too, admire fairness, sir."

"My high steward fears that you continue to admire my daughter, as well."

"Since I believe 'twas Lady Mairi herself who first drew your attention to my admiration, your grace, that cannot have come as news to you."

"Not news, no, but I did make my decision on the matter clear, I believe."

"Aye, sir, you did."

"Then that is all we need say on the subject, is it not?"

Lachlan bowed his head, saying submissively, "As you wish, your grace."

MacDonald turned to tell MacDougall of Dunstaffnage that he should take the next shot, and then signed to his huntsman, who announced that his men had found new spoor and were stalking a second stag.

Lachlan knew that in minutes the second chase would begin, although the term was inaccurate, since no one rode fast on such a hunt.

Mackinnon had slipped away, perhaps to give orders about the meat, or for some less dispassionate purpose, making Lachlan wish he knew of a way to distinguish men loyal to Mackinnon from those loyal only to MacDonald or one of his guests. He knew of no such method, however, so he kept his gaze in constant motion, searching even as Hector moved to ride beside him.

"You should stay near her ladyship or his grace," Lachlan muttered. "Mackinnon will not chance striking his liege or a member of the family."

"I will, but no one is shooting now, so a wild shot would be hard to prove. I wanted to tell you I overheard what his grace said to you, and your reply."

"Your ears are as sharp as ever then, but you need not concern yourself, because no one else was paying us heed," Lachlan said.

"Perhaps not, but I'm doubting that he'll change his mind about the matter dearest to your heart even if Alasdair—" Breaking off when another horseman drew near, he added more circumspectly, "I should say, even if the absent one should never show his face again."

"You may say it as you will. The saying will not alter my course."

"I see. You did not say you had accepted his decision."

"You noted that, did you?"

"I have much experience with your parsing, my lad. A wise man learns to heed the words and not simply hear what he expects to hear. You agreed only to say no more on the subject if that was his wish."

"You distract me," Lachlan complained as his attention shifted sharply to a man climbing a tree ahead. He relaxed when he saw that it was only a weaponless gillie looking for the stag. "Drop back and ride beside my lass. You'll be safe there, and mayhap the prattlers will watch you for a change, instead of me."

With a sigh and a shake of his head, Hector obeyed.

"Has your brother decided never to speak to me again?" Mairi asked when it appeared that Hector Reaganach intended to continue riding beside her.

He smiled. "He did not say so, my lady. Doubtless, he is but puffed up in arrogant delight at your lord father's generosity in letting him shoot the first stag."

"It was kind of him. Many of the men here desired that honor."

Hector made no reply. Indeed, she thought, he seemed more interested in one of Niall's gillies, who was climbing a tree to look for the stag they stalked.

The signal came that the dogs had blocked the stag's retreat and it soon turned, whereupon MacDonald blew his oliphant again, and the chase was on.

MacDougall brought it down, and after that, MacDonald let anyone shoot who could claim a good line, making the rest of the morning pass swiftly. Mairi found Hector surprisingly attentive, but Lachlan scarcely heeded her.

Not until they paused to eat their dinner of bread and meat, and Lachlan sat near her father, did she recall her brief hope that he would ignore her. Recalling that he still did not know she had overheard his exchange with Hector the previous night and was angry with him, she told herself that perhaps he simply had seen that MacDonald was watching them, and behaved as he did to protect her.

The thought gave her small comfort, and his behavior continued to annoy her. She did not believe he would compromise her merely by acknowledging her presence from time to time, or by exchanging a polite word or two.

Hector's behavior was strange, too. Fiona had flirted with him since his arrival at Ardtornish, as had Elizabeth, and he had clearly enjoyed flirting back. But today he had eyes for no woman except Mairi, and she could not flatter herself that his interest was amorous. She might have suspected him of trying to protect her, but no man with half a brain could think she needed protection in that company.

Since deer were plentiful, the afternoon went as quickly as the morning, and before she knew it, they had returned to the clearing and Lady Margaret was announcing that she was ready to go back to Ardtornish.

"Those who mean to accompany me should do so at once," she said. "I know many of you will want to change for supper."

Mairi hesitated, hoping to find some reason to linger.

"Mairi, you and Elizabeth go with your mother," Mac-Donald said as he dismounted.

After that, she had no choice.

Lachlan felt only relief at seeing the lass ride off with Lady Margaret and the other women. Except for MacDonald's guardsmen and body servant, the rest of the men accompanied them, because by now the longboats would be waiting for them in Craignure Bay. Everyone was to gather at Ardtornish for supper and the evening's entertainment, as usual, so the party from Duart would accompany the others, and the men were as eager for their supper as the women were.

Hector said quietly, "Do we not go with the others?"

"Nay, we'll find an excuse to stay with MacDonald. He'll wait to see most of his guests safely departed before he goes, I believe, although I did expect him to accompany her ladyship's party to the jetty, and Mackinnon as well. But surely he will accompany MacDonald to the royal galley when he goes, so we should be safe until then. I'm thinking they'll strike on the jetty, after MacDonald has gone."

"But is there not a boat for the Duart party?"

"I'm guessing it will either not show or have departed early."

"Then won't MacDonald expect us to ride to Ardtornish with him?"

"Even if he does, I want this business settled," Lachlan said. "I don't want to have to keep looking over my shoulder, watching for Mackinnon's people to carry out his orders. We'll offer to wait and go with him if the boat from Duart has gone. He may even suggest that himself. He has no cause to think we suspect him."

"Sakes, we'll be at his mercy if we wait that long."

"You forget my wee trap," Lachlan said.

"Aye, sure, I did. Perhaps you'll tell me about it now."

"Lads," MacDonald called, "do you not go with the others?"

Waving as he dismounted, Lachlan exchanged a look with Hector. "I have adjusted a part of Mackinnon's own plan to benefit us. Just be prepared to act quickly," he added, "because if Mackinnon should prove wilier than I am, we'll need all of our wits and skill at arms to emerge from my trap alive."

Chapter 15 ———————

Resisting the temptation to grip his sword and subtly test the sheath's willingness to release it, Lachlan said, "We are at your command, your grace. Can we help speed matters along here?"

MacDonald replied, "'Tis courteous of you to ask, lad. Niall, do your men have everything in hand here, or have you tasks for some of these others?"

"Nay, your grace, everything is ready. The handlers will return the dogs to their kennels, and my lads have nearly finished packing up everything here."

"Then we can all head back together," MacDonald said.

"I'm afraid I sent the Duart boat off betimes," Mackinnon said, confirming Lachlan's expectation. "Dougald MacHenry, who is also staying there, said his lady wanted to return or go on to Ardtornish and rest before supper, and since I did not expect you back for another hour, I told them to do as they pleased. I'm afraid I don't even know which destination they chose."

"I see," MacDonald said with a thoughtful frown. "I doubt the Duart boat will return for some time then, which will leave us a few places short."

"The Duart helmsman kens fine that his boat will be

needed here, so he will return," Niall said. "But you should go on ahead, your grace, and see to your guests. If the helmsman tarries, these lads are welcome to ride in my boat if they like."

"Aye, that's a good plan. Just don't let them go hungry," MacDonald said.

"No fear of that. My people have orders to serve supper an hour after your return. 'Twill be earlier than usual, but doubtless some of your guests will be wanting to retire early after so long a day."

"Then you'll ride with Mackinnon, lads, if that will suit you."

"Thank you, your grace," Lachlan said, but his thoughts were racing, and as MacDonald remounted, he added, "Since the gillies have all in train here, mayhap Hector and I would do better to ride on with your party and turn our horses over to the lads at the jetty when you do, sir. 'Twould be one thing less to delay us later."

"An excellent notion," MacDonald said. "I'd enjoy your company, and if the Duart boat returns in time, you can take any stragglers aboard with you. Niall, you will know then by their absence that the Duart boat has been and gone."

Mackinnon's quick agreement further confirmed Lachlan's belief that the steward had ordered the Duart boat not to return.

Moments later, as they turned their horses to follow MacDonald, Hector said in an urgent undertone that Lachlan hoped carried to his ears alone, "Are you daft? You said the jetty is the most likely place for the attack. If his grace leaves without us, we'll be sitting like butts in his practice field, waiting for the arrows to strike."

"We could hardly stay in the clearing with them when, for all we know, every man with Mackinnon is loyal to him alone," Lachlan said quietly. "It was one thing to ride beside him, knowing none of his louts would risk hitting him any more than their liege lord or his family. It is another altogether to let Mackinnon isolate us amongst his men. If you doubt his ability to devise a tale to explain our tragic deaths to MacDonald, I certainly don't."

"It occurs to me that MacDonald could be in league with him," Hector said thoughtfully. "Had you considered that?"

"He is not," Lachlan said confidently, noting that MacDonald was looking back as if wondering why they dawdled. "We've no more time to talk, but his grace is not a man of violence or deceit. If he wanted us dead, he'd simply hang us."

"Aye, well, that's comforting, that is," Hector said acidly.

But Lachlan had given spur to his horse.

Having sent everyone else ahead to the jetty, MacDonald rode with only his body servant and four men-at-arms. When the brothers rode up beside him, he said, "I think my guests enjoyed themselves today despite our uncertain weather."

"Aye, your grace, and acquitted themselves well," Hector said. "I noted that Lady Mairi's arrow was the first to bring down the last two stags. She has a hunter's eye and steady hands."

"Aye, the lass has many skills," MacDonald said proudly. "Often do I heed her counsel as she grows older and more experienced with things beyond those her lady mother taught her." With a steady look at Lachlan, he added, "She will make her royal husband a fine wife, indeed."

Despite yearning to contradict that statement, Lachlan maintained his part in the conversation politely as his gaze swept right, left, and back again. He might hope Mackinnon's men would put self-preservation first and not chance loosing an arrow near MacDonald, but he was not such a fool as to add trust to that hope.

He knew Hector watched too, and that Lady Axe sat loosely in her sling, ready to leap to his brother's hand at the least hint of trouble.

As they neared the bluff overlooking Craignure Bay, his gaze paused briefly at the stone watchtower. Its only arrow slits faced the Sound, as he had noted while passing earlier, but its crenellated battlements commanded a view in all directions.

A lurking enemy could easily conceal himself there.

Catching Hector's eye, he saw that the danger of the watchtower had struck him, and winked to let him know he believed all was well.

They passed the tower minutes later, and although the door at its base stood ajar, as it had not earlier, he saw no sign of life and was satisfied.

Below them, the tide neared its highest point of the day, boats were loading, and one just pulling away from the jetty carried Mairi, her mother and sister, and most of the other women. A skyward glance revealed that the clouds that had hovered in the west after the mist had cleared were nearer, darkening ominously as they gathered moisture. The wind blew from the west now, rendering sails useless for the up-wind journey back. The crossing might get rough, but the oarsmen were strong, well fed, and rested, and he was certain all the boats would make it safely back before the storm struck except, possibly, Mackinnon's.

They reached the jetty in time for MacDonald to bid the other boats farewell and to board his own. Despite the lack of the Duart boat, the departure of all the ladies with Lady Margaret had left room in the others for more men, leaving only old Cameron of Lochaber, MacDuffie of Colonsay, MacDougall, and MacDonald's body servant to ride with him in the royal galley.

"I still have plenty of room, as we see," he said to Lachlan. "You are welcome to ride back with me if you like."

"Thank you, sir, but if Niall Mackinnon finds us gone, he may think the boat from Duart returned and left with us. Then, if anyone lingers—mayhap those stragglers you mentioned—he'll unknowingly leave them behind."

"Faith, lad, his boat is tied yonder. I see no oarsman or helmsman, so they must be seeing to other tasks, but doubtless the lads with the horses will tell him."

Smiling, Lachlan said, "An it please your grace, we'll wait as we promised. It may have escaped your notice, but your steward seems to have taken us in dislike. We know not why, but we'd as lief give him no further cause for enmity."

"'Tis true that he seems to dislike you," MacDonald agreed, "but I think the difficulty more likely lies between Niall and your father, and not with you."

"Nonetheless—"

"Aye, I understand. Doubtless, I should do the same, for I've seen that you dislike fratching as much as I do. Proceed as you think best then, though I'm bound to say Niall can be a hard man when his mind is set. Still, you lads have made many friends at my court. If anyone can sway him, you will."

"Thank you, sir," Lachlan said, stifling a twinge of guilt at the turn MacDonald's thoughts had taken, and not daring to look at Hector.

Hector waited until they were alone on the jetty watching MacDonald's oarsmen pull away before he said, "Do you think that was wise?"

"Do you think I'd have been wiser to say we suspect his high steward of plotting to murder us and want to see if our trap catches him at it?"

"What I think is that Mackinnon will complain about

whatever happens after your trap springs and will tell the tale in such a way as—"

"Let us finish this conversation elsewhere," Lachlan interjected. "We'll be out of sight of the royal galley in a few minutes and should find cover before then. I suggest that watchtower."

Setting a fast pace, he led the way up the hill, but they had gone less than halfway when he saw that they were too late.

At least a score of armed men lined the hilltop above.

"We're in God's hands now, for we're open targets," Hector muttered.

"Wave," Lachlan said, looking up with a smile and a jaunty wave. "Now, turn and walk back down to the jetty, so it looks as if we were just going to see if they were in sight yet. This venture is not proceeding as I'd planned, but it will do."

"Sakes, they'll shoot us in the back if we walk away."

"If they do, how will they explain the arrow holes in our backs to his grace?" Lachlan asked. "Mackinnon can scarcely claim his men were shooting at a stray buck on the jetty and hit us instead. They'll at least come closer first. Just pray he lacks the patience to wait until we're aboard his boat to reveal his true intent."

"In troth, I'd feel a deal safer on his boat."

"Until he orders swords drawn, dispatches us, and throws us overboard."

Hector growled low in his throat as he said, "I've never cared much for your damnably clever imagination, my lad."

"You'd like the reality less."

"Aye, so what's our plan now?"

"To let him think for a few minutes more that everything is as he wants it."

"You lead the way then, because if you are wrong and

those lads let fly, at least Lady Axe can deflect a few of their arrows if I am behind you."

Lachlan did not argue, knowing it would be useless and would stir undesired curiosity from Mackinnon's lot as to why they argued. Instead, he concentrated on walking as if he were not the least bit worried, albeit continuing to seek some sort of shelter to protect them until the others were near enough for swords to count. Two unstrung bows against twenty or more would be useless.

He concluded that their sole, slim hope in a rain of arrows was to dive into the water and swim for the Morvern shore. But trying to outswim Mackinnon's galley once his oarsmen were in it would be hopeless, so he was almost relieved as he stepped onto the jetty to hear the villain shout his name.

"Lachlan Lubanach, I would speak to you!"

Turning, he gestured for Hector to step aside and give him a clear view of Mackinnon as the high steward led his men down the hill. A number of them held tautly strung bows. Several had arrows nocked.

"Walk past me onto the jetty," he muttered to his brother. "I wonder if he thinks us fools or simply did not notice the weapons his men are carrying."

"Thinks us fools," Hector muttered back as he strolled past. "Damnable cheek, but nearly do I agree with him."

With battle near, Lachlan's concerns vanished and his mind focused sharply on the moment. Watching the oncoming men, knowing Hector was doing the same, he kept his hands loose at his sides as if he had no thought of drawing sword or dirk, and waited for Mackinnon to come near enough to say what he wanted to say.

The wind was stronger now, kicking up foam on the waves of the Sound and the bay, and driving them against the jetty. Mackinnon's empty galley rocked and banged against the wood timbers.

"You have betrayed his grace's trust, Lachlan Lubanach," Mackinnon shouted with a smirk. "I have orders to take you prisoner."

"Indeed, and how is that? His grace gave me to understand that he thinks highly of me and mine."

"He leaves such unpleasantness to me," Mackinnon said, closer now.

"Faith, but I'd no notion he was afraid to speak his mind to me, let alone that he would designate a mere Mackinnon to act for him," Lachlan retorted.

"By heaven, you take life in hand to speak to me so!" Mackinnon snapped. "You can see that we have you outnumbered, so remove your weapons, both of you, or we'll remove them for you."

"First, perhaps, you should look behind you," Lachlan said gently.

Mackinnon turned to see a Clan Gillean banner waving from the watchtower battlements. Lined along the hilltop where his men had been before, well within bowshot, stood forty men of Clan Gillean, bows drawn and arrows nocked.

Mackinnon's men gaped, relaxing their weapons.

"By God, you go too far," Mackinnon snarled, snatching out his sword as he bellowed, "At them! Kill them all!" Wheeling, he lunged at Lachlan with his sword, snarling, "Your louts won't dare shoot when they could strike you or me!"

But Lachlan's sword was out, and he easily parried the stroke. As he did, the man behind Mackinnon raised his bow, arrow nocked, and aimed at Lachlan, only to collapse before he could shoot, felled by Hector's flying battle-axe.

Hector's sword and dirk were out as well, and battle

joined as Mackinnon's men strove to defend themselves against Clan Gillean's onslaught. Twice, when a man of Gillean met his match, an arrow from the tower battlements saved him. Others accounted for Mackinnons up and down the hill, because the highly skilled archers on the tower shot with the wind, and the tower protected their arrows' flight.

Lachlan continued to fight Mackinnon, and Hector ran past them to engage a pair of Mackinnon's men who had drawn great two-handed swords to help him.

Mackinnon was an excellent swordsman, but Lachlan knew he could hold his own if his clansmen could hold off the other men-at-arms. He knew, too, that the older man would tire more quickly than he would.

"You had no orders from his grace," he said, smiling as he danced nimbly back along the jetty, knowing that his smile would infuriate his opponent.

In answer, Mackinnon lunged, but Lachlan parried the attack with a two-handed, slashing stroke. Steel rang against steel, and Mackinnon showed little sign of wearying. However, as they drew alongside the empty longboat, he slipped in a puddle on one of the wide timbers.

Not wanting to take unfair advantage, Lachlan checked his stroke, only to see Mackinnon lunge hard instead of falter. Recognizing the feint in time, he flung himself to one side, but the blade of Mackinnon's sword caught his sleeve and pierced the flesh beneath.

"First blood to me, I believe," Mackinnon said.

"Aye, but you don't deny my accusation," Lachlan said, parrying the next stroke. "I say you are a liar, and MacDonald likes me well."

"Mayhap he will speak well at your funeral," Mackinnon said, his breathing labored at last. "You'll never marry his daughter."

"That remains to be seen. But you will not have her."

"His grace believes what I tell him."

"You forget the many witnesses to your attack on two innocent men who had done you no harm."

"You assume that your men will beat mine."

"They are doing so right speedily," Lachlan assured him as he lunged.

"Have you looked toward yonder battlements?" Mackinnon said, gasping, as he whacked the thrust aside. "I think you should."

As Lachlan glanced up, Mackinnon flipped his own sword, bringing the hilt up hard from the ground, aimed right at Lachlan's head.

"Aye, sir, I see that the battlements are still mine," Lachlan said, stepping aside so that the very weight of Mackinnon's heavy sword pulled the man to him as he made his own thrust. "Your men drop like walnuts from trees in a wind."

Although Lachlan's thrust went wide of its mark, Mackinnon had clearly expected his to connect, for he turned as if to look at the hill again, then turned back into the path of Lachlan's blade. Regarding him with astonishment, he clutched his chest, stumbled, and still gripping his heavy sword, fell headlong into the water between the jetty and the longboat.

Lachlan stared at his bloody sword and stepped to the edge, leaning against the boat to widen the gap and look down. The roiling water was too deep at cliffside to see bottom, and he saw only bubbles and a spreading slick of blood on the water.

He saw that Hector had dispatched at least three of the villains, and that he and the other men of Gillean would soon disarm or kill any who refused to surrender. Then a shout came from above, and the rest of Mackinnon's men, evidently noting the disappearance of their master, threw down their arms.

"Hector, I want you," he called.

"Where's Mackinnon?"

"Dead, I'm afraid," Lachlan said, gesturing toward the water. "I struck him in the chest and he fell in. He hasn't come up."

"Likely he won't then," Hector said, peering into the water as Lachlan had done earlier, with the same result. "You know as well as I that bodies don't float unless they still have enough life in them to swim or flail about."

"Could he be clinging to the longboat?"

Hector leaped into the boat and peered over the opposite side. "There's nowt to cling to unless he's hanging from the steerboard, and I can see he's not. We'll watch for him, but if your sword went into his chest, I'll wager the man has sped to the arms of God or the Devil, and I'm guessing that was no part of your plan."

"No." Glancing up the hill, he saw that his men had Mackinnon's all in hand.

"Where did they all come from?" Hector asked.

"His lads at the clearing, plus his boatmen, I suppose."

"I meant our lot," Hector said grimly.

"I sent word last night to all our people on Mull, of course. Only a few are men-at-arms by trade, but some are first-rate bowmen and most can wield swords deftly enough. I counted on greater numbers and surprising them, and when I saw the watchtower, I knew it might be wise to take control of it in order to command the field here if we survived the hunt. The jetty was always the most logical place to take a stand. I feared, however, that Mackinnon might realize that for himself."

"He did, my lord."

Recognizing the man he had put in charge of the force from Clan Gillean, Lachlan said, "What do you mean by that, Rankin?"

"When we took the tower, we found two lads here afore us," Rankin said. "We killed one, but we've got the other tied up inside."

"Let's have a look at them," Lachlan said. "Mayhap your captive and one or two of these other prisoners can help us with a wee problem we now face."

"Aye, just a wee problem," Hector muttered, giving him a look.

Lachlan responded with a half smile. The road ahead was fraught with peril, to be sure, but obstacles were familiar challenges. He had only to identify a course that would avoid the worst of them and take him to his destination.

Leaving the others to dispose of the bodies and deal with their five prisoners, he followed Rankin to the watchtower. Inside, they found the tower prisoner trussed up and gagged, lying on the spiral stairway leading to the battlements.

"He and his companion were atop the tower when we arrived, sir."

"Take off the gag and bring him out into the light so I can see," Lachlan said.

Hector jerked the lanky, dark-haired man up, trusses and all, and dragged him outside, saying as he untied the gag, "That storm will be on us soon."

"Aye," Lachlan agreed, looking thoughtfully at the prisoner. "You seem familiar. What do men call you?"

"Gil Dowell, but I've nowt t' say t' ye."

"I see. Well, I think you do have things to say to me, but we've no time for lengthy conversation, so we'll leave you until his grace's men can question you and your friends. I warrant he'll see you're treated gently, although my lads may not be so gentle whilst you wait. Still, you've set your own course."

The man shrugged.

"Take him away, Rankin. See that he behaves until I've further use for him."

"Beg pardon, sir, but where shall we keep them all?"

"Bury the dead and take the others to Amalaig. The tower there will hold them until I want them. We'll send a boat from Bellachuan to collect them later."

"Aye, sir, we'll look after them till then."

"You said you found two men here," Lachlan said. "Where is the second?"

"Yonder, wi' the dead," Rankin said, pointing.

"Show me."

The second man also looked familiar. Suddenly recognizing him, Lachlan exchanged a look with Hector, who nodded. It was Fin MacHugh, which made Lachlan wonder where Shim MacVey might be, before he recalled that Hector had told him that the third witness in Ian Burk's trial had stayed at Finlaggan.

"Rankin, I'll need oarsmen for that longboat," he said.

"Aye, sir, straightaway."

"We'll wait for them below," Lachlan said, signing to Hector to follow.

"Those two louts testified against Lady Mairi's Ian," Hector said. "They said he was with Elma MacCoun on her last day."

"Aye, and whilst they may honestly have mistaken the day, finding them here with Mackinnon makes a man think, does it not?"

"Aye, but we've more important things to consider at the moment. How, exactly, do you intend to tell his grace that you've killed his high steward?"

"We have no body to produce, which means that no one else can produce it either," Lachlan said thoughtfully.

"Aye, sure, but I don't suppose we can just forget about having killed him," Hector said. "Some of our prisoners must have seen it, and if they accuse us of murdering him, we certainly can't produce him alive to prove them wrong."

"MacDonald likes us, and we have our own witnesses," Lachlan said, speaking his thoughts as they walked rather than trying to suggest any particular solution. Since he had not thought of one, he had nothing to suggest.

"MacDonald is our kinsman and has shown us much honor," Hector said. "However, one cannot help but expect the death of his high steward to annoy him even if we could persuade him that Mackinnon attacked us rather than the reverse. Moreover, Mackinnon wielded great power in his own right. His clan is large and unlikely to believe anything we say against him."

"He has also a powerful, most untrustworthy brother who has many sons," Lachlan said. "Much as the Green Abbot flouts such rules, he will be quick, I fear, to declare a blood feud. And, too, he could well excommunicate us both."

Hector shrugged. "He is not exactly in good odor with the Pope just now."

"I do not speak of the Pope but of trouble Fingon can cause us here at home. His local power remains great, and whilst we may not hold by all dictates of the Roman Kirk, we'd find it embarrassing to be shunned by our neighbors who do. Think you MacDougall of Dunstaffnage will welcome your flirtations with his Fiona if the Green Abbot should declare us excommunicate?"

Hector frowned. "We must think of a way to avoid Fingon's displeasure. Such dissension would anger our father, but in truth, 'tis MacDonald's wrath I want most like to avoid. If he should name us outlaw, order us put to fire or sword . . ."

He let the words trail to silence, but Lachlan did not require further description of his likely future to make his fertile brain work at top speed.

"The royal galley is eminently seaworthy," he said musingly, "but she does not travel as fast as a longboat, especially against the wind. Nor does his grace have special cause to travel fast. I'd wager he is not yet halfway to Ardtornish."

Hector's eyes narrowed. "Why do you bring that up now?"

"He has but eight oarsmen, having left the others behind this morning to make more room for his guests. We will have sixteen."

Hector nodded. "I ken fine that you take note of such details, and that our lives may depend on the course we choose now. But if you are thinking we should catch up to the royal galley and kill them all to protect ourselves, I—"

"Nay, nay, for Lords Ranald and Godfrey, not to mention Mairi, would soon see us sped if we took such a daft course. Moreover, I like MacDonald and infinitely prefer him as an ally."

"Just how do you propose to keep his friendship after killing the man who was not only his friend and high steward but also chief of the Mackinnons and a councilor of the Isles?"

"We'll do what's necessary, of course. We'll abduct him and persuade him of the excellence of our character and our unwavering loyalty."

Chapter 16

The oarsmen and helmsman were hurrying down the hill, so Lachlan cut off Hector's protests until they were in the longboat, moving at speed. The sky was low and heavy with the approaching storm, and although the clouds had not begun to spit, the wind and resulting waves in the Sound made visibility uncertain.

"'Tis a mad course," Hector said. The two faced each other in the bow, leaning close to keep their words from carrying to others on the wind.

"Mad indeed," Lachlan agreed, "but 'tis our only hope."

The oarsmen, pulling hard, were too intent on rowing to heed them, he knew, but it would not matter if they did. They were loyal to Clan Gillean and he was the designated successor to their chief. They might know the brothers disagreed, but they would never let him down. Nor would Hector.

"We might as well kill MacDonald then," Hector muttered. "He'd forgive us for that, I'm thinking, more readily than for abducting him."

"You are not thinking," Lachlan said. "We have neither the right nor the disposition to kill him, and if we did, 'twould be a grave mistake."

"And abducting him is not?"

"Perhaps it is, but the other is certain, because if we killed MacDonald, we would incur the wrath of every clan, not to mention Ranald of the Isles, who would take command of his grace's men. I've already pointed out the danger the wicked abbot presents, and that was without the suggestion that we murder MacDonald."

Hector made a rude noise. "You know that I would never commit murder," he said grimly. "I kill without compunction any man who attacks me or mine, but I'd not kill to avoid deserved punishment, nor would I kill my liege."

"Nor I, so listen and heed me well. I value your trust, and you can trust me with this. If Mackinnon's men get to his grace first—the Green Abbot, for example—we cannot know what will happen. But if we capture him, I can make him hear our side of the incident, and he will judge us fairly. We simply must gain his protection before he hears from the others—"

"Most of whom are already dead or prisoners," Hector interjected.

"Only those we saw," Lachlan said. "You may be certain that Mackinnon took counsel with others, perhaps even the wicked abbot, and for Ian Burk to learn of his plan, at least one of those others must have spoken out of turn. We cannot know more until we can question Gil Dowell, or his grace does."

"Aye, that is all true, but would MacDonald not listen to both sides in any event? As you say, he is fair, and I warrant the lady Mairi would be even quicker to speak for you than she was for Ian Burk."

"Only if matters take the course they should. 'Tis more likely we'd meet with treachery before we'd face a fair trial. Recall that Mackinnon has friends on MacDonald's Council of the Isles, and recall, too, how they followed his lead in their treatment of us. Do you think they would easily accept him as a villain? Might they not prefer us in the role?"

Hector was silent.

"Now, consider this," Lachlan said, leaning closer. "Even to discuss the matter with MacDonald, we must first have his ear, and without debate from any who would undermine our position. He is not a difficult man. Nor are MacDougall or MacDuffie, let alone MacDonald's body servant. More-over, MacDonald is practical and dislikes violence. Faith, he said himself that he dislikes fratching."

Hector was peering narrow-eyed into the distance. "I'm thinking that may be a gold banner ahead," he said, "with a little black ship in its center."

"Then what say you? Think what may come of making him our ally."

"Aye, much could come of it, I agree, but whether it does or not doesn't matter. You know I'm with you, even an it means sailing into hell."

Mairi had kept a close eye on the sky as the oarsmen rowed for Ardtornish. It looked increasingly as if later boats would be in for a soaking, but more worrisome was the pos-sibility that the Sound might turn into a dangerous, boiling cauldron if the winds grew stronger. As the ladies' boat and the three behind it pulled into the sheltered bay below Ard-tornish, the waves of the Sound were just a nuisance; how-ever, stronger winds from the west could render them lethal.

On the landing, she spoke to one of the lads and learned that the Duart boat had arrived much earlier with Dougald MacHenry and his lady. More surprising was that the boat had not returned to Craignure or Duart but had gone around to MacDonald's safe harbor in Loch Aline.

Walking up the cliff stairs with Elizabeth, behind Lady Margaret and the other women, she said, "Do you not think it odd that the Duart boat would bring only two people when eight from there hunted with us this morning?"

"Perhaps," Elizabeth agreed, "but only one other woman was in that party, and she walks ahead now with our lady mother."

"That still leaves five men," Mairi pointed out.

"But only one you care about," Elizabeth teased.

"Aye," Mairi admitted, certain she was blushing.

"Do you want to marry him?" Elizabeth asked over her shoulder as they entered the laird's tower and followed the others upstairs.

"Faith, Elizabeth, what a thing to ask!" Mairi exclaimed. At least the others were well ahead of them, chattering merrily, and had likely not heard her.

"Well, do you?"

"Hush! Our father would never allow it."

"But do you want to?"

"Lachlan Lubanach can be a most irritating man," Mairi said, remembering that he wanted her only for the wealth and power she would bring. Also that he had ignored her all day except for that moment at the beginning when, without even a by-your-leave, he had lifted her to her saddle. *And* that he constantly insisted she leave everything to him as if she had no brain of her own, no skills, or capabilities.

Elizabeth smiled. "I think you *do* want to marry him."

"Even if I did, which I don't, I should still have to marry Alasdair."

"Oh, a pox on Alasdair!" Elizabeth said as they entered the great chamber.

"One hopes you do not mean that, cousin," drawled a vaguely familiar voice. "So disfiguring, the pox is, and one has one's splendid appearance to protect."

"Oh!" Elizabeth, eyes wide, clapped a hand to her open mouth.

Mairi, too, stared in dismay at the fair-haired man standing just inside the doorway, smiling sardonically at her. Alasdair Stewart had joined the court at last.

In little more time than it took Lachlan to explain to his men what he expected of them, the longboat caught up with the much slower royal galley and eased alongside.

MacDonald greeted them cheerfully. "Come aboard, lads," he said. "You've made excellent speed, but I see that Niall has lent you his longboat, and with the weather as it is, I wager he wants it to return for him as soon as it can."

"Well, sir, in a manner of speaking, he has lent us his boat," Lachlan said, obeying the command to climb aboard. "We bring sad news, however."

"Indeed?" MacDonald watched, visibly puzzled as Lachlan's men shipped oars and began boarding the royal galley. "Should we not send his boat back?"

"There is no need, your grace."

MacDonald's eyes narrowed as the empty longboat bobbed beside the royal galley on the churning waves and two of Lachlan's men lashed them together, but he said only, "Sit then. You'll be glad of a drink, I'm thinking, for I would myself."

Lachlan and Hector found places to sit between Mac-Dougall of Dunstaffnage and MacDuffie, the hereditary keeper of the records, and across from old Cameron of Lochaber, and MacDonald gestured to his body servant.

He poured brogac into five silver goblets from a nearby basket, the first one for MacDonald, and then for the others.

Accepting his, Lachlan said, "I regret that our news will distress you, sir, but to speak plainly, we have all put our trust in a traitorous villain."

"Have we?"

"Aye, sir, for although he pretended to be your friend, even to count himself one of your family, he schemed against you. In the course of that scheming, he sought to take one of your greatest assets and also to kill Hector and me."

"Am I to understand that you speak of Niall Mackinnon? I should find it hard to believe such villainy of him."

"I am deeply sorry, sir. I do speak of Mackinnon."

Lachlan realized as he said the words that his sorrow was sincere, because loyalty was the true coin of their realm, and Mackinnon had betrayed his liege lord, the man to whom he owed his greatest allegiance. "He betrayed not only you, your grace, but the Kingdom of the Isles. From the first, he was—"

"Was?"

"Aye, sir. What I must say to you would be easier if he were here to speak for himself, but as it is, you have only our word and that of our henchmen, although we did take several prisoners."

"You have never given me cause to doubt your word, sir. I do not doubt it now."

Lachlan had the grace to feel a twinge of shame, knowing that although he always spoke the truth, his phrasing might sometimes be deceptive. He said, "Thank you, sir. As you know, after you left, Hector and I waited for Mackinnon at the jetty, but when he came, he brought a small army. 'Twas an ambush, but although they attacked us, I did receive sufficient warning to prevent disaster."

"My dear fellow! God must have been watching over you, but how came this timely warning?"

"As you know, sir, I have a certain facility for acquiring information."

MacDonald's lips twitched as he nodded.

Relaxing, Lachlan said, "I received word from one of your loyal followers, Ian Burk, that Mackinnon had arranged for two of his expert bowmen to misfire before the end of the hunt, killing Hector and me."

"'Tis true Niall had no love for you," MacDonald said, frowning. "He even accused you of attempting to seduce my daughter."

"You know of my deep admiration for her ladyship," Lachlan said. Much as he would have liked to elaborate, he knew it was not the time, and went on to say quietly, "Despite the warning, I gave him the benefit of assuming he would realize that such behavior was unworthy of him. However, I took necessary precautions."

"I see," MacDonald said. "Do I understand then that it was not the simple pleasure of my company that kept you and your brother so close to me today?"

"Not entirely, sir," Lachlan admitted. "We wanted to survive the hunt."

"And evidently, Niall failed to come to his senses."

"He and twenty of his men advanced on us from the top of the hill, weapons drawn. He drew his sword on me, your grace, threatening to spit me where I stood."

"Faith, lad, I knew well his volatile temper and his dislike for Clan Gillean, but to have done such a thing to any guest of mine was dastardly."

"Aye, sir. Thanks to Ian's warning, however, I had sent messages to our people on Mull, so my kinsmen kept watch throughout the day. When Mackinnon and his men attacked, my men descended on them in force."

"Niall fell, you say?"

"I am sorry to admit that my own sword dispatched him, your grace. I meant only to disarm him. He slipped on a wet board, so I checked my thrust, whereupon he flipped his sword and tried to club me with the hilt."

"Aye, I've seen him use that trick myself."

"I leaped aside, but the weight of his sword and his own momentum carried him into my blade, whereupon he stumbled and fell off the jetty into the deep water there, still clutching the sword. With its added weight, he sank too fast for me to catch him, and he never came up again."

MacDonald shook his head. "I'm thinking it was only by God's will that you survived the initial ambush. Twenty men, you say? Against just you two."

Lachlan nodded. "As you know, sir, Hector alone is worth three men-at-arms in battle, and I did little more than talk for the short time we had to hold them at bay before our men could engage them. When Mackinnon's men saw ours, they were ready to lay down their arms, but he ordered them to fight to the death. I'm sorry he is dead at my hand, sir, but at least he is powerless now to harm you or yours."

If MacDonald felt distress over Mackinnon's death, he did not show it. Nor did Lachlan expect him to, the mild reaction being wholly in keeping with his understanding of MacDonald's character. The Lord of the Isles was a politician, even a statesman. He would want to assess his position and Clan Donald's before giving more thought to Mackinnon, let alone to his own feelings.

"We seem no longer to be sailing toward Ardtornish," he

said mildly as the galley picked up significant speed. "One of your men has taken the helm, sir."

"A necessary, precautionary measure, your grace," Lachlan said. "It is possible that Mackinnon made a secondary plan in case his first failed, as it has. Indeed, I think his clansmen will lose no time in declaring a blood feud, so the three of us must have a quiet talk about the future, somewhere other than Ardtornish."

Eight men of Gillean having persuaded the royal oarsmen to share their oars, the other eight were now climbing back into Mackinnon's longboat.

"What manner of talk had you in mind?" MacDonald asked, watching them.

"A private one, your grace, so that you, Hector, and I can decide how matters stand with us. MacDougall and these others can stand witness to some proposals we want to make that I believe will benefit us all if you agree."

The longboat, sail raised and one oarsman per oar, was pulling rapidly eastward ahead of them.

"Where have you decided to hold this discussion?" MacDonald asked.

"The fortress of Dunconnel strikes me as an excellent site."

"Faith, lad," exclaimed MacDougall, listening perforce to the exchange, "ye'll kill us all an ye try to land at Dunconnel in this storm that's blowing up."

"I admire Dunconnel, sir, and I know it well," Lachlan told him, watching two of his men set the galley's sail. "I know, too, that it stands presently unused with only a lad or two to man its beacon fire if needed. We'll land safely, I promise you, but the difficulties of landing will assure us the privacy to talk undisturbed."

With the wind behind them, the galley made excellent speed. Ahead, the longboat was nearly out of sight.

Lachlan saw MacDonald exchange a look with Mac-Dougall and knew both men were concerned for their safety, but he decided not to repeat his assurances. No harm would come to anyone aboard unless through some happenstance of nature or attack by a superior force, both of which were unlikely.

"Dunconnel has no harbor," MacDonald pointed out calmly.

"We have landed there many times since our boyhood, your grace. Hector and I know the safest approach, and my helmsman is excellent."

"Still—"

"I'll not deny that we may have some exciting moments if the wind picks up, but no harm will come to us. Moreover, I thought you would appreciate my choice."

"Why?"

"Because not only did our mutual forebear, Conal, King of Dalriada, build Dunconnel but a mere handful of men, such as ours, can defend it against a much larger force. 'Tis said that one man alone can lower the portcullis if he knows the trick, and once down, it can withstand an army. It seems the ideal place for us."

"In plain words," MacDonald said dryly, "you mean to hold me captive."

"As I said, sir, I mean to ensure that we risk no interruption. I likewise want us to be comfortable, and to that end, I have sent the longboat ahead with a few of my dependable followers to see to our arrangements. Since I know that your stores are being replenished everywhere now, I'm hoping they will find enough food to prepare a decent supper for us all."

"By my troth, lad, you seem to have thought of everything."

Lachlan hoped he had and knew Hector hoped the same. They had embarked upon a tricky business, in which a single mistake could mean their deaths. But the reward for success might be greater than even Hector suspected.

"Well, lass," Alasdair said to Mairi, "have ye lost your tongue?"

Her stomach churned at the sight of him. She had never been enamored of the idea of marrying this burly, smirking, younger version of her grandfather, but now, comparing him to Lachlan—and notwithstanding that gentleman's distressing ulterior motives—the very thought galled her.

Lacking Robert the Steward's sense of humor and a few other social graces, Alasdair simply stood watching her, waiting for her to reply.

"You should not startle people like that," she said sternly.

"Ah, but my beloved sister Margaret had no time to talk to me, lest she not be dressed in time for supper, and I found your conversation amusing."

"How much did you hear?"

"Only the bit when Elizabeth said you want to marry him, and when you said you *have* to marry Alasdair—oh, and the bit where she flung the pox my way. I own, I'm not certain from that brief exchange whether your problem lies in wanting to marry straightaway, and thus wondering if we shall ever become betrothed, or if I am the problem in and of myself."

"Well, you shall just have to keep wondering," Mairi

said, "for I do not mean to say one word to you on that subject. You might have sent a message, sir, warning us of your arrival. Indeed, you must have known that his grace's deer hunt was today. Why did you not stop at Craignure Bay?"

"Don't be stupid. I did send a message to his grace's high steward, and I did not want to hunt. I loathe grand occasions unless they are of my own devising."

"Well, your message must have gone astray, because when you did not come to Finlaggan and failed to join us for the hunt, we simply did not expect you."

He shrugged. "I went to John Og first."

Elizabeth still held her hand over her mouth, as if, Mairi thought, it had somehow stuck to her lips, but at these words, her demeanor altered radically. "Has the baby come? Oh, Alasdair, pray do not hold us in suspense!"

"Aye, it came. Neither John Og nor Freya would tell me what they mean to call it, though, for fear of fairy mischief or some such before the christening."

"But is it a boy?"

"Oh, aye, of course it is. Why would I care about the name, else? I hoped they'd name him for me."

Meeting Mairi's gaze, Elizabeth said, "Alasdair, do you *want* to marry?"

"Of course I do," he said. "All men should marry and produce bushels of children to carry on their name and look after them in their dotage."

"But do you want to marry Mairi?"

He shrugged. "Aye, certainly. She's turned out well, and her tocher will be impressive. However, my father had made no move to arrange it before now. Nor had yours, although that is about to change," he added with a straight look at Mairi. "Which makes me deduce that I must be the obstacle rather than the prize."

She knew better than to trust him with the truth, because Alasdair was sly. As a child, he had been the sort to collect information merely to use it to his own advantage, often to the detriment of others. She was glad, too, that Elizabeth made no move to go on to their room, because the great chamber was empty, the other women apparently having accompanied Lady Margaret to the inner one.

That realization made her wonder if Alasdair had even shown himself to her mother. It would be in keeping with his character for him to let the bevy of women walk right past him without saying a word to draw attention to himself. He would, she decided, have expected his sister to see him and exclaim or even shriek her surprise and delight at his arrival. Indeed, she could not imagine Lady Margaret behaving otherwise at seeing her youngest brother so unexpectedly. Yet there had been no sound at all to indicate such a discovery.

Instead, he had overheard Elizabeth's comments and Mairi's replies. Not for a moment would she assume that he spoke the truth about how little he had heard.

She tried to remember what they had said, but she could not. They had been speaking of Lachlan, but she was certain they had not mentioned his name. In any event, it would not do for Alasdair to suspect that Lachlan wanted to marry her or that she had become fond of the notion, particularly if, as she suspected, Alasdair had come to Ardtornish to tell MacDonald that Robert the Steward believed that the time was right at last to approach the Pope.

"Come," Alasdair said, grasping her arm. "I'll pour the two of us some wine from that fat jug yonder, and you can tell me all the gossip of his grace's court."

"You had better pour some for Elizabeth, too, sir. It would be improper for me to sit alone with you, sipping wine," Mairi said with a minatory look at her sister. She wished they could just snub him and leave, but she knew from unhappy experience that he would complain of any such rudeness to Lady Margaret.

She hoped MacDonald and Lachlan would return soon, because the less she had to deal with Alasdair on her own, the happier she would be. On the other hand, the last thing she wanted was for her father to agree now to betroth her to Alasdair.

With the wind at their back, the journey was swift, and the formidable rock fortress of Dunconnel loomed ahead little more than an hour later. The waves were higher than before, thunder rumbled distantly, and black clouds overhead dripped as if they were overfull and ripe for splitting.

"Ye're plain daft, lad," MacDougall growled. "Just look at that."

The sight ahead was awe inspiring, to be sure, for on the north, west, and south sides of the islet, sheer rock cliffs plunged several hundred feet straight into the sea. Lachlan's first thought was to agree with the older man, to wonder if they could land safely, or having landed, could ever get off again.

MacDonald caught his eye but said nothing. He, too, had been to Dunconnel many times and knew its secrets.

The helmsman ordered the sail lowered for more control as they swept around the north end to the shelter of its leeward side, where midway, the sheer walls opened into a pair of narrow, craggy inlets. Neither was easily navigable, and the wind had stirred up even the leeward-side water. It surged around them, and heavy seas broke in mountains of foam over the jagged rocks in the larger inlet, toward which they were heading. But the sturdy helmsman remained undeterred, taking them straight in and easing alongside the longboat, where it rode at anchor with a four-oared coble bobbing beside it.

"With permission, your grace," Lachlan said, signing to two of the larger oarsmen to descend into the coble, "you and I will go first."

At a second gesture, Hector and a third man-at-arms almost as large as he was steadied MacDonald as he swung his legs over the side of the royal galley, and then lowered him carefully to one oarsman in the coble as the other did his best to hold the smaller boat steady. Minutes later, with powerful strokes of the oars through the roiling water, the coble plunged into a narrow, sandy creek and beached hard on its pebbly shore. Two men that Lachlan had sent ahead stood waiting to assist MacDonald out of the coble.

"I suggest we not wait for the others, your grace," Lachlan said as he jumped ashore, accompanied by a loud roll of thunder. "They'll arrive soon enough, but the rain is coming down heavier, and I suspect we'll have lightning soon."

MacDonald nodded and led the way up a steep flight of rough-hewn steps to the castle's front door, while fierce winds tugged and pulled at them. As the huge door clanged to behind them, the wind's roar diminished.

The hall fire blazed brightly, and in the absence of wind, the place seemed welcoming. Lachlan said lightly, "Whilst we wait for the others, sir, perhaps you would like to show me the trick of that portcullis."

"I don't think so, lad. Not yet, at all events."

The winds raged around Ardtornish Castle, as if trying to blow it right off its promontory, and the rain had attacked with vengeance. By the time Mairi and Elizabeth had managed to excuse themselves from Alasdair Stewart's company, the need was so great to ready themselves for supper that it occurred to neither of them that MacDonald should have arrived home soon after they had.

They did not think of him until Lady Margaret entered the bedchamber to tell them she had ordered supper in the great chamber for the family and their most honored guests. Gillies would carry the food up from the kitchen in the new wing, rendering it unnecessary for anyone but servants and men-at-arms who would sleep in the great hall to venture out in the storm.

"But have you any idea what may be keeping your lord father so long?" she asked as she finished explaining her plan.

"Is he not here?" Mairi asked. "What of the others from Duart who were to follow us back?"

Lady Margaret shook her head. "The wind has grown dangerously strong," she said. "They say it blows straight through the Sound, making the water wild enough to toss galleys about like children's toys."

"Was Ranald with his grace?" Mairi asked, unable to remember.

"Nay, he came back in an earlier boat."

"I'm going to find him," Mairi said, snatching up her cloak. The air outside would be icy, and if she did not find him inside, she would have to go out.

Chapter 17

The storm struck with a fury that everyone enduring it would long remember, but nothing could have suited Lachlan's purpose better. While the wind howled around Dunconnel and heaving seas crashed below, no one could touch them or interfere. To his further satisfaction, his men had found plentiful stores of food and drink, and the meal they prepared, while simple, was sufficient and tasty.

They ate in the castle hall, which, along with the entrance chamber, occupied most of the second floor. After supper, Lachlan, MacDonald, and their companions lingered over wine and brogac at the table where they had eaten.

MacDuffie, as hereditary record keeper to the Lord of the Isles, carried a small leather bag with him everywhere, and kept it beside him on the bench now. MacDonald and Mac-Dougall sat with him, while Lochaber shared the bench on the other side of the table with Hector and Lachlan. The boatmen and the two lads who looked after Dunconnel ate at a second table.

Waited on throughout by his body servant, MacDonald looked as relaxed and comfortable as anyone in such an uncertain situation could look. Deciding the time had come to begin their discussion, Lachlan dismissed everyone to the floor below, except Hector and the three gentlemen who had accompanied MacDonald.

"What we want to discuss, sir," he said, pouring the six of them more brogac after the others had gone, "concerns the future of the Lordship. What happened today will surely stir more trouble, because unless we can think of a way to stop Mackinnon's kinsmen, they will declare a blood feud against Clan Gillean to avenge his death, regardless of its cause. You know that as well as we do."

"Aye," MacDonald agreed. "The Green Abbot's bound to demand one, and mayhap do worse things himself. He'll not sit quietly by, that one."

"No," Lachlan said. "We have all had a lucky escape from Mackinnon's scheming, for I believe he intended more perfidy once he had me out of the way. I fear that greed had overcome his good sense. What your grace needs, I'm thinking, is an absolutely loyal, trustworthy man to act as your second in command."

"Aye, sir," Hector said softly. "'Twould be a good thing, that." He had removed his battle-axe and other weapons to eat, and like MacDuffie with his leather satchel, had set the axe in its sling beside him. From time to time, idly, he stroked it with a finger or thumb. He was doing so now.

The stroking, as Lachlan knew well, was no more than habit formed over the years by a man who rarely let his great historical weapon out of his sight, but noting MacDougall's gaze riveted to the axe and MacDonald's drifting that way, he nearly cautioned Hector to mind what he was about.

The thought had no more than crossed his mind when MacDonald looked at him and said, "You suggest yourself as that alter ego, do you?"

Lachlan nodded. "I do, your grace, because I believe

such an arrangement would benefit us all, but the decision must naturally be yours."

"Exactly what do you propose?"

In another, less pragmatic leader, Lachlan would have suspected irony or at least a lack of sincerity in such a request. However, he knew the Lord of the Isles was not only practical but a realist and one, moreover, who had set aside his first wife to marry his second, in order to gain the benefits of Margaret Stewart's close connection to the Crown for the Lordship and Clan Donald. Thus, he believed that Mac-Donald would listen now and judge his plan on its merits.

"What we all want is to protect the Lordship from further strife and Clan Gillean from Mackinnon hostility," he said. "My proposal is to provide indisputable evidence that Clan Gillean enjoys your grace's favor, so any attack on us equals an attack on the Lordship of the Isles. Any of several acts might send such a message."

"Go on," MacDonald said, glancing at MacDougall, who frowned heavily.

"I believe, for example," Lachlan said, "that I could serve you well as High Admiral of the Isles and commander of your grace's armed forces."

"By God, lad," MacDougall exclaimed, "you aim too high."

MacDonald put a hand on his friend's arm. "Let him continue."

"Thank you, sir. I realize that I must seem presumptuous, but with me in command, your grace need never worry about routine military matters. Lord Ranald and Lord Godfrey are fine leaders, as we know, but they cannot be everywhere. They'd each still answer only to you, but with my vast network of political, social, and military intelligence, plus the loyal cooperation of nearly every Islesmen that would follow your grace's endorsement of me, I can promise that your men will always be well armed, well equipped, and well led, and your ships well manned and seaworthy. Your Council of the Isles would then be free to deal with broader questions of policy and strategy that often now you must set aside to deal with time-consuming, less important details."

Silence followed, but he did not attempt to break it, knowing that all four men were thinking over his words. He did not care what MacDougall, MacDuffie, or old Cameron thought, however. MacDonald was the only one who counted.

Outside the storm raged, flashing lightning and booming thunder, pounding against the stout stone walls as if wind, fire, and sound would devour them. Inside, silence reigned a few moments longer, and Hector continued to finger Lady Axe.

At last, MacDonald nodded and said, "Such an arrangement could provide a number of benefits."

"Aye, it could," Cameron of Lochaber said, his words measured, his aged brow heavily creased. "I'm thinking, though, that we may yet hear more than one version o' what took place on the wharf at Craignure Bay."

MacDougall nodded, seemed to catch himself, and then glanced at Hector before shifting his gaze with visible reluctance to Lachlan. "Dinna take offense, lad," he said. "'Tis no so much doubting your word as wondering how others will look on such a demand coming so speedily upon Mackinnon's startling demise."

"Taking offense would do naught to persuade you that my word is good, sir," Lachlan admitted. "But I'd remind you that we can produce witnesses, including at least five Mackinnon men who survived the battle."

Hector said with an edge to his voice, "One may have more to tell us than mere details of today's battle, your grace, because two of them testified against Ian Burk at Finlaggan. Only one survived, but I'm thinking, though I've no proof yet, that he may be able to tell us more about Elma MacCoun's murder."

"Faith," MacDonald exclaimed, "can you honestly think Niall Mackinnon had aught to do with that tragedy? She fell."

"What I'm thinking, sir, is that the prisoner, being one who laid information against a man who afterward proved innocent, may have more yet to tell us."

"Aye, well, we'll see then. Niall was an honorable man, and loyal for many years. Still, when we were younger, he did have a fond eye for beauty," he added thoughtfully. "He may have indulged it again after his wife's death. I saw no more than a glint in his eye, mind, but we'll question that prisoner of yours thoroughly."

Hector said, "I doubt that any of the men there today would dare lie to you about what happened, your grace."

"They would not be the first if they did," MacDonald said with what might have been a twinkle of humor. He turned to Lachlan, adding, "Such matters aside, I own that I find your argument persuasive. Naught can be gained by a blood feud between Macleans and Mackinnons, and much may well be lost."

"I was certain that a man of your vision would quickly grasp the advantages of my proposal once I had explained it, sir," Lachlan said. "'Tis plain that to be secure, the Lordship must be well and faithfully served."

"I agree with that," MacDonald said with perhaps the slightest touch of irony. "May I take it then that you have naught else to demand from me?"

MacDonald's three companions seemed to stop breathing as they awaited Lachlan's answer. This time the hitherto silent MacDuffie glanced at Hector, but that gentleman's elbows were planted on the table, his chin resting on one fist.

Taking a deep breath and exhaling, Lachlan said, "I do want to discuss one other matter with you, your grace, a matter that is more important to me than any question of high position. Nevertheless, 'tis a proposal that if put into action would send the strongest message possible of your confidence in me and mine."

"I see," MacDonald said. "I believe I can guess what that is."

"You need not guess, sir. I want the lady Mairi's hand in marriage. She loves me, and I own that I care for her more strongly than I had thought it possible for any man to care for a woman."

"So it is love between you now, is it?"

"I believe my feelings for her are as strong, if not stronger than yours for the lady Margaret when you offered for her," Lachlan said. "And, too, such a union would strengthen the bonds of our kinship, a point always counted to the good."

The glint in MacDonald's eyes was sardonic now, as if perhaps he recalled feelings other than love when he had set one wife aside for the other, but he said only, "If my daughter still desires such a marriage, I'll not withhold my consent."

Lachlan stood, picked up the jug of brogac, and refilled each man's goblet to the brim. "I propose then that we drink to your grace's good health and future prosperity, as well as to that of your council and loyal allies, the sons of Gillean."

When every man had emptied his goblet, Hector filled them again, so it was fortunate that MacDonald's body servant entered not long afterward to replenish the fire, and remained to look after it and to keep their jugs and goblets full.

After a time, in a voice slurred with drink, MacDonald said, "By my troth, lad, I own that at the outset o' this business I expected ye t' demand the entire Lordship in return for our safety, what wi' such boldness as you've shown today, and wi' Hector the Ferocious thumbing that damned great axe o' his as he were."

Lachlan smiled. "Aye, sir, 'tis a bad habit Hector has, I'll agree."

"I suppose you'll be wanting our agreement writ down now."

"That must be as you wish, your grace, but I trust our witnesses, and yourself. I know you are all men of your word."

"Aye, and 'tis no as if there were land grants involved," MacDougall said.

Another silence fell before Lachlan said, "That must also be as your grace wishes, of course, but as you treasure your reputation for generosity, I am confident that you will not be sending your daughter into marriage empty-handed. Naturally, you will want to discuss settlements at some point, so if you like, I can save time by telling you now what heritable holdings would suit us best."

Old Cameron cleared his throat and looked toward the ceiling.

MacDonald glanced at him, but said in his usual calm way, "I am curious what they may be. Is it Ardtornish or Aros that you seek?"

"Nay, sir, I'd prefer Duart, an it please you. 'Tis a better location for your high admiral's seat, commanding as it does the Sound of Mull, the Firth of Lorn, and the entrance to

Loch Linnhe. Moreover, my lass is partial to the Isle of Mull, so Duart would please her well. However—"

"Aye, we did expect a 'however,'" Cameron interjected dryly.

"As I said," Lachlan went on equably, "receiving Duart as part of her tocher would much please her ladyship. If you should likewise wonder what would please me, it would be to gain hereditary title to the four Isles of the Sea, and to serve you as captain and constable of Dunconnel here."

"As a memento, doubtless, of the pleasant hours we have all spent here," MacDougall said with a grimace.

"Just so, sir," Lachlan agreed.

"And what of Hector the Ferocious? What wee memento would he like?"

Without missing a beat, Lachlan said, "Hector is likewise partial to the Isle of Mull, sir. I wager the hereditary rights to Lochbuie would please him well."

MacDonald listened to the exchange silently, and that silence reigned for minutes afterward, broken only by the crackling of the fire and the soft, padding steps of the body servant as he moved around the table to refill goblets again.

Lachlan let his gaze drift from one man to the other as he waited. MacDuffie had scarcely said a word since they had turned the royal galley around hours earlier, and although he glanced from time to time at Hector, the hereditary keeper of the records had remained calmly observant and nothing more.

MacDougall was drinking his wine, and Cameron likewise showed deep interest in his own goblet.

At last MacDonald said, "I am persuaded that we must do all we can to prevent a blood feud, and I am likewise persuaded that conferring favor on Clan Gillean will do much toward accomplishing that end. Therefore, and lest some mischance occur in getting off this wretched rock, or afterward, if MacDuffie has his quill and some ink, he can write down what we've agreed betwixt us, as is his duty, and I'll sign it and put my seal to it straightaway."

MacDuffie nodded, reached into the leather bag beside him, and extracted a sheet of vellum, a quill, a penknife, a ball of red wax, and an ink pot, all of which he laid out on the table before him.

"'Tis kind of your grace to do this," Lachlan said sincerely.

"Aye, well, I'll stand by the agreements I've made, but recall, lad, that the marriage banns, the marriage itself, and its tocher all depend on Mairi's agreement."

"She'll agree, your grace. I am as confident of that as I am of anything."

The storm was finally abating. At least, it seemed to Mairi that the wind did not howl as loudly or the new shutters over the upper windows of Ardtornish rattle as badly as they had earlier. Still, any trip to the garderobe proved an icy penance.

She had found Ranald unsympathetic to her concerns.

"His grace is no fool," he told her. "Niall has not returned either. Do you think they both lack the sense to go ashore when the water grows too rough for safety? I warrant the winds rose quicker and struck harder on the south side of the Sound than here, and they decided to spend the night safely at Duart. Wherever they are, we'll find them after the storm has blown itself out and not before."

"Then we must prepare to leave at first light," she said firmly.

"We'll leave after we've set men to preparing that venison for roasting, and all else required for his grace's Paschal feast. He'd not thank us for doing aught else before we see to that, lass, and well do you know it. Moreover, with Alasdair Stewart here, 'tis your duty to play the gracious hostess."

"You and Elizabeth can see to those preparations," Mairi said. "As to Alasdair, I care not what manner of hostess he thinks me. I am going to order a longboat now to set out in the morning as soon as we can see."

"And where d'ye propose to go, lass?"

"To Duart, of course, since you are so certain his grace is there." She turned and walked away, lest he realize that it was not his grace but a more arrogant, more infuriating man, with a pair of twinkling blue eyes, that drew her to Duart Castle.

Supper might have been as merry a meal as any they had had since arriving at Ardtornish had it not been for the absence of MacDonald, Niall, and the sons of Gillean. Nearly everyone speculated as to their whereabouts, with most comfortably deciding that they had simply sought shelter from the storm.

But Mairi could not shake her uneasiness, nor could she discuss it with anyone else, because she did not understand it herself. Strong winds would frighten neither Maclean. Nor would an oncoming storm have terrified her father or Niall. Yet, whatever had happened had sufficed to delay all four, and all their oarsmen.

Her discomfort increased when she discovered that some but not all of the gillies who had accompanied Niall had returned. Questioned, one man said Niall had sent them to Duart in the longboat from the castle that came to collect the trestle tables and other items, and they had come on to Ardtornish from Duart.

"Faith, my lady, but we were gone from Craignure long afore the hunting party. 'Twas considerable work cleaning and putting away the things at Duart."

"But did you not see the high steward or his grace there?"

"Why should we? 'Twas all we could do to get our long-boat out o' Duart Bay and home again without the winds blowing us backward to Oban instead."

He was vague about times, and she could not be certain that he ought to have seen her father's party or Niall's at Duart, if they had indeed taken shelter there, or to have met their boats at any time. More frustrated than ever, she paid no heed to conversations going on around her until a feminine shriek snapped her out of her reveries and she looked up to see Alasdair Stewart stumble toward the fireplace.

Stunned, everyone watched as, apparently, albeit awkwardly, he pitched headfirst toward the fire, until Ranald lunged forward and caught an arm. But even his strong grip was not enough to prevent Alasdair's collapse in a heap at his feet.

Ranald's demeanor as he knelt beside Alasdair told Mairi that the latter was not the worse for drink. Rising, she motioned a gillie to her side and said urgently, "Fetch Agnes Beton. Tell her a guest is ill and to come at once."

"Aye, mistress," he said, running to obey.

Moving to Ranald's side, she said, "What's wrong with him?"

Ranald looked up, frowning. "He said only one word."

"What?"

"Poison."

"Mercy!" She looked at the bench where Alasdair had been sitting moments before, certain he had been drinking from a silver goblet, but she saw none there.

As her gaze swept the crowded room, she noted a number of gillies pouring wine or ale into outstretched goblets or mugs but no one presently carrying trays away. Moving nearer the bench where Alasdair had sat, she said casually to a nearby woman, "I thought him ape drunk, but I see he was not drinking."

The woman looked surprised. "Oh, but he was, my lady. He set his goblet on the floor before he stood up. A servant must have taken it, but 'tis plain he won't need it again tonight. Men never seem able to stop before they keel over."

Seeking out an older gillie who had loyally served Mac-Donald for years, Mairi said quietly, "Gabriel, pray discover who took Lord Alasdair's goblet away, and do not let him leave the castle. Lord Ranald will want to speak with him."

"I know who it must have been, mistress, for I've seen only one man leave since. I'll find him and keep him in the kitchen until my lord sends for him."

Agnes Beton approached then. "What is it, mistress? Who ha' fallen ill?"

"Lord Alasdair, Agnes. He lies yonder on the hearth by Lord Ranald."

"Aye, I see him. Be he sick or the worse for drink?"

"He said poison."

"Och, then the devil be amongst us! Ask Lord Ranald t' ha' a few lads carry him to a bedchamber, and I'll boil up me cleansing toddy. The man looks stout enough t' hold his own through the night, so God willing, we'll ha' the devil out o' him and himself hail again by morning—unless he dies, o' course."

Hardly reassured by these words but knowing the herb woman was highly skilled, Mairi went with her to Ranald, and when they had seen Alasdair borne off with Agnes in charge, she told her brother about the missing goblet.

He said, "That was fast thinking, lass, to look for such a thing."

"Gabriel said he knows who must have taken it away," she said. "He will keep him in the kitchen until you send for him."

"I'll go there now," Ranald said, turning away on the words.

Without bothering to ask permission, Mairi went with him.

In the kitchen, they found Gabriel standing guard over a quivering young gillie. "This be the lad, my lord."

"I didna ken it would kill him," the lad exclaimed. "'Twere just t' make him drunk, is all."

"What devil possessed you to put anything in any guest's drink?" Ranald demanded. "Who gave you such an order?"

"Why, 'twas his grace's order," the gillie said, eyes wide with fear. "I swear t' ye, m'lord, I'd no ha' put the powder in yon goblet had he no said I should."

Shocked to her bones, Mairi stared at him in disbelief. Realizing Ranald was just as stunned, she said, "Did his grace give this order himself—and the powder?"

"Nay, my lady," the lad said, visibly surprised. "His grace doesna speak t' the likes o' me. 'Tis rare that Niall Mackinnon does, but 'twas him give me them powders, and all here ken fine that when he speaks, he does speak for his grace."

Able to think of no argument to contradict that, she left the man for Ranald to deal with and went to her chamber to think. Her thoughts were no clearer an hour later, however, when Meg came to help her prepare for bed.

She could not imagine MacDonald conspiring to poison Alasdair when it was his idea that she marry him. Nor could she imagine Niall, whom she had known all her life, doing such a thing. Focusing on the puzzle was hard, though, when her thoughts kept shifting to Lachlan and the unsettling puzzle of his whereabouts.

At last, reminding herself that she could accomplish no good with pointless worry and some at least by resting before she set off for Duart, she rolled to the inside of the bed, because Elizabeth had not yet come in, and soon fell asleep.

She did not stir when Elizabeth got into bed or disturb her when she arose before dawn to dress in the warm clothing that Meg had laid out for her the night before. After dealing as best she could with laces and ties, she plaited her hair as she did when she rode early, put on her crimson cloak, and went down to the kitchen.

There she collected bread and a slice of roast lamb from a smiling cook's lad, and took the food with her, munching as she went down to the wharf, where the longboat she had ordered the evening before awaited her.

The frost-ridden air served as a reminder that winter still had a few ice arrows left in its quiver. The wind had died to a normal sea breeze and stars twinkled overhead, albeit in patches between dark clouds hurrying east as if to catch up with the departing storm.

The oarsmen were at their benches, and the helmsman greeted her respectfully as he assisted her aboard.

"We go to Duart," she said quietly.

"Aye, my lady, and swiftly too, I'm thinking, for the tide be still on its flow and running fast from the west, like yon breeze."

His prediction proved true, and twenty minutes later, as the sun rose into a clearing sky, the longboat slid into its place near two others at the Duart landing.

Mairi hurried up the hill and across the forecourt to the castle entrance. The great door swung wide at her approach, the guards having recognized the black-ship banner on her longboat, and Mairi as well. Greeting the constable of the castle as he strode forward to meet her, she said urgently, "My father, his grace, is he here?"

"Nay, my lady," the man said, clearly astonished at the question. "We've none here save Dougald MacHenry, his lady, and our own lads now."

Reading meaning in the way he phrased his words, she said, "Now?"

"We did ha' more visitors yesterday, wi' his grace's hunt, and all."

"Who came yestereve?"

"Why, only them bringing horses, my lady, and Mackinnon's lads returning trestles and such. But they stayed only long enough t' put everything away."

"So you have not seen Niall Mackinnon either?"

"Nay, my lady." He chewed his lower lip.

"What are you not telling me?" she demanded fiercely. "Come, I want to know!" Only long years of her mother's training kept her from stamping a foot.

The man swallowed hard before he said, "I doubt it be true, m'lady, but a lad did say a fight blew up at Craignure, that men attacked Mackinnon's men . . . or mayhap 'twas Mackinnons attacked them. He also said Niall fell dead o' his wounds, but I've heard nowt more o' that, so I put little store by anything the rascal said."

Mairi frowned. The tale sounded unlikely. Niall disliked the sons of Gillean, but surely he would never attack them. Then, memory of the gillie's assertion that Niall had provided the poison in Alasdair's drink set her thoughts racing again.

"Call out your oarsmen," she commanded. "Your galleys will go with me."

The last day of Lent had dawned fair, and although the seas at Dunconnel remained high and unsettled, the wind had died to a respectable level. Lachlan breathed deeply of the fresh air as he stood nursing a headache in the tower's great open doorway and tried to discover the trick of its iron-spiked oak portcullis.

As far as he could tell, it was like any other such device. One released its massive weight by knocking away a wedge or ratchet in the chamber above, freeing the windlass or winding drum used to raise it on a system of pulleys, chains, and ropes. Thus, in effect, one man could lower it quickly if alerted to do so, but any such windlass or drum required at least two men to raise the portcullis. From what he had long heard, Dunconnel's portcullis included more capabilities than that, but as yet, he had discovered nothing to suggest what they might be.

Below in the steep-sided, craggy inlet, the royal galley and longboat rocked, looking like bits of food floating in a monster's toothy mouth.

They had all slept late, and no one had shown much interest in breakfast.

Lachlan hoped the clean salty air would chase his headache away but knew from sad experience that it would linger. He was in better shape than his overnight guests, but only Hector felt well, for he rarely drank heavily.

Lachlan had drunk more than his usual allowance to keep the others drinking, knowing that he'd sleep better if they were comatose with brogac.

MacDougall winced as he stepped into the sunlight, but

MacDonald only squinted a little. He held a roll of vellum with his ship seal on it in red wax.

"Here you are, lad," he said, handing it to Lachlan. "Mac-Duffie finished it before he slept, and I signed and sealed it this morning."

"Thank you, sir."

"Don't you mean to read it?"

"I've no need, sir. I know it says exactly what you said it would."

MacDonald nodded and led the way down the rock steps to the inlet. The tide was in, and waves hitting the rocks spilled foam across their ridged tops, but oarsmen held the coble ready to launch into the creek where they had beached the night before. Lachlan signed to MacDuffie and Mac-Dougall to go first.

Handing Hector the vellum roll, he said, "You go with old Cameron and keep this safe. I'll come last with his grace to prevent any foolish notions."

Hector nodded and tucked the roll into his jerkin. Mac-Donald, in his usual placid manner, merely nodded when Lachlan said they would go last. As they were rowed into the choppy inlet, he wished again that he had not drunk so much, but he was pleased otherwise and looked forward to seeing his lass again.

As it happened, he saw her sooner than expected, because as their boat rounded Duart Point into the Sound, they all recognized the little black ship on the banners of the three longboats heading toward them. Their lone, dark-haired passenger stood in the bow of the lead boat in her crimson cloak, waving madly.

MacDonald grinned. "Evidently, at least one person was concerned enough about our absence to begin a search," he said.

Lachlan chuckled. "I doubt she is the only searcher, your grace, for if she has not turned out your sons and every other man at Ardtornish and Duart to look for us, I'll own myself astonished. She must be relieved to find us both safe."

"Perhaps, lad, perhaps," MacDonald said, gazing fondly at his daughter, now standing on the forward bench, gripping the boat's gunwale near its high prow.

As her boat bumped against the royal galley, Lachlan jumped to a rower's bench and held out a hand to her. Accepting it, she stepped up into the galley but flung herself at her father, standing now to greet her, and hugged him fiercely.

"Where have you been?" she demanded. "Ranald thought Duart, but when I did not find you there, I feared something terrible had happened to you."

"Nothing so dire, my dear," MacDonald said in his easy way. "'Tis merely that your admiring suitor here killed Niall, abducted the four of us, and carried us off to Dunconnel to resolve a small problem that Niall's death will likely present."

"Abducted you!" She stood beside MacDonald looking up at Lachlan, who still stood on the rower's bench but was no longer smiling. "Is that true?"

"Aye, in a manner of speaking," he admitted, balancing easily in the rocking boat. "In a manner of speaking 'tis also true about Mackinnon, too, but we bring good news too, lass. Your father has agreed to our marriage."

"Has he, indeed?" She looked grimly to MacDonald for confirmation.

"Only if you agree to it," he said.

"I see, and what then of Alasdair Stewart?"

Smiling again, Lachlan said, "Since the stupid fool has

not furthered his claim or even presented himself, we need not consider him."

"If you think that, you are wrong on both counts," she said. "That 'stupid fool' is at Ardtornish now, and certainly means to further his claim. Moreover, if you think for one minute that I would accept the hand of a man who has shown such disrespect as to abduct his liege lord and kill his high steward, merely to further his own selfish aims to gain wealth and power—"

"Now, wait just a—"

"No, you wait," she interjected. "Alasdair has at least been frank about his reason for wanting me. He said outright that my birthright as a daughter of the Lord of the Isles makes me worth it. I know well that your reasons are the same, for I've heard you admit as much. No," she added, raising a hand as he opened his mouth to object. "Do not say a word, not yet."

Turning to Hector, she said, "You, sir, have never given me cause to think you would lie to me, and I believe you know your brother's mind as well as he knows it himself. Can you say to me, honestly, that I am wrong in my assessment?"

Hesitating, Hector looked at Lachlan, who grimaced, knowing exactly what Hector thought, and cursing himself for having never denied it. He knew, too, however, that to do so now would avail him nothing.

Evidently, Hector's look said enough, because Mairi nodded and turned back to Lachlan, saying, "You are no better than Alasdair, sir. Indeed, you are worse."

"Now, lass," he said, bending toward her, unable to keep silent despite knowing any protest would be futile. He'd have done better to hold his tongue, though, for no sooner were the words out than she slapped both hands against his shoulders, snapped, "Don't you 'now, lass,' me," and shoved hard.

Had he simply sat, he might have saved himself. Instead, he tried to regain his balance by straightening, and the rocking boat betrayed him. He stumbled, caught a foot against the bench, a thigh against the gunwale, and plunged between galley and longboat into the icy water of the Sound.

As it closed over him, shouts of his brother's laughter rang in his ears.

His first, barely sensible thought was that at least he had had the foresight to entrust his precious document to Hector's safekeeping. His second, that his lass was going to pay dearly for her unfortunate burst of temper.

Chapter 18

Mairi stared at the empty bench where Lachlan had been hunkered down just moments before. Knowing his strength, she had not expected him to budge when she struck him, let alone to topple overboard.

With mixed emotions, she watched the nearest oarsman leap up and lower his oar to the water. Part of her feared for Lachlan's safety. Another part feared they would pull him back in before she could get away, and as the two emotions warred inside her, a third part retained a strong sense of outrage at what he had done.

The latter emotion was bracing, however, and without looking to see if he was safe, for she knew he would be, she glowered at Hector, still doubled up with laughter, tears streaming down his cheeks. "You may think it funny, sir," she snapped. "Indeed, I hope you laugh yourself to death, but you may tell that odious brother of yours that I'd accept Alasdair before I'd marry *him.*"

MacDonald put a calming hand on her arm, and much as impulse stirred her to shake it off angrily and stomp away, being on a boat limited such behavior, and the thought of tossing her father's gesture to the winds sent prickles up her spine.

She had never blatantly defied him and doubted that she would ever have the courage to do so.

Therefore, sternly repressing a strong desire to throw a childish tantrum, she said with immense dignity instead, "I pray that your grace will excuse me. Now that I know *you* are safe, I have duties at home to attend."

"Running away, lass?" MacDonald murmured dulcetly.

"Aye, sir, perhaps, but not out of fear, if that is what you are thinking."

He shook his head. "I know you do not fear him, certainly not aboard this boat. But do you not think you owe him an apology? Your behavior was unseemly."

"His was outrageous, sir. If I must apologize, I will do so later unless you insist that I do it now."

"Nay, child, I'll not insist, but if you are going, you'd do well to go quickly. I know of no man who could rise from an icy bath like that one in a good humor, and I'd as lief not have to call anyone to order over this business."

A quick glance revealing that men in her longboat were already helping Lachlan from the sea, she said, "Your grace, may I ask that your helmsman signal one of the other boats to collect me and take me home?"

With a wry smile, he nodded and signed to the helmsman, and moments later she was on her way back to Ardtornish. Arriving there, knowing Ranald and others still searched for MacDonald, she sent gillies to the parapets to light beacons that would be passed on to let them know his grace was safely home again. Then, not wanting to discuss marriage, men, or Niall's death with anyone, preferring instead to ride the fidgets out of her head, she strode to the barn in search of Ian.

Finding him brushing the gray mare, she said without

ceremony, "I want to ride, but you need not saddle her. Just put her bridle on and give me a leg up."

"Aye, sure, mistress. I heard ye found his grace and them safe and sound."

"We did."

Ian shot her a speculative look as he set down the curry brush and lifted the mare's bridle off a nearby hook.

Knowing she had sounded curt, she smiled wearily and said, "Forgive me. I'm talking as if I'd swallowed a thistle, and you have done naught to offend me."

"Ye've been that worried about his grace," Ian said sympathetically, "and doubtless about Lord Alasdair's illness and Niall Mackinnon's death, too."

"How did you hear about Niall?" she demanded. "I heard the rumor at Duart very early this morning but learned it was true only an hour ago."

He looked uncomfortable, "Och, well, it come t' me the same way as the other bits did, come t' that."

"What other bits?"

Looking more uncomfortable than ever, Ian said, "About Niall Mackinnon plotting t' kill Lachlan Lubanach and Hector Reaganach."

"What!"

Raising both hands defensively, Ian said, "I swear, mistress, I'd ha' told ye, but Lachlan Lubanach said I mustna say a word to anyone, especially yourself."

"Aye, well, of course he would not want you to trust such news to me," she said, not bothering to hide her fury at Lachlan's decision, once again, to handle things alone. "But pray explain to me, if you will, why he did not tell his grace."

"Faith, mistress, I'd guess 'twere 'cause the man didna believe it himself."

"So that is why you told me they might not ride with the hunt."

"Aye, for he did say they would take care, and since I had warned him that they'd threatened t' murder him, I thought—"

"I understand now what you thought," she said. But he had also reminded her that he had known of the threat, and Niall. "Who told you about Niall, Ian?"

He chewed his lower lip for a long moment, but when she merely waited, arms folded under her bosom, he said finally, "It were Ewan."

"Ewan Beton?"

"Aye. Said he heard them plotting but that they didna seem t' care that he heard. Said Shim had been kind t' him ever since he'd found Elma MacCoun's body after Shim told him he'd find salmon leaping at Loch Gruinart. Said it were Shim's regret at sending him there that made him friendlier than usual now, but Ewan couldna hear about murder without telling someone, so he told me."

A chill shot up Mairi's spine, and she uncrossed her arms, looked around the empty barn, and then leaned close to Ian to say in fierce undertone, "You are to say nothing to anyone else about such things, do you hear me?"

"Aye, mistress. I'd ha' said nowt t' ye did ye no command me."

"I know, Ian, and I know too that if Lord Ranald or Lord Godfrey should command you, or his grace, you will answer them, too. But heed me well, because 'twas Lachlan Lubanach who killed Mackinnon, and the Mackinnons must know all about it if Ewan told you. Doubtless, the Green Abbot will declare a blood feud against the sons of Gillean soon if he has not already done so. And if they should suspect that you had any hand in the matter, that you warned Lachlan . . ."

She paused and, seeing his face whiten, knew she need say no more.

"I'll take care, my lady," he said solemnly. "Will I put ye up now?"

She nodded, let him give her a leg up, and said, "I'm riding to the hilltop near the archery field to blow my fidgets away, so if anyone comes looking for me, tell them that, Ian." She had a second thought. "I'm thinking now that if you see Hector Reaganach, you should perhaps tell him about Ewan and Shim."

He nodded, and she rode out of the yard, past the castle, and up the hill. At the practice field, she paused, surveying the damage from the night's storm. Despite the shelter that the forest bounding three sides of the field provided, the wind had toppled butts and scattered hay everywhere, but it was nothing their men could not easily set to rights. That they had not done so yet merely indicated that everyone's thoughts were on the preparations for the next day's Paschal feast.

From the hilltop, she saw the royal galley approaching at last, followed by the other Duart boat and the longboat she had set out in early that morning. She could see Lachlan, too, hunched and doubtless shivering after his icy bath. Her father's words echoed in her mind, but she did not need the reminder to know that Lachlan would seek vengeance. The thought made her smile.

Tempted as she was to linger until she saw him looking for her—and she was sure he would—she knew Lady Margaret would expect her to heed their guests now that she had returned from her successful search. She would gallop to the end of the field and back, just far enough to exercise the mare and clear her own head.

Hector had given Lachlan his cloak, and having disdained the offer to set him down at Duart long enough to change, he sat wrapped in its voluminous folds, freezing and plotting revenge. She was furious with him, and believing what she did, she had good reason, false though that belief was. Doubtless MacDonald felt satisfaction in having explained things as he had, for he understood his daughter's nature, and had clearly known exactly how she would view his abduction.

Lachlan admitted—albeit only to himself—that he had behaved badly, but necessity had ruled at the time, and the result had been more than expected. MacDonald understood him if anyone did, because he would act in exactly the same way to gain a similar advantage for Clan Donald.

Lachlan had no regrets about what he had won. Nor did he doubt that in the end he would win all. She was angry, but he was certain that she loved him. She would not, in any case, marry Alasdair Stewart.

When the state galley eased up to the wharf, he realized that he could not have the scene he envisioned with her in wet clothing, and sought out Godfrey's body servant to beg dry clothes, Godfrey being the only man at Ardtornish of a size with him. His brother followed, and watched warily as Lachlan accepted leather breeks, a shirt, a quilted jerkin, and a dark cloak from the man.

Lachlan let Hector wait in silence, a small punishment for laughing.

Dismissing the servant abruptly, Hector said, "Art vexed with me, lad?"

"Only for laughing at me, but you'd do that any chance you get, so it does me no good to bark about it."

Hector grinned. "I ought to have told the lass you want her for herself."

"You could scarcely do that when you don't believe it."

"Still, it would have been the loyal thing to do, and would have saved you from a soaking." A half smile touched his lips at the memory.

Lachlan gave him a straight look. "Do not think you will ever please me by sacrificing your integrity to save my hide. Not with my lass, that is," he added, acknowledging that more than one situation might arise where he would not care if Hector lied through his teeth to save his hide, or Hector's own, for that matter.

Hector said evenly, "You do want that union because it will bind Clan Gillean closer to MacDonald and the King o' Scots, do you not?"

"Aye, I do," Lachlan said. "I'll not deny that."

"I'm thinking now, that's not the sole reason, though."

"No, nor even the primary one." He finished fastening the jerkin, flung the cloak over his shoulders, and headed for the door.

"You are going to find her."

"Aye."

"And what will you tell her?"

"Nothing," Lachlan said with a grin. "I'm going to wring the wee vixen's neck for pushing me into the Sound."

Mairi knew she was extending her ride for all the wrong reasons. She ought to have ridden to the far end of the field and back as she had promised herself she would, then returned to the castle to prepare for the midday meal. It might well have begun by now, but she knew he would come, and she wanted him to if only so she could tell him exactly what she thought of him for daring to abduct her father. Doubtless, he had extorted the marriage agreement out of MacDonald, too, and what that might mean in the end, she dared not think.

Moreover, she realized as she rode hard to the end of the field for the third time, she had not spared a thought for Alasdair. What would her father do when Alasdair said Robert the Steward was ready to arrange their betrothal and apply for papal dispensation? To her horror, she realized that she did not even know if Alasdair had survived the poison, but decided on the thought that had he died, the first person she had seen that day, in the kitchen, would surely have told her so.

Niall Mackinnon's countenance leaped to her mind's eye then, and another pang of guilt struck, stronger than she had felt for Alasdair. At least Alasdair was alive. Still, it was hard to imagine the stern but always watchful Niall gone. She continued to feel as if he would meet her at the door on her return, ask where she had been, and warn her not to keep her mother waiting.

Smiling sadly, she reined the mare's head toward home, only to find herself suddenly surrounded by men erupting from the forest. Although she shrieked like a banshee, they pulled her from the mare, tied something thick and dark over her head. Then one of them slung her over a shoulder and began to run with her.

"Stop," she cried, gasping at each bounce, "I'm Mairi of Isla!"

Someone muttered something, and her bearer halted and swung her down again, dumping her without ceremony onto her backside on the ground.

Anger stirred, and she readied herself to give full rein to her temper, but before she could speak or gather her wits, someone grabbed her head with two hands to control her struggling while someone else tied something tightly over her mouth that not only gagged her but nearly suffocated her in the process.

Frightened that the gag might really prevent her from breathing, she made no further protest when whoever it was hefted her to his shoulder again, relegating her energy instead to staying alive long enough to tell MacDonald what they had done so he could order all of them thrown off *Creag na Corp* to die on the rocks below.

Lachlan sought news of Mairi's whereabouts from the household servants, but when everyone he questioned said she had not returned from her search, he decided that she must have gone for a walk or a ride, and headed for the barn.

Finding Ian doing chores, he smiled and said, "I owe you my sincerest thanks, lad. Had you not warned me, I'd be dead now, and my brother as well."

Shyly, Ian said, "I'm that glad t' see ye, sir. 'Twas a devilish thing they'd planned, and no mistake. Hector Reaganach survived, too, then."

"Oh, aye, and I ken fine that you kept mum, as I bade you, because her ladyship certainly knew nothing about it." Seeing an alert look spring to the lad's eyes, he added casually, "I know well that had you told anyone, you'd have told her, and that you'd have to do so if she asked you to."

Ian hesitated, neither agreeing nor disagreeing, which

told Lachlan all he needed to know. "She has been here, has she not, and you did tell her."

"Aye, sir," he said with a sigh, "but only then. She were in a rare temper."

"Not with you."

Ian shrugged. "I'm no so sure o' that."

"Trust me, for 'tis myself who's vexed her ladyship, not you. Where is she?"

Nodding toward the hilltop, Ian said, "Yonder, at the practice field, though she said she'd stay only long enough t' clear her head. She's been gone now nigh onto an hour or more."

Lachlan chuckled. "Clear her head, indeed. She's waiting for me, knowing I'll seek her out, because she means to hand me *my* head in my lap, but we'll soon see about that. Have you a horse for me?"

"Aye, sir," Ian said, "and I'll bid ye good fortune, too. I'd no go seeking such trouble, myself, but if ye've a fondness for fratching . . ." He shook his head.

Grinning, Lachlan said, "Don't fear for me, lad. I'm looking forward to it."

But when he reached the grassy archery field, all he saw was Mairi's beautiful little gray mare, grazing contentedly.

In a heartbeat, his ardent anticipation plunged to cold dread.

Mairi had no idea what direction her captors traveled. At first, by their softly thudding footsteps, she deduced that they walked through the woods, but as most of Morvern was forested, she had no hint of their direction. She had noticed their clothing but only to note that they wore skins and kilted wraps, and were not men-at-arms. She had not noticed if they wore shoes or went barefoot.

Apparently, they had no horses, because they traveled a good distance afoot, and the man who carried her was clearly strong enough to do so without respite, although they moved at speed.

After what seemed hours but common sense told her was no more than thirty minutes, she heard a scraping sound and a rattle of pebbles, and the man carrying her shifted her as if he needed to balance her weight differently. It grew harder than ever to breathe, and her ribs and side hurt where they bumped against his shoulder. Every time she bounced, what little air she managed to inhale was knocked out of her, but she strove to stay calm, and breathed as well and as deeply as she could.

She knew that soon everyone would be looking for her. The mare would return to its stable since the men had not caught it. She knew they had tried to do so, for she had heard them, but surely had they succeeded, they would have slung her over its saddle rather than carry her.

Even if the mare did not return to the barn, men would soon be searching, for she had told Ian she would not be gone long. He would remember that and tell anyone who came looking for her. And if no one else did, Lachlan would, to wreak his vengeance on her for pushing him into the icy Sound.

The thought struck that he might be so angry he would not want even to talk to her. But that was unlikely, and in any event, her father and mother would soon wonder where she was and would begin a search. Ranald would return soon, too, if he had not already, because other castles would have relayed the beacon's signal quickly, as far west as Mingary and eastward to Dunstaffnage and Dunconnel.

Remembering that it had been nearly time for their midday meal when she left, she wondered if they would wait to search for her until after they had eaten. She had decided she was being foolish to worry about things she could not control when she heard water lapping on the shore.

Until then the men had not spoken beyond the muttering as they had gagged her, but someone said now, "I'll hand her t' ye when ye're in the boat."

She wished the speaker had mentioned a name. Names were important, because when she told his grace—

That thought ended abruptly when the man carrying her suddenly swung her outward, away from his body. For a startled moment, she thought he was casting her into the sea, but then other hands grabbed her, and a moment later she was half sitting, half lying, awkwardly and uncomfortably, in the bottom of a boat with her back against the sharp edge of a bench or some such thing. When she tried to shift to a more comfortable position, a hand grabbed her shoulder, holding her still.

She wanted to protest that she was not being defiant or troublesome, that she was merely uncomfortable, but since she could not speak, she endured.

"Hector, I want you," Lachlan said curtly when he strode into the great hall and found his brother already standing at his place, conversing with friends as they awaited the arrival of MacDonald and his lady.

Excusing himself, Hector said as soon as they were beyond earshot, "You're in a lather. What's amiss?"

"Someone's taken my lass—Mackinnon's lot, most likely."

"How?"

Lachlan explained, adding, "I think she lingered up there

because she had more to say to me. She certainly knew I'd have something to say to her."

"Aye," Hector agreed. "But are you sure she's gone? Could she not be having a game with you?"

"Ian is certain she would not leave the mare loose even if she were up to mischief, because it wanders and she has never done such a thing before. Moreover, the ground at the far end of the field is churned up as if by a struggle."

"We'd best tell his grace."

"I'll do that, and we'll want Ranald, Godfrey, and their men out when they return, too. But while you wait for them, get word to our lads, as many as you can, to listen and watch. I looked for tracks but found none worth following, so we'll need horsemen, too, to seek them in Morvern, in case they went north."

"Morvern is not Mackinnon territory," Hector pointed out.

"Aye, so I'm thinking they may go that way to put us off the scent."

Hector nodded. "Fair enough. We should check all routes, in any event."

"Aye, so do you get started, and I will tell his grace."

When MacDonald and Lady Margaret entered the chamber, he met them at the door. "Forgive me, madam," he said with a swift but graceful bow, "I would speak briefly with his grace if I may."

"Certainly," she said.

He had hoped she would walk away, but she stood waiting patiently, and when he hesitated, MacDonald said, "What is it, lad?"

Without further ado, Lachlan said bluntly, "Lady Mairi has disappeared, your grace, and I believe the Mackinnons have taken her."

Lady Margaret gasped and gripped her lord's arm.

MacDonald patted her hand, saying in his calm way, "Rest easy, madam. No one will harm our lass. If someone has taken her, it can only be in hopes of forcing us to comply with some demand or other. We'll hear soon enough what they want. Meantime, I mean to eat my dinner. Sit with me, lad. We'll discuss this further."

Ruthlessly suppressing his compulsion for haste, Lachlan said, "Aye, sir, thank you." He could take action only when he knew what action to take. First, he needed more information, a direction at least, and therefore, until Hector and their people learned something useful, he could do no more than he had done.

His capacity for patience being small, it was as well that Hector joined them before the end of the meal. MacDonald, seeing him, motioned him to the head table and ordered a space cleared for him beside Lachlan.

Thanking him, Hector sat and began piling his trencher with food as he went on to say, "I've sent a boat to collect our prisoners in the hope that someone amongst them will know where they might have taken her," he said. "That will take hours, though, and I'm thinking we should not restrict our thinking to Mackinnons. Could someone else or some other happenstance not be responsible?"

MacDonald looked at Lachlan and raised a quizzical eyebrow.

"Anything is possible," Lachlan said, repressing impatience again. "But the plain fact is that she's been safe here until today. Even should we discover some other happenstance, I'd still believe the Mackinnons responsible. We know Fingon rarely heeds consequence, and since Niall cannot be behind it, I'll wager anything you like that the Green Abbot is."

"I agree," MacDonald said. "In troth, I know no other man bold enough to do such a thing—excepting present company," he added with a sardonic smile.

"Your grace," Lachlan said, "you have been kinder to me than I deserve, and I believe I must apologize—aye, and deeply—for my outrageous tactics earlier."

"Must you, indeed?"

"Aye, sir. The document notwithstanding, you have both the power and right to punish me for what I did, and to phrase the charges against me as you will. I beg only that you will let me see the lady Mairi safe before taking any such action."

"Have no fear, lad. I gave you my word, and I'll keep it. I'd have listened to your version of the incident in any event, but I know you had no reason to believe that your words could outweigh what Niall's kinsmen said. I'd known him most of my life, and the position to which I'd elevated him would make most men think as you did. My only concern now is to find Mairi, and as you now command my men-at-arms and my fleet, I expect you to do that, and right quickly, sir."

Hector said, "It may help to know that one man with whom I spoke said he'd heard a gillie here boast of possessing facts his grace would give much to know."

"You've sent for this braggart, I trust," Lachlan said.

"Our lads will tell us the minute they lay hands on him."

The message came a quarter hour later, and excusing themselves, Lachlan and Hector went to speak to the supposed witness. They found a lad awaiting them, clearly frightened, and since Hector still carried Lady Axe in her sling over his shoulder, and Lachlan's patience was strained taut, he knew the lad had cause.

"What is your name?" he demanded.

"Sym Love, an it please ye, laird."

"What do you know of Niall Mackinnon?"

"That he fell dead this very day, God save him."

"What else? Come now, we know you've bragged that you know much his grace would like to know. I am now his first in command, and have the power to order you put to death. Do you understand me?"

"Aye, but wi' respect, laird, how can that be?"

"I mean to wed the lady Mairi, and thus his grace has named me leader of his army and his navy. My position," he added grimly, "stands above even Lord Ranald and Lord Godfrey, so do not try my patience, because the lady Mairi is missing, and we suspect that you aided in her disappearance."

"Nay then, I wouldna do any such thing! I ha' served Clan Donald and his grace all me life, sir. I'd never touch her ladyship, nor let anyone else neither!"

"Then tell me what you do know."

"'Tis no so much," Sym said. "Nobbut that a cousin o' the high steward were saying Mackinnon might be Lord o' the Isles someday, did all go well, just as Robert the Steward will be King o' Scots. And when the cousin said Lady Mairi would marry the Steward's son, *our* steward said that union would never come t' pass, that if they had to wait much longer, Alasdair wouldna want her and his grace would marry her then t' the man he trusts above all others. Then the cousin laughed and said 'twould be gey fine t' ha' the Isles and the lass as well."

"But Niall Mackinnon is dead now," Lachlan reminded him grimly. "Can you think of any other man who schemes so against the Lord of the Isles?"

"Nay, laird." Sym shook his head.

"Can you think of any place that Mackinnon's men might take a hostage?"

Sym shrugged.

"What about the Green Abbot?"

Hesitating, furrowing his brow as if he were thinking deeply, Sym said at last, "Were the abbot party to an abduction, likely he'd take the lass to Holy Isle."

Lachlan looked at Hector.

Nodding, Hector said, "It is possible, I suppose. He would know every cave and closet, and none would say him nay."

Lachlan was still turning that thought over in his mind when Lady Elizabeth hurried into the chamber, clearly big with news. "I beg your pardon, sir," she said, casting a flirtatious eye at Hector as she spoke to Lachlan, "but a man has come to me, saying that he must speak with you urgently."

"Thank you, your ladyship. I'll see him at once," Lachlan said.

"I'll fetch him," she said, hurrying away. A moment later a man came in, pulling his forelock and bobbing so obsequiously that Lachlan thought anyone would forgive him for suspecting the fellow of being an Englishman.

"What is it?" he said more curtly than he had intended.

"Beg pardon, me lord, but 'tis for your ears alone."

"My brother stays," Lachlan said. "You may go, Sym, but don't go far," he warned. "You don't want to put Hector Reaganach to the trouble of looking for you."

Paling, Sym fled.

"Now what would you tell me?" Lachlan asked the newcomer.

"Please, sir, 'tis me cousin who would tell ye. I ken nowt, and I be feared for me life just a-coming t' ye."

"Where is your damned cousin then?"

"Across the Sound, sir, at Craignure. He says he kens fine where the Mackinnons ha' taken the lady, but he fears t' come here lest one of their men here recognize him and send him t' his Maker afore his time."

"Take me to him then."

"Wait," Hector said. "We should plan a little, I think."

"Nay, sir," the man protested. "He'll wait only the hour, he said, and then he's for England and safety. He'll watch from the bluff at Craignure, and he'll meet only wi' ye, Lachlan Lubanach. He said did ye bring anyone else up the hill, he'd no show himself, but do ye come t' him alone, he'll tell ye all ye need t' know."

"A trap," Hector said flatly.

"Nay!" the man exclaimed.

"Trap or not," Lachlan said, "it is the only news we have of her so far, and if it comes from across the Sound, he knows more than he ought to know. I'm going."

Chapter 19

Mairi could breathe again and see, but she knew no more than she had hours earlier, because she had seen nothing and her captors had said little during her journey. Although she was on solid ground again, she knew she might be on any isle, or even on the mainland of Argyll.

The vaulted cellar in which she found herself seemed familiar, but only insofar as it looked like any such cellar in any holding belonging to her father or any other laird. Great storage kists that doubtless contained items for the castle above lined one rough-cut stone wall, and looked well cared for. The area itself was clean and dry, which spoke well for the castle's management, but she could recall no vaulted cellar containing an iron cage such as the one she now inhabited.

Her captors had thrown thick furs on the beaten dirt floor to provide her with a place to rest, and she had her cloak to cover her. However, after the discomfort of her journey, her muscles ached and finding a comfortable position was impossible. They had also provided a jug of water, a manchet loaf, and the promise of hot food at suppertime. With little breakfast and no dinner, she was hungry, but she decided her anger and the bread would sustain her until someone brought more food.

She had seen but two faces, those of the man who had removed her gag and the one carrying a torch so that they could see. The first had murmured an apology for "distressing" her and said they meant her no harm, that indeed, great honor awaited her. The other had said nothing.

When she had informed them both tartly—and in a voice that, thanks to their gag, was much hoarser than she had expected—that everyone involved in her abduction would pay heavily for their impertinence, the one who had apologized tugged his lower lip and walked away. Clearly, he knew who she was, and just as clearly, he was sorry about participating in her abduction. But he was not sorry enough that she could persuade him to disobey his master, whoever that might be.

Left to herself in the dark, she managed to make herself comfortable enough to think by folding the blanket in which they had bundled her between her back and the bars of the cage, and prayed the cellar contained no rats. But thinking did not help. That the Green Abbot had speedily heard about Niall's death and meant to avenge it was likely. That he had heard about it so fast was easy to accept, given that the Holy Isle all but adjoined the Isle of Mull. But how, exactly, she could figure in any scheme of the abbot's, Mairi could not imagine.

Unless . . . The thought struck with icy certainty that the one thing Fingon Mackinnon might know as well as she did was that Lachlan would search until he found her. What if that, in itself, was the Green Abbot's plan? How better to entice the man who had killed his brother into a fatal trap than to bait it with the one thing he knew his prey would find irresistible?

Lachlan stood on the wharf at Craignure Bay and gazed speculatively at the bluff above. Anyone standing up there could see him and would see, too, if a single one of his oarsmen left his post. Moreover, any watcher atop the abandoned tower would see a second boat approaching, or even one landing anywhere near enough to get to the bluff soon enough to help him. The informant might be there as promised, alone, with the information he needed to rescue Mairi. Or the man might be luring him into ambush. The cliff-top site was perfect for either purpose.

For that matter, the man might not be there at all, might not exist.

Hector had employed every argument, and Lachlan knew that all he had said was true. He was a fool to have come. He was armed only with his sword, the dirk he carried in his boot top, and his wits. Neither of the steel weapons would avail him much against an army led by the Green Abbot, and as for his wits . . . Well, they might aid him but only if the other side allowed time for thinking. Indeed, as he acknowledged to himself if to no one else, if Fingon had sent only his four oldest sons to deal with him, they would be more than a match for him.

He was not accustomed to dealing alone with such problems. Hector had been beside him at every important point in their lives, always dependable, always reliable, always ready with Lady Axe to handle any situation. But this time Lachlan was on his own, and the thought that Mairi's life hung in the balance terrified him.

He studied the landscape again, noted that the sun was diving toward the western horizon with sufficient speed that dusk would cast its cloak over the landscape within two hours at most. It had turned into a fine, clear day, but now the black cloud of fear for Mairi darkened his world, making it hard to think.

"Master Hector were right, sir," his helmsman muttered.

"Aye," Lachlan agreed, adding, "I don't know what I'll find, and I've no way to get a message to you unless I can fling my dirk or sword off that bluff."

"They'll be for killing you, sir. An I see any weapons flying, I've me horn by me, a bit o' flint and tinder from Master Hector, and arrows t' set afire and let fly. Our lads do ha' boats yonder across the Sound and men watching."

"If Fingon's men are lying in wait up there and they see one man moving toward them," Lachlan said, still studying the heights, "my life will be sped."

"Dinna forget, ye left men there, too, t' keep watch for stray Mackinnons."

Lachlan nodded, knowing he meant to be helpful, but Mackinnons littered the Isle of Mull, too many for the few sons of Gillean scattered about to keep track of all. His loyal clansmen would do their best, but if Fingon had set a trap, he was about to spring it. Trap or not, it was the only hope he had of finding out quickly where they were keeping his lass.

Hector would do what he could afterward, for him or for Mairi, but Lachlan wanted to stay alive long enough to increase the odds in their favor. In any event, he knew that standing where he was would win him nothing but distrust.

Drawing a deep breath, he strode off the wharf and up the hill path.

At the top, he slanted a look in passing at the tower but saw no sign of occupation and left it at that, having nothing to gain by letting them see that he suspected more than they had promised.

At least the door at the bottom was shut, so he should have warning if they had to open it before ambushing him.

Ahead stretched the grassy clearing through which the track passed that led from Duart to the clearing where they had met for the hunt. Beyond lay forestland covering much of the isle. No one meeting him would expect him to enter the forest alone, because only a fool would do so in such a situation, particularly after they had abducted Mairi in just such a way.

Walking to the center of the clearing, he scanned the trees but saw no one. The forest was silent until a lone bird chirped and, a moment later, a squirrel's raucous chatter filled the air. Such complete silence had not fallen on his account, so someone waited, perhaps more than one, and at least one had moved a short time ago. The knowledge heightened his tension.

Surely whoever kept watch for his arrival must have known that he would check the tower, and would have feared, too, that he might somehow receive warning of anyone entering it. His ambushers, if they existed, would not have wanted to give him any reason not to come.

The watcher had likely been circumspect, perhaps crawling to the bluff's edge, then running back to the shelter of the trees at his approach—which told him no more than before. The watcher could still be informant or ambusher, or both.

It occurred to him then that he might never know the truth because a single arrow shot from the concealment of the forest might end his speculation forever.

His skin prickled at the thought, and he swore that when he did get his hands on the lass, he would soon teach her to take an army with her whenever she rode out, particularly with enemies so clearly at hand.

He nearly smiled as he imagined the likely result of issuing such an order to her. Even before his ducking, he had learned enough about her to know that although he still meant to call the tune after they married, it would behoove him to use as much tact as he used when he had key negotiations in hand.

If they ever married.

He could not let himself dwell on such misgivings, he knew, because a man who doubted himself defeated himself at the outset.

Another squirrel chattered long and loud to his left, and as his gaze shifted abruptly toward the sound, his hand flew to his sword hilt.

A shaggy-haired, barefoot man in a long saffron shirt and skins stepped from behind the thick, heavily gnarled trunk of an ancient oak. He stood and stared at Lachlan, saying nothing. He did not appear to be armed.

Lachlan motioned him nearer, but the man did not move.

The rutted track lay between them, because it curved along the bluff for another hundred yards before bending inland toward the river ford.

The squirrel had ceased its chattering, but Lachlan heard more birdsong now.

Deciding the man's wooden demeanor stemmed from wariness of him rather than anyone in the forest, Lachlan stepped nearer. No matter what lay hidden in the trees, the two of them could not converse sensibly or safely by shouting.

Crossing the track, his gaze scanning the forest, now on three sides of him, he moved within yards of the barefoot man, who still had not moved.

Knowing the man could easily hear him now, and leery of moving closer, Lachlan said, "Who are you?"

"That doesna concern ye, sir. I ha' the information ye seek."

"Speak then," Lachlan said, keeping half an eye on him while his gaze darted through the forest on both sides of him. Beams of golden, mote-strewn sunlight pierced the canopy, lighting bits of the forest floor. He saw no one, but he knew he could miss an army in the undergrowth, or in the leafy treetops, for that matter.

The man peered across the clearing behind Lachlan as if expecting someone, but whether Lachlan's reinforcements or his own, only God and the man knew.

"Damn it, have you something to say to me or not?" Lachlan demanded.

The man's eyes widened, and he opened his mouth, but that was the last thing Lachlan saw before pain exploded in his head and darkness enveloped him.

The cellar gave no hint of daylight, but Mairi's loaf was long gone and her stomach growled frequently and with increasing fervor before she heard footsteps approach. A key rattled in the lock, and the door creaked open. Expecting to see one of her captors bringing supper at long last, she saw instead what seemed to be three men clutched together, plus a fourth bearing the torch.

Its light hurt her eyes, but she discerned that two were supporting a third bundled much as she had been, and started to get up. Before her stiff limbs would obey her, the cage door opened and the bundled one tumbled to the floor in front of her and lay still.

The cage door shut with a clang, and one of them locked it again.

"Who is this, and where is the supper you promised me?" she demanded.

"Whist now," the man with the key muttered.

His companion stepped out and returned with a sack and jug in his hands. "Here be your supper, so dinna set up a screech," he said, handing sack and jug through the bars. "'Tis bread and meat, and wine for two, if himself feels like eating or drinking at all. Tell him it'll be his last meal. Mayhap he'll enjoy it more."

"But who is he?" she asked as they walked away.

The cellar door shut with a thud, and darkness fell again.

The figure on the floor moaned, shooting shivers up her spine.

Terrified that she already knew the answer to her question, she forgot her aches and felt her way to the figure on the floor. Her captors had not tied her, but the muscular figure she touched was definitely male and had bound him tightly in a rough woolen cloth. She fought to loosen the knots, wishing fiercely that she could see.

He was moaning more by the time she untied the first knot, but there were only two, and she soon parted the cloth over his head and gently felt his face. They had gagged him, too, the cloth tight at the corners of his mouth. They had likewise bound his wrists.

She attacked the knot at the back of his head, and at the cost of a few broken fingernails, the gag fell away at last. "Oh, please, say something," she said as she tackled the knot at his wrists. At least he was breathing, albeit stertorously.

"Thirsty," he muttered, the voice ragged, unrecognizable as his.

Blinking back tears, she dipped a portion of her hem into

the nearest jug, smelling wine as she used it to dampen his lips. A moment later she felt them suck the damp material. "Water if you have any, lass," he muttered. "I'm fair parched."

"Oh, my love, I knew it was you," she said, feeling cautiously about for the jug of water they had left with her earlier. Finding it, she held it carefully to his lips.

Before he drank, he murmured, "What did you call me?"

"Never mind. I feared you would not wake up. How badly are you hurt?"

He was drinking and did not answer until he had drunk his fill.

"I can't see a thing," he said then.

"They left no light," she said. "Doubtless that is all it is, but if they've injured you severely, I don't know what I'll do."

"Kiss me and make it better," he murmured.

"Oh!" She reached to shake him, but he protested instantly.

"Easy, lass. They've already given me a devilish headache."

"How?" she asked, leaving one hand gently on his shoulder.

"Bashed me with something, I expect."

"But who would dare to strike you?"

"Faith, I don't know. I never saw him. And I was careful, too, right up until I began paying more heed to my supposed informant than to what lay behind me. I realized my error, but by then it was too late. What happened to you?"

She told him, adding swiftly, "And don't scold or say I should not have gone up there alone. We have always been safe from the north, because all of Morvern is loyal to his grace. Indeed, I cannot think what these men can want with us, since they did not kill you outright. Whoever they are and whatever their plan, they must know they will infuriate my father by what they have done."

"The villain has to be Fingon Mackinnon," he said, trying to sit up.

His groans made it clear that he suffered for the attempt, so she said firmly, "Stay quiet until your head clears. I wish Agnes Beton were here, for I have nothing with me to ease your pain."

"I've a hard head," he said, apparently rubbing it and sitting anyway, since he added, "But they've put the devil of a knot on the back. I was unconscious for some time but came to when they put me in a boat. Not knowing their intentions, I thought it wise to keep still until I knew it was safe to speak."

"I, too, suspected Fingon," she admitted. "He has likely ordered a blood feud to avenge Niall's death, but abducting me makes no sense. It will anger my father."

"Aye," Lachlan agreed. "The risk of a feud is one reason I was able to persuade his grace to agree to our marriage, to show the Mackinnons that he favors Clan Gillean. I thought perhaps they'd abducted you to force my hand, to lure me to ambush, but if that was Fingon's purpose, why not kill me as soon as he had me? He would merely have been finishing what Niall tried to do yesterday."

"Aye, I know about that," she said. "Ian told me."

He grunted, gasped, and then said wryly, "Clearly I should *not* nod my head, especially since you cannot see me when I do. I do think you'll have to kiss it, lass, although I own, the best thing for me right now would be just to lie back down and hold you in my arms. Or are you still too vexed with me to allow that?"

"I thought *you'd* be furious with *me* for pushing you into the water," she said as she began feeling about to spread the furs on the floor.

"Nay," he said gently, adding, "Oh, I was for a time, but I expect I deserved it. I am curious about one thing, though. What made you think I care only for wealth and power? I'd swear you knew better than that at Finlaggan."

"I heard you say as much to Hector when you were coming out of the hall."

"I never said any such a thing."

"He said your plan to increase Clan Gillean's wealth and power any way you could was marching smoothly. *And* he still thought that when I pushed you in."

"He did think it, because I don't confide everything even to Hector, but he knows now that he was wrong, and so should you." Before she could reply, he added, "That's the second time you've heard things by listening at doors, my lass."

"It is my besetting sin," she admitted, smoothing the furs.

"Well, it is a dangerous one, and you should stop. Someone should have smacked you soundly for it when you were young."

"Niall did," she said, grimacing at the memory. "He turned up my skirts and spanked my bare backside so hard that I couldn't sit comfortably for a week."

"The devil he did! If he weren't dead already, I'd kill him for that."

Smiling, she said, "You just said that someone should have."

"Not him," he growled.

She sighed. "What demon possessed you to abduct my father?"

"I'm sorry for that, but was necessary."

"Necessary! How could it be when he is your liege lord?"

"I learned young to recognize necessity, and to act on it," he said. "I was nine when my mother died. She spoke often of hoping—for pretty clothes, for my father to pay heed to her—but she never acted on those hopes. I wanted to prevent a blood feud. I wanted you. So, I did what was necessary, then, and when they captured me."

"I'm glad you're here," she said impulsively. "I'd rather have seen you come through that door on your feet with Hector and his battle-axe beside you, and I am sorry they hurt you, but I'm not angry anymore." She folded the wool blanket to act as a pillow, and added, "You can lie down now, sir, on these furs, and I do want you to hold me. If we get cold, we can pull my cloak over us."

"I liked it better when you called me your love, sweetheart."

Tears pricked again at the thought that their time together might be short, and she did not try to reply.

When he had made himself as comfortable as he could, she lay down beside him with her head on his shoulder and sighed, instantly beginning to relax.

"Where's my kiss?" he demanded.

"You will have to collect that yourself," she said. "If you are not strong enough, then you will just ha—" The word ended in a half scream, half laugh as he reared up on an elbow and bent over her to claim his kiss.

His claiming was thorough, and he clearly intended to refresh his memory of her body, too, as his hands roamed freely over it.

She did not protest, however, because she had not known she could enjoy even a few minutes of such contentment in such a horrid place, and because with him at her side, she felt safe despite the danger she knew they faced.

His lips against hers, he murmured, "Do you know where we are?"

"No, for I've seen only this cellar. They bundled me in as they did you."

He kissed her again before he said, "Well, I think I know, for unless they've stupidly carried us to the Holy Isle, which his grace will search thoroughly and at once, I'll wager they've chosen the same place I did, for the same reason."

"When you abducted my father?"

"Aye," he said, adding pensively, "Although I don't know how they would have found such ease of entrance as we did."

"Where did you take him?"

"Dunconnel, the northernmost of the Isles of the Sea."

She thought for a moment. She knew Dunconnel, but she had visited the rock fortress there only twice in her life, the first time when she was small, and the second the previous year. She tried to recall if she had ever seen its cellar.

"I expect it could be Dunconnel," she said. "It has but one entrance, so its cellar must be entered from an inside stairway. Why did you choose it?"

"Because 'tis well known that his grace leaves only two or three men-at-arms to look after the place. Because of something clever about the portcullis he installed, two can easily hold off an army or navy from within its walls."

"Aye, that's true, for he told me so himself," she said.

His hands still explored her body, leaving paths of fire where they touched her. She wriggled against him. "Does your head still hurt?"

He chuckled. "Sweetheart, by the way it feels, it's going to ache for days."

"Oh," she said, disappointed.

He pulled her closer, kissing her neck and then her ear, setting nerves dancing in other parts of her body.

She stroked his hip, delighting in the rough texture of the leather breeks.

"You have a fine hand for untying knots," he murmured, nibbling her earlobe. "How would you like to untie one or two more?"

"Which ones?"

"The ones nearest your hand, below."

"Your breeks? Are you sure that . . . that it won't make your head ache more?"

When he only chuckled, she kissed him hard while her hand sought the lacing of his breeks. She untied the rawhide string on the left side of the flap and was reaching for the other when footsteps sounded outside the cellar door. Snatching her hand back, she sat up and scooted away from him.

"Coward," he murmured.

Then the door was open and torchlight spilled through the doorway.

A figure stood holding the torch high, blinding her with its light after the total darkness. She realized that it could not be one of the men-at-arms, because his long robe covered even his shoes. His hair reached his shoulders, but it was another moment before she could make out his features and be sure.

Lachlan recognized him at the same time. "So it *is* you," he said.

"Aye, curse ye, and so ye should ha' known," the Green Abbot said gruffly. "When ye touch one Mackinnon, ye touch us all, and ye'll pay with all in the end."

"If you mean to kill me, why did you not do so at once?"

"'Tis more fitting this way," Fingon said. "Ye'll see the

fruits o' your labor—see that God Almighty doesna favor the sons o' Gillean."

"You have captured only one of us," Lachlan pointed out.

"For now," Fingon said, "but I'm a patient man wi' plentiful resources."

"Do you mean to kill me, too?" Mairi demanded, annoyed despite the danger at being ignored by both men.

Fingon looked at her, his narrowed, glinting gaze sending slivers of ice through her veins. He waited, saying nothing, as if wanting her to say more. She did not, and at last, he said, "Ye disappoint me, lass. Ye're such a knowing one, yet ye dinna ken friend from enemy, and cast your favor t' them who deserve nowt."

She swallowed, uncertain of his meaning but fearing he must somehow know she had given her maidenhood to Lachlan. He had the power to excommunicate her for such a sin, and would doubtless go home to his concubine and his many progeny afterward without one pang of conscience to trouble him. He was a law unto himself.

"D'ye want t' confess your sins?" he demanded sarcastically.

"She has none to confess, and neither have I," Lachlan said.

"Aye, sure, ye both do," Fingon said. "I ken fine that she's given herself to ye, ye wicked man. God kens it, too, but in the end, her wretched sin willna matter."

"Why not?"

"Because she's t' wed wi' a Mackinnon. Her father will ha' to accept the man and grant him all the favors ye hoped t' gain for yourself and that upstart lot ye call Clan Gillean, wi' its made-up history and all."

Mairi winced, fearing Lachlan would respond angrily to defend the honor of Gillean, and anger their captor more.

But she had misjudged him, because he said calmly, "I should think that if MacDonald disapproves of the man who weds his daughter, or his manner of marrying her, he would flatly refuse to grant him either favor or wealth."

"He would soon rue his refusal," Fingon said.

"You would kill her?"

"Nay, for we're not barbarians like the sons o' Gillean, who kill for the love o' killing." He turned to Mairi and said with a sneer, "I expect this wicked man told ye he couldna help killing me brother Niall."

"He told me what happened," she said, matching her tone to Lachlan's.

"Aye, well, then he lied."

"What will you do with me if you don't mean to kill me?" she asked.

"I told ye, lass, ye'll marry a Mackinnon, and he'll keep ye close and teach ye no t' grant your favors t' any but himself."

"But if I have already given my favors to Lachlan Lubanach, what if he's gotten me with child?" she said daringly.

He shrugged. "If ye carry a bairn, the bairn will belong t' your husband, no to any son o' Gillean. And Lachlan the Wily can just go t' his grave wondering did he leave ye wi' a bairn who'll grow up t' be a good Mackinnon."

"I won't marry anyone else," she said flatly.

"Faith, d'ye think we're offering ye a choice? Ye'll marry when we say and whom we say, for I'm marrying ye to the man myself, and ye'll no be gainsaying the rightful Mitered Abbot o' the Holy Isle."

"Rightful, is it?" Lachlan said grimly. "At last account, his holiness, the Pope, still had not agreed that you are anything rightful, Fingon Mackinnon."

Mairi held her breath, but Fingon said, "I came only t' tell ye, ye should enjoy this next hour together, because it'll be the last one ever for one o' ye."

"Hour?" She nearly choked on the word.

"Aye, for we'll ha' the wedding at midnight, I'm thinking. No need t' wait longer, since ye'll no need a gown or bridesmaids and such. Moreover, 'twill leave the rest o' the night for your new husband to enjoy his wedding rights."

Lachlan said curiously, "Am I meant to attend this wedding, then?"

"Och, aye, for is that no why we've brought ye here? Ye'll be our most honored witness, because we'll want ye to gaze on the stern man who will enjoy your lass's submission whilst ye slave for the devil in hell."

"Then I'll have to enjoy what time I have left with her, I expect."

"Aye, sure, you do that, lad. If ye can perform, knowing what lies ahead o' ye, the devil will surely welcome ye as his own."

As he turned away and the torchlight fell briefly on a lanky figure behind him with fiery red hair, they realized for the first time that he had not come alone.

The door slammed to, and the two were gone.

"That was Shim MacVey," Mairi exclaimed. "I thought he stayed on Isla."

"I, too, but we knew he was a Mackinnon man. Mayhap he just came home."

"But he is the reason Ewan Beton went to Loch Gruinart the day he found Elma's body," Mairi said, telling him what Ian had told her. "How could Shim have known that the salmon were leaping there that day?" she added.

"They don't leap for long, so he must have been there

shortly before, and Elma's body was in plain sight on the sand. So why did he not find it?"

"Because he killed her himself?" she suggested.

"Or because someone who had expected her body to be found much sooner told him in hopes that he or some other innocent would go there and find her."

"Perhaps," she said, moving toward him, seeking comfort, but although he put an arm around her, he said, "Hush now. I must think."

"We *both* must think," she said.

"Aye, well, if you want to help, sweetheart, pray that I know the man who comes to take us to your wedding, for he may be our only hope."

"What do you mean to do?"

"I'll think of something, but it would help if the one that comes to fetch us is one of the two who were here when I brought your father, because I got friendly with both lads. I'm hoping we can persuade one to help us escape."

"More likely it will be Shim MacVey, but even if it is not, I do not see how one or two lads could do much against all of Fingon's men," she said, frowning.

"I can talk the feathers off a duck," he said. "So you just leave that to me."

"I wish you would stop saying that," she snapped. "I do have a brain, you know. I could help if you would let me. I don't know who was with you earlier or if we are even at Dunconnel, but I do know that one of the men who carried me down here seemed unhappy about my abduction."

"Excellent news," he said. "Now, if that man and my man are the same—"

"But if they are not—"

"We'll discuss it more then," he said soothingly. "In the

meantime, kiss me again. I should hate to think of dying and never tasting your kisses again."

"I do wish you will be serious," she said. "We should certainly have more than one string to our bow."

"Lass, if the hall here is swarming with Mackinnons, it won't matter how many strings we have to our bow, or arrows. But talking may still turn the tide."

"Your talking can only work if someone listens," she said fiercely. "A situation like this requires action. What we need is an army of our own."

"Aye, sure, but I'm it, sweetheart, and I'm not by nature a man of violence."

"You just killed a man yesterday," she reminded him.

"That was necessary." His arm tightened around her, and when her body leaped as it always did, she knew that with no control over what would come, she welcomed any diversion, but particularly the one he nearly always had in mind.

She sighed and nestled more comfortably against him, but if he had interest in more than cuddling, he did not show it. She wondered if perhaps Fingon was right and the thought of impending death inhibited him.

"You're a brave lass," he murmured sometime later, kissing her neck. "If we win free of this, your family will be proud."

"Never mind that," she said, not wanting to look so far ahead. "Just think harder, sir. I don't want to marry any Mackinnon, especially since I am sure Fingon means me to marry the worst of them, if only to teach me a lesson."

"Aye," he agreed. "That's likely."

She nearly snarled at him then, but the key in the lock stopped her.

Chapter 20 ────────────────────────────

The door opened to reveal two men, one in the open doorway and Shim MacVey standing behind him with the ubiquitous torch.

Lachlan leaned close to Mairi, saying quietly, "Keep MacVey busy as we go up and give me a chance to talk with the other. He is your father's man, I believe."

"Aye, 'tis Aidan Kean," she whispered, sure now that they were at Dunconnel and trying to recall all she knew about the place.

Lachlan said, "Good, then, if you know him—"

"I should be the one to talk to him."

"Nay, because—" He broke off, having time for no more, because Aidan Kean was unlocking the cage.

Grateful that Aidan's arrival had nipped the debate short, Mairi watched as Lachlan got to his feet, groaned suddenly, and grabbed his head with both hands.

"Are you sick?" she demanded, frightened. "What is it?"

"Not sick, just weak and a bit light in the head," he said, winking at her as he straightened. "Lad, can you lend me your arm? I doubt her ladyship can support my weight, and with all those steps—" He broke off, bending to put both hands on his knees as if to steady himself.

Mairi looked at Aidan, who seemed willing enough to help, but wary.

When he hesitated, Shim said harshly, using the torch to emphasize his words, "I'll see ye up them steps, ye villain, and ye'll keep your lips tight shut the while, for me master warned me ye'd talk a hawk off its limb did we give ye the chance. And lest ye think ye can talk me round, I'll just tell ye I've orders t' gag ye an ye try it. The lad can look after her ladyship."

With that, Mairi knew she was on her own and could think of only one thing that might improve the odds against them. With no idea what actions her father, brothers, or Hector Reaganach might have taken, she had small hope of success. Nonetheless, futile or not, she had to do what she could.

Shim ordered Lachlan out, then drew his sword to follow, saying, "I should bind your hands, but the master said 'twould gall ye more t' be free." Whacking him hard on the backside with the flat of his sword as he passed him, Shim added tauntingly, "Och, and if ye're thinking t' make a dash for it, ye should ken we've a host o' Mackinnons above, all hoping ye'll do summat t' speed your trip t' hell. An ye ask me, though, ye're no fit t' fight even a wee mouse."

Lachlan said nothing, and Shim followed close behind him, putting the burning torch in a bracket. Continuing his taunts as they went upstairs, he occasionally prodded Lachlan with his sword.

Grateful for the torchlight, Mairi let them go ahead as she bent to adjust her boot, certain that Aidan would not worry about her trying to escape, and trying to estimate how easily anything she said would carry up the stairway. Turning slightly, she said, "Do you know who I am, Aidan Kean?"

"Aye, my lady," the lad said, his voice trembling. "Ye be his grace's daughter, the lady Mairi."

She smiled. "I know your parents, too, Aidan. Your father is his grace's loyal vassal, and farms land in Knapdale. He would want you to help me."

"Aye, but what must I do? I'm sore afeard o' that lot abovestairs, mistress."

"Nothing dreadful, I promise you. Do you recall when Lady Marjory married two years ago?"

"Och, aye, mistress. Everyone does."

"Well, do you remember how they passed the word that she *had* married?"

He nodded. "The beacons. Folks lit them all over the Isles."

"I want you to light the beacon here, Aidan. Can you do that without telling any Mackinnons?"

"Aye, but they'll ken soon enough, choose how. And what if one catches me?"

"You can explain that it's no more than what you did for Lady Marjory, to celebrate her marriage, and you thought it right to do now. I swear I'll see that no one blames you, Aidan. If necessary, I'll tell them you did it at my command."

"Aye, then, my lady, I'll do it, and gladly."

The footsteps ahead had stopped, and she knew she should say no more. Although she could not be sure with a dim lad like Aidan if he had truly understood what she wanted him to do, she dared not linger.

"Scold me, Aidan. Tell me to hurry."

"Get along there now," he snapped.

Smiling at him, she picked up her skirt, turned, and hurried up the stairs.

Shim waited with Lachlan at the doorway to the anteroom between the great hall and the main entrance with its great iron-tipped portcullis.

"Sakes, but it took ye long enough," he said grimly.

He stood aside as Mairi entered the anteroom, and motioned her to precede them into the great hall. She glanced at Aidan, felt reassurance when he nodded, and then walked with dignity past the other two into the hall, hesitating only as she passed through the archway, when a memory stirred.

Some twenty men were in the hall, but two drew her attention, for they stood only a few feet away, beside the huge fireplace and its roaring fire.

Fingon Mackinnon faced her in his long robe. The other man, doubtless her intended bridegroom, stood with his back to her. Since Fingon had said she would be marrying a minor Mackinnon, she had expected to see someone in a common shirt and skins, or a belted plaid, but the man facing Fingon wore a moderate-length black robe over fashionable gray leggings.

As the thought crossed her mind that the figure was familiar, he turned.

Mairi gasped as Niall Mackinnon smiled and held out a hand, saying, "Come, lass. No need to look as if ye've seen a ghost. I'm no dead yet."

Lachlan, following Mairi into the hall, saw her stupefaction and knew he must look as stunned as she did.

"But I saw you die," he protested.

Niall's smile turned sardonic. "My holy brother would prefer you to believe a miracle spared my life—perhaps even one of his own performance—but whilst one certainly credits God for one's gifts and capabilities, what saved me was simple attention to detail."

"How?" Mairi asked before Lachlan could utter the flippant retort that had sprung to his lips.

Niall said, "'Twas a matter of knowledge gained through years of meticulous maintenance of Craignure wharf, my dear. Its supports consist of great stone pilings connected by some twenty feet of horizontal planks that protect boats from banging against the stones, and provide mooring even at the lowest tide. However, below the timbers, there is space enough between piers for one to swim under the wharf."

"Twenty feet down?" Mairi said skeptically, as well she might if a man actually had to swim down twenty feet and back up the same distance before breathing, Lachlan thought, realizing she had not reasoned the matter through.

Niall said, "You forget the tides, lass. When the tide is high, scant space exists between the water and the timbers atop the wharf. Indeed, extreme tides in the Sound have inundated that wharf. But the incident occurred at mid-tide on a normal ebb, you see, so I had only to wait until everyone had gone and trust that our attackers had left no watchers atop the tower."

"Attackers?" Lachlan said. "As I recall the matter—"

"Your recollections are of no interest to anyone," Niall snapped. "The only reason you are not gagged, sir, is that we want to hear your protests, so that all here can see you powerless."

Mairi said hastily, "How did you know when it was safe to swim out?"

Lachlan had suspected earlier and knew now that she feared he would anger the high steward into harming him, but he did not care if he did. He had to extend the proceedings as long as possible if they were to have the slightest hope of escape. To let her marry Niall Mackinnon was unthinkable, and if it cost him his life, he would find a way to prevent it. But Niall was explaining that he had been able to see through the narrow spaces between the wharf timbers.

"I nearly froze to death in that water, I can tell you," he said, "but I warrant 'twas the cold that stopped my wound's bleeding. I could see enough, at all events, to be sure my murderers had left no great body of men at Craignure, and I doubted they would risk one or two to the onslaught of my kinsmen that was bound to occur as soon as my brother learned of my supposed fate."

Mairi frowned. "So you just waited for Fingon to come fetch you?"

"Shim here was in the trees on the bluff, hoping for a clear bowshot. I knew he had seen what happened and, cut off from me as he was by men of Gillean, would find Fingon. And I knew Fingon would come at once, because he would not believe me dead unless he saw my body with his own eyes."

"Such explanations are tedious," Fingon complained. "Lachlan Lubanach has no need of them, and you can tell Lady Mairi later anything you want her to know."

A knot of fury in Lachlan's throat ached to explode, but he choked it back, knowing any reaction from him would only augment the Mackinnons' satisfaction.

However, Mairi did not conceal her feelings. "You cannot truly think I'll marry you," she exclaimed. "Why, you are as old as my father, and although I do know such marriages occur, one expects to gain great advantage from them. But neither side gains advantage here!"

"You will gain much," Niall said. "For one, I shall certainly prove a better guardian than your father. He's been far too indulgent."

As often as Lachlan had echoed that sentiment, he grated his teeth at hearing the words from Niall Mackinnon, especially knowing the villain had beaten the child Mairi at least once. His fists clenched, and a low growl escaped his lips.

Shim stood watchfully, his now-sheathed sword temptingly near, had the situation not been such as to guarantee death to anyone foolhardy enough to think a snatched sword might gain him the upper hand for more than a heartbeat.

Mairi had visibly struggled to ignore Niall's comment about her father's indulgent nature, but she said now, bitterly, "I suppose you pretend to love me."

"Don't be childish," Niall said. "Love is for peasants."

"But you cannot expect to gain wealth or power by this . . . this outrage!"

"That depends on circumstance, but whether I do or not matters not one whit. I have wanted you for years, my dear, since long before my wife died."

A startled look crossed her face. Then, grimly, she said, "Doubtless since the day you spanked me."

"Before then," he said with a reminiscent smile. "Still, when I turned up your skirts and saw those little pink cheeks and watched them redden under my hand as you screamed in fury, I knew I wanted the right to guide and correct you, always."

"To punish me, rather. Indeed, I warrant you are as much of a brute as Mellis MacCoun. Is that what drew you to Elma? Oh, yes," she went on when his eyes narrowed and his expression hardened, "I know you seduced her. She tended your chamber as part of her duties. She would have been easy game for you, I imagine."

"One might more accurately say the wench seduced me," Niall said testily.

"When a man wields such power over a woman's life as

you wielded over Elma's, no one can blame her if she complies to save her hide or her house. You could easily have rejected her, but she could rebuff you only at her peril. Did you kill her, Niall? Is that what lies in store for me if I disobey you?"

"Nay, then, I did not, and that's enough," he said sternly. "No longer will I allow you to give free rein to your temper, lass, so you'd do well to restrain it now."

Not much to Lachlan's surprise, Mairi scorned that advice.

"You have no right to command me, Niall Mackinnon," she declared. "I won't obey or submit to you unless you beat me into a stupor. Nor will you ever succeed in overthrowing my father. That *is* what you hope to do, is it not?"

Shim stepped closer to her, as if he expected her to strike his master. As he did, the hilt of his sword moved even more temptingly into range.

Niall began to speak, but she talked over him, snapping, "You are despicable, sir, the worst sort of traitor, because you pretended loyalty whilst you plotted murder and destruction. Even your so-called blood feud against Clan Gillean is a lie, because they committed no murder, as your presence here testifies plainly. Indeed, aided by this wicked, so-called holy brother of yours, you foisted a fraud onto your own kinsmen and stirred trouble by pretending to be dead. The Council of the Isles will make short shrift of any claim you make to martyrdom and shorter shrift if you try to claim the Lordship of the Isles."

"By God, I'll show you who is master!"

Niall's temper had snapped, but as he reached for Mairi, she ducked under his hand and turned away. As she did, Lachlan snatched the sword from Shim's sheath, knocked him aside with a blow worthy of Hector, and stepped between Niall and Mairi, sword at the ready.

"Try showing me who is master, Mackinnon. There is no hole hereabouts to dive into, none large enough, at all events, to accommodate a rat of your size."

Niall whipped out his own sword and faced him, shouting, "To me, lads!"

His attention riveted to the other man's eyes as the best indication of his first movements, Lachlan was aware nonetheless that the atmosphere in the chamber had changed. His skin prickled at the thought of the many swords doubtless drawn and aimed at him, but he detected no such motion in the men within view.

Fingon Mackinnon, rather than leaping to his brother's aid, stepped back out of the way, but if the holy man was armed, Lachlan had seen no sign of it.

"Dinna move again, or I'll spit ye where ye stand," a voice behind him said.

"And ye, your holiness, heed his words, for I've me own sword at your back."

The first command startled Lachlan, and had he not seen Niall's blade move, he might have turned. The second command came from in front of him, and as Niall lunged and he parried the stroke, he saw a man behind Fingon, evidently holding him at sword point, and keeping everyone else thus momentarily at bay.

"Aidan is behind you, sir, with his sword drawn," Mairi said quietly, "and the other is our man, too, but I think we should all leave as quickly as we can."

The observation seemed singularly foolish under the circumstances, and Mackinnon clearly agreed, for he said snidely, "Where do you think you will go, lass? I've only to shout and the portcullis will fall in a trice, and whilst I doubt your father's contention that it makes this place impregnable, I'm thinking 'twould take an army of axes a day to breech it."

"Aye, it would, but I'd feel safer in the antechamber than here," Mairi replied with an urgency in her voice that, despite the apparent foolishness of her words, gave Lachlan time to think.

Clearly determined to slay him instantly, Niall increased the pace of his blows, and for several minutes, it took Lachlan's full concentration and every ounce of his skill to defend himself. But the strength and fury of Niall's blows soon eased, because swords being the cumbersome, heavy weapons they were, even the best swordsmen could fight with such fever for only minutes at a time.

Recognizing that the older man's strength was waning, Lachlan began pressing him and said, "You'll not best me, Mackinnon. I am not even the best swordsman in Clan Gillean, and yet I had you beat on that wharf. That's why you dove into the water, you coward, pretending to be gravely injured."

Clearly energized by the taunt, Niall slashed his sword upward, nearly catching the back of Lachlan's hand where it gripped the sword.

"A clever stroke," Lachlan said, striving to speak without gasping. "But then you're a clever man as well as a coward. I warrant you ordered Elma MacCoun killed if you did not murder her yourself."

"I had naught to do with her death," Niall snapped. "I was at Finlaggan the whole time she was missing, as anyone can tell you."

"Aye, sure, but you sent your lad Shim here to kill her and then conspired with him to blame young Ian Burk."

"Aye, well, Shim may have killed Elma. He'd wanted her for years."

"Here now, what are ye saying?" Shim cried.

"'Tis true," Mackinnon said, stepping back. He was breathing hard, and made no attempt in that moment to fight, but Lachlan, though glad of the respite, kept his sword ready and his eyes on the other men.

They seemed spellbound by their chief's accusations.

"She led you on to believe you could have her, Shim," Mackinnon said insistently, regaining his wind. "Then she married Mellis, but still she played with you, teased you, right up until she offered herself to me. And for that you—"

"'Twas ye, ye villain! She were carrying your bairn, not mine," Shim cried, forgetting Aidan in his fury until the lad pricked him with his sword.

"Niall!" Mairi exclaimed. "Is that true? Did you get Elma with child?"

"More likely the bairn was Mellis's," he said, flashing his sword up again. "He would have accepted it, and so I told her, but she wanted me to support it and take her away from Mellis's fists. Still, 'twas Shim killed her, not I."

"Liar!" Shim screamed. "Ye said t' see she didna trouble ye nae more!"

"Put away your sword, Mackinnon," Lachlan said, watching him warily. "We'll sort this out in a more peaceable way."

"Nay, then," Mackinnon snapped, lunging hard. "I never said to kill the lass, nor did he ever admit he did it until now!"

Lachlan parried the stroke easily, for Mackinnon was tired. "Put up, man!"

"Not until one of us is dead, damn you!" He lunged again, wildly.

Lachlan countered the stroke again, but this time Mackinnon stepped into the path of the counterstroke, and Lachlan's sword went straight into his chest.

Mackinnon collapsed at his feet, and Lachlan stared
down at him until a roar of rage erupted from the Green
Abbot.

"Take him, lads! Now!"

Swords clashed, and whipping toward the sound, Lachlan saw the lad holding Fingon at sword point fall, the victim of another Mackinnon sword. That Mackinnon leaped
toward him, but he sidestepped the thrust and spitted the
would-be killer instead.

"This way!" Mairi shouted as he yanked his sword free.
"Hurry!"

Others had drawn swords, and Aidan waved his menac-
ingly as he dashed with Mairi toward the archway into the
anteroom. Realizing they would all have a better chance
standing on the anteroom side of the archway, fighting one
man at a time as the others passed through it, Lachlan ran
after them, only to meet one of the Mackinnons' swordsmen
just as Shim attacked Aidan.

Speeding his own attacker to his Maker swiftly enough to
make two others approaching him slow their pace, he saw
Aidan take a stroke to his right leg that made him stumble.
Shouting at Shim, Lachlan felled him as he wheeled and
lunged, then grabbed Aidan by an arm, and dragged him
through the archway, turning as he did to meet the immedi-
ate fierce onslaught he expected.

Instead, the moment they were clear of the opening, a
portcullis he had not known existed in the archway crashed
into place.

"Hurry!" Mairi cried as she pushed an iron pin through a

hole in the wall nearby. "Men might be in the windlass chamber, so we don't have much time."

Helping Aidan, Lachlan followed her to the main door, unbarred it, and pulled it open, sword at the ready.

Only moonlight met him. No one was on guard.

"Everyone must be in the hall," Mairi said, moving past him. "Come on out and shut it. Oh, do hurry, both of you. That inner gate will not hold them long if anyone is upstairs and . . . Oh, do be quick!"

Lachlan did not question her but did as she bade, and was astonished when, instead of running to the creek path, she ran to the far side of the huge door, grabbed a rope hanging there, and pulled hard.

Nothing happened.

"Help me!" she cried.

Leaving Aidan to look after himself, he hurried to her side, grabbed the rope above her hands, and pulled with her. To his further astonishment, the great portcullis above the main door crashed into place.

Back she ran to snatch up a bar near the door that he had thought must be for men to scrape their boots. Hefting it into a slot in the wall, she shoved hard.

"Come," she said, holding up her skirts and hurrying toward the path, clearly visible in the silvery glow of a half moon. "You help Aidan and, Aidan, do try to move quickly. I do not think Niall can have known the trick to the portcullis—"

"Faith, my lady, even I did not know about the wee one!"

"Only the family does," she said, increasing her pace despite the danger that she might miss a step in the uncertain light. "My father showed me last year when we were here, but until I passed through that archway, I'd remembered only that the main one can be lowered from outside as well as in—supposedly by one person."

"One man could do it," Lachlan said. "But how does it work?"

"That rope we pulled connects to the ratchet in the windlass room. When it's pulled free, the gate falls of its own weight. But we must hurry," she added. "If anyone is in that room, the gate will be open again in a trice, and even if they are not, the pin holding the small one can be reached from inside if anyone thinks to feel for it. And two men can easily lift that gate back into place."

"'Tis a most unusual arrangement," Lachlan said, glad to see they were nearing the creek. "One usually thinks of shutting folks out of a castle, not into it."

"It was my father's notion," she said. "I don't think anyone has ever even questioned that rope."

"Doubtless, most folks seeing it expect it to ring a bell," he said. "How—"

But Mairi had reached the landing place. "Faith," she exclaimed, "they've beached two cobles here. They'll be able to follow us!"

Lachlan glanced toward the castle again to see flames leaping high on the ramparts. "Someone lit the beacon fire," he said.

"I did that," Aidan said. "Her ladyship said I should tell anyone who asked that she wanted t' spread word o' her wedding like his grace did for Lady Marjory's wedding two years ago, but I kent fine why she wanted it."

"Her ladyship's reasoning is, as always, excellent."

"Aye, but me hands did shake so I feared I'd never get it lit, 'cause that lot would ha' killed me, sure, did they catch me."

"Then it is a very good thing they did not. Can you row, lad?"

"Aye, sir. Me leg be bleeding still, but it doesna seem too bad. I doubt we can row both boats wi' any speed, though."

"No, but we can tie one to the other and sink it when we get to deep water," he said. "Help me launch them."

It took all three of them to get the two boats into the water, for they proved heavier than they looked. Mairi climbed into the bow of the first one, followed by Aidan, who quickly unshipped an oar to steady the rocking craft as Lachlan climbed aboard, and their weight lifted the boat away from the pebbly beach. Lachlan tied the second boat's painter to theirs, moved to his seat, and unshipped the oars there. The second boat's weight slowed them considerably, so they were just rowing into the inlet from the creek when the first Mackinnons appeared on the hilltop.

Shouting, the men descended fast, and Lachlan ordered Mairi to sit as low as she could behind Aidan to protect herself. "Row harder, lad," he ordered, doing the same himself. The other boat swayed back and forth, jerking the connecting rope and making it hard to gain momentum, let alone speed, but he knew that if they stopped to untie it, the others would be upon them in a flash. As it was, they would have to swim to catch them.

Several raised bows with arrows nocked, but although the arrows flew, the hill path was too far away, and the angle uncertain. By the time the archers reached the shore, the two cobles were out of range.

"It is only a matter of time, though," Lachlan said. "They'll swim for their longboat, and we can do nothing to stop them, because we cannot sink it in time or row it by ourselves. And once their oarsmen are in it, they'll soon catch us."

"Men are in the water already," Mairi exclaimed.

"And they have only to send one to the cliff top to see which way we go."

Mairi fell silent, and he needed his strength to row, so he said no more, and in another few minutes, they reached the mouth of the craggy inlet. The waves there were stronger, despite being on the leeward side, but they would meet even heavier seas when they entered the Firth of Lorn. Although he said nothing to the others, he knew they would be lucky if the first great sea wave did not overturn them.

As that thought crossed his mind, he heard Mairi gasp.

Turning, expecting to see ships full of Mackinnons, he saw three galleys heading straight for them, bright with torches, banners flying.

In the torchlight, however, he saw that the banners were gold and the device on each one was a little black ship.

Chapter 21

MacDonald himself commanded the lead ship, and after men had helped Mairi aboard, she said as she hugged him fiercely, "You saw the beacon!"

"Aye. I'd set men to searching Morvern and Mull, whilst Godfrey took boats to Iona and Ranald into Loch Linnhe, but I knew if Fingon had taken you, he'd not risk the Holy Isle. We suspected they'd gone the other way, but knew not where."

Lachlan said, "The Mackinnons had to swim to their longboat, sir, but they are right behind us. Where's Hector?"

"In my second galley," MacDonald said as he motioned the two others past them. "He was going to set out this way himself in your longboat, but my galleys are swifter, so we came together. He thought the villains would head out of the Sound as soon as they could, lest others see them there and tell us which way they'd gone. He soon came to believe they must have carried you through the woods past Duart, to a boat they had waiting on the coast to carry you south."

"That's my guess, too," Lachlan said, waving as he caught sight of his grinning brother in the galley just passing them. "They knocked me out and hooded me, but I do recall now that I came to my senses briefly in some sort of a cart, and was damned uncomfortable in it, too."

"Lighting that beacon fire was a clever notion, lad," MacDonald said.

As Lachlan opened his mouth to reveal whose notion it was, Mairi forestalled him, saying earnestly, "Aidan Kean did that, your grace, and very brave of him it was, too, because he knew he was risking his life to do it."

MacDonald turned to the lad and held out his hand. His voice shook as he said, "I thank you for your bravery, Aidan Kean, and I'll see you well rewarded for it. Your action undoubtedly saved my daughter's life, and Lachlan Lubanach's as well. I warrant the Green Abbot would have murdered them both."

Lachlan said, "As to that, sir . . ."

"My life was never in danger, only my pride and my future," Mairi interjected. "And, Father, it wasn't Fingon, not by himself. Niall was there, too."

"Niall!" MacDonald exclaimed.

"Aye, sir, but he's truly dead now, I think."

"He is, lass," Lachlan said. "I am certain of it."

"I thought you killed him at Craignure," MacDonald said.

"So did I," Lachlan said, "but apparently he just sank enough to swim under the wharf. Fingon collected him, and they abducted Mairi and captured me."

Mairi said, "The worst of it was that Niall meant to marry me and kill Lachlan. He aspired even to control the Lordship. They said if they kept me hidden, you'd do whatever they demanded. I told Niall I'd never obey him without being beaten into submission, but I think it only made him more determined. He . . ." She paused with a glance at Lachlan, and then added, "I never liked him much."

"Niall had long wanted to control her ladyship," Lachlan said. "He spoke of providing better guidance for her, less indulgence than she has hitherto enjoyed, and severe punishment for disobedience. We believe he murdered Elma MacCoun or, at least, bears great responsibility for her death."

"Aye, we learned as much ourselves," MacDonald said, adding in a louder tone, "Hold here, lads."

Lachlan had paid little heed to their course after the other two ships had passed and MacDonald's had fallen in behind, but all three were taking up positions outside the mouth of the craggy inlet. Hector's boat rocked on the near side, holding a position just beyond view of anyone coming out, while the second boat faced his on the other side. MacDonald had ordered his galley to halt behind Hector's.

A moment later the longboat they had seen in the inlet hove into view, manned by a dozen oarsmen. Hector waited until its prow emerged from the inlet, then blew his horn just as the emerging vessel's helmsman caught sight of them.

The galleys surged forward, cutting off retreat, and at the enemy helmsman's command, his men raised their oars in the classic gesture of surrender.

The Green Abbot was not aboard.

MacDonald demanded to know if the men who were there would accept him as their liege and swear loyalty to him. Not surprisingly, all of them roared, "Aye!"

Lachlan said, "Your grace, I don't think they knew until a short time ago that their masters intended to betray you. When Lady Mairi spoke her mind on learning that Niall Mackinnon expected to marry her, some of the things she said clearly surprised his men."

"What did she say?"

"That he was betraying you and had lied to many of his

own kinsmen by pretending to be dead whilst he and Fingon organized her abduction."

"But did you not say that Niall was badly injured at Craignure?"

"I did, but he showed no sign of injury in his swordplay today. So, despite the blood I saw, I believe he must have greatly exaggerated that wound to make his fall in the water look natural. Then, aided by the weight of his sword, he was able to sink low enough to swim under the landing and make good his escape." Obliquely, he added, "You said you'd also discovered his connection to Elma MacCoun's murder. How did that come to pass?"

"From one of your prisoners," MacDonald said. "Your ferocious brother had a talk with Gil Dowell."

"Did Dowell say Mackinnon wanted Elma dead, or that he killed her?"

"Nay, only that he ordered Shim MacVey to keep her from troubling him."

"That agrees with what we learned, sir," Lachlan said, explaining.

When he finished, MacDonald nodded and said with a sigh, "Gil also told Hector how she died. Apparently, Shim feared telling Niall what had happened but did tell Gil that she'd scorned him too often, when she married Mellis, when she gave herself to Niall, and there on the beach. Shim meant only to teach her a lesson, but she fought and some-how—he knows not how—she died, and he left her on the sand. The notion to cast blame on Ian Burk did not come to him until later, Gil said, after he'd sent Ewan to find her. By then, he and his two friends had forgotten Ian's brief trip to Dunyvaig and recalled only seeing him argue with Elma on the causeway."

As he spoke, MacDonald was watching his men and

Hector's take control of the longboat. When its crew had climbed aboard the three galleys, he ordered his men to take the longboat into the inlet, supported by one of the galleys, to secure the castle and collect any stray Mackinnons they might find on the tiny isle.

"Do you think they'll find Fingon?" Mairi asked her father.

He shrugged, saying, "I'd not risk a wager on it, lass. They say the abbot has more friends below than above. My guess is that he had his escape planned before he arrived, but I won't hazard a guess as to how or where."

"Sprouted wings and flew," Lachlan said with a grimace. "I doubt it's the last we'll see of him, but 'twould be dangerous to go against him publicly."

"Aye, for he still wields great power in the Kirk," MacDonald said, adding, "We'll leave the other boats and return to Ardtornish. Dawn will be upon us before we arrive, and I've guests and a Paschal feast yet to host for them."

They sat on cushioned benches along the sides of the high prow, MacDonald facing Lachlan and Mairi. When Mairi sighed and leaned back, exhausted, Lachlan slipped an arm around her and drew her close so she could rest her head against his shoulder. He expected MacDonald to object to the arrangement, but despite Mairi's murmur of contentment, or perhaps because of it, he did not.

Instead, he said, "We'll talk further, lad, when we get home."

Mairi's eyes fluttered open. "What about, sir?"

"That depends, lass. You said you'd not marry him, but seeing you now, curled like a wee kitten beside him, I'm thinking you've changed your mind."

She bit her lower lip and said nothing for several moments, stirring a strong temptation in Lachlan to demand a chance to talk with her again before they continued the conversation. He told himself he was confident, but his inner voice seemed less so than usual. Nevertheless, he forced himself to stay silent.

At last, she said quietly to her father, "If the match does not displease you, sir, I will agree to it now."

Lachlan's inner voice cheered, and a huge weight slid from his mind.

"Are you certain, daughter?"

"Aye, sir. When I refused, I spoke from my anger at his disrespectful treatment of you, his liege lord, and other, more personal matters, but I knew when they threw him into that cellar cage with me that my feelings for him had grown stronger than ever before."

Diverted, MacDonald snapped, "Cage!"

"Aye, the iron one in Dunconnel's cellar."

"I know of no cage there," he said grimly. "However did the two of you win free of such a place?"

"They took us out so Fingon could perform my wedding to Niall," Mairi said sleepily. "In the end, though, 'twas your own gift to me that saw us free, sir. You trusted me with the tricks of both the inner and the outer portcullis last year when you took me to Dunconnel."

MacDonald smiled. "So that arrangement worked, did it? Clever lass, to have remembered. I devised that arrangement myself, lad," he said to Lachlan. "Heard that attackers drove a hay wagon under the portcullis at Linlithgow Palace years ago filled with English soldiers who jumped out and swarmed the place. Reinforcements easily followed, because the wagon propped up the gate. I decided that if an enemy ever gained entry at Dunconnel, I wanted a way to contain them, and with only the one entrance, a trick portcullis seemed ideal. There's a trick to getting out, too, so an enemy outside cannot trap the occupants inside."

"Very clever, sir," Lachlan said.

"Aye, well, you asked me about that trick, lad," Mac-Donald added. "In troth, we've only entrusted the information about the second one to family members, so I expect we'll have to make you one of us now, to keep the tradition."

"Thank you, your grace. I swear to you that I'll do all in my power to remain worthy of your confidence. You and yours can depend on my loyalty and that of all sons of Gillean, both now and long after I become chief of our clan."

MacDonald turned to Mairi. "He suggested you might like Duart as part of your tocher, lass. What think you of that?"

Her smile answered him, and with the torchlight making stars dance in her eyes, her lips parted invitingly, and with her body molding softly against his, Lachlan had all he could do not to kiss her and keep kissing her all the way home.

Ardtornish loomed above them, silvery in the early dawn light, as the royal galley slid against its landing in the bay.

Mairi smiled drowsily at Lachlan as he picked her up in his arms without asking anyone's permission and stepped onto the timber dock.

"You take liberties, sir," she murmured provocatively.

"Aye, and I intend to take more before this day is done, sweetheart."

"Faith then, do you mean to carry me all the way up the cliff stairs?"

"If you want the entire household to think you incapacitated by your ordeal, I'll be happy to do so," he said, answering her teasing smile with one of his own.

"Knave," she muttered. "It would serve you right if I pretended that such a lie would not disturb me, and made you exhaust yourself, but I am too vain and too concerned for your well-being to do that. Put me down."

To her surprise, he complied at once, and as he did, she detected a lurking twinkle in her father's eyes.

"I think we'd best arrange the wedding as soon as we can, lass," MacDonald said. "I don't want to know if Niall was right about your having indulged yourselves already in the pleasures of the connubial bed, but I can see that you will certainly do so if we do not soon take steps to prevent it."

"How soon?" she demanded.

"I believe my Paschal feast can easily serve as a wedding feast," he said.

"But banns . . . and my lady mother will want to order new gowns for—"

"I will speak with your lady mother," he said as they climbed the steps cut into the cliff. "In troth, I am more concerned about Alasdair Stewart, because I did not spare time to discuss any of this with him before we set out in search of you. Nor, since he was still sick from whatever he drank, did I ask him to go with us or even tell him what had happened. Considering his supposed interest in marrying you, he may regard that as a slight."

"I don't want to marry Alasdair," Mairi said flatly. "His reasons for marrying me were the same as Niall's. But I expect you can manage him easily, sir."

"What about papal dispensation, your grace?" Lachlan asked. "Our kinship does lie within the forbidden degrees."

Mairi held her breath, but MacDonald shrugged, saying, "If one follows the rules of the Roman Kirk, nigh well every man and woman in the Isles lies within them. I'll apply to his holiness straightaway, but we need not wait. You certainly will not be the first from these parts to marry before dispensation was granted."

"Then I'm agreeable, sir, but I'd like my brother to be present."

"Of course, of course. Hector should be here shortly. He only stayed to lend the others support if they need it, and to look after the few Mackinnon oarsmen who did not return with us."

They learned upon entering the laird's tower that no one at Ardtornish was still abed. Lady Margaret and Elizabeth were in the great chamber with a number of others waiting to greet them, for nearly everyone had watched for the galleys or had commanded servants to watch and wake them the instant any came into view. The only one they might have expected to see who was not there was Alasdair.

"He left yesterday," Lady Margaret told them when she had hugged Mairi and congratulated Lachlan on his safe return. "He said he had promised to be elsewhere for Easter, but as he did not say where or mention the commitment earlier, one doubts he meant to be anywhere but here."

Elizabeth smiled. "He said he would come back for the christening of John Og's bairn, which John Og wants to do here, but I doubt he will. His man told Meg that Alasdair feared being murdered in his bed. I don't like Alasdair, but it cannot be pleasant to have been so sick, and in front of everyone!"

"I'm thinking it may well have been an attempt on his life," Lachlan said.

"Aye," MacDonald agreed. "We know that Niall ordered the gillie to give him the poisoned wine, so I'm guessing it was all part of his plot to win our Mairi and wield more power within the Lordship."

"If not to control it," Lachlan murmured.

Mairi smiled, wondering why she suddenly felt like smiling at everything and everyone. Turning to her mother, she met a searching look before Margaret shifted her gaze to MacDonald, her eyebrows lifting slightly.

"Aye," he said, grinning. "One would think that living amidst this court all her life, as she has, she'd have learned to conceal her feelings better, but she never has, and I fear you'll be vexed with me, my lady, for I'm going to let them marry straightaway, today. We're having a feast in any event," he added coaxingly.

Margaret bowed her head. "It must be as you wish, of course, my lord."

Mairi glanced at Lachlan, hoping he would not expect such unquestioning submission to his every statement and decree.

He met her look with a twinkle, saying nothing.

Meeting her mother's gaze again a moment later, she was astonished at Margaret's expression. Despite her ladyship's submissive attitude, she had expected to see displeasure. Instead, Margaret's eyes were twinkling as brightly as Lachlan's.

"You will want to change your dress, dearling," she said.

"I should think she would," Elizabeth exclaimed. "Only look at it!"

Mairi's wedding was not, as she had long expected it to be, an event preceded by months of planning and discussion, of choosing gowns and ornamentation, or those who would attend her. Instead, with the help of Lady Margaret, Elizabeth, and Meg Raith, she bathed as rapidly as one could, after gillies had carried the tub and myriad pails of hot water to her chamber from the kitchen. Afterward, she donned the ermine-trimmed scarlet kirtle and tunic she had worn the day she met Lachlan Lubanach.

Meg brushed her hair until it gleamed and left it loose as tradition required, flowing down her back to her knees in the loose waves that always result when hair that is normally plaited hangs free.

Elizabeth presented her with a garland of spring flowers to attach to the gold circlet she wore for state occasions. The rest of her jewelry was splendid as always, a profusion of necklaces and bracelets, but at Lachlan's request, relayed through her mother, Mairi wore no rings.

The hour had advanced well past the usual time for their midday meal, but news of the wedding had swept through the castle, and no guest expected the bride to produce herself before she was ready.

She descended to the courtyard to find the entire household gathered there and the yard itself redolent with aromas of the feast, those of roast lamb and venison predominating. When she appeared in the doorway of the laird's tower, everyone cheered, and she knew that the other boats had returned because Ranald and Godfrey were there, grinning and cheering with the rest.

With his piper walking a little behind him, the Lord of the Isles strode from the crowd to meet her, beaming as he extended his forearm formally, to escort her across the courtyard to the great hall.

After commanding the others to go ahead and find their places, MacDonald said, "This proceeding is coming about gey swiftly, lass, and there is no shame in a woman's changing her mind. Art sure this man of wiles is the one you want?"

"Aye, sir," she said softly, knowing she wanted him with all her heart.

Nodding, MacDonald gestured to the piper to play, and the haunting notes of the pipe began to float across the yard.

With the piper leading the way, and Lady Margaret and Elizabeth following, Mairi and her father walked to the great hall.

Inside, Mairi saw that people had been busy while she dressed, for not only had they filled the hall with flowers as usual for his grace's Easter feast and laid the tables splendidly, but an altar stood before the high table on the dais.

Lachlan, Hector, and her father's chaplain stood beside it, waiting.

The guests stood at their places as they would have for any meal, save for those whose seats were on the dais. No one stood there but the bridegroom, his brother, and the chaplain. Those others who would sit at the high table afterward stood nearby at the side of the hall.

Her father's piper led the way onto the dais and stepped aside.

MacDonald escorted his daughter to her place and stood behind her as the chaplain began to speak the words of the ritual.

Conscious of Lachlan at her side, Mairi tried to listen to the words, but she felt as if he were touching her, and she could think of nothing but him and the fact that soon they would be married and not have to seek private places anymore.

The chaplain turned to Lachlan and nodded, whereupon he removed the gold ring from his little finger and said as he slipped it on her finger, "With this ring I thee wed, and with my body I thee worship, and with all my worldly chattel I thee honor."

Mairi's promises followed, and she repeated them after the chaplain, ending with the promise to be bonnie and buxom in bed and at board until death parted them, "from this time forward, and if holy Kirk it will ordain."

"What if the Pope does not ordain it?" she asked her new husband minutes later as they took seats of honor at the table and MacDonald's grand feast began.

"He will," Lachlan said. "And even if he does not, it will not matter. We have each other now, so eat, my love. You will need your strength later."

His voice and words stirred her senses as they always did, and willingly she obeyed his first marital command to her.

The Lord of the Isles had sent servants across the Sound to Duart to prepare the castle for their wedding night, and when Mairi arose to leave the feast first, as tradition required, her new husband rose with her. Everyone else did, as well, for his grace had arranged a parade of boats to escort the newlyweds to their new home.

At Duart the servants came out to meet her, the children with flowers. Ian was there, her own gillie now, to look after the horses she preferred to ride.

"We've brought food for a wedding supper an ye want one, lass," MacDonald said, giving her a hug.

"Ye can eat your supper wi' the lass in hell, MacDonald!"

The words, issued in stentorian tones, shocked everyone to silence.

Fingon Mackinnon stood at the entrance to the castle in his canonical robes, his arms spread wide. A host of armed Mackinnons stepped forth from the woods near the castle, their swords unsheathed.

Lachlan put a protective arm around Mairi, and Hector stepped in front of them both with battle-axe in hand as MacDonald snapped, "By God, Fingon Mackinnon, 'tis yourself that will burn in hell. Lads!"

"Hold, sir, if you will," Lachlan said, laying a hand on his arm. "With your permission, I would speak to him."

"Aye, if you think to slay him and his evil lot with words," MacDonald said. "He goes too far this time."

"He is still a priest, your grace. You do not want his death on your hands."

Touching Hector's arm next, Lachlan nudged him out of the way, faced the Green Abbot, and said in a voice audible to all, "Fingon Mackinnon, just as his grace does not want a priest's blood on his hands, you do not want to answer to man or to God for his death or those of these wedding guests. You swore loyalty to his grace on your knees, and your brother did likewise. Both of you betrayed him, but only you still have the opportunity to repent and do good."

"I have not come to do murder but to put a fatal curse on the house of MacDonald. My men accompany me only to see me safely home again."

"With your great power, 'tis murder all the same, and on a sacred occasion, as you must know it is, since you meet us here. You can have known we would be here only had you likewise known of our wedding. Have you considered what his holiness will make of such an act leveled against the Lord of the Isles and King of the Hebrides? 'Tis to betray your prince, Fingon. Think you the Prince of the Roman Kirk will look lightly on such a foul deed against a fellow ruler, or have you forsaken all hope of ever becoming Mitered Abbot of the Holy Isle?"

"My curse will shrivel MacDonald," Fingon snapped.

"Only if others believe in it as you do. If those others choose instead to believe his holiness, you will no longer wield power here or elsewhere. I stand fearless before you now. Do you think others will not stand with me?"

Mairi stepped up to stand on one side of him, Hector on the other. MacDonald moved up next to Hector with Lady Margaret's hand in his, and Ranald and Godfrey moved to Mairi's side. Moments later, every man and woman of their party stood with them—a silent, strong force, gazing solemnly at Fingon.

Rustling sounds behind Lachlan, followed by clinking steel, made it nearly unbearable for him not to look, so certain was he that Fingon's men-at-arms must be closing in. Only Hector standing quietly by him made it possible to do the same.

The silence lengthened until Lachlan said, "Your powers now are still great, Fingon. Consider that, and unless you mean to curse all here, or kill us, think hard."

Fingon lowered his hands. Moments later, he and his men were gone.

Mairi moved into Lachlan's arms, sighing deeply as they closed around her. Having feared that they had won all only to lose all, she wanted to stand right where she was until everyone else left. But courtesy and duty required that she lead the way into Duart Castle with her new husband, and smiles of welcome.

The great chamber walls were draped with colorful arras

cloth. A fire roared in the hooded fireplace, and against the nearby wall, the bed that stood ready to receive them was lush with blue and gold curtains, coverlets, and pillows. On two gold silk pillows, someone had embroidered little black ships. She smiled when she saw them, recognizing Elizabeth's work and realizing that she had worked them for their father but had decided to give them as wedding gifts instead.

The men carried Lachlan off to another chamber to prepare him, while the women undressed Mairi and helped her beneath the coverlets, where the fine linen sheets were so soft as to invite the new owners of Duart to linger often in bed.

The women laughed and chatted as if it were an ordinary day, but the men soon returned, laughing even louder, many of them merry with too much brogac or wine, pushing Lachlan ahead of them. He wore only a thin robe, but when one man a bit the worse for drink reached to throw back the coverlet, he caught the fellow's arm and held it with ease.

"If you would please me, sir," he said gently, "do not touch that bed. 'Tis my privilege, and I would look most unhappily on the man who stole it from me."

The other shook his head but moved away, still laughing, and Lachlan climbed into the bed beside Mairi, his robe still covering his body.

MacDonald's chaplain stepped forward to bless the bed, and then at a word from MacDonald the company abandoned them. Thus, the great chamber, filled with people, laughter, and chatter one moment, was utterly silent the next.

Lachlan got up and looked around as if to be certain no one had lingered. Finding a jug of wine on a nearby table, with two goblets, he filled the latter, set the jug back down, and returned to the bed.

For a long moment, he stood beside it and gazed lovingly at his bride.

Her cheeks glowed, her eyes sparkled, and her lips were slightly parted. She showed none of the shyness associated with maidens, and despite her previous acquaintance with coupling, one could scarcely think her anything more.

He wanted to savor the sight of her, but even more did he want to feast on her beauty. This woman he had won was not what he had expected her to be the day she had walked into him, thinking only of saving another man's life. On learning her identity, he had believed her no more than the spoiled, indulged daughter of the most powerful man in the Isles, a chit of a girl who would preen and demand all a princess could demand, and think herself greater and grander than all other females.

Instead he had found a warm, vibrant, compassionate woman, determined to do what she believed was right, even in defiance of those she cared most about.

"What are you thinking?" she asked, her voice husky with desire.

"I'm thinking I offered for a girl and won a woman," he said. "I'm thinking I negotiated for a prize and won more than I'd ever imagined."

"What did you win?"

"You," he said simply.

"But you wanted me from the outset."

"I wanted MacDonald's daughter, sweetheart. Hector told me I was a fool."

"For wanting me?"

"Nay, you know better—for seeing wealth and power as necessities and you only as the means of gaining them."

"But power is seductive, sir," she said with a teasing smile, "and you will wield great authority now, for his grace told me he means to name you to take Niall's place as High Steward and Master of his Household. Moreover, the lands he has granted you will not be mere vassal's holdings at his pleasure but will bear hereditary rights, as well. You will wield all the power you could hope for."

MacDonald had already told him as much, but it was with heartfelt sincerity that he said, "Sweetheart, no power that I ever wield can compete with yours." Pulling back the coverlet, he dropped his robe to the floor, and climbed in beside her. "You wield more power over men with a smile than I could wield with a thousand galleys at my command."

She held out her arms. "Be quiet now, and kiss me."

Readily he complied. Her body was warm against his, and soft, her skin like silk. He sighed, thinking of the years ahead of them together, and as he stroked her and bent to taste her breasts and belly, he slid a hand beneath her to cup one soft cheek of her bottom. She was delicious, and he savored his delight until the thought of Niall Mackinnon turning up her skirts and smacking her intruded on his pleasure.

"I'm glad Mackinnon's dead," he murmured. "I did not mean to kill h—"

With two fingers on his lips, she silenced him. "Niall wanted to die, my love," she said. "He stepped into your blade. He knew he would lose all and he could not bear it. Put him out of your head now, for I would be your wife in all ways."

His body ached for her, and hers was ready for him. Their coupling was swift, fierce, and powerful.

Afterward, they lay quietly for several minutes before she turned onto one side and kissed him lightly. Then, with her head in the hollow of his shoulder, and her body molding itself against his, she said, "It is very strange, is it not, that love makes one look at the world and all who inhabit it as utterly delightful. You make me feel wonderful. Faith, I like everyone right now. I can even forgive Fingon for all he did—aye, and Niall, too—and perhaps even offer a prayer for their souls."

"You are kinder than I am, sweetheart, but I have little worry that your prayers will make any difference where Niall is now."

"That's sacrilege," she said, tapping his nose with one finger. "For that you must pay a penance, I think."

"Willingly," he said, grabbing her by both arms and pulling her close. "I shall begin my penance by kissing every inch of your beautiful body."

Laughing, she rolled to her back. As he began his penance, she said with a chuckle, "I've decided that submission to one's husband is occasionally acceptable."

He murmured a response, but his kisses had reached a spot by then that rendered further sensible conversation impossible.

Epilogue

Loch Gruinart, Isle of Isla, July 1367

The tide had turned, but still he did not come to her, although he had sent word promising to be at the loch early if she would meet him to watch the sunrise. Already they were going to be late getting back, and considering her present moodiness and uncertain temper, it would be as much as his life was worth if he did not show himself soon.

She walked barefoot along the sand toward the north shore cliffs, dangling her boots by their rawhide laces and thinking about Elma MacCoun and what her last moments must have been like, focusing on Elma so that her impatience for him would not be the first thing he would see. As always, just thinking of him brought his twinkling image to mind, and jolts of desire shot through her at the knowledge that his impatience would match her own.

He would come soon. He would be aching for her and for the bairn, too, but she had moved to Kilchoman days ago, wanting to enjoy his homecoming with him alone. He had promised to meet her, to watch the dawn break through the twilight here, and he kept his promises. Still, things did happen, unexpected events that altered the course of one's life in a heartbeat. But no such thing had happened today. She would know if it had, and her mind was at peace, her world safe for now.

As the sky continued to lighten in the east, she stood facing the sea, letting her body relax, delighting in the way the changing light brought the water's colors to life. Fluffy white clouds floated overhead and would soon bloom with roses as the sun began to touch them directly.

Hoofbeats sounded at last on the hillside behind her, and she whirled, filled with eager anticipation that swelled to joy when she saw the galloping horse and its rider. Dropping her boots, she snatched up her skirts and ran laughing to meet him.

Just as he had the last time they had met at the loch, he reined his steed in sharply before it reached her, then leaped from the saddle and ran to meet her, catching her up in his arms and whirling about, holding her close.

"You're really here!" Mairi said happily, hugging him.

"Aye, sweetheart," Lachlan agreed, "I'm here, and I've missed you sorely."

"Did you get it?"

"I've the document in a bag on my saddle," he said. "You can see it when we reach Kilchoman, and although 'tis written in Latin, I'll tell you what every word means. But first I want you all to myself for a while."

"We are to be alone at Kilchoman for a fortnight, are we not?"

"Aye, for your lady mother promised as much, but 'alone' in a splendid summer palace with servants all around . . ." Clearly seeing no need to finish the thought, he added abruptly, "Kiss me, lass. I'm fair parched for the taste of you."

She obeyed with alacrity, and the kiss was long and deep.

A second one followed, and his hands moved over her body in their strong, possessive way, stirring deep contentment within her.

When he held her a little away and looked into her eyes as if to reassure himself that the reality matched his memory of her, she said with satisfaction, "So we are legally married now even in the eyes of the Roman Kirk."

"Aye, and his holiness was kind enough to mention our wee Hector in his dispensation, to protect him from any threat of bastardizing or excommunication. In fact," he added, grinning, "the document protects the 'children' conceived of our union before the dispensation's date, so he allowed for more than one, just in case."

"The Pope is a wise man," she said archly.

"What?" He gripped her shoulders. "Do you mean to tell me—"

When she nodded, a huge smile split his handsome face. "Art sure, sweetheart?" he asked foolishly.

"You've been gone two months, sir. I'm very sure. And I'm thinking 'tis another rowdy lad, for mornings I'm sick as a cat, just as I was with wee Hector."

"Faith, you didn't ride out here alone, retching all the way, I hope!"

She raised her eyebrows. "And if I did?"

He struggled visibly with himself, then said with a twinkle, "If you did, you'll have to pay a wee penance for your foolishness, my love, but if you are well enough, we can celebrate your excellent health instead."

"And what would be the difference betwixt the two, sir?"

"Why, none, lass, none at all," he said. "'Tis a rare bargain, you'll agree."

She laughed, and he hugged her tight. And then he was kissing her again, and soon he spread his cloak on the grass nearby for them to lie on, and she reached for him. Their clothing quickly discarded, she squealed and he chuckled when the cool morning breeze from the sea kissed their naked skin, but they quickly forgot the breeze in the heat that consumed them both.

Gulls prattled overhead, and birdsong erupted in the heather, but the two of them were oblivious, their bodies too hungry for each other to care about anything else. Behind them, to the east, the sun peeked between the Paps of Jura, spilling warm golden rays across the landscape.

Their new day had dawned.

Dear Reader,

The idea to write a book about the first Lord of the Isles stirred when I came across the story of Mairi of the Isles and Lachlan Lubanach Maclean in a collection of bards' tales [*West Highland Tales* by Fitzroy Maclean, Edinburgh, 1985]. Needless to say, Clan Mackinnon's view of the events described in *Highland Princess* differs dramatically from the Maclean version. However, in general, the Maclean version seems to have more supporters among historians, and truthfully, it was more romantic and more fun to write.

There was in the fourteenth century, as there is in my book, only one Mac Donald (sic), and he was the Lord of the Isles. Mac Donald was not a surname but a title, meaning the son of Donald, and there could be only one at a time. Eventually, the name evolved into the various spellings used today, but in 1367, it was still written as two words on official documents. I used the modern spelling, MacDonald, to avoid both reader and proofreader confusion.

Few surnames, as such, were used in the Highlands or Isles until much later, but I chose to use some, sparingly, to help us all keep track of who is allied with whom in the story. One never appreciates surnames more, however, than when one tries to write without them. For example, a proper fourteenth-century introduction of the hero of *Highland Princess* would have been "Lachlan Lubanach, son of Ian Dubh, son of Gille Coluim, son of Maol Iosa, son of Gille eoin, son of MacRath, son of Maol suthan, son of Niall, son of Cu duiligh, son of Ceallach, son of Rangce, son of Old Dubhghall of Scone"—in other words, his entire known genealogy.

When characters in *Highland Princess* refer to the Macleans as upstarts, they do so because of an unfortunate four-hundred-year gap that separates the Macleans' known (confirmable) history from the seventh-century brother of a king of Dalriada that they claim as progenitor of the clan. Clan Donald, on the other hand, claims a pedigree confirmed to Somerled and Colla Uais, legendary High King of Ireland and one of three traditional founders of the fourth-century Irish Kingdom of Oriel.

Fingon Mackinnon, the Green Abbot, had to wait forty years from the date he proclaimed himself Abbot of Iona before a friendly Pope finally came along in 1397 and agreed to let him style himself the Mitered Abbot of Iona. And experts disagree about the actual death of Niall Mackinnon. Some say he lived long after the battle with the Macleans (an "ambush," according to Mackinnons, and they may be right). Other experts insist that Niall died at Craignure Bay.

Those of you who have visited the nearly treeless Western Isles of Scotland may be wondering about all the forests in *Highland Princess*. Let me reassure you, sadly, that the fourteenth-century Isles were lush with forestlands. Until the sixteenth century, Mull and the other western isles boasted more than forty thousand acres of trees. The trees vanished there, as elsewhere throughout the British Isles, through an unfortunate habit of denuding forests to provide fuel and building materials.

For readers interested in pursuing the history of the Lords of the Isles, I suggest the following books: *House of Islay* by Donald Grumach (Argyll, 1967); *The Clan Donald* by Reverend A. MacDonald, (Inverness, 1896); *History of the Macdonalds and Lords of the Isles* (with genealogies) by Alexander Mackenzie, (Inverness, 1881); *Warriors & Priests* by Nicholas Maclean-Bristol (Tuckwell, 1995); *The Lords of the Isles* by Raymond Campbell Paterson (Edinburgh, 2001); and *Lord of the Isles* by Nigel Tranter (London, 1983).

For those of you interested specifically in Maclean history, Lachlan the Wily is the progenitor of the Macleans of Duart, Hector the Ferocious that of the Maclaines of Lochbuie. The change in spelling did not occur until after 1745, and according to the present Chief of the Maclaines of Lochbuie, the traditionally accepted split between the two houses never occurred but was simply a device the Macleans used, in common with other extended clans, to establish "openly" that elements of the clan were "not out" (i.e. not Jacobite supporters of Bonnie Prince Charlie). When the inevitable defeat occurred, vengeful Hanoverians and their non-Jacobite Scottish allies could not take lands from clans that had refused to join the rebellion, so by claiming publicly that one line was "out" while the other was not, all Macleans were able to retain most of their holdings.

Aside from documents such as land grants and papal dispensations, little written evidence exists of fourteenth-century Isles' history, so one's imagination can run free. However, once again, I've had lots of help from the amazing Donald R. MacRae, for one, and to him, again, I extend many, many thanks.

I also want to thank Duncan Staffa Maclean, FSA (Scot) of the California/Nevada Clan Maclean Association; Rob Goodson, Webmaster of Gillean.com and his wife Elena; Linda MacArthur of the Finlaggan Trust (and other members of the committee who took an interest); Nicky Pendry of the British Ordnance Survey; Brian Palmer, who connected me with the folks at the Finlaggan Trust; and last but very much not least, Alasdair White, whose extraordinary knowledge of twelfth- through fourteenth-century Scotland has been particularly helpful.

And, as always, I thank my wonderful editor Beth de Guzman, my long-suffering and indispensable agents Aaron Priest, Lucy Childs, and Lisa Vance, and everyone else in my life who does so much to ease the writer's angst.

If you've enjoyed *Highland Princess*, please look for *Lord of the Isles*, the story of Hector Reaganach Maclean and Cristina Macleod at your favorite bookstore in May 2005. In the meantime, *Suas Alba!*

Sincerely,

Amanda Scott

http://home.att.net/~amandascott

About the Author

AMANDA SCOTT, best-selling author and winner of the Romance Writers of America's RITA/Golden Medallion and the Romantic Times' awards for Best Regency Author and Best Sensual Regency, began writing on a dare from her husband. She has sold every manuscript she has written. She sold her first novel, *The Fugitive Heiress*—written on a battered Smith-Corona—in 1980. Since then, she has sold many more, but since the second one, she has used a word processor. More than twenty-five of her books are set in the English Regency period (1810–20), others are set in fifteenth-century England and sixteenth- and eighteenth-century Scotland. Three are contemporary romances.

Amanda is a fourth-generation Californian who was born and raised in Salinas and graduated with a bachelor's degree in history from Mills College in Oakland. She did graduate work at the University of North Carolina at Chapel Hill, specializing in British history, before obtaining her master's in history from California State University at San Jose. After graduate school, she taught for the Salinas City School District for three years before marrying her husband, who was then a captain in the Air Force. They lived in Honolulu for a year, then in Nebraska for seven years, where their son was born. Amanda now lives with her husband in northern California.